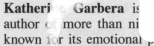

Katherine Garbera is ~~the~~ author of more than ni~~ne~~ known for its emotional ~~punch and ...~~ She lives in the Midlands of the UK with the love of her life; her son, who recently graduated university; and a spoiled miniature dachshund. You can find her online at www.katherinegarbera.com and on Facebook, Twitter and Instagram.

A former job-hopper, **Jessica Lemmon** resides in Ohio with her husband and rescue dog. She holds a degree in graphic design, which is currently gathering dust in an impressive frame. When she's not writing supersexy heroes, she can be found cooking, drawing, drinking coffee (okay, wine) and eating crisps. She firmly believes God gifts us with talents for a purpose, and with His help, you can create the life you want. Jessica is a social media junkie who loves to hear from readers. You can learn more at jessicalemmon.com

7/23

Discover more at millsandboon.co.uk

THE TROUBLE WITH BAD BOYS

KATHERINE GARBERA

SECOND CHANCE LOVE SONG

JESSICA LEMMON

MILLS & BOON

First Published in Great Britain 2021
by Mills & Boon, an imprint of HarperCollins*Publishers* Ltd
1 London Bridge Street, London, SE1 9GF

www.harpercollins.co.uk

HarperCollins*Publishers*
1st Floor, Watermarque Building,
Ringsend Road, Dublin 4, Ireland

The Trouble with Bad Boys © 2021 Harlequin Books S.A.
Second Chance Love Song © 2021 Jessica Lemmon

Special thanks and acknowledgement are given to Katherine Garbera for her contribution to the *Texas Cattleman's Club: Heir Apparent* series

ISBN: 978-0-263-28289-4

0421

MIX
Paper from
responsible sources
FSC
www.fsc.org
FSC™ C007454

Printed and bound in Spain
by CPI, Barcelona

THE TROUBLE WITH BAD BOYS

KATHERINE GARBERA

This book is dedicated to my wild, crazy family who kept me sane with weekly family video chats. Rob, Courtney, Lucas & Georgina, Tabby, Josh & Darcey, and Bobby & Brooke. Love you!

Thanks to Stacy Boyd for her insightful edits on this book, making it really shine.

One

Lila Jones looked at her phone for the hundredth time as if she could magically will a big-name Instagrammer to respond to her request. It wasn't working. If she weren't such a people pleaser, she never would have volunteered to do a task that was so obviously outside of her wheelhouse.

After all, she was a classic girl next door with her unhighlighted long brown hair, thick bangs and a tortoiseshell barrette that kept the sides off her face. She dressed for comfort rather than style and was totally okay with that. Men always wanted to be her friend and confide things to her. Women liked her, *genuinely* liked her, because she was never going to compete with them for attention once they were all in a room.

She loved that about herself. *Honestly.* But she'd volunteered to get some high-profile social media influencer interested in *Soiree on the Bay, the luxury food, art and wine festival* being held on Appaloosa Island, located about three hours from Royal, Texas. But the truth was, despite her good intentions, she wasn't someone that a famous social media personality was going to respond to. Pictures of Whiskers, her elderly friend Winifred's cat, and her favorite books stacked up by her cup of Earl Grey had garnered the usual seven likes by her parents and some of their friends and the Royal Chamber of Commerce account that she managed. And that was it. She wasn't bringing anything exciting or relevant to the table.

She had her planner open in front of her, jotting notes as she sipped her iced coffee. While she knew it was going to be an uphill battle, she wasn't going to fail at this. Because more than anything, Lila didn't want to let the committee down. In fact, that was one thing in her wheelhouse: she was dependable. She opened her social media direct messages and her heart leaped to her throat when she saw that Zach Benning had read her message. Wow. *Seriously?* Although she'd known it was a long shot, she had optimistically added the address of the chamber of commerce and an invite for him to drop in whenever.

Then she saw that he had given the message a thumbs-up.

What did that mean?

Was he going to come to Royal?

He wasn't her top choice of influencer to help promote their event because he was a little too wild—favoring fast cars and women over sensible ones. She had hoped they'd get someone they could rely on. But still… if he did show up and he tweeted or posted one thing, they'd probably get a million likes and that would really help to give the festival worldwide attention.

Now she needed to sweeten the deal. But how? She clicked on his image and tried to ignore the fact that his bright blue eyes were smiling intriguingly at her... well, not at *her*. At anyone who clicked on his profile, Lila noted. He was, after all, all about his image. And that photo screamed, *look at me and my fabulous life*.

Hmm. How could she use that to her advantage?

Billy Holmes had said that Royal was an undiscovered gem. And that Soiree on the Bay was just the first step to getting more influencers and money into their town. She wasn't sure that Zach or any other influencer would see it that way. Because as sophisticated as some of the residents of Royal were, it was still a small town in Texas, and Appaloosa Island was remote... Perfect for a Coachella-type event, but she was going to have to convince them of that.

Direct message to Zach Benning:

@Zach You've probably seen everything and been everywhere, but I guarantee you've never experienced anything like the southern glam of Royal, Texas. The Soiree is just one small part of what we have to offer. Drop me a DM soon. You're our first choice, but there are a lot of others waiting to—

"Hey, Lila. It sure is hot here today. Do you mind if I join you for a minute? I'm waiting for my takeout order."

She glanced up to see Charlotte Jarrett. Charlotte was a renowned chef and was working on the advisory committee for the Soiree along with Lila. Charlotte had been living in Los Angeles and recently returned to Royal and reconnected with her baby daddy, Ross Edmond Jr. That had caused a bit of a scandal around town and Rusty had gone so far as to disown his own son over the incident.

"Not at all. I could actually use your input on this text… I'm trying to up the ante and get Zach Benning to our town."

"Let me see what you've got," Charlotte said.

Lila pushed her phone across the table, and as the other woman read the message, she heard the roar of a powerful sports car coming down Main Street. Looking up, she saw it pull to an abrupt stop in front of the chamber of commerce building, directly across from the coffee shop where she and Charlotte were sitting.

As soon as the cherry-red Ferrari came to a halt, a tall blonde woman hopped out of the convertible, slamming the door so hard that in a less luxurious car, the vehicle would have rocked.

"You're a total asshole!" she fumed. "I hope you rot in this Podunk town. Because I'm not the only one done with you. LA is, too."

The blonde stalked away from the car in impossibly high heels at a furious pace that Lila had to admire. If she were wearing heels that tall she'd have probably twisted her ankle.

"Wow. You don't see that every day."

"No, you certainly don't," Lila agreed. "I wonder who is driving…kind of reminds me of something Rusty might do."

"Ha. You're not wrong," Charlotte said.

Lila chuckled, glancing back over at the car as a tall man emerged from behind the wheel. He put on his sunglasses, running one hand through his thick brown hair, and it fell immediately back into place. Leaving him looking artfully ruffled.

Her gaze raked over him, taking him in from head

to toe. He wore jeans and a skintight designer T-shirt that showed off his muscled chest and biceps. Sheesh. The dude looked like he hadn't missed a date at the gym—ever. Honestly, if he went to her gym she knew she would be there every day, too. Probably just to stare at him.

He was hotter than the May heat surrounding them on this Texas afternoon. He moved as if he had all the time in the world...like he knew all eyes were on him. She'd never in her life walked with that much confidence.

He moved toward them with intent.

Don't be silly, Lila, he's walking to the coffee shop.

She forced herself to look back at her friend. "What do you think? Should I send it?"

"Uh, no. I don't think you will need to do that," Charlotte said.

She was staring over Lila's shoulder toward the Ferrari and Mr. Hottie.

The closer he got, the easier it was to see his trademark dark sunglasses, and there was no mistaking that cut physique. OMG. It was Zach Benning.

Well then.

The waitress called Charlotte's name for her to-go order. "Let me know how this goes."

She left the table. Lila wondered if Zach was going to stop and see her or go to the chamber of commerce first. But he surveyed everyone sitting outside, his attention focused on Charlotte, who frankly was gorgeous, so she didn't blame him at all.

Then he pulled out his phone and glanced at the screen before once again looking at the people who sat in front of the coffee shop. In person, he was even more dynamic, she thought. And she was at a distance. What would it be like to be up close and personal with him?

A sizzle went straight through her. Dang. It had been a long time since she'd felt a physical reaction like this. She rubbed her sweaty palms against her napkin.

Be cool.

He turned and walked over to the chamber, and she started trying to wave down the waitress to get her check. She was a little bit afraid that if she wasn't in her office he might just leave. She wanted to make a good impression on Zach because she needed him.

Or rather, the Soiree needed him. The only way they were going to really start generating word of mouth was with someone of his stature attached. And if he was kept waiting in the lobby of the chamber of commerce…well, that wouldn't be impressive at all.

The waitress still hadn't noticed her and for the first time in her life, Lila tossed some bills from her wallet on the table. Then she hurried across the street to the chamber offices and slammed into a solid chest.

"Sorry," she said, bracing her hand on the firm biceps and looking up into those mesmerizing blue eyes. Up close she saw that he had a firm jaw and his lips were full. She licked hers.

She'd finally run into Zach Benning.

"Well, hello there," Zach said, staring down into a pair of big brown eyes behind some of the largest horn-rimmed glasses he'd seen in a long time. The pretty brunette was tiny in his arms and smelled of summer flowers. Her hair was long and lustrous, and he felt the ends of it brush the backs of his hands as he caught her.

She had a cute little nose, but her mouth was full, making him wonder what she'd do if he kissed her. He was tempted, but the last time he'd followed his gut it hadn't worked out so well.

Zach set her on her feet and smiled. Very aware that he had to always be on. He lived his life in the spotlight and had no regrets about that, but at the same time he could never let his guard down.

"Hi. Um, I'm Lila Jones… I think you might be here to see me," she said, giving him one of the most guileless smiles he'd seen in a really long time.

He raised his eyebrows, smiling back at her. There was something so fresh and pure about her but also downright hot. Next to her the scandal that he'd left behind in Los Angeles made him feel…jaded and dirty.

"Yes, I am here to see you. Should we go somewhere and get a drink so we can talk?"

"My office?" she suggested.

Definitely not. He wanted to be seen in public. Actually, needed to. He should be lying low but didn't want to seem like he *was* lying low. And while being photographed with this sweet, wholesome-looking girl probably wouldn't hurt his reputation, it would definitely help hers.

"It's such a nice day, be a shame to spend it inside. I noticed a coffee shop across the way," he said, putting his hand on the small of her back.

"Are you sure? I noticed that blonde lady storming off when you pulled up…"

"Don't worry about her," he told her with a shrug. Tawny would be back when she cooled down. The fact was she liked the attention that being with him brought her. There were times when he wondered why they kept hooking up when they knew it would fail, but that was part of the charm. Both of them were too used to being the diva to give it up.

"Well, thank you for coming," she said, looking both ways before crossing the street, then putting her hand on his arm to keep him from walking until it was clear.

He couldn't remember the last time someone had done that. There was something so innately kind about her that it struck a chord with him. He tucked that information away because it was different from what he was accustomed to, and he wondered why he'd even noticed it.

Zach followed her and she gestured for him to sit down at the table she'd picked.

"I've been meaning to check out the Lone Star State for a while," he admitted. "My grandfather was born in Texas and used to tell me stories about growing up here."

"In Royal?" she asked curiously.

"No. Dallas. So not too far from here. You just gave me the perfect excuse to come to Texas."

She wrinkled her nose at him as if she didn't buy that. But he wasn't going to let her see any cracks in his story. If there was one thing he was good at, it was making sure everyone saw only what he wanted them to see.

"So tell me a little bit about you and your event."

"Me? There's not much to tell. I work for the Royal Chamber of Commerce, I spend my evenings reading or bingeing shows, and I have brunch with my mom and dad every weekend. What about you?"

Lila was cute and honest. She wasn't grabbing her phone and asking for a selfie or trying to pretty herself up for him. He liked that confidence she had in herself.

He felt a zing of awareness.

Why?

She wasn't his normal type. He didn't sleep with women who went home to their books and had brunch with their parents in a quiet little town. On the contrary, he was attracted to gals who knew the score. Who were used to taking what they needed and using it to get ahead. He had the feeling as much as Lila had reached out to ask him to help with this event, she wasn't a user.

"Me? I'm an open book. Tell me about the Soiree." He didn't want to talk about himself; he wanted to listen to her voice instead. It was sweet and melodic.

"Well, there will be two main stages and some smaller venues for music acts. The lineup is still being put together and I can't reveal any names yet, but there are some big ones on it."

"Good. So is it a music festival?"

"Yes, but so much more. We will have three restaurants at the event."

"Where are you holding the festival? I know your text said Appaloosa Island, but I've never heard of that."

"It's in Trinity Bay, only a three-hour drive from here. We can go and check out the festival site if you'd like."

"I would. Then I'll know what we are dealing with," he said. "Is it only accessible by car and ferry?"

"We? Does that mean I can count on you?" she asked.

Count on him.

Not likely. He had to see more of this event. Right now, it sounded like some sort of small-time festival… though he knew that the Edmond family had put their weight behind the event, which should help bring in some big bucks. But it still didn't sound like the kind of thing his followers would be interested in.

"Let's see," he said. "I like to have all the facts first."

She smiled at him then. "Me, too. Everyone wants a snap decision, but it takes time to weigh all the options. To answer your other question, the island has a private landing strip and can be reached via private plane or helicopter."

She really was too adorable for words. Suddenly he felt another jolt of pure desire go through him. He wanted her. How was that even possible? While there was no doubt she was smart—he could easily read her intelligence in the questions she asked and the way she talked—she wasn't for him. They came from two different worlds and had little in common. Too bad his body didn't seem to care.

"Are you married, Lila?"

"No. Why?" she asked, appearing startled by the question.

"Boyfriend?"

She shook her head. "I don't think that is relevant."

"It is to me."

She looked as if she wanted to ask more questions, but he stopped her by standing up. "Should I drive us to Appaloosa Island?"

"No, I'll drive. I can expense the mileage. I don't want you to have to pay for the gas."

That made him laugh. He'd needed a change, which was why he'd left LA, but even he couldn't have guessed how much he'd enjoy this break.

Inviting Zach to ride in Milo might not have been her brightest idea. Watching him fold his large frame into her passenger seat would be interesting. She'd never been much for following famous Instagrammers and had maybe been a bit judgy thinking they'd be shallow—because this guy certainly wasn't.

It had almost seemed as if he were flirting with her. But no, he couldn't have been. She was nothing—*nothing*—like the blonde who had stormed away from him. In fact, the more she thought about it, the more she was sure she'd imagined the flirting.

She sighed inwardly. He did have that kissable mouth and honestly he looked better than she imagined Jane Austen's Mr. Darcy in her head. And he was the guy she always pictured when she thought of hotties. But she had to nip this ridiculous little infatuation she had for him in the bud. *Now.* Before she made a complete fool of herself.

Her convertible Mini Cooper was in good condition but a bit old. And she'd never really concerned herself with the appearance of her vehicle before she led him to it in the parking lot behind the chamber of commerce building.

She pulled her prescription sunglasses from her oversize cross-body bag and held her keys loosely in her hand. Zach had stopped walking when they'd gotten close to her car as his phone started dinging. He looked at the screen of his device and then back at her.

"Give me a minute, doll," he said. "I've got to take care of this."

"Take as long as you need. And my name is Lila, not doll," she said, smartly. She had the feeling that this was the real Zach Benning. The kind of guy who used a nickname for all women so he didn't mess up their names.

"Fair enough… I didn't mean any insult," he said. "Bad habit."

"Due to the frequency with which you change girlfriends no doubt," she remarked. "Take care of your business. I'm going to get the air running in the car."

Though it was only May, it was Texas and they'd already had a few sweltering days. It wasn't too bad right now but her car, which had been sitting in the lot all day, would need time to cool down.

She got behind the wheel and took a few moments to put her purse on the floor behind her seat after removing two refillable water bottles that she'd put ice and water in for them both. Three hours was a long drive and she wanted Zach to get a good impression of Royal's hospitality.

"Zach Benning is in trouble again. Busted coming out of a nightclub with the wife of record exec Dom Deluca," the radio deejay said. "Apparently there was a confrontation...more to come."

Zach opened the door just as they moved on to the latest drama between two *Rich Wives* who were feuding. She looked over at him as he slid into the passenger seat and put on his seat belt. He'd had a fight with the husband of his lover. Even if he had in fact been flirting with her, there was a lot more to Zach than she wanted to invite into her life.

"I guess the married woman question makes sense now," she said.

He arched one eyebrow at her.

"Deluca."

He shook his head. "I had no idea she was married or whose wife she was."

"So you decided to start asking?"

"Yeah. Don't want any more of that kind of trouble. My old man cheated on my mom, and while I know their marriage wasn't perfect and they both had faults, that's one thing I've always tried to avoid."

"Fair enough. You moved on pretty fast with that blonde, though."

"You are fixated on Tawny, aren't you?" he asked drolly.

"You asked me some personal questions, *doll*, you've got to expect the same in return."

He almost laughed again, which made her smile. She wasn't going to let him walk all over her. That wasn't her way. She really wanted the Soiree to succeed and she was going to do everything she could to make that happen. Even flirting with Mr. Million Followers.

"Tawny isn't my girlfriend—she's sort of one of my most loyal fans. I posted in my Benningnite group that I was coming to Royal and she pinged and asked to tag along," he said.

"*Benningnite* group?" she asked as she started driving toward Trinity Bay. This man was way out of her league. He was charming and of course had that underlying sexuality that made it impossible for her not to want to stare at him. But she wasn't going to. Zach was here for business and that was it. She'd never had a problem keeping men and business separate, she didn't want to start mixing the two now.

"Yeah. I know how it sounds but some of my most loyal followers started it," he told her. "I like it."

"Okay, I think it's odd but that is your world. So, did you come here because you were interested in the festival or to avoid Deluca?" she asked. "I mean, we don't really want any negative publicity."

"What do you think he's going to do? Come to Royal and challenge me to fight?"

She shook her head. When he put it like that, she sort of felt foolish for asking, but she didn't like taking risks. He had followers which was great, and what she needed for the event, but if he was going to bring negative publicity—she'd wait and find someone else. "Make fun all you want but I have to ask these kinds of questions."

"You do? For who?" he prodded. "Is this committee worried about my personal life?"

She shrugged, a little embarrassed because she knew they weren't. The truth was, *she* wanted to know the deets. "Probably not. I mean, I don't want any trouble, but if I'm being totally honest here, it's also for myself. I usually just listen to Hollywood gossip and this is the first time I actually have met someone who is the focus of it."

"It's not as fun as you might think," he said gruffly. "But you do get used to it. So you like tea?"

She knew he meant tea as in spilling the dirt on someone famous. "I do. I hate drama in my life, but I really love listening to it in others'. Does that make me a bad person?"

"Not in my book. If you weren't interested, some of those people wouldn't have a career."

"Probably," she conceded with a laugh. "That entire world of social influence seems strange to me. I mean my parents have real jobs where they go into work and get paid. But I love the *Rich Wives* shows...those women are paid to let a camera follow them around doing outrageous stuff. It's hard to comprehend."

He laughed at that. "Yeah, I know. I am on the periphery of that. I have a lot of followers due to my lifestyle and I make money for promoting products, but I do have a real job."

He did?

"You do?"

"Yeah, having fun and giving everyone a lifestyle to aspire to."

She shook her head. "I'm not sure that's a real job, but I'm glad that you have all those followers."

"Why?"

"So they will come to the Soiree," she said. "If one of your groupies took a ride with you from LA to Texas, imagine how many will flock to our event if they know you will be there."

"So you're using me?"

"Yeah," she admitted, taking her eyes off the road to grin at him. "But I think you like that."

"We will see."

Two

They got out of her car when they got onto the ferry that would take them from Trinity Bay to Appaloosa Island. Mustang Point was an elite waterside community, and he was impressed by the yachts moored in the marina. This was his type of place. And hopefully it would distract him from Lila—the drive down had only heightened his awareness of her. He was trying to find the chink in her armor but so far, he hadn't. To be honest, he wasn't looking that hard.

She paid for their tickets and chatted with the man who was selling them. If Zach had learned anything on the three-hour drive, it was that Lila was open and friendly. There was something almost innocent about her and it was refreshing after the LA scene, where everyone was trying to outshine one another.

Lila walked back over to him, her wide-leg pants undulating with each step. His eyes drifted upward to assess the rest of her outfit. She had on a slim-fitting Breton shirt, which showed off her slender waist and the curve of her breasts. Again, he wondered why she was single. He wasn't going to make the mistake of asking her another pointed question…or was he? She intrigued him.

True, he was bored and at loose ends while he figured out his next move, but still he tried to reassure himself that he would have found her interesting even if he wasn't in this rather small Texas town. He knew that was a lie and while he had no problem putting on a facade for his followers, he had always tried to never lie to himself.

That was a path that he had long ago realized if he started down, he'd never come back from. His life was all about showing off; he knew that it was smoke and mirrors, and most of the time that didn't bother him. *Oh, hell.* Was he getting melancholy? He shook his head. It was just being here in the state his grandfather had talked so much about, stirring up old dreams that were better left in the past. And of course, Lila stirring up new desires that he knew had no future.

"The ferry will be leaving in ten minutes," she told him. "There aren't a lot of facilities on the island so if you need…well, it's over there."

She sort of blushed when she gestured and he turned to see what she was pointing to.

The ferry offices were there, and he noticed a restroom sign. He almost laughed again. She was too much. Just so *different*. He liked it. A little too much, he thought. He was in Texas to lie low, not start something with this small-town sweetheart.

"I'm fine," he said.

"Okay. So, um, now that I'm not concentrating on driving, do you have any questions for me?"

He did. But he knew she wasn't inviting him to probe into her personal life. He was also curious about how she'd feel in his arms and what her kiss would be like. Prim and proper...or hot and unrestrained? She was a mix of both things and he wondered if there was something in her past that made her hide that side of herself. "I'll wait until I've seen the facilities. The pdf you supplied was interesting." A bit dull. But perhaps that was only because of the document. He wanted to see the venues before he made any judgments.

"That's fair. I haven't been out here since all of the construction has been completed. I'm really impressed by the committee so far. I don't want to let them down," she said.

"You won't."

"I wish I had your confidence...and your followers," she confessed.

His *followers*.

He seemed to have an instinct for posting the right sort of photos and wording his text in a way that people liked. A lot of the time, especially in the beginning, he'd been sarcastic, and his audience had thought he was joking. They loved his sense of humor. Which in a way had given him carte blanche to be himself. Or this version of himself. Speaking of which, he hadn't posted for almost twenty-four hours on his social media channels. He'd needed time to think. To regroup and figure out his next move. He enjoyed his bad-boy reputation, but he had always felt that he was a good man...until now.

He wondered if he'd become too inured in his lifestyle and lost a part of himself. Sleeping with a married woman—that was a line too far. And Ms. Jones was the balm for that.

His mom had texted him as he'd left LA…one of her little nudges. She always couched it as "hope you are okay," but he knew she wanted him to get a real job. To stop making money off influencing people. So he'd just texted back a smiley face and left it at that.

"Followers are good, but if I burn them by recommending something that's not up to the normal standards, they will turn on me. And rightly so. They've put their trust in my platform and I have to make sure that I deliver."

"What exactly do you deliver?" she asked. The ferry pulled in and she walked back over to the Mini Cooper.

He followed her and got in, thinking about her question. What *did* he deliver? "A lifestyle that is fun, sexy and luxurious. I give them something to dream about and an escape from their everyday lives."

Lila nodded as she carefully drove onto the ferry. "That's perfect for our event. I hope you will agree to share it with your followers."

She pushed her sunglasses to the top of her head, and he couldn't help noticing her pretty brown eyes. They were big and wide and she smiled easily at him. That mouth of hers tempted him, too. The full lower lip seemed to beckon him closer, but then he noticed it moving.

She was telling him something. Probably something important. Probably nothing to do with where his mind was heading.

"I'm sorry…what did you say?"

"Just that I don't think you are going to be disappointed."

Oh, hell.

He knew he wasn't going to be disappointed in the woman, but the event had *snoozefest* written all over it from what he'd read. Now he was in a quandary. Did he stay here and help her out in the hopes of getting into her pants? Or was he going to be honest and go back to LA where an angry husband was waiting for him?

No choice really.

He was going to have to find a way to make this work, because he wasn't ready to leave Lila Jones. Not yet.

"Oh, I'm sure you and I can come up with something to keep that from happening," he said.

She blushed and nodded. "I'll do whatever I have to in order to make this event a success."

"Perfect."

Lila found Zach charming and easygoing. After the drive down she'd stopped feeling nervous about being around a man who was so famous. Well, mostly. It was hard because as she drove them off the private ferry toward the eastern side of the island, she saw people watching the car. Even when she'd been buying the ferry tickets, people had noticed him.

Mostly younger people. The young, well-heeled mon-eyed crowd were exactly who they wanted to attract to Soiree on the Bay. They had the energy to share on social media the charities that the committee was promoting.

"The western half of the island is famous for its pristine beaches and a small boutique hotel. There are a few large vacation homes as well," she explained. "After we see the venue, I can drive you by them if you'd like."

"Sure."

She drove away from the ferry toward the festival

grounds. There hadn't been a lot on the island before they'd started constructing them. She parked in the dirt lot and put her keys in her pocket as she got out, slinging her bag over her shoulder as she waited for Zach to join her.

"This is the parking area, obviously, and that field over there beyond will be for overnighters. I'm talking to a company that does glamping pods right now."

"Glamping?"

"Yes. Well, not everyone who attends will be able to stay on their yachts, and the community of Mustang Point only has 750 hotel rooms. And the boutique hotel is very small. They do have a golf cart and Jeep service to pick up guests and bring them from the landing strip or this side of the island back to the resort."

"Um-hmm," he said.

She wasn't sure how to respond to that, so she put on her best tour guide voice and smile and led him around the island. "This is the second music venue, sort of the smaller stage. I was thinking, like Glastonbury, it will be a place for up-and-coming artists to showcase their talent."

"That's a good idea. Have you talked to any record companies?"

"I have some feelers out," she said. Not wanting to let him know that once he was on board and they started generating some real promotional buzz, she would make the calls. She didn't want their top choices to turn the Soiree down before she had done this kind of work.

"Over here will be the first of the three restaurants. It's sort of based on a sports bar with a fusion menu. It will be open 24/7, serving both in the restaurant and some takeaway basket–type prepared meals."

"Do you have a celebrity chef doing the menus?"

"I'm not sure. I think so. I can find out and let you know. I know that another member of the planning committee is handling that."

He nodded again. Then waited for her to go on.

Lila wasn't sure what he was thinking. She kept getting distracted by the spicy scent of his aftershave and the way that the sun brought out the highlights in his thick brown hair. The breeze on the island swirled around them, ruffling his hair, but it always landed back in the perfect spot. Her own mane, on the other hand, felt like it was growing with the humidity. And she was pretty sure that it was getting frizzy despite the products she'd put in it earlier in the day.

She showed him the rest of the venue and he asked a few questions but not really that many. Tension gnawed at her. She was worried that he wasn't impressed, and she had no idea how to wow him. But she was determined to do whatever she had to in order to get him on board with the event.

"How do you feel about grabbing a drink at the hotel?" she asked. "We can discuss your thoughts there."

"Sounds great," he said.

She drove them over there, and they were seated on the patio of the restaurant, which afforded them an unspoiled view of the bay. He ordered a Jack and Coke. She had sparkling water with a twist of lime.

Finally she couldn't wait any longer. "So what do you think? Will you let your followers know about the Soiree on the Bay?"

He took a sip of his drink, then leaned back. "There are a lot of festivals out there. Why should people come to yours?"

Well, he had her there. Why *should* they? They

weren't Coachella, but she felt with the right planning and people in place they could be. "I don't know. I'm not sure I can figure that out on my own."

"Don't worry, I can. What you need is sizzle."

Sizzle.

"I mean I can guarantee some sizzle from the Texas heat, and the food is going to be great, but I'm sure that's not what you meant."

"It isn't."

She knew it. She looked into Zach's blue eyes. He had sizzle. Oodles of it. And sex appeal. But there was no way she could figure out how to get that into the event. Not on her own. She'd tried to do sexy one time and it had backfired—big-time. Convincing her to stick to what she knew. Who she was. And she was that quirky, smart girl whom everyone liked. Not a hot fantasy woman.

"So what should we do? I mean you are absolutely right. We don't have anything that makes us stand out."

"Don't worry, Lila, I got this."

"You got this?" she asked. "Sure, you have your own brand of sizzle but I don't see how that's going to translate to Soiree on the Bay."

"You think I have that?" he asked, leaning in, and she noticed the tiny gray flecks in his irises. He smiled at her and wriggled his eyebrows.

He liked to flirt, and she had to admit she wasn't used to that sort of attention from any guy. She was the reliable woman everyone turned to in order to get things done. But Zach acted like...well, like she was that hot blonde who'd stalked away from his car. Okay, that might be an exaggeration, but he seemed to actually see her. And that was new. She kind of liked it but at the same time, she was scared. No one had ever really seen through her quirkiness. She knew she used it as a shield. And now she was wondering what she was going to do with Zach.

"You know you do," Lila said, taking a sip of her sparkling water. She'd put on those thick-rimmed sunglasses of hers so he couldn't see her eyes. Only himself reflected in the lenses. He looked good in this light, but he wanted to know more about *her*.

"You're right, I definitely do," he admitted. His mom had always said that he was born with the spotlight on him. He just had naturally gravitated to attention. And yeah, he liked it and had luckily found a way to cultivate that into the life he wanted.

"So humble."

"Listen, why pretend that I can't see what I'm good at?" he asked, grinning at her. He wasn't like Lila— he didn't want to blend into the background. And to be honest, he wondered if she wanted that for herself. Though she was a plain dresser, her attitude and her personality were anything but. Lila Jones was born to sparkle, but for some reason she hid that side of herself. He wanted to know why.

She just smiled and shook her head. "Why indeed. Actually, that is why I contacted you. If you promoted our event. Just talked about it…"

He could. But he wasn't sure that he was going to be able to spend the kind of time in Texas that he needed to in order to help her that way. It would be better if she had a following that she could use to promote her cause.

"What's your social media account?" he asked.

"What? Um… I messaged you from it. LilaJones93."

He pulled it up and there were a grand total of twelve pictures listed on the account. The most recent had been last Christmas and a photo of her tea in a Christmas mug that said I've Been Good. The account seemed like it would belong to, well, a grandma and not the young hip kind, but one who was ninety-three. "No offense, but your account screams crazy cat lady."

"Okay. Calm down. Not everyone is so obsessed with themselves that they feel they need to post a selfie four times a day."

"It's six, actually," he said. "And you reached out to me. So I'm guessing you wanted feedback."

"Feedback on the event. Not a personal critique of my own social media presence. Or lack thereof. But that is my life. I have my job and my quiet life. I know it's not going to bring the 'sizzle' you're talking about. But I'm not you."

No, she wasn't him. But she could be with a few tweaks. He shouldn't have been so blunt in his assessment of her Instagram account and he knew she'd taken it as an attack on her way of life. Which was as foreign to him as his was to her. But as she'd so aptly pointed out, it was *her* life.

"I'm sorry for what I said," he apologized. "I never meant to hurt your feelings."

"It's okay. I'm glad you were honest with me," she admitted. "It's just who I am."

This was who she was? No way. Lila was so much more than a few pictures of teacups and books or the PBS Masterpiece screenshots she posted. She was funny, witty, smart and someone people would find engaging...if she changed a few things.

And she was the perfect distraction, he thought. No use trying to pretend he wasn't doing this for himself. He wanted her, but the way she was right now...well, there was a very real chance he'd hurt her if they had a summer hookup. But if he helped her out of her shell, showed her how to be that sassy woman she kept hidden behind her plain clothing and thick glasses, maybe a few nights burning up the sheets with him would be enough. And maybe, along the way, he'd start feeling like himself again.

"I have an idea," he said. The thought had come to him suddenly. He knew how to make anyone famous in the social media world and then translate that to the real world. He'd done it for many of his protégés. And he could do it for her.

"Great. That's why I asked you here."

That smart mouth just made him want to kiss her. But he wasn't going to. Not yet, anyway. Zach wanted to prove his point that she was hiding her true self behind her girl-next-door persona. He knew she believed in herself, so why was she shy at times and feisty at others? His eyes roved over her, drinking in every gorgeous facet. He wanted to pull that dynamic woman to the surface. Show her the sizzle she had deep inside and for some reason was afraid to show the world.

"What if I told you that I could make you famous? That you could promote the Soiree on the Bay without me."

"I'd say the Texas sun has gotten to you," she said, laughing. "I promise you right now that won't happen."

"If you put yourself in my hands it will," he assured her. "In fact, I bet you right now that if we go into the shop in the lobby and get you a different outfit, I could post a picture of you that will get over five hundred likes in the first hour."

"And if it doesn't?" she asked. "Will you give up this notion and promote the event from your own account? And attend all of the press events?"

He narrowed his eyes. She was fighting this change. He got it. For as much as he put himself out there every day, there were still pockets of truth he hid from the world. Was he urging her to do this for any reason other than as a sop for his conscience so he could feel okay about seducing her?

He turned away from her. Forced himself to be real for a minute. As much as he wanted Lila in his arms, he wanted the world to see that beautiful, quirky, sassy woman.

He saw what she was doing but he knew that under his guidance he could create a social media image for Lila Jones that would garner more attention than she ever dreamed possible. "You have to do exactly what I say. That means clothes, hair, *everything*…and I'll tell you what to post until you get the hang of it. No quibbles."

"No quibbles? Exactly what does that mean?" she asked.

"That I get final approval on everything you wear and eat and talk about on your account. I get to mold you."

"Mold me? I like me."

"I like you, too, Lila. But no one is noticing you the way you are now. I'm not talking about changing you, I'm talking about dressing you and photographing you in a way that shows the world the real Lila. That way the success of the event is yours." This was his hard sell. She hadn't come to him asking to be Insta-famous, and if he was honest, a part of him expected her to turn him down. But another part, that deep-seated masculine part, sensed she'd rise to the challenge. His gut told him there was a part of her that wanted to stop blending in with the background.

"I don't need the success to be mine," she said. "The committee has a lot of really talented people on it."

"Including you." She was too quick to hide her own sparkle and he didn't understand what made her do it.

But regardless, he wanted to change that. Of course he knew once she started getting the attention she'd change. Maybe lose a little of that innocence, and then he wouldn't feel so bad about flirting with her and maybe getting her in his bed. Then they'd be a part of the same world and understand that nothing lasted.

He felt a pang.

Did he want to do that?

She was more complicated than he wanted her to be. But then so was life. And it was her decision. "So what'll it be? You in?"

She didn't answer immediately and he wondered if she would turn him down. He was asking her to change a lot about herself and he could tell she wasn't unhappy with her life.

He wanted to get back to that himself.

"Okay, doll, you've got yourself a deal."

Three

Lila felt foolish as she stood in the dressing area of the chic boutique in the island resort. Zach had nudged her toward the changing area, asked the shop attendant to get her a glass of champagne and told her to wait.

She'd declined the champagne. That wasn't her style, but she went and sat down. Everything in this shop was totally out of her budget. She hoped that they would be amenable to some sort of payment plan where she put the pieces on different credit cards. Ugh. Why had she agreed to do this?

Truth be told, she had never really been that interested in fashion. She liked her clothes comfortable, and she kept her hair trimmed and occasionally wore lipstick, but that was it. That one time she'd tried to be different—no. She wasn't going there. She liked herself just as she was. This makeover was all about Zach. Because she needed him to help promote the Soiree, and if this was what she had to do to get him on board, then so be it.

Bottom line? They had gotten a lot of charities involved and they wanted to get A-list stars and chefs at the event, so she needed to do this. She wanted the event to be successful. Also, she was honest enough to admit that she liked Zach. His challenge was silly but the thought of having his full, undivided attention was…*intoxicating*.

"Where's the champagne?" he asked when he came into the dressing area with another shop assistant she hadn't seen earlier following him with a wheeled clothing rack.

"I decided water would be fine. Who's that?"

"This is Georgia. She's one of the Benningnites. She spotted us when we were having our drinks and volunteered to help out."

"It's no problem at all, ZB. I'm so thrilled to do it! Who is this?" Georgia asked, pointing at her.

"This is the woman I am making over," he said. "She and I have a little bet that I can't get her five hundred likes in an hour."

Georgia raised her eyebrows as if "ZB" had bitten off more than he could chew. Lila bit the inside of her cheek to keep from smiling. "I don't know if these clothes are going to be enough to do that."

"Trust me," Zach said. "Georgia, will you go and see if we can get some champagne?"

"Love to, ZB. Back in a mo," she said, turning and dashing away.

"Now, let's see," Zach said, turning back to the rack. He pulled off a pair of tiny tropical-printed shorts and a lacy top and handed them to her.

"Uh, I'm not letting you photograph me in something this…small."

"This is just so I can get an idea of your shape. Those pants and that shirt don't really tell me enough," he said. "Also, I'm offended you think I would pick something that wouldn't flatter you."

She wondered if he were pushing to see how committed she was to this makeover. She didn't blame him for picking something that was so totally different from what she was wearing.

She shook her head and took the clothing from him, going into the changing room without saying another word. He'd asked her for her sizes, so she knew they'd fit. She'd been a solid size 10 since eighth grade and rarely fluctuated. She knew it was trendy to be 00 but Lila liked food and not worrying about her figure too much to try to fit into that size. Her mom had once joked that the Jones women had hips; no use trying to pretend they didn't.

She took off her shoulder bag and placed it on one of the hooks on the wall. Then turned back and looked at herself in the mirror. Was she going to do this? She felt like she could back out at any time, but she knew if she did Zach was out the door.

Lila stopped debating and got changed. The shorts were shorter than she normally would wear but they were cute and the top…it was flattering, too, revealing her arms and scooping down over her breasts.

What would Zach think when he saw her? Oh, gosh, what if he didn't see any difference? Or if he was like—*no*. She couldn't let her mind go there. The clothes didn't change who she was at her core.

She forced herself to open the changing-room door and stepped out find Zach nowhere around. But she could hear his voice in the other room, and he was laughing and joking with someone. She went to peek out and see who he was talking to. A group of men and women were smiling at him and snapping selfies.

Oh, for Pete's sake.

At this rate, she was going to be here all day waiting for him.

"Hey, ZB, if you can spare a minute, I'm ready," she called to him.

"Later," Zach said to his fans, and came back over to her.

He took her hand in his, pulling her arm away from her body as his gaze scrutinized her from head to toe. She felt a tingle as if he were touching her as his eyes moved over her neck, lingering on the curve of her breasts, before he finished looking down her body.

She shifted her legs as his gaze lasered in on them. She pulled her hand back and put it around her waist. This was a mistake.

Of course she never could resist a dare, and this had felt like one. But standing here, feeling so vulnerable...

She hated this.

"Nice legs, Lila," he said. His voice was deeper, huskier. "You look fabulous. I really like this on you. Do you?"

She scrunched up her mouth. His words washed away some of the self-consciousness that had settled on her. She turned back to the full-length mirror and saw herself this time without the fear and doubt. If she was doing this, she needed to be honest. Both with him and herself. "Yes, but not for a photo. I'd prefer to have my legs covered to mid-thigh, and the top is light and airy but the scoop is lower than I like."

"Okay. I can work with that," he said. "Now what about shoes?"

"These are fine," she said. "Already I'm going to be paying off these clothes for a few months."

"Oh, this is all on me," he said. "Then if you are as popular as I think you will be, the rest of your wardrobe will be gratis."

Gratis.

Who did he think he was? She wasn't going to argue with him just now. "Wardrobe?"

"Yes. If this works, one photo won't be enough. You're going to have to keep posting. Every day, Lila, not just at Christmas."

She laughed at him, tossing her hair, and for the first time she really let her guard down with him. There was something about Zach that felt very open and real, as if he were just what she saw. Though she knew everyone had hidden layers. "If it works. If not, then you will be posting about the Soiree."

"If this makeover fails…then yeah, I will fulfill my end of the deal. But I'm sure it won't. Now give me a minute to think about what will look best on you. Can you wear a heel?"

"Yes, I like the added height."

"I thought so. I noticed those chunky Mary Janes you were wearing."

"They are comfortable. Shoes have to be."

"Agreed."

She waited while he went over the rack of clothing and then put several things in the dressing room. Georgia came back with a waiter from the bar and a standing ice bucket with a bottle of champagne in it and three glasses. Lila left them to their drinks and went into the changing room to try on the clothes he'd put in there.

She shook her head. The colors were bold and eye-catching. Not her normal muted navy, peach and cream.

"Come out when you have the first outfit on. Wear everything I provided, and oh, here are some shoes."

He pushed a pair of strappy gold sandals under the door.

What had she gotten herself into?

Zach waited for Lila to change, trying to forget how hot she'd looked in those shorts. He had suspected she had a killer body under those sensible clothes, but he hadn't anticipated how turned on he'd get just from seeing her in clothing that fit her.

The sooner he got Lila out of her shell the better. Though he wondered if she was going to really let herself be comfortable in anything he chose. Speaking of which…she was taking a lot longer in the dressing room than he'd expected.

It had been funny to him that she hadn't believed him when he'd said she'd be popular. He knew the way followers reacted online and he was steering Lila to the sort of persona that would have the maximum effect. Also, his gut was seldom wrong.

Once she was popular, once she was like all the other women he knew, then…well then, he'd know how to handle her. He'd feel comfortable just being his flawed self around her. Instead of the guilt mixed with lust he felt right now.

Zach glanced toward the dressing room again. He wasn't nervous, but he was anxiously waiting to see her in the clothes he'd selected.

He'd settled on a classic A-line dress with a halter neckline. It was universally flattering and had a timelessness to the look, which he suspected Lila would appreciate. Georgia was chattering on about her summer and how she felt so lucky she was on Appaloosa Island when he'd arrived.

"Why are you here?" Georgia asked.

"I heard there was going to be a luxury food, art and wine festival here and wanted to check it out," he said.

"Are you coming back for it? I've heard about it, too, but I thought it was going to just be another event in the Mustang Point social calendar."

"It's going to be big," he stated, with a certain vagueness. He wasn't willing to commit to attending the event yet. There were still too many unknowns. Like if it would be a success or not. He wouldn't endorse something that might fail.

"I'll tell all my friends," she promised.

Her phone chimed and she groaned. "I have to go. Will you be here for a while?"

"Heading out in a short while. But it was great to see you," he said. "Maybe I'll see you at the Soiree."

She smiled and waved as she left. He took another sip of the champagne and waited. Scrolling through his social media feeds, he noticed that he'd been tagged in a lot of photos this afternoon. Well, he wasn't off the radar. Which was fine.

Zach grimaced when he saw a DM from the husband of the woman he'd been caught with. He wasn't about to open *that*. Instead, he delegated it to his assistant. That was why Dawn worked for him.

He heard the door of the dressing room open and glanced up and nearly lost his breath. The transformation wasn't complete, but in clothing that actually fit her and with those heels on... Lila Jones was a knockout.

He was trying to make it physical but when their eyes met and she smiled at him, he felt something...

something he'd never felt before. But he refused to let this be anything other than fun and flirty. That was it. All he had to give to anyone.

A therapist he'd seen after his parents' divorce had pointed out that he was reluctant to create any lasting bonds and Zach had shrugged it off. But those words lingered in his mind and he felt more and more that he'd never be able to be anything more than the photos on his feed.

And damn, she was hot. He had sensed it when he'd seen her in the shorts and scoop-neck blouse but this was next level. The confidence she'd always had was suddenly front and center. She wasn't trying to wrap her arms around herself like she had earlier.

He had included a headband and some various hair accessories that he'd seen in the shop, and he was pleased to see that she had pulled her hair up into a high ponytail, which left her shoulders bare. She'd even put on the earrings he'd selected.

He stood up, putting his champagne glass down before he walked over to her. God. How was he going to hide his reaction? Did he *have* to? "Damn, I'm good."

"*You're* good? I'm the one wearing it."

"And you wear it well," he rasped. "Step up here."

He gestured to the step situated in front of the three-mirror setup. Offering her his hand as she stepped up there. The mirror gave him every angle of her outfit and honestly there wasn't a bad one. Well, except for those rather large glasses, but they were cute and Lila. IRL—in real life—they'd be okay, but not for the photo he had in mind.

"Wait here."

He turned and went back into the main store area and sorted through the designer sunglasses on the rack. Finally settling on a pair of black cat's-eye frames. They weren't too big and would be perfect on her heart-shaped face. He brought them back in and stood next to her on the step in front of the mirror.

"Turn toward me," he commanded.

She did and he reached for her glasses, taking them off. She blinked at him as he did so. For this one moment when she couldn't see he let his guard down. Looked at her with the hunger she'd stirred deep inside him.

"What are you doing?" she asked. "These aren't for show. I need them to see."

"Trust me," he said. He needed her trust…needed her to follow wherever he led. And he honestly didn't want to go much farther than back in that dressing room so he could kiss her until they were both breathless and naked.

"You ask that a lot, don't you?"

"Just of you. Most people inherently do," he said.

"Most people are waiting to be told what to do," she retorted.

"Not you," he said, reaching up and pulling a few tendrils out of her ponytail to frame her face and then decided that they were too much and tucked them back behind her ear. He was trying to make her look like other influencers he knew but even in the same outfit she was still Lila Jones. Still so different from them. It wasn't the clothes, it was the woman.

Then he put the sunglasses on and stepped back. "Perfect."

"If I could see myself, I'd let you know if I agreed."

He almost laughed at the way she said it. "Put your glasses on and then step down and we'll find a good place to photograph you."

"Sure."

She took her glasses from him and a tingle went up his arm as their hands touched. He wanted to pretend it was just static electricity. But he knew it was more. He wanted her. He'd wanted her before when she'd been sweet and shy little Lila, but with the fashionable new clothes and hair…she was making him hard and addling his senses.

He was thinking that he wished he'd brought his private jet instead of his Ferrari to Texas, because then he could have swept Lila onto it and taken her someplace exotic and intimate.

"Zach…?"

"I'm sorry, what did you say?"

"I asked if I should leave my clothes in the changing room?"

"Yes. We are coming back."

She dashed in and grabbed that hideous bag of hers and he shook his head. "Not that sack."

She almost hugged the purse to her chest. "What's wrong with it?"

"Too much to explain. We will find something suitable before we leave. Let's go take a photo and see if this works."

"Oh, okay. But I'm not giving up my purse."

Zach didn't argue with her. Instead, he told the shop assistant they'd be back in a few minutes and led Lila out into the lobby, where he found the right background for the photo. He took her hideous bag and put it by his feet and then took her glasses and made her put on the sunglasses he'd found.

"I don't know why I'm wearing sunglasses inside," she complained.

"And that's why you have so few people following

you on social media." As he moved back to take the picture, he noticed that the men and women in the lobby were watching them. He heard someone ask who the woman was and smiled to himself.

This bet was in the bag. But he knew that this was never about winning, it was about getting Lila into his bed. About making her into the kind of woman that he could hook up with and not have regrets. He felt that twinge again deep inside. Why was he trying to take someone who had been unique, beautiful and natural and make her into a woman like so many others'?

Because he was selfish and wanted her more than he should.

Lila felt silly posing in the lobby of the chic boutique resort on Trinity Bay. It was odd, but when she'd been alone with Zach, she hadn't felt silly. As soon as she filtered out the other people and just concentrated on him, her nerves settled. Of course, once he'd taken her glasses from her and insisted she put on the sunglasses, she couldn't really see anything but blurry images.

That was oddly freeing.

She didn't worry about what anyone else was thinking about what she was doing because she couldn't see them. All she could truly concentrate on was Zach's voice. He told her how to stand and how to pose and when to smile, and she did it.

He took—no lie—about a million pictures. Or at least it felt that way to her. She wondered if he really thought that he was going to be able to make her into a social media star with just a change of outfit.

But she knew he didn't. He'd said *wardrobe*. Yet while he wanted this change to be permanent, she wasn't sure she did. He finally stopped and came back over to her.

"We are done for now," he said. "Here are your glasses. What do you think?"

He handed her his phone and at first she barely recognized herself. She'd felt sort of different when she'd seen herself in the mirror, but not being able to see everyone else in the lobby had been more liberating than she'd imagined. There was a playfulness and a confidence to her poses that she'd never seen in herself before.

"I like them."

It made her wonder why she hadn't thought to try this before. But she wasn't interested in delving into her psyche at the moment. "What now?"

"Well, I'm going to reach out to Warby Parker after we get your photo trending and ask them to make you some new glasses and sunglasses," he said. "But first let's pay for these clothes and then I'll show you how to post your picture to get the maximum likes."

Lila doubted that Warby Parker was going to want her wearing their glasses, and as much as the photo made her feel different, she still wasn't sure that Zach's confidence wasn't misplaced. She followed him back across the lobby and noticed that people were watching them. Of course they were. She was with Mr. Über Famous who just took it all in stride. But the eyes on her…well, it was flattering, but she was used to a certain amount of anonymity.

Zach had her old clothes wrapped up and put in a bag, which the shop attendant handed to her with a smile. "You look great."

"Thanks."

He led her back outside until they were standing with the bay to their back. "Put your sunglasses on."

She did it and he put his arm around her waist and pulled her close.

"What are you doing?" she asked. Trying to ignore the fact that her heart was beating faster and that she could feel the heat of his hand through her dress on her waist.

"Taking a selfie. We are about to start your social media climb," he said.

He put his sunglasses on, stretched his arm out and snapped a picture of the two of them.

"So never post a photo without editing it. Every platform has its own size that works best. I'll AirDrop you the dimensions when we are done. Next you want to find a filter that works best for you. I'd try this one... it's my favorite."

She leaned in closer, resting her hand on his upper arm so she could keep see the screen. A little tingle went straight up her arm and her nipples tightened. She wasn't going to pretend she didn't want Zach.

But she was his project...

"Then when you are satisfied with the image, you need to think of the right caption. What do you think we should say?"

"This is on your account?"

"Yes, I'm going to tag you," he said. "Tell the Benningnites to follow you."

"Fun day out with @lilajones93," she suggested.

"Maybe. How about this?" he asked.

She saw he captioned their photo with, "@lilajones93 is bringing the sizzle this summer in Texas. #SoireeontheBay."

"Now what?"

"Now we wait for the likes to come flooding in. One of my followers suggested a great seafood restaurant in Mustang Point. I'll treat you to dinner before we drive back to Royal."

Dinner?

She didn't have any plans tonight, but wasn't sure she liked that he thought she didn't. "I might have plans."

"Do you? I'm hungry. I just thought eating would be nice before we went on a three-hour drive."

Now she felt silly for even saying anything. "I was just being defensive. I hate when anyone assumes I don't have plans."

"Me, too. Do you want to eat with me?"

"I do," she admitted.

"Is seafood okay or do you have allergies?" he asked.

"Not allergic to anything but BS," she said.

"Good to know we have the same allergies," he deadpanned. "Let's get out of here."

"I'm going to have to put my prescription sunglasses on to drive," she told him.

"I'll allow it, since I'm not sure we want to be in a car accident."

"So glad you'll *allow* it… I'm a grown-ass woman, ZB," she said. "I make my own decisions."

"Oh, I know you are, LJ. I was teasing."

"Fair enough. But you've been very bossy today," she reminded him.

"It was to help out Soiree on the Bay."

She nodded and didn't say anything else but couldn't help wishing that he'd helped her out for herself and not the event. That made her face the fact that she might have agreed to the makeover because it had brought her into Zach's spotlight and she liked it more than she wanted to admit.

Four

Lila valet-parked the car and then followed Zach into the Republic of Texas Steak and Seafood House. He smiled at the maître d' and did his charming Zach thing while she hung back watching him. She wasn't sure how she felt about the afternoon. So much had changed in so little time.

Honestly, it rattled her. Probably because she didn't hate it as much as she thought she should. She had the feeling if she'd been dressed like this, Zach would have noticed her when he'd pulled up.

Her phone pinged and she saw it was a text from her mom.

Honey, you look great in that picture. Are you dating that guy?

Thanks, Mom. He's a work friend. For Soiree on the Bay.

Try to make him a friend friend. He's cute. ;)

Mooooom.

[kissing emoji] Have fun. Text me tomorrow. We can meet for lunch or coffee. Love you.

I will. Love you, too.

"Phone blowing up with likes?" Zach asked as he came back over to her.

"Uh, no. That was my mom."

"What did she say?" he asked. "Did she approve of your look?"

She rolled her eyes. "She liked it. Said you were cute."

"I like her already." Zach grinned. "You should be getting some notifications from the post…let me see your phone."

"Why?"

"I want to make sure your notifications are turned on," he said.

"Is that important?"

He looked at her as if she'd started speaking a different language. "It's *massive*. When we are seated, I'll show you. I've already gotten a ton of likes. So I'm sure you've gotten a few."

The maître d' offered them a glass of champagne while they were waiting to be seated and Lila almost groaned. "I have to drive home."

"What if you didn't?" Zach asked.

"Then I'd love a glass. It kind of feels like a champagne kind of day," she said. And in all honesty, Zach bought the good stuff, not the bottom-shelf grocery store sparkling wine that Lila usually purchased. "But I don't think you are going to skip drinking."

"I'm not," he said, winking at her. "Leave the details to me. We will get home safely and your car will be in your driveway in the morning."

"How?"

"Leave it to me," he repeated. "Can you do that, Lila Jones? Just stop worrying and planning and let go for one night?"

"Of course I can. I just might not want to," she huffed. But she *did* want to. She caught a glimpse of herself in the mirrored panels behind the maître d' stand. This was new Lila. "Fine. But my car better be there in the morning. I have a meeting at ten."

He just shook his head and laughed, turning to the waiter. "We'll have a bottle of champagne. Two glasses here, the rest at the table."

"Of course, sir," the waiter said, turning away.

Zach led her to a padded velvet bench and sat down next to her. "So, if you go in your app and hit the settings button you can turn on notifications."

He showed her on his phone, and she was surprised to see she already had way over five hundred likes on the photo that Zach had tagged her in. She turned on the notifications like he demonstrated and then went back to her profile to notice that her actual followers were increasing, too. By a lot.

"Uh, what's going on?" she asked Zach, showing him the increasing likes.

"You're going viral, LJ. Prepare to be famous," he said. "I need to make a quick call. I'll be back and then we will celebrate."

He got up and she stared at her phone. She couldn't believe one photo could change her online presence that much, but it had. A thrill shot through her. Zach was going to do wonders for the Soiree on the Bay. This was what the event needed. The kind of publicity that was in essence free.

Well, not really. Because no matter what he said, she'd have to pay him back for this outfit. And in regard to her "wardrobe"…she'd have to do some secondhand shopping and see what she could find. She'd never admit it to Zach, but she liked the new clothing he'd selected and she might even spring for new glasses. After all, she'd had this pair for almost five years now. Thankfully her vision had finally stopped worsening so she didn't need a new prescription, but maybe something a little trendier would be nice. Or even contacts… She could take the extra ten minutes in the morning to put them in.

"Oh, you're Lila Jones, right?"

She glanced up to see a group of three college-aged women standing there. "I am."

"We saw you with ZB. That's fab! What's this event he was talking about? Where can we buy tickets?" one of them asked.

Lila stood up and reached into her large bag to pull out the flyers she'd made up for the event. But as she started to, Zach returned and put his hand over hers. Stopping her, and she realized why. Those flyers looked like they were made in the office. They weren't slick or professional-looking.

"Ladies, hello. Lila has a website that you can check out. Soireeonthebay.com. She's still working on the print promotion."

When he winked over at her, she felt a connection. Like they were a couple. She liked it, but she cautioned herself that it wasn't real. Zach was a man used to lots of attention and he immediately made everyone feel at ease. She was nothing special.

"Great, ZB. Can we get a selfie with you both?" one of them asked.

What was going on? This was nuts. She found it hard to believe these women wanted a picture with her. Earlier today she'd had trouble flagging down the waitress for her check…and now *this*?

"Of course," Zach said, pulling her into his side and looking down at her with an impish grin. She felt a connection with him. As much as they were in this group, they were also just the two of them. Sharing a smile over the way these women were behaving around them. He told the girls to come around behind them, then took the phone and snapped a photo.

Their waiter came back and let them know their table was ready. *Thank goodness*. She wasn't sure she was ready for the amount of attention being with Zach garnered. He loved it, she noticed, but he didn't shove her to the side. He included her, which she liked. He seemed to want to share the spotlight with her.

"See you at the Soiree," he murmured, putting his hand on the small of her back as they followed the waiter.

She felt an electric tingle go down her spine and she realized how long it had been since her last date. This was business, but she couldn't help herself. She liked Zach and a part of her wanted this to be personal. Though that was crazy, because his life was on a different level than hers. And changing her clothing and her look was one thing. She wasn't interested in changing her life.

* * *

They'd been seated at the best table in the house next to a large glass window that provided spectacular water views. As the sun set, the lights from the marina reflected on the bay, the yachts that were moored in the water came to life, and for once, Zach didn't feel that gnawing need to be somewhere else. He'd always had something worse than FOMO—fear of missing out— and had always struggled to be content with what he had and where he was.

But with Lila sitting across from him, gazing alternately at her phone, which kept lighting up with notifications, and then out the window at the bay, it felt different. She *enchanted* him. He knew it was because she was new. It had happened before. He also knew he was going to just go for it. Follow this feeling for as long and as far as he could.

In a way, dating one girl had always stirred that feeling of missing out, like there was another woman that he'd have more fun with. One woman couldn't tame him. He loved women, but he had never been satisfied by just one. For now, though, Lila was enough.

"What are you thinking?" he asked. "You keep staring at the yachts."

"Just wondering where they have been… Actually, that's not true. I'm staring out there because when I look at my phone, I can't believe that people liked our photo that much and then I panic thinking how am I going to sustain that kind of thing. Is it a fluke?"

Zach couldn't remember a time when he worried about anything like that. He'd been famous since he was in his early twenties…and knew that he was luckier than most. Born into an affluent family with connections, it had been easy to make his social media account one that people would follow. He was doing stuff most people could only dream of. But Lila wasn't *most* people.

"Don't worry. Tomorrow we will go shopping and—"

"I have a meeting at ten," she reminded him.

He normally didn't get up until well after ten, but just nodded. "Not a problem. Afterward, we will get your new wardrobe. I have some friends—other influencers—who do glam for me and I asked them to come to Royal and give you a few tips."

"Glam? Zach, I'm not glamorous, and I think everyone in town will be shocked if I start dressing like this every day."

"Why?" he asked. "You're wearing a pretty summer dress, not haute couture. Is it that you won't be comfortable?"

She tipped her head to the side. "Do we know each other well enough to have this kind of conversation?"

"We don't. But I've always found that deep subjects are better discussed with strangers."

Lila nodded and looked away again, back out at the bay. He had the feeling he'd disappointed her. *Get used to it, honey*, his subconscious jeered. He shut down that annoying inner voice. But the thought lingered. He knew that as much as he might say that he liked to keep moving, a part of him had learned early on that he wasn't good in relationships.

A part of him felt like that stemmed from his father. The old man couldn't commit, and neither could Zach. But another part knew being a bad boy just worked for his brand. Kept him on target and raking in the money.

"I only meant it's easier to unload your secrets when you have no agenda. And usually with strangers there isn't one. You don't have any expectations from me... other than helping you promote your event."

She looked back at him and her brown eyes seemed a little nervous. "I don't like being the center of attention. I'm sure that's not a shock to you. I took the job at the Royal Chamber of Commerce because I love my community. But I usually work behind the scenes."

"And you thought this would be another behind-the-scenes role?"

"Yes, and let's be honest—my role is definitely behind-the-scenes," she murmured. "It's you and your dare making me step out of the shadows. I never expected to be doing this."

"Do you want to stop? Go back to your old self?" he asked. "You haven't done anything except get tagged in a photo with me."

"I know that." She sighed. "But I have to admit I like it. Those women in the lobby asked about the event and were ready to book tickets… This is the kind of promo I was hoping to generate."

Their food arrived before she could say anything else and he noticed her phone was still blowing up with notifications and text messages. She looked at it and then smiled.

"What is it?"

"Nothing. Everyone on the committee has noticed the likes. I think I'm going to have to keep doing this. But if I do, we need to establish some ground rules," she said.

He took a bite of his sea bass, nodding at her and trying to figure out what kind of rules she was talking about. Like missionary position only? He had the feeling she'd be more adventurous in bed, but knew that wasn't what she'd meant. His mind was just going to filthy places.

"Like what?"

"You can't buy me clothes. I'm not comfortable with that. I will pay you back for this... It might be in installments, but I *have* to pay you back," she insisted.

"Fine. But the truth is, we won't be paying for many of your clothes," he said. "Usually stores and labels gift them to me as long as I tag them in the photos. And it will work the same for you."

"How does that make them money?" she asked curiously.

"Well, all of your followers are going to want to be like you," Zach explained. "So we tag the brands, the shop you purchased it in, and then we let the likes and human nature do the rest. People will start snapping up the items. You'll be gifted more stuff than you have ever imagined."

She shook her head, that high ponytail swinging with the motion, drawing his eye to the long, graceful line of her neck. "All because of a few pictures?"

"No. All because of your image and your influence. That's how you are going to wow your followers and make them want to meet you at Soiree on the Bay."

Just like she was wowing him with her honesty and charming him with her smile, he thought. Now he needed to step up his game and start wowing *her*.

Lila stopped worrying after her second glass of champagne. It was so delicious, she started to wonder why she didn't drink it more often. Zach suggested a walk along the pier at the marina after their meal and looped her arm through his as they walked. She tipped her head back and looked up at the stars in the night sky. It was so vast and clear tonight.

She watched them twinkling and then caught her breath as she saw a shooting star. She made a quick wish that this night would be as magical as she felt it was in this moment.

"What is it?" he asked.

"Shooting star. Quick…make a wish!"

He didn't look up at the sky as he stopped walking but turned and looked down into her eyes. "I wish for one kiss."

She gazed up at him. His thick eyebrows, the tanned skin and the full mouth that easily smiled. *One kiss.*

She wanted that, too, on this night. With him. It had been so long since she'd wanted a man. She had been on dates and even slept with a few guys in the last year or so. But honestly, it had been more just to get out of the house. It hadn't felt like *this*.

Her rational mind shouted it was the champagne and the moonlight, but she didn't care. She wanted that kiss as much as he did.

She put her hand on the side of his jaw, felt the rough abrasion of his stubble, and then he turned his head and kissed the center of her palm. A shiver ran up her arm and her breasts felt fuller, her heart beat faster again and everything feminine inside her seemed to wake up and say, *Yes, girl, let's get some more of this guy.*

"There's your kiss," she said.

"Damn."

She looked up at him from under her eyelashes and shook her head. "You missed."

"I did?"

"Yes, you did," she whispered, going up on tiptoe, balancing herself with her hand on his shoulder and kissing him.

The first brush of her lips against his was everything she'd hoped it would be and more. The giddy butterflies in her stomach took flight and she brought her other hand to the back of his neck, pushing her fingers up into the thick hair at the back of his head.

His hand was on her waist, pulling her into his body, and his chest was solid against her torso. He lifted her slightly and then shifted so that his back was to the walkway, keeping them from prying eyes.

As he leaned down over her, she felt his lips part and his tongue brush over hers. She sighed. He tasted so good. Of champagne and that minty thing he'd had for dessert. His arms around her were solid and she clung to him, realizing how easy it would be to fall under his spell. She pulled back and looked up at him. Something shifted inside her and she wondered if she'd be here in his arms if she hadn't agreed to his makeover.

Ugh.

She hated that notion. Where were these thoughts coming from?

The smart part of the brain and not the hoo-hah, her subconscious reminded her.

Stop.

"What is it?"

"Would you have kissed me if I was still wearing my regular clothes?" she asked.

Oh, great, now she decided to start dropping truth bombs instead of enjoying the champagne glow of the evening.

"Yes. I wanted to kiss you in the doorway of the chamber of commerce building when you first ran into me."

Was he lying?

She realized she didn't know him well enough to be able to judge the truth from the lies. And did it matter? Deep conversations, like white-hot sex, were probably best exchanged between strangers. Or at least that was her experience. The hot flame of lust often didn't last in relationships and it had been a really long time since… Was she going to let this chance slip away?

"What are you thinking, Lila? No woman has ever looked at me the way you do," he confessed.

She put her hand on the side of his face again because she liked touching him. Liked the feel of his stubble against her palm. Liked the way he met her gaze squarely and didn't hide from her. Liked…him.

Danger, girl.

She knew it was dangerous. Didn't need her subconscious to warn her. Zach wasn't a stranger to her anymore. He was starting to become real. She already wasn't sure how she was going to work with him and still keep her head straight. Now she was kissing him in the moonlight and making wishes on stars that weren't sensible.

"Lila?"

"I was just wishing that this was real. That this night wasn't just magic and make-believe," she said softly. The words meant as a reminder to herself but ones that she was struggling to make herself heed.

He quirked a brow. "Why isn't it real?"

"Really, ZB? You know why. I'm your flavor of the moment, and don't shake your head and pretend it's anything else."

"I wasn't going to. What's wrong with that?"

"Nothing," she told him. "If I was really the girl in that selfie you snapped. But I'm still me inside."

He stepped back, nodding his head a few times and putting his hands on his hips. "You're you on the outside, too. You just haven't adjusted to the new look and the new attitude. I can wait until you do."

"What if I never do?"

"Then we will have had this one kiss in the moonlight, and I will count myself a lucky man," he said.

Her heart wanted to melt but that stubborn part of her psyche pointed out that he was good at making people believe what he said. She needed to remember that.

Five

"So how exactly are we getting home?" she asked as they walked back to the restaurant and met the Uber he'd called.

"I thought we'd take a helicopter," he said as the driver took them to the small airport and helipad where the chopper he'd rented waited.

"Really? I've never been on one. I mean, I've wanted to, but oh, my gosh. Is it scary?"

He shook his head, smiling at her. "Not scary... unless you're afraid of heights. I should have checked first. Are you?"

"No. Not at all," she said. "My parents took a helicopter tour in Hawaii for their twenty-fifth wedding anniversary. I have been wanting to try it, too."

"Then I'm glad I booked it," he told her.

Soon they were seated with their padded headphones

on and the helicopter lifted off. Lila grabbed his hand as it did so. Squeezing his fingers.

"Are you okay?" he asked.

"Yes," she replied, her voice full of excitement. "Sorry about that."

She let his hand go and then leaned toward the window to look out as the pilot took them over Trinity Bay and Mustang Point.

"It's so pretty from up here."

"It is," Zach said, but he was looking at her. He realized that he might have made a colossal mistake by waging this bet with her. He thought he was making her into a woman who could run her own brand campaign, but he knew it was more. His jaw flexed. Was he trying to make up for the sin he'd committed in Los Angeles?

A part of him wanted to play it like he was too jaded to care if he'd slept with another man's wife, but he knew he wasn't. Helping Lila wasn't going to erase that mark on his soul, but it would give him something positive to focus on. He knew he wasn't one to just use someone for his own gain…and while he liked to live life on the edge, deep down he'd always felt like he was a fairly decent person.

Lila was helping to give him a bridge back to that.

But at what cost?

"Oh, wow. I love this! The sky is even bigger up here," she said.

"It is," he agreed. She kept up a running commentary over the different sights they passed and he listened to her. He'd given her this. To him this was just a quicker way of getting from place to place. But to Lila this was an *experience*. He let that thought settle in his mind. What would she do if he took her on his private jet?

She'd probably be over the moon. But this was also a reminder of how different they were. There was an innocence to Lila that he didn't want to ruin. Yet wasn't that inevitable?

Making her over was just step one in creating a new Lila. The kind of Lila who would easily fit in and thrive in the spotlight the way he did. He wanted that for her. But he also liked it for himself, too. Helping people like Lila find their own brand and style had always appealed to him. She grabbed his leg as the lights of Royal came into view. "I can see the chamber building from here. I always knew Royal was a beautiful city, but seeing it all lit up makes it even more magical."

They landed at the helipad in the neighborhood where the house he'd rented earlier was, while she'd been getting changed. There was a golf cart waiting to take them to the house. He tipped the pilot and then led Lila to the golf cart.

"Whose house is this?"

"Mine. I rented it."

"What?" she said, her eyes widening. "I thought you'd be heading back out of town as soon as you made a few posts about the event."

"I'm not ready to leave yet," he told her.

"Why not?"

"Well, I have to finish helping you pick out your wardrobe, and I want to meet the rest of the advisory committee," he said. "Find out a little more of your world."

She twirled a long strand of her hair around her finger as she tipped her head to the side to stare at him. "My world? It's not as exciting as anything we've done tonight. It's just sitting on the back porch listening to the fountain my dad helped me install in the backyard and reading one of my favorite books. Or going to a night class at the community center and learning how to make origami birds."

There was a note in her voice that didn't sound dismissive. Lila liked those things. She liked that quiet pace, he could tell. He wondered if, in his selfishness to make it okay for him to go after her, he'd lured her into a bargain she might regret. But would that make it his fault? As she'd said, she was a grown-ass woman.

"I'll be the judge of that," he said. "Do you need to go home now? Or do you have time for a nightcap?"

She seemed to debate her answer, sitting next to him in the golf cart in front of his house. There were two cars in the drive. His Ferrari and an Audi sedan that the driver he'd hired would use. He was a brand ambassador for Audi, so the car had been sent over from the local dealer.

"I don't think I should drink another thing tonight. Like I said, I have work in the morning and then I have the meeting with the advisory committee on Friday," she said. "I'll let them know you want to attend."

"Good. Then I will have my driver take you home."

"You have a driver?"

"Yes. I have an entire team," he answered.

She rolled her eyes at that.

"I hope you will forgive me, but I did order a few things for you to wear to the office tomorrow." He flashed a grin. "And FYI...you're all mine after your 10 a.m. meeting."

Her gaze shot to his. "I—I am?" she stammered.

"Yes, you are. I am taking you to Dallas for a shopping spree in the afternoon."

"I can't…"

"Why, do you have something scheduled?" he asked.

"No. But—"

"We made a deal. Five hundred likes in an hour and you put yourself in my hands."

"I put my *wardrobe* in your hands," she reminded him pertly.

He winked at her. He wanted all of her in his hands. "Of course. That's what I meant."

"Oh, good," she said. "Can't we go shopping here in Royal?"

"We could, but then your friends and family would be around. I thought you'd be more comfortable in Dallas."

She nibbled her lower lip, which just made him remember how soft her mouth had been under his and how much he wanted another kiss. One hadn't been enough.

Five hundred likes on one picture was what he'd used to buy that kiss, and he wondered how many likes it would take for her transformation to be complete. For her to suddenly be like him.

"Okay. Yes. We can do that. Can we take your helicopter again?"

"Yes. Meet me here after your meeting," he said.

Lila had a restless night's sleep dreaming of Zach and that hot kiss they'd shared. She'd wanted more but at the same time, this situation was reminiscent of that time she'd changed her looks for a man and been burned by him. She shook off those thoughts. Zach wasn't using her. If anything, she was using him—for work.

Stay focused, she reminded herself.

There were several packages waiting on her front porch step, all from Neiman Marcus. Her mom, who lived two streets over from Lila, had come by for coffee and to find out all about Zach. The last thing she wanted to do was have a chat about a guy she still wasn't sure about.

But as her mom helped her bring in all the boxes, she knew she was going to have to tell her something.

"I made a silly bet with him and that's what this is," she said as her mom watched her opening all the boxes.

"What kind of bet? You're normally not a gambler."

Her mother sounded concerned. Lila hoped she wasn't remembering Peter and that disastrous time she had tried to make herself into a different woman for him. The only thing that would make this embarrassing was to have to discuss that and what was happening with Zach. Or maybe it would help. Make her have to focus on how this situation was different.

For one thing, she wasn't changing anything to please him. It was for herself. Truly she liked the way that she'd felt in the new outfit Zach had selected yesterday.

So as long as it felt right, she thought her mother would be okay with this.

"I know, Mom. He said that I wouldn't need him to promote our event if I started using my social media accounts in a different way. He said he could get me over five hundred likes in an hour if I just changed my clothes and took a selfie with him."

"And he did it, didn't he?"

"Yes. But now he thinks if I just keep doing this, taking photos of myself..." She cringed. "Oh, Mom, what have I gotten myself into?"

Her mom had gotten up and was helping her open all of the packages with an amused smile on her face. She pulled out a cute, trendy outfit and held it up. "I don't know, but I like it. This is the first time I've seen you…well, excited about a boy."

Boy.

Ha.

Zach wasn't a boy. He was a total superhot man as evidenced by the steamy dreams that he'd starred in last night. She almost blushed and turned away because she knew her mom would notice. "It's not him per se as much as it is…just the thought of doing something new."

"Good. Do you want this change?"

Her mother always had a way of asking the shrewd questions that Lila tended to avoid answering to herself.

"I think I do. I really liked the way I felt yesterday, it was fun, and when I saw myself in the mirror—it was like I was the girl I see in my head, you know what I mean?"

"I do," she said. "And there is nothing wrong with dressing up and liking what you see. You've always seemed to shy away from all of this. Just make sure you haven't made this decision for someone else."

She shook her head. "Of course not. I think this will help with my job, which you know I love. And the Soiree, which I want to be a success."

"Then great. I love it. Wish I could stay and watch you try on all these clothes, but your father booked us an earlier tee time than normal. I swear, that man is trying to make me crazy now that he's retired," her mom said with a smile as she kissed her on the top of the head and ran out the door after saying goodbye.

Lila watched the door close behind her and then looked back at all the clothes. She was still young but there was a part of her that wanted the loving partnership her parents had found. While she knew there had been a lot of ups and downs between them and she was very happy in her single life, there was something to be said for sharing a life with another person.

Of course, she probably needed to figure herself out before she tried a relationship, she thought.

Which led her right back to the fashionable new wardrobe awaiting her. Her mom had been supportive—honestly, she and her dad always were—and Lila knew she was blessed to have that kind of family. But she'd also been right when she'd said this kind of change couldn't be for likes or for followers. It had to be for herself.

Lila sighed. She wasn't like Zach, who moved blithely through the world, changing looks and lovers with the seasons and trends.

No matter how exciting that helicopter ride and her mini photo shoot had been, that wasn't real. Royal was real. She pulled the bright-colored designer outfit that had caught her eye out of the tissue and took it with her to get ready for her day. This was the kind of thing she'd have purchased for herself if she had the money. So she felt no guilt in wearing it.

She left the house, her hair once again in a high ponytail because she hadn't had time to do anything else with it, and drove to the office.

"Morning, Lila."

She smiled at Josh Peterson, one of her coworkers at the chamber of commerce, and waved at him as she walked over to the coffee shop to grab her morning java. Several men and women all smiled and waved at her, even strangers. Hmm…perhaps there *was* something to dressing differently, she thought.

"What have you been up to lately?" one of the guys who'd gone to high school with her asked.

"I'm helping organize the Soiree on the Bay," she said. "Have you heard about it?"

"Rumblings. Isn't that something that Rusty Edmond and his family are putting together?"

"Yes. It's going to be *fabulous*! Check out our web-site for more details. Hope to see you there."

"You will. Hope to see you again before then," he said, winking at her as he walked away.

Had he been flirting? She wasn't sure. In high school he had pretty much only talked to her when he wanted to cheat off her in English.

Lila got her coffee order and then went to her desk, realizing that no matter what else had happened yes-terday, Zach had given her a boost in confidence that she was definitely able to use in her job and in her life.

She wasn't going to tell him because his ego was big enough already, but these changes might have been long overdue.

Zach's crew all started arriving around ten, but he didn't get out of bed until noon normally. He'd always been a bit of an insomniac, so staying up all night and thinking about Lila and then her media presence had been a nice distraction.

He had to force himself to stop remembering how she'd felt in his arms, so instead he'd developed a plan and even sent several emails to his team to get them thinking. He wondered what she'd think about the clothes he'd had sent from Neiman Marcus and had half expected her to text him and tell him that she couldn't keep them, but she hadn't.

He had checked his phone a few times waiting for something from her and then realized what he was doing. *Likes* mattered, not people. But he'd thought she was different… Maybe she had been until he started making her over. Yeah, he knew that sounded cold but whenever he'd relied on a person…well, he'd been let down. He'd therefore learned to keep things bright and breezy. But some part of him was always sort of hoping for more.

"Hello, Mrs. Smith," he said, coming into the kitchen. His housekeeper always flew to wherever he was staying. She was fifty-six but looked younger and had been married to her high school sweetheart for three years before she'd been widowed. Mrs. Smith had no kids and said she'd learned that being married wasn't for her. She was motherly without smothering him and she knew how he liked his meals fixed. His housekeeper also had her own media account and a huge following, mainly folks who wanted to style their houses and food. She was a genius when it came to that.

"Morning, ZB. I staged your lunch at the table by the pool if you want to snap a pic before we talk about dinner. You mentioned a guest in your email. Fancy or simple Texas fare? I found a recipe from your great-granny Benning's notes that I could use."

"I like your thinking," he said. "Let me post my lunch and then we can discuss. Are the rest of the team here?"

"Vito and Dawn are. Shantal made a coffee run."

"We have coffee here," he reminded her.

"Oh, she knows, honey, but she wanted to check out Lila in person. Everyone is intrigued."

He just shook his head. He felt protective of Lila, he realized. "She's not a toy."

"Isn't she?" Mrs. Smith asked. "You kind of made it seem like she was something new and shiny for everyone to play with in all those emails."

"I'm helping her build her presence and you all can help with that. But that's it," he said. "Sorry if I sound cranky."

"It's all right, honey. Take your coffee and go do your thing."

He took the steaming mug with him and walked out onto the stone patio, which was covered with reclaimed railroad timber, spaced apart with some kind of purple flowering vine growing on them. Zach stopped and took a deep breath. It was fresh and not too sweet-smelling. He saw the area that Mrs. Smith had staged for him. As he walked to the table, the waterfall into the land-scaped pool came on. The table was laid with his mono-grammed tablecloth from a luxury British maker and the plates were from an exclusive designer.

He lifted the cloche off his lunch and had to smile. Mrs. Smith knew how to capture summer with her lob-ster rolls, coleslaw and peach iced tea. His tripod was set up from last night when he'd prepped for the day. Taking his camera out of the bag that had been left for him on the chair, he fiddled with the settings until he had the look he wanted. Then he took his seat, donned his sunglasses and stared off in the distance.

Normally he thought about his latest girlfriend or next big project, something to make him smile. Un-bidden, an image of Lila just as he'd leaned in to kiss her the night before danced through his mind. He re-membered the sound of her laughter and the way she'd smelled of lavender, the way her mouth had felt under his and her body pressed against his. He couldn't wait to see her again.

He hit the remote trigger for the shutter release on the camera, but he was distracted by her. Why hadn't she texted him this morning?

Had she regretted yesterday? Was she going to tell him to hit the road?

And why the hell did that matter? There were a million other ladies waiting in the wings...well, not a *million*, but a few. If she wasn't interested in him, he'd find another woman and go back to Los Angeles, face the paparazzi and the moral police, and deal with his own conscience.

But he didn't want to just disappear. He wanted Lila. He wanted her to need his help. He was kind of addicted to her excitement and her smile. He wanted to see it again. Wanted to kiss her again. And so much more....

Hell.

What was he thinking?

They could have fun. For a while. But this other stuff, this gnawing need deep inside him, needed to be quelled and quieted. He wouldn't let himself become obsessed with her.

She was his project...that was all. Not someone he was using; someone he was helping. That was it.

But was it ever enough? He'd helped other people and companies before but there was always something in it for him. And this Soiree thing she was planning, there wasn't anything in it for him. He was a bigger draw than anyone she'd mentioned to him so far. What did he need to feel compensated?

Her.

He wanted her. He intended to seduce her. But he knew that wasn't going to happen. She was way too smart to fall for him. He knew that. So could he just do this for her? He wasn't sure that he wasn't also doing this for himself. He'd said he liked her but just now it hit him that he wanted her to like *him*. The real him, not the million followers kind of like but the man he was away from social media.

Would that be enough?

He had no idea, but he also knew that unless she told him she didn't want his help anymore, he was going to be right here in her life for the foreseeable future.

Six

Arriving at Zach's rental house after lunch, Lila was determined to do this on her own terms. She'd talked to the rest of the festival advisory board and set up a meet and greet for them with Zach on Friday night at Sheen. Charlotte had promised them a quiet, private table at the back of the popular restaurant where they could talk. And being in the public would both suit Zach and generate publicity for the event.

Along with Charlotte, the advisory board consisted of Jack Bowden, whose company had done all of the construction at the festival site, and Valencia Donovan, a sort of bohemian cowgirl who was drop-dead gorgeous and ran the Donovan Horse Rescue. Brett Harston had also been on the committee but he was booted after a run-in with Rusty Edmond over the fact that he'd started dating Sarabeth, who was Rusty's ex-wife. There was never a stop to the drama that surrounded the Edmond family. Billy Holmes was sort of advising the advisory committee. He was a family friend of the Edmonds…well, sort of. Seemed he and Ross had been college roommates. Billy really was the only one who got the cantankerous Rusty Edmond under control, and had been overseeing the event.

The Soiree was in July, which meant she really needed to get some word-of-mouth promo that wasn't just everyone in Royal. And she'd do whatever it took to make that happen. Even if it entailed changing her image and hanging out with Zach. Her mom's words were a warning in the back of her mind about making sure the change was for herself, but for the first time since she'd been meeting with the rest of the advisory committee, she didn't feel like she was just there to take notes. Not that anyone had ever treated her that way, but today she'd felt more confident and had spoken up, telling everyone that she was in talks with documentary filmmaker Abby Carmichael, which was only half true.

The front door opened, and she realized she was still sitting in her car in front of his large house. The circular brick driveway led up to the imposing modern abode, which had large glass windows and beautiful stonework.

She saw Zach standing there—he had his sunglasses on and behind him were three people. They were crowded around him and leaned out as if to catch a glimpse of her. There was a tall guy with spiky brown hair with blond tips. A curvy woman with curly hair who waved at her. And finally, a woman who was taller than Zach with hair down to her butt. She crossed her arms over her waist and said something to the others.

This must be his team. His "glam team." Oh, goodness, what had she gotten herself into?

Confidence. That was what she'd gotten.

Get out of the car, Lila, she told herself.

She turned off the engine, grabbed the large cross-body bag that Zach hadn't loved and got out.

"Hi," she said as she walked up the drive. "Sorry about that. I was finishing up a call."

"Sure. This is Vito, Dawn and Shantal. They are on my team and will be helping you with a few tips. Have you had lunch?"

She nodded as she followed Zach and his team into the foyer of his house. It was large with marble floors and modern decor. She took a moment to look around and realized that he'd picked a place that would photograph well in his posts.

"Good. Then we get straight to it. Vito is one of the best hairdressers in the country."

"Excuse me? Did I hear that right? I'm the best in the *world,* honey," Vito said. "This man was a ragamuffin until I did his do. I mean shaggy might work for the just-from-bed posts but not for the red carpet."

She laughed with Vito as Zach just shrugged. "Sorry, V. You know I'm nothing without you."

Vito patted him on the shoulder. "That's okay, hon. So what do you want to do with her hair?"

"Nothing," she said.

He raised both eyebrows at her. As he came over he touched the length of her hair and then walked around behind her to look at the ends. "You have great hair. I have some ideas that will give you more of a modern look but keep most of your length. Is that what you meant?"

She glanced over at Zach and found him watching her. He had that same look on his face as he had last night when he'd kissed her. She couldn't help remembering how his mouth felt on hers. Was he going to kiss her again? Or had he regretted it?

"Lila?" Vito asked.

"I am really not much on fixing my hair. It takes forever to blow-dry and curling it has always…well, not worked out. I'm okay to cut some of the length. Really when I said nothing, I meant I don't want to spend an hour getting ready in the morning."

"Got it. Let me pull some photos together while you and ZB are in Dallas shopping. Highlights?"

She scrunched her nose. Her hair was dark brown with natural highlights in it. And despite the fact that this was Texas and every time she went to the salon, they suggested lightening it, she'd resisted. "I don't think so."

"Got it. Want to keep your look more you," Vito said. "This is going to be fun."

Vito dashed off up the stairs and then Shantal and Dawn both stared at her. "Dawn will help you with writing your posts and using the right hashtags. Shantal is going to do your makeup."

"I'm guessing the easier the better?" Shantal asked. She was tall with hair all the way down to her butt and had a deep timbre to her voice. Her eyes were bright green. She wore minimal makeup, but she had such lovely bone structure that honestly, she didn't need it. Her skin was a deep olive complexion and her high cheekbones and full mouth made her stunning.

"Yes, for every day. But could you also show me how to do something for going out? Right now, I just swap my lip balm for red lipstick and some mascara."

"Girl, don't worry. I'll give you a couple of different looks."

"I'll start working on some posts for you," Dawn said. "Have you taken any photos today?"

"No. Should I?"

"Yes. I know you are promoting the event, but we also want everyone to see how fun and one-of-a-kind you and Royal are. While you and ZB are shopping I'll go scout some locations and have some ideas when you come back."

Dawn and Shantal left after that.

"How are you doing? Was that too much?" he asked.

She smiled over at him. It was as if he was seeing the real her, the one behind all of these new facades. She wanted to just be honest with him. But at the same time, she felt exposed now. She didn't have her normal clothing to hide behind. If she let him all the way in, would she regret it?

"It was a little overwhelming. Are you sure we need all this?" she asked, though the idea of a makeover was exciting. She'd always wanted to wear more makeup but had never been sure how to go about it.

"It is. But it will be fun. Ready to head to Dallas with me?" he asked.

More ready than he was aware. After dreaming of him all night, then waking up to the new clothes he'd sent, it had been hard not to text him before coming over today. A part of her wanted to know if he'd been thinking about her as much as she'd been thinking about him. Not as his pet project but as a woman.

She wrapped her arms around her waist. This was it—she was going to have to face that fear deep inside her that she wasn't woman enough for him. No matter how confident she was at her job, or in planning the Soiree, one-on-one with Zach, she stumbled.

"Yes," she said. She'd been looking forward to seeing him again all day. Now that they were alone she was both excited and a little bit scared.

"I can't believe they just gave us all of this stuff!" Lila exclaimed as they got back on his private plane at the small airport near Love Field.

It had taken all of his willpower to keep his hands to himself while they'd shopped today. She'd tried on outfit after outfit and modeled them for him, her grin growing bigger each time.

She had been reluctant to hand over any of the bags of stuff that had been gifted to her. She sat on the large leather couch in the main part of the plane as the pilot and attendant got it ready for them to fly back to Royal.

They'd had dinner at a revolving restaurant that had afforded them a view of Dallas at night. Lila had gotten a like from one of the *Rich Wives* that she followed and spontaneously hugged him. He'd hugged her back, gotten a boner and realized he needed some space. So he'd stepped away from her and turned the conversation to being a brand ambassador. As if talking was going to turn him off. It hadn't worked, but she hadn't seemed to notice. Lila hadn't stopped talking since they'd gotten back on the plane.

They'd taken care of her glasses first and she now wore a pair of chic-looking frames that no longer dwarfed her face. She kept her hair in the ponytail, but some strands had slipped and now curled around her face. Her cheeks were flushed, and she kept looking at all the bags that were piled on the other couch.

"I told you. In exchange for a mention in a post and tagging them each time you wear an outfit, they don't mind writing off the price of the clothes and accessories. It's way cheaper for them to do this than to shoot a commercial or pay for print advertising."

"I know but *still*. I'm going to send thank-you notes to all of them," she said.

He almost laughed but knew she might take that the wrong way. So instead he only smiled. There was something so refreshingly innocent about her. That was what had drawn him to her in the first place. She was making him feel good just by being with her. "I'm sure they will appreciate that."

"Manners are never wasted."

"I agree," he murmured. "Also, I have a present for you. This wasn't gifted to me. I purchased it for you."

"What is it?" she asked.

He reached behind the leather armchair he was seated in and pulled the orange Hermès box out, handing it to her. She took it and put it on her lap, slowly opened the box and then pulled out the Birkin bag that he'd had monogrammed with her initials. It had an adjustable strap so she could wear it across her body as she did that hideous thing she'd been carrying all day.

She caught her breath as she stared at the high-end bag. She'd never received anything like this before. She was almost afraid to touch it.

"Zach…are you sure you want to give this to me?"

"Yes. I am positive," he told her. "I want you to transfer all of your stuff into it right now and then we can burn that other one."

"I am *not* burning my favorite bag. But thank you for this. I will start using it."

"Good," he said.

She set the box aside after they were in the air for the thirty-minute plane ride. He'd told Jennifer, the flight attendant, that she wouldn't be needed so she was sitting in the cockpit with the pilot.

"Thank you for all of this. I always thought that fashion wasn't anything but a waste of time but earlier today in a meeting... I felt more confident than I normally did. Started speaking up more. That's not what I expected."

He got up and went to sit next to her on the couch, stretching his arm along the back of it and toying with the hair in her ponytail. "I'm glad. I think we are changing the outside Lila to match the inside one."

She turned to face him, putting her hand on his thigh. "I agree. But I'm still wondering what's in this for you."

A shiver of awareness went through him. His skin felt too tight and it took all of his control to just keep from reaching over and pulling her into his arms.

"Can't I just be a good guy who is doing this because I'm nice?" he asked. But no one thought of him that way. Not even himself. He was the bad boy who kept the gossip sites and paparazzi busy following his latest scandal.

"Yes, of course. It's just that many people do that these days. I mean even the Soiree on the Bay isn't just for charity. There is a lot of money to be made by the vendors who are participating."

"I get it. But this...this is for you, Lila."

She furrowed her brow. "But you don't know me."

"What do you want me to say? That I'm using you?" he asked. Had she somehow gleaned that he wanted her to fit into his world? Honestly, he was not sure what he wanted from her. He knew he wanted her naked, writhing under him, but there was an emotional component to this he wasn't used to dealing with. Wasn't sure he *wanted* to deal with.

"I want the truth," she said, her words direct, just like she'd been from the beginning.

He stopped. This. This fire and passion. These were the things he'd sensed in her from the beginning and this was what he wanted from her. But how to show her without revealing his hand? Without allowing himself to seem too...needy?

"It was a bet. Remember? And I won. I'm not someone who reneges on a bet. That's not my style," he said. The truth was it was so much more than that. Plus it was fun watching her excitement at the new stuff and designing her new look. But just being around her aroused him. It wasn't like he needed to see her naked to get turned on.

Hell, he'd gotten a hard-on from a hug.

A *hug*.

He normally had more control and more finesse, but this was Lila and nothing was what he expected.

"You're right. But why are you sticking around?"

"I like you," he admitted gruffly. "One kiss wasn't enough for me."

"What if it was for me?" she asked.

Damn him.

Honesty, straight from those guileless big brown eyes, and he wanted to say the hell with it and grab her and pull her into his arms. But he couldn't. Because he was starting to feel things and that wasn't him. He got a rush from driving fast—acceptable feelings. He got turned on by women—especially Lila—again acceptable. He felt all gooey inside when she told him she was sending thank-you notes to the stores that they'd been gifted things from—not acceptable.

Not *him*.

Ruefully, he nodded at her. "Then I'm out of luck."

She took his hand in hers, threading their fingers together. "I like you, too, Zach, and that kiss was amazing. But I'm not sure about this kind of lifestyle. The novelty of it is fun for right now, but I think this would wear on me after a while."

And that was probably that. His lifestyle wasn't for everyone and he knew what she was saying in that super polite way of hers. It was nice while he was here in Royal, but she must have sensed what he hadn't said. That he was hiding from the world, giving the scandal time to die down. So this wasn't real. No matter how he tried to make it so in his mind.

Lila wasn't sure what she had wanted Zach to say. Something like it had started out as a bet but was much stronger now? She knew that she was wildly infatuated with him. How could she *not* be? He was funny, generous…and hot. He made her feel like she could be herself and achieve things that honestly she'd never expected.

It was so much more than the fact that he'd given her the keys to a luxurious lifestyle that she'd never thought in a million years she could be a part of. But Zach was slowly taking away the mystery of jet airline travel and high-end shopping.

She felt like Cinderella with her own ZB fairy godfather. And that was fantasy; there weren't fairy godparents in the real world. So she'd had to bring it back to reality. No matter how attracted he might be to her in the moment, that was all this could be. A *moment*.

She'd always prided herself as being someone who was grounded in reality, but she was forced to admit that she was being swayed by him. When he touched her, even accidentally, she felt a rush go through her entire body. She wanted more, wanted to fall into his arms and his life, but she had to remember that they came from two completely different places. She lived in Royal. He lived online and in LA. He'd pulled her into a world where she wasn't sure how she'd survive yet at the same time she wanted to try. He'd said he liked kissing her, but he was a playboy who changed women as often as he posted on social media, so she wasn't building a future for the two of them. But she was building a relationship in her head.

However, she couldn't help but wonder how much of it was because of what he could do for the Soiree. She wanted to prove herself to the Texas Cattleman's Club members as well as to the Edmond family. Now that she'd had a taste of how people treated her with her new look, she knew she didn't want to be that little unremarkable Lila from the chamber of commerce. She wanted to be noticed and taken seriously. She'd always been smart but she'd also always been quiet. Now she needed to *shine*.

She wanted to change more than her clothes.

She shifted on the couch and leaned over to kiss Zach. Just to see what he'd do. She knew that it was forward and polite ladies didn't do this. But she was on a private plane that had a freaking bedroom in it with a roguishly sexy bad boy. And she'd been sitting next to him like his chaste *sister*. She wanted for once in her life to have a story that was exciting. She wanted an experience that she knew she'd never have a chance at again when Zach walked out of her life. And he was going to walk out of her life.

She knew that.

So she was going into this with her eyes open and taking this for herself. For the man who'd shown her how to be Lila 2.0.

"Lila…" He said her name slowly in that husky tone he'd used just last night when he'd kissed her by the bay, and she looked up into those gorgeous blue eyes of his, waiting and wanting so much from him. And so much for herself. She'd always told herself she was happy and that she had the life she wanted, but she also knew that she'd been afraid to take any risks.

This was the riskiest thing she'd *ever* done. Kissing a famous bad boy on his private plane…this wasn't the Lila Jones she'd always been.

And that brush of his lips against hers was sending chills through her. The good kind that made her pulse race and her breasts feel full. Lila put her hand on his shoulder and he wrapped his hands around her waist and lifted her, pulling her onto his lap. She wound her arms around his shoulders as he deepened the kiss, his breath mingling with hers. She sucked his tongue into her mouth.

Wanting and needing more from him. This was changing from doing something risky to doing something that she'd always wanted but never been able to find for herself. She hadn't ever been this bold, she thought. Then, shifting on his lap to straddle him, she felt his erection between her legs and pushed herself against him.

Lila cradled his head in her hands and deepened the kiss even more as he cupped her butt and urged her to rock more solidly against his hard-on. She did. Waves of pleasure rippled through her as she felt one of his palms on her back, moving up and down, then he grabbed her ponytail with one hand as he pulled his mouth from hers.

She closed her eyes and realized how close she was to coming. Just from this. But she couldn't. That would be too much for this jaded, sophisticated man. But then he kissed her neck, nibbled at her sensitive flesh. His hand was under her shirt and he whispered in her ear, his breath hot and his words turning her on with each one.

She rocked harder against him, felt his solid shaft between her legs, catching her right where it felt so good.

She did it again and then he whispered into her ear. "Come for me."

And she did. She bit back a guttural sound and continued riding him until she collapsed in his arms. He held her as she rested her head on his shoulder, his hands moving languidly up and down her back.

"I want you. But not now. We will be landing soon. The team is at my place…can we go to yours?"

He was thinking through the variables and she knew he needed to figure this out for himself. As much as she might have felt like they were together in this, he wasn't. Not really. She was a temporary diversion for him. "I'd like that. I don't have protection."

"I'll take care of it."

"Don't tell me you have a sponsor for those," she said, feeling vulnerable to him at this moment. Even though she'd been the aggressor, now she was having thoughts…all kinds. Like wanting more of him and also afraid that if she had more of Zach she might not want to let him go.

"No. Definitely not. Some things are just for me and not for my public persona," he said.

Me? She didn't ask but she wanted to know. She had the feeling that it was better not to know and instead maneuvered back into her seat as they landed in Royal.

Zach looked at her as if nothing had changed while inside she'd felt a huge shift, and maybe that was because this was his life. Things like women throwing themselves at him happened every day.

God.

What had she gotten herself into?

Seven

Lila's house was tucked into a cute neighborhood of older homes. She gave him directions in that quiet, direct voice of hers, which let him know she hadn't changed her mind. This woman was an enigma and it had been a long time since he'd allowed himself to be drawn into something like this. He stopped at a convenience store and ran in for protection along the way. Then a short time later found himself pulling into the alleyway that led to the garage at the back of her house.

"The garage door opener is in my car. Let me go inside and I'll open it for you, so you won't have to park in the driveway."

"Trying to keep me a secret?" he asked. A little bit because he wasn't sure if she was embarrassed to sleep with him and a little bit because it sort of seemed like something she'd do. Lila was a private person by nature. He suspected she wouldn't want her neighbors to know about them.

"Yes. My mom is good friends with Mrs. Anderson, who lives one street over, and if she spots a car in my drive in the morning my mom will hightail it over here."

He wouldn't mind meeting Lila's mother but he wasn't sure the morning after was going to be the best time for that introduction. "Go on and open the door."

She hopped out of the Ferrari and opened the wooden gate on her fence. A few moments passed before he heard the garage door open, and then he pulled in and parked before getting out of the car. Her garage was super neat with metal shelving on one wall and well-labeled tubs on each shelf. She opened the door to the house and stood there watching him as she closed the garage door.

He swung his keys around on his finger and realized he was nervous about the emotions she stirred in him. Not about the sex. Sex he could handle. But nervous that the real Lila hadn't really changed enough yet. That if he slept with this woman she was going to change *him*.

"This is very organized."

"I'm sure your garage is, as well."

"Actually, it is. I have several cars that I keep in it so it's large. I also have a driver and a mechanic back in LA who maintain everything so it's neat, but I'm not responsible."

"Fair enough," she said. "Want to come in or are you going to keep admiring my garage?"

"I want to come in…if you still want me to."

"I haven't changed my mind. Have you?" she asked. "I know I'm not your usual glam girl."

"No, you aren't." Zach was beginning to see the

chink in his plan. He had been trying to change her, make her into someone who looked like the women he normally associated with, never noticing that he wasn't changing the woman inside. She was so much more than those self-absorbed women who were sort of mirror images of him. Wanting to be famous, craving some kind of influence over the world around them and seeking just the pleasure of the moment.

Lila had substance.

He had to remind himself that she was different. Because he didn't want to be the same with her as he'd been with everyone else. But could he change?

Did he really *want* to?

Or was this feeling just something new that once he'd experienced it would fade?

"So…"

"I haven't changed my mind," he reassured her.

"Then come on in, ZB," she said, stepping back and holding open the door.

ZB.

Zach walked in and put his keys on the round wood-and-tile table in the breakfast nook. A lot of lovers had called him that before, but he didn't want her to. Hell. This right here was what he'd been hoping to avoid. Maybe once they had sex he'd regain his perspective.

"Don't call me ZB. Unless… Are you hoping to have sex with ZB?" he asked.

She shook her head, her long ponytail bouncing. "No. But I'm nervous. You've had a revolving door on your bedroom forever—not judging you, but I've only had sex three times. And let's just say it was sort of beige."

"I can promise tonight won't be beige."

"Good. I'm glad to hear it. Zach, are you sure about this?"

"This? Sex or something more?" he asked.

"Sex. This can't be something more. You are not staying in Royal and I am. I want… This is fun, and you turn me on. I like who I am with you."

"Good," he said. "I like who you are with me, too."

He took off his suit jacket and hung it over the back of the chair and then toed off his shoes. Leaving them next to the same chair he'd hung his jacket on. "Give me the tour?"

"The tour? Sure. It's not fancy like your place."

"You're not me, so I wouldn't expect it to be," he said, putting his hand on the small of her back as she turned. She'd said she was nervous and that bothered him. Sex should be fun, hot, exciting…no place for nerves. He knew he was going to have to put her at ease and luckily, he was good at that.

She sort of half turned so that her shoulder brushed against his chest and then she put her soft, delicate hand on him. "This is the kitchen… I was really excited about the double ovens when I saw this place and pretty much that's why I bought it."

"Double ovens?"

She sighed. "I like to bake. This way I can do bread in one oven and cookies or cakes in the other."

He leaned down closer to her as she tipped her head back and their eyes met. She was shy about her life around him, and he knew that was his fault. He'd pointed out how her social media stream made her seem, well, boring. But he knew she was anything but.

He rubbed his thumb over her cheek and knew he had to keep his guard up with her. She was already making him think and feel things that were unexpected. He wondered if he would need reminding that this was just sex.

Because when she talked about baking and he looked at her sweet, cozy house, he realized that she'd stirred some long-forgotten dream in the back of his mind. So much of Lila was tied to Royal and when she talked about the town, she made him see it through her eyes. A dream that was foreign and not his reality. But when he was holding this beautiful woman in his arms, he craved it.

Lila's nerves dissipated as soon as Zach touched her. She'd never been wishy-washy about what she wanted. And she definitely wanted Zach. The more time she spent with him the more dimensions she was coming to realize he had. He was so much more than the bad boy with the millions of followers on social media. He was complex and caring. Charming and sexy. And way more real than she'd have expected.

There was something so solid about him, and while showing him her kitchen wasn't exactly what she'd had in mind when she'd invited him back to her place, it was giving her the time she needed to shake off the lingering anxiety that had been plaguing her since she'd realized that her neighbors might see his car.

Not that she cared what anyone else thought.

But so much of her time with Zach had been played out in the spotlight that she wanted this night just for the two of them.

He leaned in and she could smell the mint on his breath that she'd seen him pop in his mouth when they'd gotten off the plane. He had the softest lips but his mouth was firm. Out of all the men she'd kissed he was the best. And there was something about how his mouth moved over hers that made her stop thinking and just want to let herself go.

He kissed her slowly, as if there were no time and nothing existed outside of her and him and this moment. And for the first time in her life, she shut off the running list inside her mind. Instead, she put her hand on the side of his neck, her fingers brushing the thick hair at the back of his head.

She didn't have to hurry through this in case he came to too quickly or changed his mind. Zach wasn't going anywhere tonight. Tonight he was hers and she wanted to use every moment of that time. Experience everything he had to give her.

He put his arm around her waist and pulled her more fully into his body. Lila felt his strength as his biceps flexed and he turned until he was leaning against the island in the middle of her kitchen. She was sort of reclining on him, her arms around his neck, her breasts pillowed on his chest and her hips resting against him.

She felt his erection against the bottom of her stomach and she remembered that shirtless picture of him that she'd seen when scrolling through his social media feed. He was totally ripped...swole in the best way possible. And she wanted to see him naked in her kitchen.

She stepped back and he raised both eyebrows at her.

"Would you mind taking off your shirt? I want to see if you look as good in real life as you do in your photos."

He threw his head back and laughed as his hands went to the buttons of his shirt. "I look better."

She bet he did. There was no shame in Zach and he undid the buttons of his shirt with a casual elegance that turned her on as she watched those long fingers moving down the front of his body. He let the sides hang open, giving her a tantalizing glimpse of his rock-hard abs and muscled pectorals as he undid the cuffs. And then he shrugged out of his shirt and once again walked over to one of the kitchen chairs and draped it carefully over the back.

He turned to face her. Putting one hand on his hip as he stood there. Flexed and waiting. "What do you think?"

"Me-ow!" she said. "You *are* better in person."

"Yeah, because you can touch me."

"I can," she murmured, walking over to him. His expensive cologne was subtle and delicious, she thought, breathing in the scent. She reached out to touch him, drawing her finger over the pads of muscles on his chest. His flat, brown nipples hardened as she drew her finger over his skin. He had a light dusting of hair on his chest and she brushed her fingers over it, following the path over his abs and to his belt buckle.

She noticed the bulge against the front of his pants and reached down to stroke him through the fabric. He reached for the button at the back of the halter top she wore and she felt him undo it before he drew the hem of the blouse up and over her head. Then he folded it in half and set it on the table next to them.

He touched her then. Using his forefinger, drawing it down over her collarbone, following the lacy fabric of her bra as he skimmed his touch over the globes of her breasts and then lower over her stomach to her belly button, where she had a piercing. He fondled the diamond stud she had there.

"This is surprising."

"I guess there is a lot about me you don't know," she said. But she was the first to admit that she wasn't at her wittiest right now. Her heart was beating faster and faster with anticipation and really all she wanted to do was get naked and feel him moving inside her.

"Babe, you're not telling me the news. I think I could spend a month of nights with you and still not have you figured out."

Ditto. But this wasn't about figuring each other out. This was about being young and living in the moment instead of always trying to be the smart, sensible woman.

She took his hand in hers. "Want to see the master bedroom?"

"Yes," he said, following her as she led him through the formal living room to her bedroom.

Lila's bedroom was large and decorated in the same cozy style as the rest of her house. She had a queen-size sleigh bed with a summer-patterned quilt on it. Next to the bed was a table with an antique lamp and over the headboard was a photograph of Texas bluebonnets in a field. She had hit the overhead light when they came into the room and the ceiling fan turned on with it. She had a hope chest at the end of her bed.

The room smelled of gardenias. She toed off her shoes and then reached for the side zipper of her pants and let them slide down her thighs. He stopped looking around her room, fixated by her long legs, her curvy hips and the tiny bikini underwear that matched the icy green bra she still wore. She had a nipped-in waist and a small pouch of a stomach, but she was fit and she was clearly comfortable with her body.

He took the box of condoms he'd picked up and tossed them on the bed behind her while he removed his socks and then undid his belt and looked around for someplace to put his clothes. Opting to just drop them on the floor, he flung them down, then stalked toward Lila, taking her in his arms. He skimmed his hands down her back and felt the goose bumps on her skin as he caressed her.

Her fingers were chilly against his chest as she ran them down his stomach and he felt her fingers at the button of his pants. She undid it and then the zipper followed a moment later and they fell down his legs. He didn't wear underwear, which he could tell surprised her as she gasped when she touched his naked erection.

She tipped her head back and he took her mouth again as she wrapped her hand around his shaft, stroking him. He undid the clasp of her bra and then tugged the garment from her body before pulling her back into his arms. He felt her hard nipples against his chest and she shifted her torso, wriggling against him. He reached down, pushing his hands inside the back of her bikini panties to cup her naked butt, lifting her off her feet and rubbing his hard-on against her.

Then he turned, walking backward until he felt the edge of her mattress against the back of his thighs, and sat down on the bed. She stood there in front of him, lips swollen from his kisses, her chest rising and falling with each breath she took. Then she pushed her underwear down her thighs and stepped out of them as he reached for the box of condoms and put one on.

She licked her lips as she watched him and he groaned, feeling himself harden even more. He reached for her hip, pulled her toward him. "Straddle me."

She did. He groaned as he felt her warm, hot center rubbing over his abdomen and then over his shaft. He held her butt in his hands and pulled her toward him as he shifted his hips until he was poised at the entrance of her body. She put her hands on his shoulders and their eyes met and something electric passed between them. That he hadn't been expecting, but she smiled at him as she straddled him, slowly lowering herself until he was deep inside her. He pulled her head to his and thrust his tongue deep in her mouth as she started moving up and down.

He let her set the pace for as long as he could but soon her thrusts weren't enough and he needed more. Needed to be deeper inside her. He shifted back on the bed.

"Wrap your legs around me," he commanded.

She did and he lay back and then rolled over so she was under him. Lila raised both eyebrows at him and he could tell she was going to say something, but he couldn't talk. Not now. Now he needed to have every part of her. He took her mouth with his. Then he cupped her breasts, flicking his thumb over her nipple as he drove himself deeper and deeper into her.

She clung to him, her nails digging into his back as she arched under him. And he kept thrusting, propelling them both higher and higher until she tore her mouth from his and screamed his name as her body started to tighten around his. He pounded into her harder and deeper until his orgasm washed over him and he collapsed against her. Careful to brace himself on his arms so he didn't crush her.

She wrapped her arms and legs around him and held him to her until their hearts stopped racing. Then he rolled to his side and pulled her close. Cradling her against him, he stroked her back. And as she ran her finger in a random pattern over his body, and he found himself listening to the sound of her breathing, a feeling of peace washed over him.

She didn't say anything, which was telling, he thought. She always had something to say and he wondered if it was a good or a bad thing. But he was afraid to find out.

He who had never let anything scare him was afraid of what he'd see when he looked in Lila's eyes. When had she wielded this power over him? He hadn't remembered giving it to her.

He was fixing her. She was his project.

She propped her chin on her fist and looked up into his eyes, and he realized that no matter what he'd been telling himself, tonight had been about more than sex. And he had no idea what to do about that.

Eight

Lila woke up alone in her bed the next morning. She knew she shouldn't be surprised and told herself that she was cool with it. But she knew she wasn't. She had a text from Zach on her phone telling her he looked forward to seeing her later that morning when she met with the glam squad.

She read the message several times, looking for some nuance that she might be missing, but the truth was she was a little pissed that he'd left and simply texted her. Why didn't he stay?

Oh, hell. How was she going to get to work? She'd left her car at Zach's place. This was…a mess. She had a feeling she was going to have to call her parents and ask them to give her a ride.

No.

That wasn't happening. She wasn't going to call them. Coffee first, then she'd figure this out.

When she got to the kitchen there was a pastry box on the counter next to a ZB coffee mug and a hand-written note.

You were sleeping so solidly I didn't want to wake you, but I figured you needed your car—it's in your garage. Also you probably didn't want the neighbors to see me leaving. Wish I could be here with you to share these croissants.
ZB

Well…okay. So maybe he wasn't a total douchebag. Lila opened the box and saw there were two freshly made croissants. She put the pod in to make her coffee and went to check for her car, which was in her spot. Her keys were on the breakfast table, so she knew he'd taken them to bring it back.

That was a lot of work for early in the morning. It was a nice gesture and she tried not to read too much into it but he'd totally changed her Friday from manic and crazy to a good one. She ate the buttery croissant, which was delicious with her coffee, and then got ready for the day.

She was smiling as she left her house and realized that Zach was responsible for today's good mood. It wasn't just the fact that she was wearing the new clothes that he'd helped her pick out the day before and…damn. Was she supposed to take a photo of the breakfast? Or the outfit? She was going to need some advice. She phoned her office and told them she'd be out until lunchtime at a meeting and drove to Zach's place.

The guard at the gated community had to check before he let her in but then he cleared her and she drove to the house. She realized that maybe she should have called first but honestly, she knew she needed to start putting all of Zach's efforts to good use. And she also needed a checklist. Some sort of routine so she did all the things she was supposed to.

She rang the doorbell and an older lady she hadn't met the day before answered the door.

"Hello, you must be Lila. I'm Mrs. Smith, Zach's housekeeper. I wasn't sure when to expect you," she said.

"I hope I'm not too early. But I ate those delicious croissants and then worried that maybe I was supposed to photograph them…"

Mrs. Smith started laughing. "Welcome to my world. Glad you liked the pastries. I miss Paris. Normally we go there in the spring. So I made the dough yesterday and whipped up a batch this morning."

"You *made* them? Wow, can you show me how? Is it hard? My mom would literally die if I made homemade croissants," Lila said.

"I can. But not today. I think you are scheduled for hair and makeup and "

"Everything, Mrs. S," Zach said, coming down the stairs. She couldn't help but remember how it had felt to be in his arms last night. This morning, he looked perfectly put together in his designer suit, body-fitting shirt and no tie. He smiled when he saw her, but she noticed that he hesitated when he reached the bottom of the steps.

She smiled back. She wondered if he felt as unsure of how they moved forward as she did. But then reminded herself this was Zach Benning… ZB…the bad boy who always knew what he was doing. Even when he was doing her? She didn't want to cheapen herself or what they'd shared, but was it just fun or did he have some other motivation?

Ugh.

Why was she having all these doubts this morning?

"Good morning, Lila," he said, kissing her on the cheek and whispering in her ear, "You look gorgeous."

"Morning, Zach," she murmured back, looking into his eyes and realizing that she felt way too vulnerable. Even in these new clothes.

"Come on. Vito wants to show you some hairstyles and then get to work. I'm afraid Shantal is like me and doesn't usually stir before noon, so she'll be down later."

Mrs. Smith disappeared, Lila assumed to the kitchen to make more fabulous food, and she followed Zach down the hall to a side room where Vito and Dawn were drinking coffee and chatting. They both looked up when she walked in and she wondered if they knew that Zach had spent the night at her place.

Someone would have had to drive back over with her car… She took a deep breath. She had to be like Zach. Like these new clothes projected. A woman who didn't worry about who knew what and just lived her life.

Yeah, she'd do that.

"So glad you are here," Vito said. "I have a couple of options for you. Ready to get started?"

"As I'll ever be," she answered, removing her bag from her shoulder. Zach took the Birkin he'd given her and winked at her as he put it on the settee.

"Love this bag."

"Thanks. It's a bit showy but so is the man who gave it to me."

He threw back his head and laughed and for the first time that morning, Lila felt like she was where she needed to be. She was herself again.

"Let's do this."

* * *

Zach sat on the settee with Dawn discussing upcoming ad campaigns that he'd agreed to do, sipping a mimosa and trying to ignore Lila and Vito. He hadn't slept a wink last night but that was his normal so no biggie, right? Except as he'd held her he'd felt a new kind of longing awaken in him. Which was definitely not his normal, so it had weirded him out. So there he was with too much time on his hands and too many thoughts in his mind. He'd gotten out of her bed and her house and driven around Royal, which wasn't that busy at three in the morning.

Nothing was clearer as he'd driven so he'd taken care of getting her car back to her place and dropping off breakfast. Still, all of that busy work hadn't changed the fact that he still couldn't get Lila off his mind. And that was disturbing because usually he was thinking about himself.

He made no bones about being a truly self-absorbed man. It was one of his key strengths and had brought him his entire career. So he wasn't going to be apologetic about it. Everyone around him knew he was always thinking about himself. Except this morning he kept getting distracted by *her*.

"I went ahead and created some branding for Lila's page and took a stab at updating the Soiree graphics as well," Dawn said. "They used a pretty decent font on the webpage, so I just tweaked the kerning to make the letters look the same but unique. I think it should work. I'll use it for your account when you post about the event."

"Great," he replied, taking another sip of the mimosa and admitting to himself that he wished it were later in the day so he could have a real drink. That might clear

Lila from his head and allow him to get back to worrying about himself for a change.

"ZB? You okay?" Dawn asked.

He turned to face her. "What? Of course I am. When have you ever known me not to be?"

"Um…well, you know that Candi's husband is tweeting about you…"

"I blocked him," Zach said. He wasn't going to have a flame war on social media about an extramarital affair. "He sounds like a lunatic."

"Agreed. Want me to try to…" She trailed off.

"Exactly. What can you do? I already told him when he punched me outside the club, I didn't know she was married. There's nothing else to do. Let's ignore it. If he tweets about me again, I'll just say talk to your wife."

"ZB…"

"Yes?"

"Nothing. If you want me to help out let me know."

Dawn wouldn't post a cutting message like that and he didn't want her involved in something this seedy. What was wrong with him lately? First, he slept with Candi and got punched by her husband. Then Lila. Maybe that was why he was obsessed with her. She wasn't Candi; she was different.

But so far making her over hadn't stopped him from falling for her, and sex had just made him more aware of her.

"I need to make a call," he said, getting up and leaving Dawn and Vito with Lila.

He walked down the hall to the office area in the house, where he'd asked for his favorite desk and chairs to be flown in and set up. Mrs. Smith had taken care of arranging everything yesterday and the room was almost a mirror of his office in Malibu. But there was no sea view and he knew he was in Texas.

What had Grandfather seen in this place? He wondered if he got in touch with his roots…then what? He'd suddenly be a better person?

Because he knew deep down that was what was bothering him about Lila. There was no way he could be good enough for her. And he was changing her to make her more like him. Was that a conscionable thing to do? And did it really matter to him if it was? He had always taken what he wanted. Why was Lila different?

Did he want to know? Fuck. No. He didn't want to know unless somehow it helped him get back to himself.

He picked up the phone and let everyone know he'd be back in Los Angeles in one week's time. Enough of Royal. He should be done making Lila over by then and once he was back in his world—throwing parties and attending media events—he'd be back to himself.

It was just *this* place that had him all out of sorts.

"Zach?"

He glanced up and caught his breath. Lila stood in the doorway. Vito had taken a few inches off the length and it now curled around her shoulders. The hairdresser had also gotten rid of the heavy fall of bangs on her forehead and swept them aside. She didn't have any makeup on but she looked beautiful.

He stood up and walked around his desk, drawn to her as he'd been drawn to nothing else in this life. He stopped as that thought entered his head and straightened his suit jacket and started to assess her. The outfit she wore today was Dolce & Gabbana; her hair was perfect. But it was the woman he saw in her eyes that really got to him like a gut punch.

"Vito did a great job. I like it. Once Shantal shows you some makeup tips, you'll be Insta-ready."

She furrowed her brow as she stared at him. "I like it, too. It's pretty easy to do. What do you think? Is it more me?"

It *was* more her. But the Lila Jones he was turning her into made him suddenly unsure whether he should have started doing this in the first place. He felt like all the worst epithets that had ever been hurled at him.

But he ignored that.

Enough with this bleeding-heart nonsense.

"It is more you. Dawn has been working on some posts for you, and a font. Go and check in with her. I'll be back in a few minutes," he said. "I have some work to finish."

Lila caught a glimpse of herself in the ornate mirror in the hallway as she left Zach's office. She stopped and stared at herself. Wow. She looked so different. It was hard to believe that just taking a few inches off the length of her hair had made it feel so much lighter, allowing it to curl naturally around her shoulders in soft waves. Vito had added some product and shown her how to do it but he assured her it shouldn't take her too much time or effort.

This woman…she was someone that Lila had always wanted to see looking back at herself, and yet at the same time, someone different. Not better, just more comfortable about showing the world who she was. Before she'd had confidence, but now she was *owning* her space and not fading into the background. On the contrary, she was finally enabling everyone to take notice of her. But the one person she truly wanted to see her had done the complete opposite. She thought about how

Zach had dismissed her from his office. He was already doing her so many favors that she hated to quibble, but yeah, it had stung.

She went back and rapped on the open door frame before walking back in. He was staring intently at his laptop but looked up as she entered the room. She cleared her throat.

"I wanted to make sure you remembered we are meeting the advisory committee tonight at Sheen," she said. "I know you don't want to miss that."

"I don't. I'll pick you up. Wear that vintage Chanel dress we got yesterday."

"I was thinking of wearing the Balenciaga pants with the halter top," she told him. "I like the silhouette it creates."

He smiled at her. "I like it, too. But the dress will show off your legs and make everyone in the restaurant take notice. It's up to you, of course."

Of course.

"Thanks for letting me know I can choose my own clothes," she said sardonically. It hadn't escaped her that Zach was different today. She was trying not to let her own doubts cloud her judgment, but a part of her wondered if he was losing interest now that they'd had sex.

"Every choice is yours," he replied. "I am just here to help you navigate and build your social presence."

She stepped into the room and closed the door behind her. "What's up with you, Zach? Last night you were different. More open. Today it's like you see yourself as the mastermind directing all my moves."

He stood up and walked around the desk. Leaning back on it, bracing one arm on the surface, caused his suit jacket to fall open and revealed the powerfully muscled chest under the dress shirt. Her mouth went dry.

Immediately she remembered him naked and what it had been like to kiss him. Caress him. Make hot, passionate love to him…

"I don't know. I am not suddenly going to be a different guy. Last night was fun, but today we have to get down to business. You have your event and your job and I have a life waiting for me back in LA."

A life back in LA. That had to be important, but she wasn't sure how. Or why he was mentioning it now. Except maybe he thought she'd read more into sleeping with him than she had. Maybe that was an occupational hazard for good old ZB. "Of course you do. That doesn't mean you can't be nice to me. I'm not trying to make you stay. I'm asking for some respect, of course, and good old-fashioned manners."

"I'm sorry. I didn't sleep last night," he mumbled.

She walked over to him and had to ball her hands into fists to keep from reaching out and touching him. "I'm sorry. Thank you for thinking of me and leaving when you did. But you could have stayed."

He nodded. "Thanks, babe. But it would have been a complication for both of us."

One he didn't want.

"Fair enough. Is there anything I can do to help you out? You said you have a lot going on and I'm really good at organizing things."

He stood and pulled her into his arms, hugging her close to him. "Don't let me wreck you."

She glanced up at his face, putting her hand on his jaw. "You won't. You're not that kind of man."

He shook his head. "How can you be sure?"

"I'm starting to get to know you. Also you have some really nice friends. Good people here with you."

He swallowed and just nodded. "The team is the best. Let's go and see them."

He took her hand as he led her out of his office and back to the room where Dawn and Vito were, and she noticed that Shantal had joined them. They all started talking to her and Zach, and she got swept into the makeup chair, realizing that he had never really answered any of the questions she'd asked.

She tried not to let that seem important, but she knew it was. He didn't want to wreck her. She knew that there was a side to him she didn't know. *Couldn't* know because this wasn't his world and truly, did she want to be a part of that?

He was helping her grow her online presence and this makeover was something that she knew she'd take with her for the rest of her life. Lila had seen how the right clothes and hairstyle and some subtle makeup could change how she felt about herself. She was curious how everyone on the committee and in the Edmond family would react to her now.

But she was bothered by the way that the more she changed the less Zach interacted with her. He said that he hadn't slept the night before and she knew from experience that she was out of sorts if she didn't get a good night's sleep, but at the same time this felt like something more.

As if the more she changed into someone from his world, the less open he was with her. He'd suggested this makeover but he might not actually like the woman he had helped create.

Did that matter? She had to like this for herself, and she did. She wanted to be the woman she saw in the mirror and not the smart, nerdy girl she'd always been.

Nine

Lila had suggested Sheen for the advisory board meeting because she knew that the added publicity from having Zach tweet about it wouldn't hurt. And Charlotte was her friend and she loved the food there. But now she was second-guessing herself.

Vito and Shantal had come to her place to show her how to get ready with the tools she had. Vito had laughed at the drugstore curling iron she owned and gifted her his Dyson styling tool. Shantal had already given her all the makeup she'd need and now she took her time creating an understated smoky eye.

The Chanel dress that Zach had suggested she wear was a simple black number and she'd paired it with her grandmother's strand of pearls and a Gucci watch that her mom had passed down to her. She had on the Louboutins she'd fallen in love with yesterday. Lila thought she looked both bold and sophisticated in them, but she also couldn't wait to see Zach's reaction to her. When she looked in the mirror she saw the woman she always was in her head, but now the outer packaging matched that inner woman.

She knew she owed that to Zach. He might have helped her out so he didn't have to promote the event on his own, but he'd given her something so much more than she'd anticipated. Who would have thought letting down her guard would net this kind of confidence?

Vito and Shantal had agreed she looked "fabulous" before they left. They'd taken a photo of her putting on her lipstick, and then using the post that Dawn had written for her earlier, she put it on social media. Tagging all the retailers but also #SoireeontheBay.

Lila heard the roar of the Ferrari and then her doorbell rang. Her pulse raced a little bit and she licked her lips at the thought of seeing him again.

She smoothed her hands down the sides of her dress, her hair bouncing around her shoulders in a way it never had before. And when she opened the door, she found Zach standing in front of his car in a navy suit with a white patterned shirt on under it.

He let out a wolf whistle and winked at her.

Zach had been quiet and almost moody when she'd left his house but was more like his regular self now—vivacious and charming. This was the Zach Benning who'd roared into town with a leggy blonde in a vintage Halston dress. It wasn't lost on Lila that she was wearing vintage as she walked down her driveway to get in his car. She saw two of her neighbors out for their nightly walk and waved at them as nonchalantly as she could as Zach held the passenger door open for her.

He waved at them, too.

"You look gorgeous. Sorry if I was an autocrat about

the dress," he said. "But damn, babe, you are making me want to take you back inside and skip this dinner."

She arched her eyebrow at him. She wanted that, too. Seeing his reaction had given her a new kind of sexual confidence. "I'd let you, but this meeting is too important to skip. Play your cards right and maybe I'll invite you in later."

"Oh, I'm very good at playing my cards," he rasped, stealing a quick kiss before she seated herself in the car. He closed the door and she put on her seat belt.

"The ladies haven't stopped staring at us since you waved at them."

She blushed. Dammit. When was she going to be able to control that? "It will give them something to talk about at the clubhouse when they take the kids up there to swim."

"Do they gossip about you often?" he asked as he fired up the powerful engine of the car and drove out of the neighborhood.

"Not usually. But I have heard them gossiping about everything from the other parents in the neighborhood to whatever Mandee Meriweather brings up on *Royal Tonight!*"

"*Royal Tonight!*?"

"It's a local television program, sort of entertainment-news. Mostly gossip about everyone in town. I have been trying to book some time on there to talk about the Soiree on the Bay but she's shut me down so far."

"We'll see what I can do about that," he said, putting his hand on her leg as he drove out of her neighborhood to Sheen.

Sheen had a diverse staff of women who ran everything from the front of house at the restaurant to the kitchen where Charlotte was the head chef. Charlotte worked hand in hand with the staff to ensure it wasn't a gimmicky place. The food was innovative and mouth-watering and its reputation for excellent service was making it "the place" to dine in Royal. Lila was pretty sure the fact that she'd asked Charlotte to book them a table was the only reason they'd gotten one on such short notice.

"I'm not sure where we are going—"

"Lila Jones?"

She turned to see Jack Bowden walking toward her. He was a tall and muscly man who had made his fortune working with his hands. He had an easy smile and normally sort of nodded at her instead of talking to her.

"I thought that was you. You've done something different…with your hair?"

"And a few other things," Zach said, holding out his hand. "I'm Zach Benning, and you are?"

She almost smiled at the way Zach had done that. Was he jealous? She could have told him that Jack wasn't interested in her but was madly in love with Lexi Alderidge. However, the novelty of having anyone jealous over her was interesting.

"Jack Bowden," he said.

"Lila showed me the event grounds that you built. Very impressive," Zach said.

"Is Valencia here yet?" Lila asked.

"I don't think so. But Rusty, Gina and Asher are," Jack said. "Follow me… I'll show you where everyone is."

He turned to lead the way and Zach grabbed her wrist to stop her from going.

"What?" she asked.

"How many men are on this committee?"

"Just Jack and Asher. Ross was but he and his father are having some issues. Then Rusty and Billy are overseeing the event. Why?"

"I just realized I don't know who's on the committee. And the Edmonds?"

"They are royalty right here in Royal. Kind of the money and the brains behind the event. You'll like them, they're your kind of people—movers and shakers."

"Great. Lead on," he said.

She turned to do so and realized, as she walked through the restaurant to the table that had been set aside for them, that for the second time tonight people were watching her.

Lila Jones, nerdy girl next door, was suddenly catching everyone's attention.

She didn't hate it.

The room they were led to was large with a huge chandelier over the long table set for ten. There was a large mirror at the end of the table, and drapes that could be drawn to give them privacy, but Zach noticed they'd left them open while the group was mingling. Which was a great way to get people wondering what they were talking about.

"Let's get a selfie before the meeting starts," he said, putting his arm around her.

"Where should I look?"

"At the camera. Smile and look like you are about to have some fun," he directed.

She made a face, which made him laugh, and he couldn't help it. He hit the shutter button to take a photo. She grimaced. "I looked horrible."

"You looked cute as always. Let's do it for real now," he said, taking a photo.

"Lila, could we see you for a minute?" Jack asked.

She turned to him. "Go ahead," he told her. "I'm going to post this and go see if I have any followers in the restaurant who will help, as well. I'll be back in five?"

"That sounds good," she said, moving away from him toward Jack and the others.

Zach liked the vibe of the restaurant. It was upscale but also somehow welcoming. He heard the entire staff was women and he supported that, but this felt like more than just some gimmicky one-off. The dishes both smelled and looked delicious and as he went to the bar to grab a drink, he was stopped by a few followers. He took selfies with them and mentioned Soiree on the Bay.

That's for your conscience, he thought.

He wasn't just using Lila; he was helping her. *And* falling for her. It was the combination of heart and hustle that she brought to everything. The way that the clothes just made her more Lila instead of changing her. He hadn't created a safe bridge to cross when he'd helped her with her makeover; he'd created a woman who was too close to what he hadn't realized he actually wanted until she'd opened her door to him and he'd seen her standing there. And he wanted her more than ever, he thought as he took a sip of the dry martini he'd ordered. Just what he needed to get through this meeting. It had been a long time since he had to socialize like this. Normally everyone was there to see him.

He saw someone walk into the restaurant who looked familiar. He knew him from somewhere. Maybe LA?

The other man saw him and smiled but didn't seem to recognize him. He continued back to the private room where Zach had left Lila. Zach tipped the bartender and then went back to the group. They were starting to settle into their seats and he noticed that Lila had saved him a seat next to her as the waitstaff drew the curtains around them to afford them privacy.

Once the appetizers had been served and drink orders taken, Rusty Edmond, who was the patriarch of his family, stood up. Everyone immediately stopped talking.

"Thanks to everyone for your hard work. I think we should start with a toast to Jack for all the hard work he put in. The event site is great."

Everyone toasted Jack, who looked humble as he swallowed his drink.

"Lila, darling, do you want to introduce Zach?" Rusty asked.

"Yes, sir. This is Zach Benning. I'm sure y'all have heard of him. He's been tagging the Soiree on his social media accounts and it is working to get the word out. He's also helped me to figure out how to add some pizzazz to our posts."

"Welcome, Zach," everyone said.

Zach nodded. "It's nothing, I'm happy to help out. I do have a few questions about the event, however."

"We will be happy to answer them after the dinner," Rusty said. "Do you know everyone here?"

"Um. Well, I met Jack on the way in," he answered.

"That's my daughter, Gina, stepson Asher. This here is Billy Holmes. Family friend. Valencia is on the end and next to her is Charlotte."

"Billy, have we met before?" Zach asked. The other man looked very familiar.

"I don't think so," he said. "Unless you went to college in Texas?"

"Uh, no. UCLA for me," Zach murmured. "You sure do look familiar."

Billy laughed and nodded at him. "I have one of those faces. Everyone thinks they know me."

"Everyone thinks they know Zach, too," Lila said. "I mean his followers are always swarming around him."

"Are they?" Charlotte asked. "Do you think you could get them to swarm here?"

Charlotte Jarrett was smart, sassy and a great dinner companion. She was the head chef here at Sheen and told him she had a son named Ben who was two. She was engaged to Ross Edmond, who wasn't at the dinner because his father had disinherited him. Sounded like there was more to that story, but Zach didn't ask.

"You don't need my help. This place is packed," he said.

"Yeah, but having a line out the door never hurt a restaurant," she countered.

"I have a few ideas. I already tagged the restaurant and took some selfies with your customers. That should help get the word going," he said.

"Thanks. Now about Lila..."

"What about her?" Zach asked.

"I saw you blaze into town with that blonde and now, what, less than a week later you're here with her? Lila's a friend and I don't want to see her get hurt," Charlotte said.

"I don't, either," Zach promised. "I'm just helping her learn how to promote the Soiree without me. She needs to be able to do this on her own."

"It looks like it's more than that."

"She's a grown woman," Zach reminded her.

Charlotte narrowed her eyes at him. "All right. Just don't come back around here if you hurt her."

Valencia asked her a question and she turned to answer it. Zach was left in the middle of one of those dinner party silences where the people on either side of him were engaged in other conversation. He heard Billy laugh and shook his head. He was sure he'd met the other man somewhere. It would come to him eventually.

He looked over at Lila, who was in her element, talking about the town and the upcoming event, and he knew that Charlotte was right. He couldn't hurt her. She wasn't used to his life, and he might have changed the outer packaging, but he didn't want to change anything else.

"I love those shoes," Gina raved as they were all standing in the bathroom fixing their lipstick after dinner.

"Thanks. I thought they'd be uncomfortable, but they aren't," Lila said. For the first time in her life, she'd gone to the ladies' room with the other women at her table. She never had a reason to freshen up after dinner as she usually didn't care if her lipstick had worn off.

Charlotte had dashed to the kitchen to check on her sous-chef and make sure that everything was running smoothly. Valencia finished touching up her lipstick and they ran into Charlotte as they walked out. Lila knew this would be a perfect photo for her to post.

"Ladies, do you mind taking a selfie? Maybe with the Sheen logo behind us?" Lila asked.

They seemed surprised that she was suggesting a selfie, but all were game. Lila realized her arms were too short to get a good photo but Valencia offered to hold the camera and they got one of them all. She followed the women back toward their private table, remembering the tips that Dawn had given her for posting. She was toying with some different hashtags when Mandee Meriweather stopped her.

"Lila Jones, you are all that everyone is talking about tonight…well, you and Zach Benning. His Benning-nites have been bombarding me, demanding I inter-view him. I'd love to have you both on the show. What do you say?" she asked.

"Oh, Mandee, thanks. I have been wanting to come on and talk about the Soiree," Lila said. "Let me talk to ZB and I'll let you know when we can do it."

"Oh, ZB…so are you part of his inner circle?" Man-dee asked.

Lila knew that Mandee was absolutely the biggest gossip in town—Lila's dad referred to her as the Mouth of the South. No doubt, she'd love to get the inside scoop on what Zach was doing here.

"We're friends," she said. "I'll message you a time that works."

She smiled her goodbye before she turned and walked away from the woman who'd been ignoring her requests for months. It felt good to be the one in this position. Lila had never experienced this before. But she knew she had something that Mandee wanted. For once, the other woman had to come to her.

She finished writing her post but didn't post it; she wanted to get Zach's feedback first. He came over to her when she entered the private dining area.

"Everything okay?"

"Yes. *Royal Tonight!* wants to interview us. Probably just you but she wasn't about to say that to my face. I told her we'd get back to her on a time. Can you look at this? I want to post it."

She handed him her phone and he scanned it, added a hashtag and then nodded. "Looks great."

She glanced down at the hashtag he'd added—#soireefoxyfour. "What if the other women don't want—"

"It's fun and it brands you four. I think it will work. If you want to get their approval first, then let's ask them."

He put his hand on the small of her back and took her over to the rest of the group. Everyone stopped talking when they joined them. "What do you think of the ladies being branded as the Soiree Foxy Four? Just a fun hashtag that the team can use when they post?" he asked.

"I think it might be a bit much for Royal, and the Soiree *is* a charity event," Gina said.

"I agree," Valencia said. "But thanks for thinking of us as the foxy four."

Lila deleted the hashtag and then sent the post as Asher came over to talk to them.

"Zach, I like your thinking. You are just what this event needs," he said.

"You were already in good hands with this advisory committee. I'm impressed with everything you have brought to the table."

"Yeah? It's fun to see something go from concept to reality," Asher said.

"It is," Lila agreed. "I can't believe we are only two months away. Zach, you came at exactly the right time."

"Well, if I'd known how charming Royal was, I would have been here sooner," he admitted.

Zach glanced at his watch and she wondered if he was ready to leave. Normally she would have lit out after dessert but here she was staying for drinks with the group. As much as she enjoyed it she wouldn't mind some quiet time with Zach. A lot had happened today, and she still wasn't sure where they stood.

But she was going to be chill. She'd made up her mind sometime during the afternoon when Shantal was showing her how to do a cat-eye with eyeliner. She couldn't be that small-town girl who clung to the bad boy. But the problem was she wanted more from Zach. More of what she didn't know. But definitely more.

"Where is Billy from? He looks so familiar to me," Zach said.

Lila shrugged. She didn't know his history. "He doesn't remember meeting you and I'm pretty sure if you had met that wouldn't be the case."

"Why is that?" he asked, pulling her closer to him.

"You're unforgettable, ZB," she said, forcing herself to be flirty, but inside she knew she meant those words. That they were a truth bomb that she should pay attention to. No matter what happened between them, she knew she'd never forget him. How could she?

He'd changed something in her, helped her see her life in a new light and sparked her desires for something that she'd never considered before. That this craving for a lifestyle that she'd never dreamed possible could be so tantalizing and fun with the right man by her side. She wanted to say he'd given her a glimpse of life beyond what she'd had but honestly, he'd made her realize how much she loved her city and her life here, and that maybe she wanted him to love it, too.

Ten

Zach dropped Lila off at her house after their dinner at Sheen. She was getting a bunch of likes from being featured on his social media account and he was getting DMs asking if she was his flavor of the week. He had to think about that, and not with Lila.

"Are you sure you won't come in?" she asked.

She was breathtakingly gorgeous, and he wanted nothing more than to come in and hook up with her again. But that wasn't going to help either of them. Either she was his pet project or she was his girlfriend. But she couldn't be both, and a part of him was beginning to realize no matter how he spun it, there was no way to keep people from seeing her as his latest arm candy.

"I don't think that's a good idea," he said.

"Why not?" she asked, quirking her head to the side, but keeping her expression blank.

"Just for once don't ask the questions I'm not sure I can answer," he bit out.

"Why can't you answer that?" she asked.

It was almost ten o'clock and her neighborhood was quiet. Everyone in their homes watching TV or sleeping. Just a quiet domestic scene that was as foreign to him as tagging a post had been to Lila. This was her world.

Zach wanted to repeat it to himself, but he knew he wasn't stupid and he already got it. He didn't fit in here. Part of him didn't *want* to. The only thing he wanted was Lila... What if he took her to his place? Enough of this sleepy little suburban neighborhood.

"Want to come and stay with me?"

"No. You have your team there and they already think we are sleeping together," she said. "Come inside so we can talk. I can see one of my neighbors pretending not to stare at us."

"Fine. But we are already sleeping together," he reminded her as he turned off the Ferrari and followed her into her house.

As soon as the door closed behind him she turned to him. "I know that. But I don't want them to know."

"You should know everyone who has liked our posts where I tagged you also thinks we are sleeping together."

"Ugh! I need a drink."

She tossed her purse on the antique table in the hall and walked toward her kitchen. He put his keys on the table and followed her. Lila had pushed a chair over to the fridge, kicking off her Louboutin pumps, before he realized what she was doing. She started to climb up on it, but he caught her by her waist and set her aside.

"I'll get whatever it is you are trying to reach," he

said, pushing the chair aside and opening the cabinet. There was an unopened bottle of bourbon, a partially drunk bottle of Jack Daniel's and two bottles of Casamigos tequila. One of them was almost empty and the other hadn't been opened.

"Tequila?"

"Yes," she said stiffly. She had moved to another cabinet and taken two lowball glasses from it. Then she used her hand to get ice from the ice maker and dropped two cubes in one of the glasses. "Do you want ice?"

"Yes, ma'am," he said. He wasn't 100 percent sure what had set her off but he guessed learning that most of his million followers had figured out they were doing the horizontal mambo was it.

"Lime?"

"Please."

She opened the fridge and he poured them both a few fingers of tequila. Then she squeezed a lime wedge over one of them and handed him the other one. She lifted the glass and took a hard swallow. Then she put the glass down.

She nodded a bunch of times and put her hands on her hips. "Okay. I got this. We are sleeping together, and everyone knows… It's the twenty-first century, so who cares?"

She did. It was very obvious to him that Lila Jones didn't like anyone to know her personal business. He hated to see her like this. This was what he'd wanted to avoid. He hadn't expected this to bother her as much as it did because she was so open about other things—hell, pretty much everything else.

"*You* do," he said gently. "I should have warned you. But to be honest, even if we hadn't slept together, people would still think we had. You know my reputation."

"I do. But you're not—hell, yes you are. You are as tempting as everyone thinks you are... I don't want to be your flavor of the week," she said. "There, I said it. I don't need promises of forever, but I don't want to be someone you forget as soon as you drive out of town in your fast car, either."

He looked over at her and knew that she needed something from him. Something real. Not a glib statement or another diversion. "I could never forget you, Lila."

She shook her head and took another healthy swallow of her tequila. "I bet you even said that to that blonde who was with you when you got to town—oh, my God, that was only a few days ago!"

She was losing herself in this spiral.

He removed the glass from her hand before she had another sip and took her hand in his, drawing her back into the hallway and down to the mirror that hung there. He turned her to face it and stepped behind her, putting one arm around her waist.

"Lila Jones, look at yourself in the mirror," he said.

"I'm the woman you made me," she whispered.

He kissed her temple. "I wish I could make someone as strong, smart and sophisticated as you are. I did nothing but help you find a way to wear well-made clothes and get other people to notice that. There is nothing about you that wasn't already there."

She leaned closer to stare at herself and he waited. He felt her settling down, but he knew she needed more from him. Something *real*. Not the facade that ZB provided to his online followers but something authentic that Zach could give to Lila. He wanted to just do it, but deep down he was afraid. Afraid to lower his guard and let her see that he wasn't all shiny and perfect away from his online accounts.

"Everyone believes what they will because of me. But anyone who has met you will probably come to the same conclusion that I have."

"What is that?" she asked, turning her head slightly to meet his gaze over her shoulder.

That she was too damned good for him. That if anyone was the flavor of the week it was him and not her.

"That we are one hell of a pair," he said. Chickening out because the truth wasn't going to do anything but leave him weak to her.

Lila felt so unsure of herself and this wasn't like her. She turned in Zach's arms and hugged him. He hugged her back and she knew she'd probably freaked him out. She hadn't meant to. It was just that tonight had been filled with so many highs and the adrenaline rush had been exhilarating.

And then…she'd started to let doubts creep in. Did she only belong because of him? Zach had the contacts and the pizzazz that they needed, and sure, he was showing her how to bring that limelight to herself and the Soiree, but she wasn't going to kid herself that she was really part of that world. She liked the way she looked and how it felt to have everyone's attention, but there was another part of her that wasn't too sure she'd want it forever.

"Brown Eyes, please don't be sad. I can't do sad," he said as he tipped her head back.

Brown Eyes.

That was the first nickname he'd used that she actually didn't mind. She smiled at him. "I won't. Sorry for that. I am pretty sure this is the only time my personal life has been interesting."

"It's not boring to me," he said.

She tried not to let it matter that he had once again turned the conversation to himself. But Zach lived his life in front of the camera. Living the scandals and gossip-worthy life 24/7. "You were never like this?"

She gestured to her normal house, and herself, really hoping he'd understand she meant her normal life.

"No. I mean this house is really nice, but I have never lived in someplace as quaint as this one," he said. "I kind of like this. It's so homey and comfortable. I feel like…well, like I can just let my guard down while I'm here."

She snapped her fingers. "You know what I could do?"

"What?" he asked, sounding a bit wary.

"I could show you this life. Show you how to chill and not post every detail of your life. That way…it would be more even."

He stared down at her as if she'd grown a second head and she held her breath. She needed this and she wasn't sure how she'd missed it before. But her relationship with Zach was always going to be lopsided until she could give him something he couldn't buy for himself.

"I'm not sure…why wouldn't I post it all?"

"Just try it. Put your phone away for the rest of the night. And hang with me. Just doing fun stuff."

"Sex?" he asked. "I wouldn't need my phone for that."

Sex. Sure, she wanted him again. She doubted that she was ever going to tire of having him in her bed and ravishing her body. But she wanted something else. "Yes, but more than that. How about you park your car in my garage and we chill out. Doing the kinds of things that everyone does but no one posts."

"I can't even fathom what that would be."

"Watching TV, reading, playing spit."

"Okay, I'm intrigued. What the heck is spit?"

"Park your car and I'll show you."

She wasn't sure he'd do it. As much as she'd freaked out and drunk tequila, he seemed a bit like he was unsure, as well. But he just nodded and went to move his car. She opened the garage for him and then waited. Twenty minutes later they were both dressed in un-post-worthy clothes—Zach in his gym clothes, Lila in a pair of Looney Tunes boxers and an oversize tee—eating popcorn she'd topped with Parmesan cheese and butter, and she was giving him an overview of playing spit.

"We don't take turns but both play at the same time. Since it's your first time when we are ready to begin you can say spit. Then we will both start placing our cards down. You can only put a card on top that is either one higher or lower than the card showing."

"Okay, I think I got that. Can we play on each other's cards? How does one of us win?"

"Yes, we can. We keep going until one of us runs out of cards. If we get blocked then one of us says *ready spit* and we get sort of a free card," she said. "Ready?"

"Spit!"

They played for thirty minutes and she soon realized that Zach wasn't paying attention to the cards at all but watching her.

"Do you like playing cards?"

"I like poker, but that is about it. Nothing this exciting."

"You are totally teasing me," she said.

"I am. But I love how excited you are," he admitted gruffly. "It turns me on."

"*You* turn me on. You aren't even trying to win," she pointed out after he missed two obvious plays.

"My mom taught me it wasn't polite to beat a lady at games," he said. "Especially a lady you want to take home."

He had his own version of manners. "What else did your mom teach you?"

Lila knew his father had cheated and that he'd grown up with his mom. She could have googled him and found out more about his past but when she'd been researching Zach that hadn't mattered. All that mattered at the time were his followers. But now...well, now she wanted to hear his story from him and not read it on the internet.

"The usual stuff," he said. "How to throw a great party. You have to have the right mix of people. Talkers, listeners, shit stirrers and peacemakers."

"Huh, I never thought of it that way, but you are right. That's a good mix. Which one are you?"

"I can be all of them depending on the party." He grinned. "Like right now, I'm listening."

"You were. Now I am."

"Yes. Everything is give-and-take. Not like you said earlier. I'd never just let you use me."

"You wouldn't?" she asked, finally getting to the heart of what was bothering her.

"No."

"So what are you getting?"

"You," he said, pushing himself up on his hands and knees and kissing her.

Zach hadn't meant for this to happen. But somehow, he felt even more vulnerable to her as she sat across from him playing this card game that made no sense and had no reason to it. He was also getting more and more aroused as she continued to play cards, point out ones he'd missed and generally just let her guard down.

Until this moment he hadn't realized how much of herself she kept locked away. But now he knew. She'd let him in a few times before, and then tonight when she'd been afraid that everything about him was just for show, she'd kind of lost it. But him sitting here with her had somehow reassured her.

Which he wouldn't allow himself to analyze. He'd been staring at her breasts under that large T-shirt since she'd sat down next to him. They were under the fan and he could tell the exact moment when she'd gotten cold. Her nipples had hardened and then *he'd* hardened.

Her mouth under his was soft but the angle was wrong, so he pulled her into his arms and rolled until they were both on their sides staring into each other's eyes. She put one hand on his hip and the other on his chest. Her breath smelled of lime and tequila and it wasn't unpleasant, but it served to remind him of how fragile she was right now.

Zach hugged her close because he had no idea what to do next. He could take what he wanted—her body. He could turn her on enough that she'd stop worrying about the fact that everyone knew they were sleeping together.

"What am I going to do with you, Brown Eyes?"

She tipped her head back, lightly bumping his chin as she did so. "Make love to me."

Make love.

Those were words he never applied to sex. He called it everything but that because love…well, he knew it didn't really exist. That it was as hollow as the likes he racked up with each new post, yet at the same time… tonight he wished he could make love to her.

He swiftly took her clothes off and then stripped his off, as well. Before he realized he'd left his condoms in her bedroom.

"Be right back."

He hurried and got one. When he returned, she was lying in the middle of the blanket where they'd been playing cards, propped up on her elbow, her hair falling around her shoulders.

"Hey there," she said.

Something emotional surged to life within him and he quickly quelled it. Shoved it deep down inside so he didn't have to acknowledge it. Instead, he got down on his hands and knees and crawled to her feet. He kissed her delicate ankle and then slowly worked his way up her body, pushing her onto her back when he reached the apex of her thighs. He moved between them and lowered his head. Tasting her first with his tongue in slow licks and then as she started to move under him, her hips undulating with each probe of his tongue, he sucked her clit into his mouth. She grabbed the back of his head, holding him to her while she pushed herself up against him.

He reached up with one hand, finding her hard nipple with his fingers and pinching it as he continued to eat her. She pulled on his head and he lifted himself up, looking up her flushed body.

"Take me now," she said. "I need you."

He slid up her body and shifted his hips until he was poised at her entrance, then drove himself deep inside her. As that tightness inside him started to unravel with each thrust, he pounded into her again and again until he felt the skin at the back of his neck tingle and his balls felt full and tight. Then he came, thrusting into her a few more times as she tightened around his shaft and called out his name.

He kept moving until he was fully drained and then collapsed on her, careful to use his legs and his arms to keep from crushing her. He rolled to his side, pulling her with him and holding her cradled against his side. She put her hand on his chest right over his heart and did that thing with her fingertip she'd done before.

She looked up at him.

"I guess they are all right."

"They?"

"Your followers who think we are sleeping together," she said.

"Does that matter?" he asked. He wished he could say the words that would make this easy for her. But they would be a lie, and he had never lied to anyone. He might be a bad boy, but he'd never been a bad man. He sort of prided himself on that.

"I don't think it does. I would rather be in your arms than not because I was being spiteful."

He smiled down at her. "Spiteful to who?"

"I guess myself. I don't know where this is going, Zach, and I might have regrets later. But for now, I'm going to enjoy being with you."

They weren't words he wanted to hear but he'd heard them before. He was the kind of man who knew his place in a woman's life, and it was temporary. No matter how much he might wish that it could be different.

Eleven

Lila was amazed the next day at work by the number of calls she got about the Soiree by the Bay. Not only that but her social media posts were racking up likes—the ones *she* posted, not just the ones that Zach tagged her in. She knew a big part of that was due to the fact that many people thought they were a couple.

Of course, they were a couple, but she also cautioned herself not to buy into the show. Zach traveled with a team and everything he did was for his followers. He had invited her to join him for lunch and taken her on a helicopter ride to a field of bluebonnets. And when they got there Shantal, Vito and Dawn were waiting with Mrs. Smith and several cameras. So the romantic lunch she'd thought she was having was actually a business lunch.

She knew that she had to start thinking that way. Like tonight when they went on Mandee's show, she had to be ready. Zach had texted her that he was coming by her office to introduce her to a media expert who would prep her for being on television.

Lila found herself pulling out her makeup and touching it up before he arrived. Her phone vibrated on her desk, but she was getting so many notifications now that she didn't even bother checking it. Probably more likes.

What a difference a few days made! She used to have seven likes—*seven*—but on her posts now she had thousands.

"Hello, babe," Zach said as he breezed into her office, accompanied by a beautiful woman who was immaculately dressed in a black business jacket over a button-down shirt and a pair of loose-fitting jeans.

She was beginning to read his signs. He called her *babe* when he was working. When they were alone... *Brown Eyes*. So this was a business call, which she'd known.

"Hey, ZB."

"This is Bree, the media expert I told you about."

"Hello," Lila said.

"Hi there. I have been checking out your social media feed and you seem pretty savvy so I'm not sure how much I can help," Bree said as she and Zach took seats in the guest chairs in her office.

"That's all ZB and his team's advice," Lila said. "I've only been on TV once before."

"Really?" Zach asked, giving her a quizzical look. "I didn't know that."

"Well, it was when I went to Congrès in high school and got first in the dictation contest. It's a French-speaking competition."

"Wow, I had no idea you *parles français*," Zach said.

"That's because I don't anymore. I mean I might be able to conjugate a few verbs for you but that's about it."

He laughed.

"Don't worry about your lack of TV presence," Bree told her. "The important thing is to be prepared and to remember your message. ZB already filled me in on the Soiree but he didn't need to. I've been hearing about it all over the state. It is going to be *the* event of the summer season."

"Thanks. We have all been working so hard and I'm excited to see it come together. So my message should be about the event. Just facts?" she asked.

"Facts, yes, but also why no one should miss the event," Bree said. "Who is performing there?"

"We have Kingston Blue lined up. He's so hot right now. I think just saying his name will get everyone excited," Lila said. The musician had been one of the first to respond to the event—he was tall, with gorgeous dreadlocks down over his shoulders, and a flashy dresser.

"Okay, so instead of just saying we've booked Kingston Blue, lead in with the 'Song of Summer,' Kingston's latest hit, and say you've had it on repeat on your playlist. Something along those lines," Bree suggested.

"I can do that," Lila said. "And it's not a lie. I mean that song is as hot as summer in Texas. So sensual and sexy. Should I do that with everyone?"

"Well, don't do the same thing each time. Just look at the facts you want to get out. Booking tickets and promoting the website…don't need an anecdote but maybe a few festival stories or something. And Zach will be there with you. How well do you two know each other?" she asked.

"Uh…" Lila began.

"I know the gossip, but that's all publicity. What I'm trying to say here is that if you know each other well then Zach can lead you to the topics," Bree said, turn-

ing to look at him. "My man ZB is an expert at directing the conversation where he wants it to go."

Lila let out a breath she hadn't realized she'd been
holding. She hadn't expected that there would be people
who would just dismiss the gossip about the two of them.
But she should have. It made her feel better to know that
most people weren't going to be thinking of them doing
the nasty each time Zach tagged her in a photo.

"I do. And I'm going to be pretty strict about not
talking about Candi. I think I already mentioned that
to Mandee's people. We are on the show to discuss the
Soiree and of course all things fab."

She smiled, but she knew him well enough now to
hear the edge in his voice. Zach wasn't prepared to discuss his affair with a married woman. He hadn't mentioned it to her, either, and she honestly wasn't too sure
she wanted the details. But she did wonder how he was
going to keep Mandee from asking about it. She was
known for getting the dirt she wanted.

Bree left her with a few more tips and Lila told her
she would do her best to implement them. Zach closed
the door behind Bree and then turned to face her.

"Ready for this?"

"No. I'm so nervous, but I will give it my all."

"I know you will," he said. "I don't want any of the
scandal from my life to touch you. I'm going to let you
take point on the interview. Just be your besotted boyfriend."

"Is that what you are?"

He had no idea. The longer Zach was in Royal and
with Lila, the less clear a lot of things were. Even his
online life had started to take a back seat to this time
he was spending with her. He'd been trying to stay fo-

cused and ignore the emotions that Lila stirred in him and so far he'd been shooting above par. Which wasn't good. He wanted to at least be on par.

"Isn't that what you want me to be?" he asked, pulling her into his arms because he'd been wanting to kiss her since he'd walked into her office. Her new glasses suited her face and when he'd entered and seen her sitting there, he had a few racy fantasies involving her and that desk of hers.

She put her hand on his chest to keep some distance between the two of them. "Don't be glib. I want to know how you see yourself."

Glib. That was his life. It was how he managed everything and normally no one dared to call him on it, but he might have let Lila get too close. He wasn't even sure how he'd done that. After all, he'd been making *her* over, dammit. But at the same time, without him being aware, she might have made a few changes in him. Because he knew he didn't want to hurt her feelings. Didn't want to say something that was going to make those big brown eyes of hers regard him the way so many disappointed people had.

"Brown Eyes, please. I'm doing my best here."

"I'm not sure that you are," she said. "I'm going to be honest and lay it all on the line, Zach. I'm not an influencer, and those pictures I post? Well, as much as I'm following the tips that Dawn gave me, they are my life. I'm not tagging you to get followers but because I like the pictures of the two of us. And before you say anything, I do know that it's for show. In my mind, I know that. But I'm also starting to buy it. To buy *us*."

Zach took a deep breath. Was that it? Were they both starting to buy into the image they created to build her followers? Was he falling for the ruse the same way that she was? This was fun. But he knew that if he said that to her right now, she wouldn't appreciate that.

"I don't know what to say. This is so not my normal scene. Royal is different. *You* are different. Maybe… I have to be back in LA soon. Why don't you come with me?" he asked.

She turned out of his arms and walked around behind her desk, sitting down. She was thinking about his offer. He remembered how the blonde—he couldn't even remember her name now—had just jumped in his car when he'd asked her to come with him to Texas. But Lila didn't make decisions that way.

Zach leaned against the wall. He could only imagine what she was thinking, probably running the pros and cons of the trip.

"It will be a lot of fun and I'll introduce you to more people who you can invite to the Soiree. The kind of people you need to get on board if you want this to be a big international event."

"Are you bribing me?" she asked.

He held his hands out to his sides. "I'll do whatever it takes to get you to come to my home with me."

"Just ask me," she said.

That honesty.

Damn.

She killed him with that. *Just ask her.* Well, now he couldn't because he knew if he did, she'd know he wanted her there. *Yo, idiot, she knows.* His subconscious was giving him a hard time lately.

"Come home with me," he said, forcing the words out as fast as he could.

"Okay."

What?

That was it?

"Seriously, that's all you needed to give up your lists?"

She shook her head and smiled at him. "How do you know I was making a mental list?"

"It's you. That's what you do."

She stood up and came around the desk, leaning back against it as she looked over at him. "You're starting to know me."

"I am," he admitted thickly. Which was why he had to get them back to LA. Back to the place where the world made sense and he could forget about these feelings that were stirring inside him.

"So we can leave tomorrow… Do you have to clear it with someone here?"

She groaned. "I do. In fact, you should leave because I have to do some work before the interview, and I want to try to get an appointment with Abby Carmichael. Do you know her?"

"Uh, no. Serious documentary filmmakers don't dig my scene," he said. But he'd heard of her and knew she'd do a great job when Lila convinced her to come and film the event.

He knew Lila would get Abby on board, too. She was good at getting people to do what she wanted. He left her office and went to the coffee shop across the street but was mobbed by his followers and left after agreeing to a few selfies. Then he found himself driving away from Royal until there was nothing but flat Texas landscape on either side of the road.

He pulled over.

Had Lila been manipulating him? He had to wonder about that because he wasn't acting like himself. It was easy to say she was making him feel things. Really, he had to figure out his emotions and stop referring to them as something he couldn't define. But this was the first time he'd experienced them.

And it was down to her.

Was that part of her plan?

Hell. He didn't know or care. He liked her. He liked the time he spent with her. He knew it would end; everything did. So he was going to enjoy the ride for as long as he could. He knew that once she saw him in LA her opinion of him would change. She'd fall in love with the lifestyle and forget all about the man who had introduced her to it.

Mandee Meriweather was very attractive and sort of made for the spotlight. Lila was in the greenroom by herself waiting for the show to start. Zach had texted he was on his way.

"Oh, all alone?" Mandee asked. She wore a black sheath sundress with large straps that left her shoulders and neck bare. She was followed by a cloud of Chanel No. 5 as she entered the greenroom and looked around expectantly.

"ZB is on his way. And his team are looking for a parking spot."

"Sorry about that. I didn't know there would be so many different vehicles. So exciting about the Soiree. I know that you have been on the planning committee from the beginning. Quite the coup for you. Little, shy Lila Jones."

She'd known Mandee in high school…well, more like known *of* her in high school, as the other woman was popular and had run with a different crowd.

"I don't think it was anything like that. I mean it is my job to promote Royal at the chamber of commerce."

"Of course it is, silly. So when did you say Zach would be here?"

"Now," he said, walking in and coming straight over to Lila and giving her a one-armed hug. "Sorry for being late."

"That's okay," she murmured, glad that he was here. Mandee was the kind of person that Zach was an expert at dealing with.

"Mandee, you look gorg tonight," he declared, turning to her.

"Thanks, ZB—is it okay to call you that?"

"Only my closest pals do," he said, flirting with her. "So of course you can."

"Ooooh, thanks for that. How about a selfie before the show?" she asked.

Lila was trying not to be jealous of the way Zach was flirting with Mandee. A part of her knew it was just the way the two of them interacted, but at the same time, Lila couldn't help thinking that the flamboyant reporter was more the kind of woman that Zach was used to.

"The Benningnites will love seeing me with you two," Zach said, pulling Lila along with him.

Mandee got in close on his other side. "Maybe it would be better if Lila snapped the pic?"

Lila smiled to herself. "It would be. You two get close."

She had to give it to Zach—he looked like he was really interested in being photographed with Mandee, and she knew that was part of his charm. He loved this life. It wasn't something he was doing for a lark. As he chatted with Mandee and his team arrived to touch up her makeup and do some final details on Zach's hair, she saw him sort of getting even more electric. Everyone in the room wanted to talk to him and be near him.

He had a real gift. She might think this was all an illusion, and for her, she reminded herself, it was. But for him this was *real*.

Mandee had to leave to go and prep for their segment, and the team departed along with her. When a production assistant came to get her and Zach a few minutes later, Lila realized her hands were sweating.

She wiped them on her hips and he caught the movement. "Don't worry. You're going to be great. Just remember to smile, to breathe and that I'm right by your side."

Impulsively she hugged him. "Thank you."

"It's nothing."

But it wasn't nothing, she thought as she sat next to him on Mandee's guest couch to talk about the Soiree. She got in the information she'd practiced with Bree and a few other facts, as well. The crew for the show all responded to her stories so she thought that went well.

"So word on the street is that you two are Royal's hottest new couple," Mandee said.

"Lila is a gem," Zach replied, flashing his trademark grin. "I came to town because of the event and that is down to the hard work of the committee, but especially Lila. She has a way of making Royal seem like the only place I want to be."

"We are pretty special here."

"Yes, but it's also Lila herself. She's got the kind of Southern charm that I've always heard about but found in short supply," he said, reaching over to take her hand in his and lifting it to his mouth to kiss the back of it. "It's easy to fall for her appeal."

Fall for…

Her heart stuttered in her chest. Was Zach telling her how he felt? It would be just like him to do it in the spotlight, but at the same time, the Zach she knew was very private. This had to be for show. To keep the numbers of her followers up because she appeared to be special to him. That was all it was.

She had to be very careful not to fall for this silver-tongued rascal. He was merely doing the job she'd asked him to do.

"Of course, ZB's pretty special, too. I can't wait for everyone to meet him at the Soiree on the Bay," Lila said, trying to bring the conversation back to the event and to force herself to remember that was the real reason he was here.

"It will be one hot July on the bay," Zach declared. "And I can't wait."

"I think we all want to be there," Mandee said. "Ticket and festival information is available at the website shown on the screen right now, and make sure to follow Lila Jones and ZB on all social media platforms for behind-the-scenes deets. Until next time, this has been *Royal Tonight!*"

The closing music played and they all stayed seated and smiling until the stage manager called cut.

"Thanks for having us on your show," Lila said.

"It was a blast," Zach added.

"I hope you will come back again closer to the event," Mandee said. "Want to grab a drink?"

"Love to, but can't," Zach replied. "We are heading to LA in the morning and I promised Lila we'd have a quiet night."

"Lucky girl," Mandee said.

Zach slipped his hand into hers again and now she wasn't sure if this was all for show or for real. She knew that she needed to figure it out, however, because she was starting to fall for him.

Twelve

"Welcome to my home," Zach said as he swept into the large foyer of a huge mansion in Beverly Hills. "I am throwing a party in Malibu in a couple of days, but for today it's just us. I want you to have a chance to get used to the time change and all that."

Lila stood next to him, her Birkin bag over her shoulder, just turning slowly in a circle and taking in the entryway of his house. The marble flooring was Carrara and had been flown in from Italy. And the art on the walls were some of his favorite modern artists, including a print on canvas of Edvard Munch's *Vampire*, or as it was originally titled, *Love and Pain*. It was a conversation starter when people came to his home.

For the first time he saw the image through different eyes. He had hesitated to say he was in love, but seeing the couple bound together in the image made him think of himself and Lila.

"I'm not sure about this painting. It's so dark but also so sensual," Lila said when she came to a stop in front of it.

"That's why I picked it," he said, coming next to her and returning his attention to the portrait of the couple. The man had his head in the lap of the woman as she cradled him. He knew from his study of the artist that Munch had been dealing with his own psychological issues, but this portrait had spoken to him.

Next to it was one of his favorite pieces—a bright neon sign that spelled out *You Wish You Were Me!*

"Nice. I guess it takes a humble man to hang that up."

"It was a gag gift from a friend. It makes me laugh and not take myself too seriously." Zach knew that he could come off as totally self-centered, but he also didn't really take himself too seriously. He wanted the chance to show Lila his world. To see if what he felt for her was just a Royal thing or if those feelings were something different, something deeper and more intense than he wanted to admit.

They stowed her bags in the master bedroom. "Are you tired or do you want to go sightseeing?"

"I don't know! I've never been to California before. Did you grow up here?"

"I did. In Bel Air. It's not too far from here," he said. Thinking of his childhood always stirred bittersweet memories. His younger self hadn't realized everything wasn't about him, and it wasn't until it was too late that he cottoned on to the reality of his parents' marriage.

"Oh, do you want to show me your childhood home? I like that idea. And then you can take me somewhere super posh for lunch and we can try shopping again," she said.

"I've created a monster," he joked. His childhood

home wasn't a place he went to often and it was odd that he had brought it up now. But there was something about Lila that made him feel and remember things that he'd ignored for too long.

"Ha. You wish," she said. "Should I change?"

"Yes. Put on that cute BCBG Max Azria outfit you modeled for me," he suggested. "It shows off your arms and makes your legs look a mile long."

"Oh, I will."

She dashed into the bathroom and got changed while he waited. Normally he would be on the phone going live for his followers trying to drum up a crowd to follow him that day, but he realized he wanted this first day in LA with Lila just for himself. He loved her excitement and wonder when she experienced something new and couldn't wait to see her face when they drove past the Hollywood sign. He knew she'd love it.

She liked all those things that people were jaded about out here. Lila got riveted by a pretty sunset or the way the bluebonnets smelled. She was just so genuine in liking the little things and well, let's be honest, the expensive things, too. But he wanted this day for them.

And he knew why. He wanted to see if the hollow aching part inside him would be satisfied with just Lila. This trip wasn't just to see if his feelings were real outside of Texas, they were to see if Lila fit in here, too. He wasn't sure if he wanted her to. If she did, how was he going to deal with that? He was so used to hiding his emotions behind the flashy lifestyle. If he had someone to share it with—if he shared it with *Lila*—he'd have to be real all the time. He'd never been able to quiet that need to find the spotlight and draw strangers to him, but with Lila he suspected he had a chance.

"How do I look?"

Drop-dead gorgeous. She had on a sleeveless knit top that came to a deep vee over her breasts and a pair of wide-legged trousers and some wedge sandals that made her seem even taller than normal. She'd pulled her hair back at the sides and her old fall of bangs were back. He hadn't realized how much he'd missed the woman he'd first met until now.

"Fab. Ready to take LA?"

"With you by my side? Always."

She pulled out some large shades from her Birkin and put them on before looping her arm through his. He walked her to the garage and she pulled her sunglasses off as the motion sensor lights slowly came on, illuminating the five cars he kept there. She pulled her arm from his and turned to him.

"I can't believe this! My dad would go nuts for that '69 Camaro."

"Give me your phone and we can send him a photo of you with it," he said. "Is that the car you want to take?"

She didn't even bother looking at the rest of the vehicles in the garage, just nodded. "Oh, yeah."

He snapped her photos in front of the white car that had been lovingly restored with the bright orange racing stripe down the center of it. Then he put the ragtop down on the convertible before he fired up the V8 engine. He seldom drove the classic muscle car because his followers preferred the newer Audi or Aston Martin, but for Lila he'd drive this.

It wasn't until they had driven past his childhood home and headed toward Rodeo Drive that he realized how much he was enjoying himself in this simple moment with her. No one was clamoring for a selfie or asking him questions. It was just the two of them with the wind blowing around them and the California sun beating down. Could he be happy like this forever or was this just another illusion he had created? One that would be a way to get over the guilt that had driven him from LA in the first place?

Lila was loving being in California, but she had to admit that what she loved most about it was being here with Zach. He was showing her his world and she relished it. When they'd driven past his childhood home, he hadn't stopped, just sort of gestured to it with a nod of his head and slowed down slightly.

She'd wanted to ask him about it, but he'd left the residential neighborhood of mansions behind and drove them to Rodeo Drive, pointing out some of the hills that had been damaged during the wildfires the year before. There was real pain in his voice as he talked about the devastation and the fear he'd felt as the fires spread in an unpredictable pattern.

She almost forgot about how he'd been so quiet at the house until they were seated for lunch at 208 Rodeo. The menu proclaimed it was Italian American fusion and she couldn't wait to see what that was. She had to admit there were things about California that she liked but there was no way this place would be better than Charlotte's cooking at Sheen.

They placed their order. Zach had asked for a seat overlooking both Rodeo and Wilshire and for the first time she understood the term *pretty people*. Because they were all around her. Walking, shopping and being seen.

"Is this everything you hoped it would be?" he asked.

"It's a bit fake, isn't it?"

He threw his head back and laughed. "Yeah, everyone is here for a reason."

"Not lunch, right? I mean it does seem like people have really…well, my mom would say *made an effort*. And she means when you take your time with your look and everything. Kind of like what I'm doing for my social media posts, but this is real life."

"It is," he said. "I think Rodeo really captures that aspirational lifestyle vibe. Of course, we'll make a few posts."

"Can't wait."

"OMG, is that Lila Jones? It is," a woman about twenty said as she came up to their table. "I love that photo you posted yesterday of that cute little coffee shop. I'm loving the vibe of your feed right now. So on point but not too in-your-face with retailers. Can I grab a selfie?"

"Sure," Lila said, standing up and putting her arm around the woman. "What's your name?"

"Kylie. I'm from Oklahoma and have been out here for about six months. Until I saw your feed, I didn't realize how much I missed home or how cool it could be."

Kylie snapped her photo and then noticed Zach. "Oh, you're really with ZB? That's awesome. I'm not really into the jet set but you are a total hottie.

"Take care of my girl," Kylie said with a wave as she walked away.

Lila sat back down and looked over at Zach. Feeling a little excitement and then embarrassed that she was excited at having someone recognize her. "I can't believe that just happened! Someone *recognized* me… I mean—here."

"I know. What did you think?" he asked.

"I liked it. I'm not going to lie. I can see why you are addicted to this lifestyle."

Zach leaned in close and her heart raced faster.

"Thinking about making this permanent?" he asked.

"What? I mean I couldn't. I'm just a novelty, right?" she asked, because she wasn't really sure of anything at this moment. Not this newfound celebrity. And especially not Zach. All she knew for sure was that her feelings for him were getting deeper with each day she spent with him.

"You are whatever you want this to be," he said, taking her hand in his. A shiver spread up her arm as it always did when he touched her. "It can be as real as you make it."

She nodded. "Like us?"

"I'm not sure what you mean."

"Are we as real as I make us," she said. "Or are we solid?"

"I showed you my childhood home. That's pretty deep," he reminded her.

"You did, but you didn't say anything," she said. "Was it a happy place for you? Do you miss it?"

"It was okay. I went to boarding school from the age of eight, so not too attached to that home. Prior to that, I was in a private school across town. Seems like most of my childhood until I went away to school was spent in the back of the Lincoln Town Car that Cissy drove."

She was learning more about him in this moment than she had previously. How did this all fit into the man who lived his life in the spotlight? The LA bad boy who slept with other men's wives and made bets with shy, small-town girls and changed lives.

"Who is Cissy?" she asked.

"She was my nanny. Actually, she was an au pair from Limoges. She was pretty funny and I liked her. My dad did, too, so she left us after a year and my mom found a dour woman to watch me." Zach shrugged.

"And to be honest, I can't even remember her name now."

Lila leaned forward across the table, taking Zach's hand in hers. The one woman that he'd been close to as a child had been taken from him. It kind of made her wonder if that was the reason he had a hard time making a real connection. Was this the missing piece she'd been searching for?

"I'm sorry." Her heart broke for his life. No wonder he needed the adulation of his followers. He'd been alone for so much of his formative years, there had to be something inside him that needed the attention. That gave her pause. Made her realize that he might never be able to step out of the spotlight.

"Ah, don't sweat it. I'm not a poor little rich boy," he said. "What about you? Happy childhood?"

"Yes. Really happy. Only child, and my parents spoiled me."

"Glad one of us had that. So, what do you want to do this afternoon?" he asked. "I got an invite for a party at an exclusive nightclub later tonight. It should be fun. Want to hit it?"

A party. Did she? Normally she wasn't—stop, she warned herself. She had to stop comparing herself to who she was and just go for it. Let her hair down and enjoy every moment of this.

"Yes. I mean I think so. I've never been to that kind of party."

"You'll love it," he promised. "We are going to set this town on fire, Brown Eyes. By the time tomorrow comes you'll be trending on the internet."

She sat back in her chair, smiling. She liked the sound of that. And she especially liked that she wasn't shy Lila Jones anymore. When she was with Zach, she felt like she was the exciting, vibrant woman in the social media feed that he'd created. And the more she lived this life, the more she was coming to love it and the man who'd brought her into it. Another part of her wondered if this could last.

After nearly four days being in California, Lila was really turning into a party animal. But this morning she had a meeting with burgeoning documentary filmmaker Abby Carmichael at a coffee shop near the Santa Monica Pier. She'd left Zach sleeping in his bed and driven the Mercedes C-Class convertible that Zach had told her to use while she was in California.

She spotted the documentary filmmaker immediately from her photo as she walked up to the café. She waved at Lila as she approached. Abby had long dark brown hair and a light brown complexion, and was wearing a thin flannel shirt paired with skinny jeans.

"Hi, Abby. I'm Lila. Thanks for meeting me in person." She had on her prescription sunglasses and was still slightly hungover from a party last night. But she was determined to use her newfound fame to help the Soiree. That was why she'd taken the bet, after all. Somehow that reason had faded the more time she spent with Zach. She had been finding it harder and harder to relate to her life in Royal as she'd been swept into Zach's world. To that end, she'd been ignoring calls from home because she didn't want her mom to tell her that it was time to stop this nonsense and come home.

"Nice to meet you," Abby said. "Um, I checked out the website for your event, but tell me more about it."

"Of course. The Soiree on the Bay is the brainchild of the Edmond family of Royal. So far, we have a lot of the members of the Texas Cattleman's Club involved. They are the elite, moneyed crowd."

"Sounds like there should be some good stories there. What about Zach Benning? Is he coming to the event with his posse?" she asked.

"Yes, he is," Lila said. "And we also have Kingston Blue and his entourage, who are always a lot of fun."

"You kind of have a following now, too, right?" Abby remarked.

"Yeah, but that's just kind of a subset of ZB's fans," Lila explained. She didn't want to build herself up too much. Especially since she still wasn't sure how long her followers would stick with her.

"ZB? I thought you two were a couple," Abby said.

Lila took a deep breath, looking at this woman with the clear gaze and the straightforward manner. She had her shit together in a way that Lila used to. This new lifestyle and California were confusing her. Making her want things that weren't really true to herself. On the drive to Santa Monica this morning she'd had plenty of time to think. And she'd started to realize that she wasn't getting closer to Zach, which had been what she'd hoped for when she'd agreed to take this trip home with him.

The parties were fun, of course. She had met people that she'd never thought she would even bump into at the airport. Talking to them had just made her more confused about Zach and herself and the life they had. The celebrities she'd talked to had either been all about themselves or genuinely real people gobsmacked by their fame.

Sure, they were sleeping together and the sex was hotter than ever and they partied every night and went to A-list events, but she'd learned more about him in five minutes that first day at lunch at 208 Rodeo than she had the last four days.

"We are together," Lila confirmed. "But it's complicated."

Abby laughed a little. "When isn't it when there is a man involved?"

Lila just shook her head. "I know. Normally I date guys that aren't…well, Zach."

"I'm sure you'll figure it out. You look like a woman who has her stuff together," Abby said.

Appearances can be deceiving, Lila thought. And it resonated with her.

"Thanks. I hope you'll come to Royal to film. I can get you access to the Edmond family and Billy Holmes—he's sort of an unofficial member of the family. Also we have a really cool chef, Charlotte Jarrett, who is overseeing the menus for the event. You'll have a lot of good people to talk to."

"Okay. I think this sounds like something interesting," Abby said. "Let me think about it, okay?"

They continued chatting over brunch and then Lila left her to drive back to Zach's place. Her phone was blowing up from the photo she'd posted of herself and Abby at the café and she shut it off. She was starting to feel fatigued from this. While she knew that somehow Zach thrived under the spotlight, it was taking a toll on her.

Or maybe it was simply the fact that when she was out with Zach they had to be photo-ready and always on for his followers and now hers. It was hard. Complicated.

Lila remembered her thought that appearances could be deceiving. She yearned for something simpler. Like playing spit in her living room with Zach. Just the two of them in their most comfy clothes not staging the evening for followers.

She was pretty sure she'd been duping herself each morning when she looked in the mirror. Trying to convince herself that this new Lila was better than the old version of herself. But the truth was she was simply different. She was *tired.* Lila hadn't wanted to admit it to herself, but she was tired of faking it for others. And she just realized she had been faking it as much as she'd been genuinely enjoying it. She wanted Zach to think she could fit into his life. But had she lost herself for him?

No.

She enjoyed this feeling of being free and living in the moment.

But it couldn't last forever. Nor did she want it to. She wanted to go home to Royal…with Zach…and have her new image in her hometown. But this glitzy, hard-partying world that he was a part of? It wasn't for her. And that was the problem. She wasn't sure that Zach could want the quiet life that she craved.

The May California sun was bright and should be cheering her up, but as she turned onto Zach's street in Beverly Hills, she knew it wasn't. That this was never going to feel right or feel like home.

Maybe if she and Zach were *more.* If he truly cared about her and she felt like together they had something real, then she could enjoy this. But whenever she got too real, Zach backed away.

Was that it?

She decided it was. When she got back to his place she was going to talk to him, to figure out what was happening between them, because she wasn't willing to keep going like this. She missed her quiet neighborhood and the Texas heat. She missed just eating a meal when it was still hot and not making sure she posted it for the world to see. But she also knew she would miss Zach if he didn't come back with her.

Somehow when she'd been changing herself, something real had emerged and it wasn't just her love for high fashion. She had started to really care for Zach Benning. The vulnerable man behind the bad-boy image that he was always rolling out for his posts.

She had to find out if that man was real and if he cared about her, too. And that was what she was determined to do today.

Thirteen

Zach woke alone to find a note from Lila telling him she'd gone to take a meeting with a documentary film-maker. He scrubbed his hand over his face, felt the stubble that had grown in overnight and tried to force himself to look at his phone. He had been nonstop par-tying, giving Lila the lifestyle that she'd sounded so excited about that first day. But to be honest, he was tired and somehow having her by his side was making it harder to keep up the illusion that his life was perfect.

He especially felt the hollowness in it with her here with him in California. He wondered if it was because she was too real. Too Texas for this life. He had no doubt that she would have already sent a thank-you gift to the host of last night's party. It was the talk of his set that she did it. Everyone felt that it was an anachronism but at the same time appreciated the thoughtful gifts she sent along.

And they were well-thought-out gifts. He had overheard her talking to Lil Dominator last night about his kids, and he suspected that Lila would include a gift for them when she sent his thank-you gift. She genuinely cared about people. He recalled her telling him that all those years of blending into the background had made her a good listener. And that was 100 percent true. People liked to talk to her and now that his spotlight was on her as well, she hadn't stopped listening.

But he had. He'd never been good at it. Frankly if something didn't involve him, he'd never seen the point in it. But this was Lila and she might be more important to him than anyone had been since his French au pair. Which was sad but also very true.

He showered and shaved and wondered if she'd go for a quiet day at home just lounging by the pool. He wanted to talk to her. To be the one that she was listening to. It had been all about her since they arrived, and he needed some of her attention just for him.

Zach blew out a breath. He had a lot of DMs to go through but he wasn't ready to deal with them until he had coffee and maybe something to eat.

"Morning, Mrs. Smith," he said as he breezed into the kitchen. "What do we have to eat?"

"Breakfast burrito?" she asked.

"Perfect, and a large coffee. I'll take it by the pool, maybe with some of that fresh fruit salad you made yesterday, too?"

"Certainly. I'll get it right out to you," she said.

He walked through the house, realizing how quiet it was without Lila by his side. She was always sharing what was on her mind and talking to him about the upcoming Soiree on the Bay and, well, everything. Yesterday she'd told him about an article she'd read about Los Angeles when it had been just orange groves everywhere.

He missed it…missed her.

He wasn't about to let this continue. Somehow, he had to get her to focus on him and then this empty void would go away. She was stirring feelings that it was getting harder and harder to deny he had for her. Feelings that he didn't want to name because frankly he wasn't a lovable man. He knew that. Had known it from the time he was very young. He had always been too blunt, too self-focused, too *Zach*.

He sat down and noticed that Lila had posted a new photo. She looked good, a bit fatigued but still good. Some of the sparkle that he'd noticed in her early photos wasn't there. But her likes were larger than ever so her followers weren't catching on.

He'd seen another protégé of his self-destruct and completely go off-grid. Lila was made of stronger stuff and that would never happen with her, but at the same time he was concerned.

He didn't know how to move them forward. And a part of him was afraid to see if he had anything to offer her without the social media boost. Would she still like him when she tired of this? And he *hated* that he was worrying about it.

He was Zach fucking Benning, not some wimpy, insecure dude who couldn't keep a woman. That was the damned feelings. He knew it. He needed to stop obsessing over how he felt about her and just do him.

Sex.

Parties.

A fabulous life.

That was it. That was what he had to give her. She could come along for the ride or not. He wasn't going to let himself get drawn further into this downward spiral.

Mrs. Smith dropped off his breakfast and Zach refused to look at Lila's social media account anymore. He was going to go back to being himself.

He'd allowed himself to be drawn into this couple-dom thing without thinking it through. He was smarter than that. He DMed a few of his most loyal followers and set up a party that night for just them. Something exclusive on his yacht that he kept moored in Marina del Rey. He'd bring Lila along, but starting tonight, he had to put some distance between them.

She was becoming too important to him. And he knew that once she got over the novelty of this life, she was going to start to look harder at him, and Zach was afraid she'd see who he really was.

A hedonistic man who lived for his own pleasure.

Not a man she wanted to spend the next week with, much less the rest of her life.

Hell, did he want the rest of her life?

He shook his head. That wasn't the kind of thing someone as self-absorbed as he would want.

But he did, he thought.

When she walked through the patio door a few hours later, he realized that no matter what lies he wanted to tell himself, the truth was that he wanted her. Not just in his bed but also in his heart. He wanted that with his entire soul.

Lila sat down across from Zach and put her Birkin on the table next to her. She was never going to admit it, but she loved the bag that he had given her way more than her old canvas messenger bag. Mostly because she remembered the look on his face as she'd opened it and how he'd teased her about her "beast" of a bag. In fact, there was a lot that he'd given her that she loved.

"How'd the meeting go?" Zach asked.

"Great. She's going to come to Royal soon I think," Lila said. "I told her all about the main players and she thought there would be a lot to work with. She asked about you...so I imagine she'll want to interview you."

"You know I love the camera."

"I do," she said with a smirk. The paparazzi were at every party and event they attended. At first, she was just an unnamed partner for him but then they had found out her name, too.

"Your post is doing good. I almost feel like I don't have anything left to teach you."

"Is it?" she asked. "I turned off my phone. It's always blowing up and honestly, I needed a break. Don't you?"

"Not really," he said.

She pulled her phone out and turned it on, waiting for it to boot up. There was a note in his voice that made her wonder if he was being honest about that. But before she could ask him about it, her phone was back on and she saw she had seven missed calls from her dad and twenty-one from her mom. There was a text message from both of them that read simply: URGENT. Call home.

"Oh, my God. I think something happened," she said. "I have to call my parents."

"Okay. Do you want me to go inside to give you some privacy?"

"I really don't want to get bad news alone. Would you mind staying?"

"Not at all," he said, reaching over to take her free hand as she pushed the button to dial her mom's phone.

"Lila Jones. Where have you been? I've been trying to reach you all day," her mom said as she answered the phone.

"I just turned the phone off. Mom, what's wrong?"

she asked. And, truthfully, she'd been ignoring her mom's texts and calls because she hadn't wanted to face reality. Hadn't wanted to think about the fact that she missed home. That she knew deep inside that there was probably no way to move forward with Zach. He didn't miss Texas or what they'd had there.

"Winifred Williams passed away on Friday. I tried to call you then. Her funeral was today," her mom said. "You were one of her favorite people, Lila. I thought you'd want to be there. And it looks like all you've been doing is hanging out and drinking with that Zach guy."

"Mom, I'm so sorry," she said, tears burning in her eyes as she thought of Winifred being gone. That sweet older lady had been like a great-auntie to Lila. She'd been the one to nurture her love of books. "I can't believe I missed her funeral. I didn't mean to not call you back, but with the time difference…"

She stopped talking because it sounded like an excuse, like a lie even to her own ears. "I didn't call you back because I didn't want to talk to anyone from home. I was afraid you'd point out that I don't fit in out here."

"Well, you did miss the funeral. If you'd looked at your phone it wouldn't have happened," her mom said. "Why would I say you didn't fit in? You changed for yourself, right? Not for a man."

Her mother was mad at her and Lila couldn't blame her. But she was also saying all the things that Lila needed to hear. "I did change for me, but it's overwhelming, Mom. I can't believe Winifred is gone—"

She had to stop talking because she had started crying and her throat had sort of closed up and no matter how she tried to talk all that came out was a sort of sob. Zach took the phone from her, rubbing her back as he did so.

"Mrs. Jones, this is Zach Benning… Fair enough…

I'm sorry, ma'am. I will get her home today. It's my fault that she missed the calls from you. You know how much of herself Lila puts into her job. She was trying to make as many connections for the Soiree as she could."

He listened and nodded as he continued to rub her back. "I know she does work too hard."

But she didn't. No matter what Zach said, she knew she should have seen those messages and responded to them. She held her hand out for her phone.

"Lila wants to talk to you again," Zach told her mom. "I'll see you soon. Again, I'm sorry for my part in this."

He handed her back her phone and then reached for his own.

"Mom, I'm sorry."

"Me, too, sweetie. I should have realized you were working hard and trying to do everything to help the Soiree. I know that's why you went out there." Her mom sighed. "But we were worried about you. Some of the pictures we've seen online looked like you were party-ing hard."

"A little bit, but that's where the A-listers hang out," she said, but inside it felt like a lie. She'd been having fun as much as she'd been talking up the Soiree. She couldn't hide from that. And a dear lady that she'd loved had passed and been buried and Lila hadn't been home for it. She'd been so caught up in living the Hollywood life and being what Zach needed her to be that she'd missed something that was important to her.

"I'm glad you are coming home. Zach said he'd ar-range a flight for you today. Coffee tomorrow to catch up and then we can go to the cemetery and put some flowers on Winifred's grave?"

"Yes. That sound fine to me. I'll message you when I'm home."

"Safe travels, honey. Sorry I was rude about Zach," she said. "Love you."

"Love you, too, Mom," she murmured as she hung up the phone.

Zach put his phone down as she finished the call with her mom. He was watching her with the most serious look she'd ever seen on his face. She wondered if she'd gotten too real for him, crying like she had. It hadn't escaped her notice that he didn't do emotion, not really. Sexy feelings yes, but anything too real, too deep, he shied away from.

"I've got the pilot getting the jet ready. We can leave as soon as we get to the airport. I'm sorry you missed the funeral."

"Thanks," she said. What she was doing out here? It was as if she was just waking up from the glitter-covered fantasy she'd fallen into. The lifestyle and the environment that had seemed so fun when she'd gotten here now felt draining and fake.

"What's the matter?" he asked.

"I'm just wondering what I'm doing here."

"Building word of mouth for your Soiree. Spending time with me. Having fun."

"This isn't real. None of this is. I don't know what I was thinking," she said, standing up.

Zach turned to her with a frown. "I'm real, Brown Eyes. And so are you. Don't beat yourself up over one missed hometown event."

"It's not a missed event. It was the funeral of a woman who was like a granny to me. She was important and real."

Zach was a little bit offended at the way she was dismissing him, mainly because he felt her slipping away. This had been his chance to see if he could hold on to something solid, something real, and not a pho- tographed image of the perfect life he'd concocted for his followers. "This *is* real. I don't know how you can't see it."

"To you," she said. "This isn't me. Somehow I for- got that."

"Isn't it?" he asked. "I have my private jet lined up to take you back to Texas. Will that be real enough for you?"

"Don't be a jerk. I wasn't insulting you," she said. But she had.

"Sure, whatever," he retorted. "I'm going to go with you, so I need to pack a bag and get things lined up for myself in Royal."

"Zach, I'm sorry if I sounded ungrateful," she said. "It's just—don't you get tired of being *on* all the time?"

"I don't. I live for it. This is what makes me feel alive," he admitted, turning and walking back to her. "And if you are being completely honest with yourself, you'll admit that you like it, too."

"I do like it. But that doesn't make it something solid," she said.

"But it is," he reminded her. "Was Lil Dominator not real? His kids and that conversation with him?"

"That's not fair. Of course the people are real," she said. "I wasn't saying that."

"No, you weren't. You were trying to point out that your lifestyle is somehow more grounded because you work at the chamber of commerce and my taking pho- tos of my life and helping people escape their everyday routine with my posts isn't."

He knew he was hitting this too hard, but it was like all the stuff he'd been thinking about her was now coming out. Lila didn't like him or his lifestyle. She found it shallow and probably thought the same about him. He was seeing her and feeling like his life could change for the better with her in it, and she was writing him off.

"No, I wasn't," she said. "That's not fair. Your life is hard. Even you have to see that it's not perfect. How do you handle having to get up every day and make the perfect post?"

"It's a job," he pointed out.

"Touché."

"I'm not trying to one-up you. I like you, Lila. I like this thing we've got going," he said. "I don't want it to end."

She nodded at that. "I don't see how it could continue. I can't live out here. I don't think I even want to."

"Okay. That's fair. But are there options?"

She shook her head. "I don't know. I think we are very different people. You were right when you said I enjoyed talking to Lil Dominator and getting to know his family. But that's not why you go to those events. Honestly, I'm a little tired of it."

He wanted to tell her he could change, but he knew he wouldn't. This was his reality. Yes, his social media girlfriend was breaking up with him. He'd find another.

But a part of him didn't want to. He wasn't ready to let go of Lila Jones.

"What is so bad about this?" he asked. "You like the clothes and the bags and the—"

He felt defensive and he knew he was using the luxury merchandise as a front. He wanted her to like *him*. Didn't she like him? Or was she following the same pattern as everyone else in his life? Was he not enough? Hell.

"Stop. It was fun, but it's not me. I'm pretending to be a version of myself that I don't like. I'm not this woman. As much as I like the stuff, it's just stuff. And I like my parents and Royal and you more. I like *you*, Zach. The real man, not ZB, and I want to figure out a way to have a life with you but not if you can't be real with me. I'm not sure that to you I'm anything other than this @LilaJones persona you created."

Her words stung. He liked the woman she was now. But he hadn't not liked her before. He might have started out wanting her to change so that he could feel better about sleeping with her and going back to his life afterward. But that had changed. *He'd* changed. He hadn't wanted to, and honestly, he still wasn't sure about it. Especially not now when she was saying she didn't like anything about this world.

"You are more than that. I think you are trying to deflect the guilt you feel about not returning those calls. But the truth is more complex than you want it to be. As much as you think I'm just about the posts and the paparazzi, you know that you liked this life. You liked being out here and standing in the spotlight with me."

God, please let that be true. He'd thought that they were starting to be a real couple. That's why he'd planned a party—he'd gotten scared and wanted to put distance between them—but now that she was talking about leaving, he realized he didn't want her to go.

"I liked being with you in Royal, too," she said quietly.

He hadn't liked it. Being there, being with Lila, stirred too much. Too many old desires and feelings that he'd learned to live without.

"That's not my life. Take my jet and go back to your home but never pretend that I only liked you because I made you into someone who would fit my profile. I liked you before you agreed to the makeover. You might want to ask yourself why you did that."

She shook her head but didn't say anything else and he turned and strode into the house. He asked Mrs. Smith to have his driver take Lila to the corporate airport where his jet was kept and then went into his private study and closed the door behind him.

He needed to shake this off. This was no different than Tawny getting out of his Ferrari in Royal and walking away from him. But he'd never lied to himself before and he didn't want to start now. He was going out and he was going to find another woman and in a few hours, he wouldn't even remember Lila Jones.

But that lie was hard to swallow. He knew the instant she left his house because he felt as if the air had been sucked out of it. No matter how he was going to act on social media, losing Lila had hurt. And he would've tried to fight for her but she'd been right. He was as hollow as his lifestyle.

Letting her go back to the life she loved was the honorable thing to do. He sneered at himself. The man who'd always put himself first had finally let someone else have the spotlight by themselves. He would miss her. Not just today but whenever he remembered this time in his life when he'd had something good and solid but had been too cowardly to hold on to her. Because he'd been afraid if he let her in, she'd see that the real man was a hollow version of the ZB he sold online.

He poured himself a Jack Daniel's neat and downed it in one swallow. Yeah, he was going to get drunk and party like nothing had changed tonight. He canceled the meetup with his followers and texted his hard-partying friends instead. He needed a few nights of oblivion and then he'd figure out his next move.

Fourteen

Lila was still tired when her mom rang her doorbell at 8:00 a.m. the next morning. She had cried most of the way home on the plane trying to find peace with the decision she'd made to leave Zach. She knew it was the right thing to do. They couldn't continue the way they had been. But it still hurt.

She opened the door to her mom, who had a travel coffee cup in her hand and gave it to Lila before hugging her. She saw over her mom's shoulder that her dad was sitting in the car. Even though she'd thought she'd been doing a good job of getting herself together she started crying again.

"Sweetheart, what's the matter?" her mom said.

Lila heard her dad turn off the car as she sat down on the rocking chair on her front porch. "I'm sorry I wasn't here for Winifred and that I let you down."

"You didn't let us down. I was a little harsh," her mom admitted.

"She was. But we were worried about you," her dad said as he joined them. He leaned down and hugged her and she stood up to embrace him back because her dad gave the best hugs.

Lila was still crying and had to admit to herself that it was about more than disappointing her parents and missing Winifred's funeral. She wanted to go back to a world where she knew how to handle everything. Bottom line? She hadn't realized how different her life would be when she let Zach into it, and how much he would change not just her public persona but also her.

"I'm sorry about that."

"How about we go put those flowers on Winifred's grave and then go home and I'll make my famous blueberry pancakes," her dad suggested.

"Okay. Let me lock up."

Two hours later she was sitting in her parents' kitchen somehow telling her mom and dad all about Zach. They'd been to Winifred's grave and eaten her dad's pancakes and now she was still a little weepy but getting herself together.

"So, what does he do again?" her dad asked. "I don't see how posting stuff is a way to make a living."

"I didn't, either, but he has a huge number of followers and most of them want to have this glitzy lifestyle, so they are willing to buy a few products or go places that he talks about," Lila said. "He's done a lot for the Soiree, really helped to drive up not only word of mouth but ticket sales."

"Okay, well then, what's the problem?" her dad asked. "I can tell you really like this boy and he's got a job."

"Leo, there are important things other than a job and liking him," her mom said.

"Well, not every man can have my special talents of being charming, sexy and supersmart."

Her mom shook her head and playfully smacked him. Lila smiled, too. Her dad had gotten straight to the heart of the matter. What *was* the issue?

"He lives in LA, for one. The other is that he really likes that entire lifestyle he's selling, and I don't mind taking a few pictures now and then but I want something a little quieter. I mean, I really like him, but we are just too different."

She had hoped they weren't. That after she laid it all on the line that he'd want to be real with her. Find a life away from his Benningnites. But she'd gotten on that plane by herself and come back to Texas.

Which pretty much said it all, right?

"That's too bad, sweetie," her mom said. "I wish it were different."

"Me, too," she admitted. "But it's not. And even though I'm sitting here like I have nothing to do all day, I do need to head into work. Would you mind driving me home?"

"Not at all," her dad said. "Want to come for dinner tonight?"

"Sorry, I can't." She was meeting the advisory committee later on to bring them up to speed on her meeting with Abby, and also needed to fill them in on the new ticket sales thanks to Zach's online posts about Soiree on the Bay. "Working on the event."

"Well, then over the weekend. I'll text you," her mom told her.

"Thanks," she said, hugging her mom and dad. As she did she realized that Zach had never had this. That he didn't trust in anything other than followers because that was the only time he'd had some kind of affection other than in the sack. She wondered if there was a way to show him how special and extraordinary love could be coming from one person instead of from the masses.

That thought was in the back of her mind as she went back into the office. Everyone commented on the parties she'd attended and the photos she'd posted. They wanted to know all the details of her glam time in LA.

She shared it with them but kept the details of her time with Zach to herself. That was private, and she realized that she'd seen him do that with the two of them, as well. Maybe she'd overlooked something…or was she just grasping at straws, trying her best to get back together with him because she'd never had a broken heart before?

"Is Zach here with you?" one of her coworkers asked.

"No, he had to stay in LA for some events he had lined up. But I'm sure we will see him at the Soiree."

"I can't believe we are only like a month away. This event is really coming together. You did a great job," her coworker raved.

"Thanks," she said, but she knew she wouldn't have been half as effective without the social media and personal makeover that Zach had given her. He'd introduced her to people she'd never have met without him. She could say that he'd made her into someone he wanted to like but she knew those words had come from her own fears. She'd wanted to be someone who fit into his world, but then she'd been afraid to stay there.

And her biggest regret? That she'd never had the courage to tell him she loved him because she was afraid that she really didn't fit in his life. Could never be the kind of woman he would love.

* * *

Zach lay on the deck of his yacht moored at the yacht club in Marina del Ray. He had tried to drink Lila off his mind but that hadn't worked. He couldn't stop thinking about what she'd said. She wanted him to be real for her. In fact, he'd done all of his usual moving-on tricks, picked up a hot chick and tried to hook up but he'd called her Lila as he was kissing her and she'd pulled back. He'd left her with some friends and come here.

Where he could be alone. His team were at the house and had all been trying to reach out to him but he wasn't in the mood to talk. What was he going to say? It seemed as if he'd screwed up the one thing that might have been real in this life of his.

He wanted to figure out a way forward but honestly, he had been doing this for so long that he had no clue how to move on.

"Dude, please tell me you are at least wearing massive amounts of sunscreen," Shantal said as her shadow fell over him. He looked up to see his makeup artist flanked by Dawn and Vito.

"Of course, I'm not a total idiot," he muttered.

"Just a partial one, right? I mean, I assume this is because we're here and Lila is in Texas," Vito said, sitting down on the lounger next to Zach. Vito had on a baseball cap, linen pants and a long-sleeved linen shirt.

"Maybe," he admitted. "So why are you guys here?"

"You need us. Or maybe, more precisely, you need Lila," Dawn said, pushing his legs to the side and sitting down on the end of his lounger as Shantal did the same to Vito.

"She doesn't like this lifestyle."

"Do *you*?" Shantal asked. "We know you like the

adoring followers and the parties, but you were different when she was out here. It seemed sort of…"

"Like you were finally growing up and realizing there was more to life than partying," Dawn said. "If I'm out of line, fine."

She wasn't out of line and he suspected she knew it. "You're right. But I have no idea how to show her that."

"You'll think of something, boss," Vito assured him. "You're smart when you're not being dumb."

Zach laughed for the first time in days. His team weren't just employees, he realized, but also friends who understood him. "I've been thinking about how to win her back and the future. What do you guys think of a sort of brand company who does what we did for Lila but for businesses? I'd need my number one team with me."

"OMG! I love it," Shantal exclaimed. "But how would it work?"

"We'd give our clients social media makeovers, help connect them to influencers that they want to work with or help mold someone from their company into the influencer they want them to be."

"Yes, that will work," Dawn said.

"Now what are you going to do about Lila?" Vito prodded. "She's going to be a hell of a lot harder to win back."

"I have a few ideas, guys. But I'm going to have to do this on my own," he said.

"All alone?" Shantal pouted. "I was hoping we could all head back to Texas."

"Oh, no worries, we're all going to Royal. I'm going to base the new business there. And I really could use some help finding a permanent house."

"Mrs. Smith and I already found a few that we think

you'll like," Dawn informed him. He shook his head as he looked over at her. "What? It's not like I had much else to do since you've gone completely silent on social media. Which I have to say is making the gossip sites and your fans go wild. They are sure you are announcing something big."

He almost laughed. Even when he tried to disappear it just continued to feed the need for him in the media spotlight. He was going to have to try very hard to convince Lila that he'd changed. This might look like a gimmick to her. But he wanted her to know he was real.

Which meant he was going to have to just strip back all the layers he'd been using for years to build his following and his influence. He was going to have to be humble and show her that there was one thing that mattered to him in this world, and it was her.

Zach was pretty sure that he loved her. Hell, he *knew* he did. He'd been hedging around her and pretending that he didn't know what the emotion was but only because he'd never said those words to anyone since he'd been an adult. And he knew he was going to have to tell her how he felt.

"If I can't win Lila back… I still want to stay based in Royal. There's a lot of good stuff happening there, and we'll be centrally located for the entire US."

"That's fine with me, boss," Vito said. "I've been looking for a change."

"Me, too," Shantal concurred. "And my mom lives in Dallas, so she'll be over the moon that I'm closer to her. And Dawn has her own reasons…"

"What?"

"I met a guy at the diner. We've been texting. It might be something, I don't know. I mean, moving there is a good thing but I'm not moving *for* him."

As Zach chatted with his friends, it struck him that his life wasn't as hollow as he'd thought it was. His heart started racing. All along he had thought he'd been protecting himself and keeping everyone at arm's length, but saw now that wasn't true. He'd created some strong bonds over the years, and he knew that what he'd felt and found with Lila was solid, too. He just had to get her attention the *right* way this time.

And he had an idea how to accomplish that. In fact, the more he thought about it, the more he loved it.

He told the team and they all were surprised but thought it would work, too. Now he just had to get back to Royal and pray that it wasn't too late to convince Lila he loved her.

Lila got dressed in one of the outfits that she'd gotten with Zach, realizing how much she had enjoyed their time together, and drove her new red VW convertible to meet the advisory committee. She'd decided to trade in Milo for a new car because she'd always wanted a convertible and she was tired of denying herself. She'd kept the group apprised of everything that had gone on in California in their group chat, but they were getting together for some drinks and to finalize some details tonight.

She took a photo of herself, tagged the brands she was wearing and used #SoireeontheBay before leaving. Gina and Valencia were there when she arrived, and she ordered a skinny margarita from the bar before joining them.

"California looks like it was good to you," Valencia said after she'd sat down.

"I tried to make the most of my time there. Everyone was really interested in the event and thought we were doing something groundbreaking," she replied. "And the best part? Lil Dominator is going to come, and he offered to perform if we have room on one of the stages." She'd really enjoyed meeting him and his wife Tisha. They had texted her photos of the kids playing on the ride-on mustangs she'd sent them.

"That's great. Zach's notoriety has really given the Soiree a boost. I hope he will continue to keep it going," Gina said.

She nodded. "I'm sure he will."

Really, what else could she say?

"Is he coming tonight?"

"Uh, not tonight. He had to stay in LA."

"Really?" Charlotte murmured as she joined them. "His account has gone dark. The social world is all abuzz about what's coming next from him."

"It is? He's probably got a new account or brand partnership he's going to announce. He never does anything without a plan," she said.

"Who doesn't?" Jack asked.

"Zach," she said. "How have you been? How's Lexi?"

"I'm good and so is she," Jack answered, turning to Charlotte. "How's Ross?"

"Good. He's doing good," Charlotte said.

"I can't believe that he is still estranged from Dad," Gina lamented.

Lila couldn't, either. But then men didn't always make sense to her. "You'd think standing up and being a father to little Ben would have been something that Rusty would support."

"You'd think," Charlotte said. "But there is a lot of ego to Rusty and he likes to think he runs the world."

"Ha. So true. To be honest I wish I ran the world," Jack quipped. "But Lexi keeps me grounded."

Billy showed up and they all chatted about the event and life stuff while they waited for Rusty. Lila only half paid attention to the conversation, pulling out her phone to check Zach's account. Not only had it gone dark, it had been suspended.

That worried her. What was going on with him? She told herself she was going to give it some time to try to figure out what to do next but what if he needed her? Heck, forget waiting. Zach loved all of his followers and to shut down his account, something had to have happened. She texted him.

Hey, hope you are okay.

I'm good.

Well, there it was. That wasn't exactly a chatty invitation for more texts but she couldn't let it go.

I'd love to talk sometime.

Me, too. Can't now.

Okay. Text when you can.

He gave her message a thumbs-up and that was it.

Lila tried not to feel sad that this was what they were reduced to. She still cared so much for him. And while she was trying to be strong and move on, this was a sign, right? It had to be. She sent him a text and he sent back a thumbs-up. *Let him go, girl.*

The rest of the committee were laughing and talking about stuff at the Texas Cattleman's Club, trying to stretch out the conversation while they waited for Rusty.

Then Charlotte did a double take toward the door and they all turned to see what had caught her attention. Lila was shocked to see Ross walking toward them with his father by his side.

Billy got up first. "Ross, great to see you. This is a surprise."

Charlotte went to her man and gave him a sort of quizzical look, but he just kissed her and took her hand in his.

"Sorry we are late," Rusty said.

"I'm just glad to see you both here," Lila told them.

"Me, too," Gina agreed. "Lila has some news—"

"Before we get to that," Rusty interrupted. "Ross has something you all need to know."

Lila didn't like the sound of that. Seems like there was something going on that none of them had an inkling about. It must be something big for Rusty to have brought his estranged son to the meeting, because despite them showing up together it didn't seem as if they were super close now. But Lila wasn't privy to the inner workings of the Edmond family.

Ross took a deep breath, putting his hands on his hips. "There is money missing from the festival's bank account."

"*What?* Are you sure?" Jack asked. "I haven't turned in my last invoice. Do you think there is something you missed?"

"I'm sure and I haven't missed anything. Someone has been stealing from the account."

What did that mean for the Soiree? "Will it affect the festival?"

"Yes, I think it will. We need to find out who has taken the money and put an end to it," Rusty said.

Lila listened to the others who discussed what the

next steps were. She had no part in the money so she wasn't sure she could add anything. When the meeting finally broke up, she was a little worried about why someone would steal from the festival.

Was it simply that they thought no one would notice? And who would be ballsy enough to take from a charity event? That was simply creepy.

She went home unable to think of much besides this new development and Zach. He hadn't texted her again. What did *that* mean? She hoped it wasn't that he was over her and had moved on. Not now, when she was ready to do whatever it took to win him back.

Fifteen

Lila got an account recommendation when she checked her phone the next morning for @LJLVR21. It sounded like one of those spambot accounts, but she clicked on it anyway while she was making her breakfast and getting ready for work.

The feed looked very similar to how hers used to pre-Zach. There weren't many photos and the most recent was one of a stoneware mug that had the state of Texas on the side of it and a heart where Royal was with a teabag in it. The caption read: "Left my heart in Texas. Going back to find it."

How cute. There were two other photos on the account. One of a breakfast plate with just crumbs from some kind of pastry and the other of a slightly askew photo of the Hollywood sign. She clicked follow and then immediately felt a pang for Zach and his California life.

Enough of this missing Zach. She had somehow made herself believe that without her makeover she wouldn't have been enough for him. And maybe she hadn't been. But she *loved* Zach. She wanted him in her life. Thinking about how different they were actually made them so good as a couple. The fact that she wasn't like all the other people in his life, and that he wasn't like the ones in hers, made them unique and special. And ultimately, it came down to one undeniable truth: she was crazy about him and was tired of acting like they couldn't be together.

Lila texted him but it was undeliverable.

Uh, what?

Had he *blocked* her?

Well, that was going to make getting back together with him hard. She'd insulted his lifestyle, to be fair. Maybe he had gone dark because he was moving on. Moving away from the life he'd had because of her?

Lila wasn't sure but knew it would have to wait until she got to work. She was running late and there had been an email from Rusty to the festival advisory committee with some questions about expenses and who had access to the account. It seemed that he was determined to get to the bottom of who had taken the money.

She wanted to respond to him as soon as she was at her desk. And sure hoped he didn't think it was her. After all, she'd been wearing a lot of expensive clothing that she couldn't afford on her salary and bought herself a brand-new car. She might have to explain how brands worked with influencers to him the way she had with her dad.

She was mentally composing her email to him when she pulled up in front of the chamber of commerce building. Glancing at the coffee shop, she saw the regulars at their tables and then a guy in the corner with hair that was the same shade of brown as Zach's. But Zach would never be out in public in the jeans and slouchy T-shirt that guy had on. Also he had on some sort of bucket hat with a pair of large blue-lensed sunglasses.

Dude, she thought. He needed some tips on how to style it up.

She parked her car and tried not to stare at the guy as she walked inside the coffee shop to get her morning cuppa. But the closer she got, the harder it was not to gawk. Unless she missed her guess, that guy was Zach.

She stopped thinking about the email she needed to send, her heart beating faster as she walked over to his table.

"Zach?"

"Hiya, Lila," he said with a tentative smile. "I was hoping to catch you before work."

She pulled out a chair and sat down. He took off the sunglasses and as soon as their eyes met she felt that electric thrill go through her as it always did when she was with him. God, she'd missed this man. But what the heck was he wearing?

"Hey, what are you doing here dressed like this? Are you okay?" she asked with a laugh. He looked so silly and so sweet and her pulse sped up as she tried to figure out what this meant. Zach never did anything without a plan.

He tried to look…well, if she were being honest, he tried to *be* less himself. He kept sitting up straight and then seemed to remember something and then slouched and leaned over himself. As if he were trying to keep himself small so no one would notice him. Which was so not Zach that she almost laughed.

"I'm here for you. I heard what you said. That we

are too different, but I've changed. Look at me. I'm like you were. Just a regular Zach blending in."

She shook her head. "You could never blend in. You're not meant to. When I said real, I mean the real Zach and the real Lila. I want you to be that larger-than-life man who loves the spotlight and selfies but also…" She trailed off. For a minute she had to stop and gather all her courage. It took a lot to tell Zach that she loved him. But she was going to do it. *Also a man who loves me*, she thought.

Before she could say the words, he started talking.

"I'm trying to show you something and because I'm who I am it's harder than I thought."

"What are you trying to show me?" she asked.

"If my lifestyle isn't right for you then I have come to realize that it's not right for me. I do like attention and the spotlight and yes, everything is usually about me, but I don't like me without you."

She held her breath, almost afraid for him to continue. "I like you."

"I know you do, Brown Eyes. I love you."

He breathed in deeply after he said it, the next words coming out in a rush.

"I tried to convince myself that it was only the novelty of you, but the truth is you have made me see the spots in my life where I was doing things to try to feel alive."

"Try to?" she asked. "What do you mean?"

"I mean that if I hadn't come to Royal, I would have been content to keep partying and sleeping with hotties and just going about that life. Not really looking around me and noticing things like pretty brunettes with sassy attitudes or the sunset or the flowers around me. You made me wake up and see that I was filling my days with so much stuff and standing in the spotlight because I wanted the world to see me.

"And *you're* real, Lila. You want me to be real, too. I've been afraid of that for so long. But I want to be real with you."

Being back in Royal was different than it had been before. He remembered how arrogant and sure of himself he'd been when he'd arrived. A bad boy running from a scandal of his own making. He'd come a long way since then and he knew it was because of Lila's influence. Regardless of what she said back to him, his life had been changed for good by her.

Zach had laid it on the line and kept talking, but now he had run out of words. He'd told her he loved her, and she hadn't said it back. His heart was racing like it never had before. It was all he could do to keep from pulling her into his arms and kissing her. *Thoroughly.* Then, if she was willing, he'd scoop her up and whisk her away to someplace private where he could make love to her. And he knew it would be making love, not just sex.

Because it was Lila Jones. The woman he'd made over but who had truly transformed him.

"Zach, I like your true self. You are such a generous, caring man. And I've changed, too. Realized that I was sort of just existing and not living. You showed me how to make the most of every moment. I love you, too," she said at last. "In more ways than you'll *ever* know. But I can't go back to California. That life is not for me."

Yes! She loved him. He didn't listen to the rest; he'd heard the only thing he needed to hear. They would sort this out but right now he needed to hold her. To make sure that she didn't change her mind. He stood up and pulled her to her feet and into his arms, kissing her long and deep, not caring if the morning commuters saw them.

She clung to him, holding on to his shoulders, and when he lifted his head, he saw in her eyes the sincerity of the love she'd professed. His heart felt full for the first time in his life.

"I didn't know how much I needed you until you were gone," he whispered as he pressed his forehead to hers. "I love you."

He hadn't meant to say the words again, but they were right there. The emotion so real that it was making him want to do and say things that he'd never considered before.

"I love you, too. Oh, Zach. I thought you'd moved on when you switched off your account," she said.

"I switched it off and created a new profile because my life is with you and not for my followers."

"Really?"

"Yes, really," he said.

"How will you make a living?" she asked, stepping back.

He laughed as joy filled him. She was so practical, his little Lila Jones. "I don't have to work to support myself, but I'm going to be starting a Texas-based brand makeover company to help businesses and folks who want to grow their social media presence. The team insisted on coming with me. We are going to be right here in Royal."

"Are you sure? I don't want you to do this and then regret it," she said.

"I am sure. From the moment you ran into me and I held you in my arms right across the street in front of the chamber of commerce, I knew you were different and I wasn't sure what that meant at first. But over the last month you have opened my eyes to so much that I had missed before. I can't wait to see what the future holds for us." He tipped her chin up and stared into her eyes. "Will you marry me, Lila? Help me start a new life filled with love and experiences that aren't for the masses but just for *us*?"

"Yes!" she said, throwing herself back into his arms.

The people around them applauded and he kissed her again.

She called in sick to work and they spent the day in her little house making love and making plans for their future together, living in their authentic selves in the real world.

* * * * *

SECOND CHANCE LOVE SONG

JESSICA LEMMON

Prologue

10 years ago
Florida State University

Sparks sizzled along Presley Cole's skin with each stinging raindrop falling from the sky. She felt as if she might go up in smoke—or up in steam, given they'd been caught in the downpour.

She could hardly believe she was standing outside her dormitory building making out with Cash Sutherland. *The* Cash Sutherland who, by some miracle, had essentially become her boyfriend.

Sure, they'd been out a few times—to dinners or parties—but she'd counted herself lucky to simply be in his presence. She'd never dreamed he'd stick around for innocent nights ending with them still wearing their clothes. Not when there were so many other beautiful girls at this school who would gladly sleep with him.

Especially when Presley had let him know she wouldn't. Oh, she wanted to, but her feelings for him were too big, too frightening, to wrap her head around. She was scared they would overtake her and drag her down, especially if she crossed that boundary. And then, if the worst happened and he left her, how would she recover?

You're worth the wait.

He'd told her so last night, after delivering a hand-in-her-pants orgasm that rivaled any in her limited sexual past. She'd apologized for not going further, for making him wait, for leaving him hanging. He'd pulled her into his arms and kissed her some more, the sturdy ridge of his erection pressing the side of her leg, and told her to stop worrying about him.

Seriously, he was too good to be true.

He pulled his lips from hers and smoothed her wet hair away from her face. They were leaning against the brick wall, the overhang not doing much to keep them dry. Not with the wind blowing the way it was. Hurricane season was upon them.

Her eyes caught the splint bracing his middle and ring fingers. She tipped her head back to admire his soulful dark eyes and sharp nose, his full mouth that usually smiled at her. He hadn't smiled much lately. As if the injury had stolen his joy.

"Does your finger hurt?" she asked. He'd broken it on the field, which put him temporarily out of the game. Not good for a senior who could be scouted by the NFL any day now. And yet his biggest complaint was that he couldn't play guitar while wearing a splint. His passion for singing and songwriting had blown her "hot jock" theory out of the water the first time she'd spoken to him. She'd thought she had him figured out, but he surprised her at every turn. The gorgeous guy who played a gruel-

ing, demanding sport quite well was also capable of singing tender lyrics with the rawest emotion. No wonder she
was crazy about him.

"Pres, I have to tell you something."

That statement was delivered in an even monotone,
so she lied and told herself he wasn't about to share bad
news. But, somehow, her body knew. Her arms began to
shake and her teeth chattered like she was standing in a
blizzard instead of a Florida rainstorm.

"Do you want to come up?" she asked, hoping to delay
whatever damning news might come. "It's pretty wet
out here."

His mouth hitched to one side, not quite returning
her nervous smile. Then he took a deep breath, one that
expanded his chest and lifted his shoulders. It was late,
it was dark. They'd spent all day in class and then most
of the evening studying at the library. She was tired and
so was he. Maybe that's what this was about, she lied to
herself some more.

"Come up." She grasped his uninjured hand. "I'll heat
some cocoa and we can curl up on my bed and talk." She
pushed to her tiptoes, planted a soft kiss on the side of
his mouth and then whispered, "Or not talk."

He looked like he might say no but nodded instead.
She took it as a win as he walked with her up the stairs,
as they entered her dorm room, as she traded her wet T-
shirt for a dry one. But when she pulled him toward the
bed for a make-out session, his stormy mood returned,
and with it came her teeth-chattering worry. Something
was definitely wrong.

Moments later she found out what.

He'd broken up with her that night, leaving her crying on her bed. The storm outside grew more intense, but
it had nothing on the one inside her. Lightning flashed,

and she watched out the window through puffy, gritty eyes. Thunder raged, the sound drowning out the sound of her sobbing.

The most beautiful relationship she'd ever had, with the most beautiful man she'd ever seen, was over. He was leaving for home next week. For Tennessee. He wasn't interested in a long-distance relationship. He wasn't interested in her.

It was *over* over.

If it had been real to begin with.

One

Presley, dressed smartly in a fuchsia skirt and floral-print blouse and a pair of peep-toe kitten heels, wrapped her folded hands around her knee to keep her leg from bobbing up and down like a sewing machine needle. She was overcaffeinated, thanks to a virtually sleepless night, but when inspiration had struck, she hadn't wanted to waste a single second sleeping.

The smile she'd glued into place was starting to shake at the edges, so she coughed into her hand to give her mouth a rest. When her boss, Delilah, looked up at her again, Presley grinned anew.

Say yes. All I need is a yes.

Presley had longed to escape Florida for as long as she could remember. She'd always wanted to travel the world, visit other countries, meet new and interesting people. But traveling cost money, which had been in short supply. Instead she'd been stuck in Tallahassee as if an invisible force field was keeping her here.

When her boss announced a "friendly" competition for their branch of Viral Pop a month ago, Presley's ears had perked. All she had to do was write an article that would go viral and grab lots of new eyeballs. The winner earned a pay-and-title bump—*hello, Senior Staff Writer!*—and a transfer to any of Viral Pop's offices in the *world*.

Pres had practically foamed at the mouth from excitement. She'd been trying to come up with a winning idea over the last week and a half but nothing came. Until her drive home from work last night, when her ex-boyfriend's song had come on the radio.

Cash Sutherland had left Florida a football star, and was now a country music superstar. Upon hearing his most popular song, a fresh idea had hit her like the title, "Lightning." Out of nowhere and with enough force to split her in two.

Admittedly, she was a tad torn. She didn't relish the idea of revisiting the painful breakup she'd swept under the rug years ago, but on the other hand she really wanted to win. Like, really, *really* wanted to win.

So she'd sat up until 2:00 a.m. last night writing the proposal Delilah was reviewing this very second.

"This would require you to be out of the office," her boss stated, her eyes traveling to Presley. Delilah's usual brand of curiosity-slash-interrogation never failed to intimidate, but winning this promotion and the opportunity to escape Florida was Presley's lifelong dream. She could handle a little intimidation.

"I've worked remotely before," Presley replied. At home, but still. "I am very good at time management. Especially when it's my own time. Or the time here at the office," she was quick to add. "I value your time, as well. More than mine. More than anyone's." She pressed her lips together to keep from sounding desperate, the sticky gloss she'd swiped on this morning helping with that endeavor.

Delilah hummed, set her tablet aside and narrowed her eyelids. Then she dipped her chin. "What makes you so sure Cash Sutherland is going to tell you his biggest songwriting secret when he's dodged that question from every reporter who's spoken with him?"

Nervously, Presley licked her lips. She wasn't *at all* sure Cash Sutherland was going to confess his biggest songwriting secret. Ever since "Lightning" hit the Billboard Top 100, scads of press had been trying to solve the mystery of whom the song was written about. Rumors were rampant. Article after article had named this starlet or that, this singer or the other, and really, given his copious dating history, it could be any *or all* of them.

"We're old friends," she told her boss. "We went to college together. I also visited with his younger brother Gavin to write that article about Elite Records two years ago."

She had no qualms about seeing Cash again. Not really. That long-ago breakup was in the past and she'd done her best to bury it, complete with a tombstone. She had no idea how Cash would feel about her showing up out of the blue, but Gavin had suggested not telling his brother she was coming. "Come to the show," he'd said of the rooftop bar concert Cash was scheduled to play. "Once you're here, he won't have a choice but to talk to you."

Okay, so their plan was a little underhanded, but she couldn't risk Cash turning her away.

During that first visit to Beaumont Bay, she'd made damn sure he was out of the state before scheduling the interview with Gavin and William Sutherland. She hadn't been ready to see Cash then, but couldn't resist chasing the story of how Elite Records had been successfully relaunched by the eldest Sutherland son. She'd been the first to break the news about the resurrected record label in Beaumont Bay. Readers had eaten up the article about four hot brothers in the exciting music town just outside of Nashville.

At the time she'd worried the visit would bring up unpleasant memories, but the lush, rich town hadn't reminded her of the Cash she used to know. She figured she really didn't know him at all. Not anymore.

"It was a small assignment back when I was a content curator," she explained when Delilah didn't comment.

Back then her job had been to compile stories and news to share on social media. Pulling photos and links for articles like "10 Superchic & Supercheap Clothing Finds" wasn't exactly groundbreaking journalism. The piece on Elite Records, the family business run by the Sutherland brothers, gave her a chance to showcase her talents. She'd interviewed Cash's three brothers: producer, Will, lawyer, Gavin, and even bar-owner Luke. She'd mentioned Cash and his accomplishments, if only to appear that she wasn't ignoring his existence entirely, wording it so that it seemed like they'd spoken when in reality they hadn't. That article's success had bumped her status up to staff writer, but she was still chained to her desk in Tallahassee. Lately the most invigorating article she'd written had been titled "10 Times You Wished You Were Taylor Swift."

She was itching to sink her teeth into something juicier.

"Gavin Sutherland told me about a private concert Cash is performing," Presley added. "No other member of the press was invited."

She'd left that nugget out of her proposal, which was

mostly a cost analysis showing how inexpensively she could travel—including forgoing the company's per diem. She'd do anything to leave her dinky desk, including paying her own daily expenses. "Elite Records wants to put a positive spin on Cash's DUI and since we know each other, the family trusts me."

Well, Gavin did anyway.

Delilah craned an eyebrow. "Isn't Cash a bad-boy type? Why does he care about a DUI?"

Cash *was* the bad-boy type. Back when they'd dated, he'd shared how he'd stirred up a whole heap of trouble in his hometown of Beaumont Bay. He ran wild as a teen, had once "stolen" his dad's truck to joyride on the back roads. By the time he'd landed a football scholarship to FSU, his parents had breathed a sigh of relief that his days of troublemaking were over.

Now it seemed Cash had returned to his roots—both to his hometown and to his former bad-boy ways. His brothers had even signed him up to tour with good-girl country singer Hannah Banks to help smooth the edges of his otherwise rough reputation.

Cash was a love-'em-and-leave-'em type when it came to women, and Presley knew that from experience. He'd loved and left her when they were in college. Although, "love" was overstating it. Other than a few heavy makeout sessions in her dorm room, they'd never escalated to "love."

Or at least he hadn't.

An inexperienced twentysomething, she'd been completely smitten with him. She'd interviewed Florida State University's unattainable star football player for an assignment, figuring she'd never be closer to him than the six inches separating their seats in the stadium. Color her surprised when he'd asked her to dinner a week later.

She'd been equally surprised when they'd become inseparable. Well, until he left Florida and never spoke
to her again. Not only had he left the state and football
behind to pursue a music career, but he'd also left her.
He'd burned the ships, leaving her with not so much as
a life raft.

"Do you think he'll open up to you about the DUI?"
her boss asked.

Nooo idea.

"Definitely." Presley nodded. "He's in the process of
writing and recording a new album." One that would include a duet featuring Hannah, country music's newest,
brightest starlet. "He's going to need the press to help
spread the word about the album. He has to know he
needs a makeover."

Though not literally. She hadn't bumped into Cash in
person in forever, but she'd seen plenty of photos of him
online. *Yowza.* He was as beautiful as she remembered.
Dark, dark brown hair, golden-brown eyes that sparkled
in the sunlight. A strong nose, angled jaw and a smile
that could melt the panties off a nun. And that was just
above the neck. Add in his height, his rounded, muscular
shoulders and biceps, washboard abs and thick, strong
thighs and the man was a recipe for an orgasm. In a recent photo, she'd noticed a tattoo on one of his arms. The
ink hadn't been there when they'd dated. No doubt one of
many changes that had occurred since he'd dumped her.

"I'll give you one week." Delilah slipped her glasses
onto her nose and regarded her laptop. A moment later
she started typing and Presley wondered if she'd imagined the two words that sounded a lot like approval.

"Was that a…a yes?"

"Yes." Delilah smiled, although it was a few degrees
cooler than Presley's own. "I expect a juicy reveal about

the woman who inspired 'Lightning,' a deep dive into the bad boy of Beaumont Bay, and the saucy gossip surrounding his DUI. Do you think you can do that?"

"Of course. Absolutely." Presley sprang out of her chair. Delilah's requests sounded a touch invasive, but Presley knew she could write an article that was both informative and respectful. She had no interest in exacting revenge for a breakup that'd occurred eons ago. Her only goal was getting the hell out of Florida.

"And," Delilah said before Presley could escape the office, "I expect you to email your progress to my assistant, Sandra."

"No problem." Presley considered saying something generic like "You can count on me" or "You won't regret this" but decided to save the platitudes. Given her rocky past with Cash, there was a good chance Presley might fail and that Delilah *would* regret sending her on assignment and then realize she *couldn't* count on Presley. She dismissed the thought with a flick of her hair. She'd do everything she could to ensure that didn't happen.

Presley keyed in a text to Gavin Sutherland as she walked through the office to her desk. It read: I leave Friday.

She didn't have to wait long for his response. Perfect. See you then.

Her stomach flopped. She was about to drive eight hours to Tennessee to interview her ex-boyfriend about the women in his past. About a recent DUI. About fame and fortune and his bad-boy ways. *About why he left her.*

Buried past or not, there was a small part of her that longed to know why. Partly for closure, and partly to satisfy her own curiosity. It was a big ask on top of everything else, and she knew that. If she didn't achieve magical "closure" by the time she left, she would console herself with champagne and a first class flight straight out of Tallahassee.

Thankfully, she had the rest of the week to fortify herself for the trip. She hadn't seen him in so long and was already feeling like the younger version of herself. The girl who'd been consumed with him…and then *by* him. She knew better than put herself in that precarious position again.

No, this wouldn't be an easy assignment. But she wasn't missing the opportunity to move up and move on. She'd delayed her dreams for far too long.

Plus, he owed her. He'd left her behind without warning or regret. He was half the reason she'd been trapped in this town to begin with. The internship options she'd considered while they'd dated were in either New York City or Tallahassee. She'd chosen the latter because Cash was in Florida. He'd had a football scholarship and the promise of a professional sports career. He wasn't going anywhere.

Boy, had she been wrong about that.

It was her turn to selfishly focus on her dreams. The title of senior staff writer as well as a position in a Viral Pop office *not* located in Florida awaited her. She could travel to New York, Los Angeles, San Francisco, London…or even Rome. All while keeping her seniority, and without starting over as a new hire at another company. If she loved it, there'd be nothing keeping her from transferring there permanently. Her family could visit, or she could fly home for the holidays. Other than that, she was unattached.

Her heart pattered, keeping time with her fingers as she typed on the keyboard.

She could do this. She *would* do this.

Come Friday, she'd fire up her Jeep and drive to Beaumont Bay to pay her famous ex-boyfriend a visit. She'd draw his secrets from him the same way he'd drawn her into his arms when they'd dated. And, like he had done back then, she'd turn around, drive away and never look back.

A shadow had stretched over Cash Sutherland's life two months ago and it didn't seem to be receding.

He'd hit hard times before, in business and in his personal life, but he'd always sprung back. The reaction from the trolls on social media about his so-called DUI was insane. It was like they were trying to tank his career. The press would do anything for a story.

Vultures.

At the epicenter of the shitstorm was, unsurprisingly, Mags Dumond. The woman had dubbed herself the First Lady of Beaumont Bay years ago when her late husband had been mayor. The Dumond family had founded Beaumont Bay, so he supposed Mags came by the moniker honestly. After a failed attempt at fame in Nashville, Mags had moved back to the Bay, married the mayor and proceeded to host posh parties that'd become a town— and industry—tradition.

The night that would live in infamy for him was the Black & White ball-slash-fundraiser. Everyone who was anyone in the Bay—and that was nearly everyone—had been in attendance. Cash had sipped champagne while milling around in the crowd at the mansion. Around midnight his brothers had begun advancing toward the door and he'd been right behind them. Mags had stopped him, put a drink in his hand and insisted on a toast. After a final cheers, and taking a single sip of the drink he didn't want, Cash climbed behind the wheel of his Bugatti Chiron.

He'd *felt* sober when he happened upon the random sobriety checkpoint in the short jaunt from Mags's hill-top mansion to his countryside house. But according to the officer who pulled him over, Cash had been one-tenth of a point over the legal limit.

The memory of the whole evening chafed him. Mags had harassed him much of the night, a habit she'd perfected over time, and one he'd grown tired of. She'd been pressuring him to sign with her record label, Cheating Hearts, for years. The company was her pride and joy—and the result of her own lost dreams of stardom. While Mags was failing at becoming a singer, Eleanor Banks—Hannah's grandmother—had become Nashville's sweetheart. Tail tucked, Mags returned to the Bay and fell in love. The mayor had promised her the world, and purchased a record label for her.

When Cash's brother Will relaunched well-respected Elite Records, Mags hadn't hid her resentment. She'd made it clear that the Sutherland boys were traipsing on hallowed ground. No one had the audacity to compete with the queen of the Bay. That is, until Will had taken on Elite, Cash recorded an album with the label and subsequently won the industry's top award. There was no stopping Elite's success now that Will's fiancée, Hannah, was on board. Plus, their brother Luke had launched many a new performer's career by inviting them to play at one of his bars and Gavin, a music attorney, worked exclusively with Elite Record artists.

Town and industry history aside, the only history that mattered now was the fact that Cash's mug shot was decorating the internet like the toilet paper he'd once strung into the trees outside of his high school. His angry expression in the photo made him appear guilty—or, if the Breathalyzer could be trusted, guilti*er*.

Up until that point, he'd been a bad boy with an unstoppable lucky streak. First, a hit album, then awards, soon a new tour and album with Hannah to solidify his new status, and then *the world*. A public shaming pulled the emergency brake on those plans.

While his biggest fans supported him, his corporate sponsors hadn't been as loyal. A famous shoe brand canceled his contract and following that, a popular game app he'd already filmed a commercial for let him know they would not air it. Suddenly "the bad boy of country music," who'd filled stadiums to capacity last summer, had been labeled unsafe for public consumption.

His mind a million miles from where it should be, he finished singing the final note of the song into the microphone.

Behind the glass of his at-home studio, his oldest brother, Will, stood, arms folded, a scowl on his face. His brother's scowl had taken up residency years ago, but had receded some after he'd begun dating Hannah. Cash had thought those two would've been oil and water, but it turned out they had a lot in common and had fallen in love. His stoic, powerful, rigid brother in love with an explosive rainbow of color and energy like Hannah Banks? It was the stuff of fairy tales. Which was what romantic love was to Cash. A fairy tale.

Will, behind soundproof glass, pressed a button so Cash could hear him. "I'd say go again but you should save your voice for the concert on Friday night." He made a wrap-up motion and Cash pulled off his headphones.

"Can't wait," Cash grumbled to himself. The concert on Friday night was a publicity stunt. He was not thrilled. When he'd imagined a shiny new career as a beloved music artist, he'd expected to glide through each and every day doing what he loved. He'd walked away from football, college, and worse—his girlfriend at the time, Presley. He'd convinced himself that breaking her heart would be worth it for both of them.

As far as Pres was concerned, he knew she was working for a huge media conglomerate. Her article on Elite a few years back seemed to do well and had painted the Sutherlands in a favorable light. Clearly, she'd moved on. He had too, though it'd been ten times harder than he'd imagined it would.

He loved performing, loved to hang with fans, but the rest of his duties could be exhausting. Living his passion came with a heap of bullshit like marketing, interviews with reporters and a recent press conference where he'd publicly apologized for being drunk when he damn well wasn't.

Cash rested his guitar on its stand, bypassing Will, who was studying his phone.

"Want to grab dinner?" Will asked. "Gavin and Luke are at Silver Marmot."

Not one to turn down filet mignon and lobster, Cash nodded. It'd been a long day. A long *month*.

"You'll be all right," Will encouraged as they walked upstairs and through Cash's house en route to the front door. "The aftermath of DUIs don't last forever."

No, it just felt like it.

Cash wanted to believe Friday night's performance would be the magic bullet that erased everyone's memory of his mug shot, but he knew better. While it might not last "forever" as his brother said, it could shadow them for months to come. Or years.

God help him.

For his brothers' sakes, Cash hoped recouping wasn't far off. Elite Records didn't need the bad press, either.

"Want me to drive?" Will stroked the hood of Cash's

ice-blue Bugatti, its sparkling paint glittering in the setting sunlight.

"No way your ass is touching the driver's seat of my baby." Cash unlocked the doors and slid in. "Not like I'll be drinking alcohol tonight anyway."

And in public, possibly never again.

Two

Presley arrived in Beaumont Bay much later than she intended, after nine hours of road-tripping, traffic-sitting and rest-stopping. She dashed into the Beaumont Hotel, a dress protected by a plastic dry-cleaning bag draped over her forearm, and past a few bodies in the lobby on her way to the ladies' room. She shouldn't care about what Cash thought of her driving outfit, but there was no way was she interviewing her ex while wearing stretch pants and an oversize T-shirt.The hotel was as luxe as she'd expected, with huge columns and marble flooring, patterned rugs and clerks dressed in white shirts with smart black vests and pants.

She'd planned to arrive a few hours before the rooftop concert being held in this very hotel, but Fate had other plans. At least Gavin had tipped her off about the service elevator, a secret passage of sorts that would take her to the venue without her having to file upstairs with ticketed guests.

She changed in one of the bathroom stalls and then regarded her reflection in the attached sitting room, pausing for a scant second to absorb what she was seeing. The room was large, furnished with a pair of stuffed chairs and a settee. A glass table with a carafe of coffee was available for guests.

It's the Taj Ma-Powder Room.

After brushing her teeth and freshening her makeup, she made quick work of finger-combing her auburn hair, which had wilted from the heat of the day. She hadn't dared take the top off her Jeep, and was glad for the decision now. She'd driven through a hell of a rainstorm.

She tucked the dry-cleaning bag into the trash can and rolled her driving clothes into a wad before stuffing them into her bag. As she was preparing to walk out, a woman entered, a cacophony of voices following her in from the lobby.

Presley recognized the slightly desperate, demanding tone of the press when she heard it. She stepped aside to let the woman pass and then burst into the lobby, her purse on her shoulder as she waded into a sea of people.

Men and women with long-lens cameras, and others with cell phones in hand, shot photos and video of their subject. The one, the only—

"Cash Sutherland!" one reporter shouted. "Cash!"

A few others tried their luck with "Over here! Cash!" and at least one went the lowbrow route of inquiring loudly about his DUI.

Tacky.

Presley pushed through the crowd, catching sight of the top of Cash's dark head, eyes hidden behind sunglasses, mouth a grim line.

Her world froze.

He was even grander in person than in her memory—

and far more potent than his photos online. Memories threatened to surface, but she shoved them down as she wedged her way through the crowd. Memories would slow her down. If she wanted her life to finally begin moving—if she wanted to travel to places beyond her hometown—she needed to focus on the future, not the past.

An opening cleared thanks to a bellman trying to help with crowd control. Presley nestled in near a woman waving a concert T-shirt in the air. Cash scribbled his name on the shirt with a black marker before handing it back to her, never spotting Presley. The woman gazed longingly at her prize and Presley took advantage, slinking between her and the bellman to chase after Cash. A security guard just missed her, holding up his arms and shouting to the crowd to "give Mr. Sutherland some space!"

Sorry, Mr. Sutherland, ain't gonna happen.

She skirted the front desk and caught up to a clerk shooing Cash into the service elevator. When the clerk nearly plowed into her, he frowned. She beamed up at the waifish man, her smile at full wattage.

"Thank you so much." She pressed a hand to her chest. "I nearly lost him in the crowd. It was terrifying."

The clerk waved her through, either not knowing she'd lied about arriving with the singer, or not caring. Just as Cash pressed a button on the panel on the elevator, she slipped inside. The doors whispered shut behind her, caging them in—literally since three of the walls were outfitted with iron bars over glass with a view of the elevator shaft.

"What the hell—" he started, his thick eyebrows lowering over his nose. Then his anger faded into surprise.

His low voice skipped over each and every one of her vertebrae, sending chills through her limbs even in the stuffy elevator car. She tried to speak but her tongue wouldn't work while in such close proximity to the man who used to turn her inside out with merely a look.

He blinked. "Presley?"

In spite of every pep talk she'd given herself before this assignment, her mind wandered back to how his broad hands felt on her body. To how his firm lips used to turn her inside out. He'd given her more than one orgasm without kissing her below the waist. It'd been the thrill of her life at the time. Sadly, it still might be.

"Hi." She licked her lips, preparing to say more, but the elevator car bumped and jerked like they'd boarded an amusement park ride instead. She grabbed hold of the nearest solid surface, in this case, stacks of glassware in large plastic racks destined for the bar.

Cash also gripped the rack of glasses, and her eyes moved from those long, talented fingers to his attractive hands and then up his arm to the ink that vanished into the sleeve of a black T-shirt.

There it was. The tattoo of music notes wrapping around a guitar she'd seen in photos. Or part of it anyway. Half of the colorful design was hidden.

The elevator jerked again, but rather than complete its ascent to the roof it bumped and whined in place. Overhead, the lights flickered.

"Service elevators. Yikes," she said to break the silence.

Cash was not amused. She wasn't sure if the fluorescent lights were to blame, but he appeared slightly green in color. A fine sheen of sweat coated his upper lip. His knuckles, wrapped tightly around the rack of glasses, stood out in stark contrast from the rest of his tanned skin.

"Are you… Are you okay?"

He didn't answer, his eyes turning to the ceiling where the light flickered again. His nostrils flared, the column of his throat moving as if he was trying to swallow a bowling ball.

"Cash?" She moved to touch him but he sliced her in two with a hard glare.

His voice a low warning, he growled, "What the hell do you think you're doing?"

Presley didn't hesitate answering, but whatever she was saying was coming at him like they were underwater. Or buried in wet cement.

The only sounds he could concentrate on were the whine of the elevator cables, the stacked glassware rattling away beneath his white-knuckled grip, and the concrete shaft visible through the iron-and-glass walls surrounding him. Who's bright idea had that been?

He rode elevators *never* if he could help it. He'd been stuck in one with his mother when he was five years old. They'd sat sweating in that box for what had felt like days, but Dana Sutherland assured him it'd been a "mere forty minutes" before help had arrived.

There was nothing "mere" about forty minutes trapped in a vertical coffin if you asked him. The only reason he was in this godforsaken cracker box on cables was because hoofing it up flights upon flights of stairs right before he went on stage would affect his performance.

And not in a good way.

Presley hadn't taken kindly to him asking what the hell she was doing. She was answering him, in a clipped, sharp tone and with plenty of gesticulating. He supposed he shouldn't be surprised by her reaction. Seeing him for the first time since he'd left her crying in Florida likely hadn't filled her with warm fuzzies.

He'd wondered if she'd forgiven him for leaving her. Considering the sparks that shot through her blue eyes, he guessed the answer was no.

She looked different from how he remembered her, but also the same. She had the same fire-red hair, and the same delicate freckles dotting the bridge her nose. Her black dress was more professional than party-girl, but no less tantalizing. Presley Cole had always been gorgeous. Still was.

"…not to mention I drove all the way from Tallahassee to *help you*," she was saying. "You're welcome."

"Help me," he repeated between clenched teeth. At least arguing took his mind off their predicament. "With what?"

"With your DUI, you idiot. There are a hundred reporters downstairs, and if you think a single one of them would give you the benefit of the doubt about your drunk driving—"

"I wasn't drunk," he snapped.

"Tell that to the judge."

"I did." The elevator jerked, Cash's stomach along with it. Before he could do something seriously emasculating, like yip, Presley lost her balance and touched him. It was an innocent forearm grab, but her painted pink nails and the pale freckles on her arm reminded him of times not so innocent. Times he'd unhooked her bra before kissing her chest. Times he'd flicked open the stud on her jeans and slipped his hand inside…

Snap out of it.

"You're here for an interview?" he asked.

"Yes. For Viral Pop. It's a huge media conglomerate."

He knew all about Viral Pop. It was a step sideways from the gossip magazines.

"No interview," he growled, desperately trying to pull himself together.

"Oh, you're granting me an interview." Her laugh showcased high cheekbones, her eyes, as blue as the Gulf Stream, flickering in challenge.

"Not even if we're trapped in this rickety tuna can for the remainder of the evening," he told her, his stomach souring at the thought of being stuck in here. This was his worst nightmare come true.

Her arm shot out and her hand slammed the emergency stop button. The elevator lurched to a halt and a buzzy alarm began blaring.

"Listen here, Mr. Big Shot. As I have it tallied, you owe me at least a few minutes of your precious time. I'm not here uninvited, by the way. Gavin understands how a positive spin on your recent crisis could help you, and the record label." She searched the inside of the elevator with obvious impatience. "How do I turn the alarm off?"

"You don't." He swiped his brow with the back of his hand, feeling woozier than before. This was just what he fucking needed. His ex-girlfriend, looking as hot as he remembered, yelling at him in an elevator stuck between floors.

"Cash, seriously. Are you okay?" Her harsh tone gentled as her other hand joined the first on his arm.

Stunning blue eyes inventoried his face, and the elevator walls faded. He recalled, with frightening clarity, the feel of her mouth on his, the way their tongues tangled as he plucked her nipple into a turgid peak. She'd orgasmed from that alone. He'd loved hearing her sweet cries in his ears while she tugged on his hair. His good girl, shirt rucked up, bra on the floor.

Yeah, his minor bout of claustrophobia was competing with another sensation entirely. Like the semi stirring to life behind his fly. She'd been polite and careful and as sweet as saltwater taffy back when they'd dated. Now, he sensed that same sweetness, but she'd added pure fire to the mix. Concern mingled with curiosity in her eyes. She was still touching him. Her black dress hugged demure curves, making him remember all he'd seen—and tasted—underneath.

The speaker crackled and a voice announced itself as "Rod from Maintenance." Presley looked over her shoulder at the panel, then turned back to Cash, a question forming on her pursed lips.

He didn't let her ask it. Instead, he leaned down and captured her plush mouth with a firm, unyielding kiss.

Three

Presley was fairly certain she was having an out-of-body experience.

Or maybe the elevator had plummeted several stories and she'd died and gone to heaven. Considering how amazing Cash's mouth felt on hers, she couldn't dismiss the possibility outright.

She'd shut her eyes, so the rest of her senses were on high alert. She moved her hands to his biceps, brushing her thumbs over solid muscle beneath smooth flesh. His mouth was firm and warm, and when his tongue touched hers, she lost the strength in her knees.

He must have noticed because next he steadied her with his hands. Oh, those talented hands. How had she forgotten? They were talented at strumming a guitar and *really* talented at turning her on. His lips still on hers, his fingers tightened around her waist and he tugged her close. Her breasts flattened on his chest, but when she lifted her arms to capture his neck, she lost his mouth.

His gaze was hazy, almost shell-shocked, as he sucked in a gulp of air. She did the same, unable to tear her eyes from the perfect vision of Cash up close. Dark scruff surrounded his luscious mouth, his lips damp from their kisses. Long eyelashes shadowed golden-brown eyes that appeared darker in the meager light.

He broke the spell by swearing. *Loudly.*

Setting her body aside, he went to the panel on the elevator, pressed a button, spoke to the crackling voice and then pressed another button.

Her heartbeat sloshed noisily in her ears as she descended to earth, still tingling from the kiss she hadn't even tried to stop. Which made no sense, as she was completely over him. *Completely,* she silently reminded herself.

The elevator started with a jerk and she gripped the rack of glasses to steady herself, her knees still weak.

You know, from making out with him.

Cash faced the doors for the remainder of the short ride. He sent her a dark look over his shoulder when the elevator opened on the rooftop. His last words to her were "Gavin, really?"

"What's that supposed to mean?" she mumbled. To herself, since he was no longer anywhere around. She stepped into the bar, angry, but mostly with herself. Yes, he'd kissed her first, but she'd kissed him *back.*

On her long list of "things to do" while visiting Beaumont Bay, kissing her ex wasn't on it. She'd once been weak for him. She couldn't let herself be that weak again.

She understood why Gavin had suggested not telling Cash about the interview ahead of time. Cash definitely hadn't been happy to see her.

The kiss hadn't been an "I want you" or an "I missed you." No, it'd been about something else. For her, an unwelcome visit from her past. For Cash, who was moving damn fast in black cowboy boots, the kiss had acted like a release valve on a pressurized container.

The posh, luxe bar was half indoors, half out. Shining wood floors stretched through the interior, couches and chairs surrounding low tables with lit candles. The bar was more like a really large living room. Outside, the patio's high glass walls offered a view of the city buildings and lake and trees beyond. Golden hour was upon them, bathing the stage where Cash would perform tonight in a warm, buttery light.

She walked in that direction, but a beefy security guy held up one massive mitt. "I don't think so, lady."

She opened her mouth to shout Cash's name. He had some explaining to do. Namely, why he'd kissed her and run away. Before she could, Gavin Sutherland materialized in front of her.

"It's okay, Irv, she's with us." Gavin's warm smile was a welcome sight. "Welcome to the Cheshire bar. How are you, Pres?"

What a question.

"Late." She adjusted the bag on her shoulder.

"Nah, you're fine. You took my advice about the service elevator, I assume?"

"Yeah." That'd been a bang-up plan, hadn't it?

Two years ago, when she'd visited Beaumont Bay for the Elite Records interview, she hadn't known what to expect. She knew she wouldn't run into Cash since he'd been on tour and was somewhere on the East Coast— North Carolina if she remembered right. But she hadn't been sure what his youngest brother, Gavin, would be like.

Turned out Gavin was open and easy to talk to. He was kind, and reminded her of the Cash in her memory—the one who had been running toward her briefly before he ran away.

A habit he'd never fully kicked, it seemed.

"Don't worry about Irv. He's just doing his job. I'll grab you a backstage pass later." Gavin placed a hand on her lower back and guided her away from the stage. He was a looker, from his contagious smile to the open-placket white button-down shirt. "How about a cocktail?"

"That would be great." As handsome and kind as he was, she didn't feel the same ripple of attraction as she felt for Cash. Which was alarming since she wasn't supposed to be feeling anything for Cash. "It's pretty empty up here. I'd have thought he'd pack the place."

"We don't open the doors for another fifteen minutes. How's the lobby looking?"

"Like a shark tank with chum in the water." She smiled when Gavin laughed.

"I noticed Cash rushing in like his ass was on fire. He's usually late, but not this late. Wonder what the holdup was?"

She knew, but she wasn't saying.

"He's never been much for rehearsal. Likes to be spontaneous."

"So I've gathered," she said under her breath.

Gavin gestured to a female bartender wearing a leather vest, an exposed red bra beneath it. A streak of red decorated her blond hair. "Christy, can you shake up something special for Presley while I fetch her a backstage pass? She's a friend of the family so put whatever she wants on my tab."

"Sure thing, hon." Christy's eyes crinkled at the corners, hinting she was a touch older than her outfit suggested. "How about a Lightning Bolt, sweetheart? It's Cash Sutherland's signature drink."

"Named after his famous song, 'Lightning,' I presume."

"The one and only. The girls go wild for that song—and the drink."

Just what she needed. But, what the hell. "Sure. Why not?"

Turned out the Cash Sutherland's signature drink was blue and fruity…and served in a martini glass with a cherry in the bottom. Which had her musing about her own intact virginity back when she'd dated him, and the likely color of his balls as they took things far, but never went all the way.

Her stomach rolled, regret and relief switching places, but she thanked Christy for the drink anyway.

Boots hooked on the rungs of a stool backstage, Cash concentrated on tuning his guitar while the band readied their instruments. He'd assumed tonight's set would be as rote as they came, given they'd performed it at least once in every state in the country, and in several countries outside the United States. Then again, after what'd happened in the service elevator, anything being "rote" tonight was a big assumption.

He hummed as he plucked the strings, his mind not on his music but on every agonizing, skin-tightening, ball-seizing second of kissing Presley in that elevator. Her truncated breaths, the feel of her small hands on his arms as she sealed her body to his. The incredibly confident way her mouth moved beneath his, slanting when he would have backed off, diving deeper when he *should have* backed off.

They'd been kids when they'd dated—her nineteen-going-on-twenty to his should've-known-better twenty-three. But she wasn't nineteen-going-on-twenty any longer. She was thirty to his thirty-three, and his sweet

Presley had bloomed. Sneaking into that elevator and implying she was here to save his career was not the Presley he remembered.

Cash would strangle his younger brother for keeping this from him.

"Set list, boss." Mikey, his bassist, handed over a sheet of paper.

Cash reviewed it, nodded and handed it back. Mikey taped it to the floor next to the microphone stand and ambled off to finish setting up.

Cash didn't know how the hell he was supposed to perform "Lightning" knowing Presley was out there watching—and preparing to report on—his every move. Especially after the kiss that had stopped the world. And the elevator.

He was used to the wolves coming for him in the form of paparazzi and press, but the last person he'd expected to take advantage of his fame was her. She had shown up a few years back to interview his family, without so much as an email to alert him. Not that he blamed her for not contacting him. Not after how things ended between them…how *he'd* ended things.

He'd been a senior at the time, itching to finish school or drop out entirely. He didn't care, so long as college was *over*. If it hadn't been for a football scholarship, he never would have gone to Florida. Never would have met Presley Cole. At the moment, he couldn't decide if that would have been better.

Anyway, he'd broken his finger on the field, an injury that had since healed but still caused him pain after a long show or hours of practice. He hadn't been able to play football immediately following, which was a huge relief, but he also hadn't been able to hold a pen or play guitar, and that had been the ultimate deal breaker.

His dad, Travis, had high hopes for Cash to play for the NFL. Cash hadn't wanted to live out his father's dream. He'd had his own dream. The decision to leave Florida State was easy. Leaving his budding relationship with Presley was not.

The break from football gave him a lot of perspective. He saw how he'd influenced Presley and not in a positive way. More than once, she'd broken curfew while they'd dated. She'd gone to parties she had no business being at, and had skipped hanging with her friends to watch him play ball.

She hadn't been the only one affected negatively by their relationship. He'd done his share of skipping class, sleeping in after spending the night with her in his arms. He'd respected her wishes not go all the way sexually during their heavy make-out sessions, but wanting her had become a type of torture the longer they were together.

She'd probably never know how much it'd gutted him to give her the "it's not you it's me" breakup speech. To watch her eyes fill with tears and then walk away like he didn't care. He had cared. Way too much.

After he'd decided to stop chasing his father's dream and chase his own for a change, Cash knew what coming home to Tennessee meant. It meant dedicating all his time to succeeding, and that hadn't left any time for Presley.

When he broke up with her, he'd reminded her that she had big dreams of her own. To be a writer, to travel. He knew she'd turned down an internship in NYC to stay close to him. The last thing he wanted was for her not to follow her own dreams in exchange for being with him. But in reality, he hadn't been as magnanimous as he'd made himself out to be. He'd been selfish, and she deserved better. Then and now.

Sad as it was, their brief relationship, honest and loving at the start, heartbreaking and lonely at the end, made for great country music fodder.

Too bad the song he'd written to help him get over her only seemed to reopen the wound every time he sang it.

"Ten minutes," Mikey called out.

Cash nodded that he was ready. If there was one thing he could do it was compartmentalize. And as far as pushing thoughts of Presley into the past went, well, he'd had a hell of a lot of practice.

Four

No wonder the man won awards.

Presley was sitting at a high-top table with Gavin and a few of his friends, trying not to stare at Cash. She failed when he performed his signature song. And she wasn't the only one who couldn't tear her eyes off him. A reverent hush fell over the crowd and goose bumps chilled her arms as he sang "Lightning."

Cash had been the one to encourage her to follow her dreams of becoming a journalist and traveling the world. She should probably thank him. Once he'd left Florida, she became focused entirely on her schoolwork. She'd put relationships on the back burner, spending more time with her laptop than she ever had a boy. In a way, losing Cash had galvanized her. She'd become bulletproof since. Or so she'd thought before he sang the knife-twist final line of his biggest hit.

How I wish, oh how I wish, lightning struck twice.

There was a sacred pause between the strum of the last chord and the audience erupting in applause. Slightly stunned, she joined in and clapped, as well. That hour had flown.

"What now?" one of the women at their table asked. "Do we rush the stage and tear his clothes off?"

Gavin laughed. "I'd love to see you try. Go for it."

The woman and her friend laughed and then dared each other to do it. Presley's stomach twisted into a knot. She wasn't sure if she was feeling melancholy that she'd had access to quite a bit of Cash's body back in the day, or jealous that other women had access to it now.

"You okay, Pres?" Gavin asked, and she remembered that she was supposed to be.

"Yep! Does he come out and mingle now?"

The crowd was small, but there were enough drooling women to form a mob if they banded together. Currently, one woman was begging for a peek backstage while the burly security guy's head swept left and right like a pendulum.

"Not usually," Gavin answered. "Even an intimate crowd can be rowdy. Women go nuts for him."

"Yeah," Presley mumbled, disappointed to learn that her reaction to him was far from unique.

"He'll come out after a majority of the crowd has dispersed. Usually we meet up in the VIP lounge. Luke's probably already back there. Will and Hannah were planning on coming out, too."

"Hannah Banks. Right." Country music megastar and a surprising match for the most serious of the Sutherland brothers. "I look forward to meeting her."

"You'll like her. You know, you're good with fame." Gavin sounded amused. He sipped from his lowball glass.

"Is it because you knew Cash from way-back-when, or does your line of work make fame commonplace?"

"Bit of both." She shrugged. "Celebrities are people. And you can't be a blithering idiot if you want to interview them successfully. You have to play it cool."

She nearly burst out laughing at herself. Yes, she'd played it *soooo* cool when she'd slipped into an elevator with Cash and then tangled her tongue with his.

Anyway. She cleared her throat.

"Let's go to the VIP lounge now and ditch the masses," Gavin suggested. "You down for some gourmet fried appetizers?"

Fluttering her lashes, she touched her décolletage. "You had me at *fried*."

They sidestepped a cluster of people who were pressing toward the stage, drawn in by Cash's ridiculously universal appeal. She passed two women who were crying and saying they'd "give anything to meet him."

Been there. Done that. Burned one of his T-shirts.

She hadn't known what she was walking into when she'd dated him years ago, but she did now. At one point she'd given up an internship to New York City to stay close to him, something she'd grown to regret. Leaving him had been unthinkable. He hadn't shared her feelings.

Well, it wasn't like she had come here to rekindle their relationship. She was here to find out who "Lightning" had been written about, and then share that news in an exclusive article that would go *so* viral Viral Pop would be tempted to name the company after her. In other words, she had a job to do and she intended to do it well. Being distracted by Cash's incredible…*everything* was not on the agenda.

In the VIP lounge, Gavin led her to a roped-off area where Will Sutherland stood, his nose in Hannah Banks's blond hair. She was more gorgeous in person, especially since she was grinning ear to ear. When Will emerged from her locks, so was he.

Ah, love.

At one point, Presley had thought she was in love with Cash. Now she knew better. What the women in this crowd—and at least one guy—felt for the singer was adoration, and had nothing to do with "love."

She understood now that she'd been caught up in adoration, too. Cash had been an incredible quarterback who could play the guitar and sing any woman into an orgasm. He had an irresistibility about him that, unfortunately, hadn't gone anywhere.

But resist him she would.

Once upon a time, he had been singularly focused on his own career and damn the consequences. Now it was her turn to nurture her career and leave him in the dust. Granted, she wasn't very good at being selfish, but hey, maybe Cash could give her a few pointers while she was here.

Five

Cash sucked in a breath through flared nostrils and kept his carefully trained half smile in place while the woman in front of him tried to keep from sobbing. She was happy—he assumed—but it was hard to tell when both a cry and a laugh overlapped.

"I...j-just wanted to tell you that y-your music changed my life and that I luh-love you. I love you s-so much."

This was the most uncomfortable part of meeting fans. He thought he'd be used to this sort of display by now, but for him it never got any easier.

"I appreciate that, Tabitha," he said in a low, soothing voice.

Her eyes widened, lashes blinking away tears as she grinned. When he'd first begun performing, women like Tabitha had flattered his pants off. Literally, in some cases. Thankfully he pulled his head out of his backside before he became a regular with the groupies.

Those hookups had been less satisfying than they were awkward, for both parties. He'd stuck with actual relationships instead, though he kept them short. That way he could take care of the physical ache while avoiding the "what was your name again?" conversation the next morning.

"Time's up, miss." Irv, who ran security for the Cheshire, was large, slightly frightening and gruff. In other words, exactly what Cash needed. He winked at Tabitha and told her to have a good night. Then he and Irv moved as one through the bar until Cash was deposited in the VIP lounge.

Safe at last.

Then he spotted Presley talking with Hannah and thought maybe he wasn't safe. She had tried to kill him, after all. If not by pressing the emergency button that stopped the elevator, then with the kiss that damn near stopped his heart.

Her blue eyes sparked like flint striking stone as he stepped into the room. She wasn't happy with him, though he didn't know if that was because of recent events or their shared past.

Hannah, her hand linked with Will's, turned for the bar. His brother gave him a nod of greeting and Hannah smiled her perfect, pearly smile. Cash liked her, always had. It wouldn't be a hardship touring with her when the time came. Both Hannah and her twin sister, Hallie, were from the best kind of stock. Their grandmother, Eleanor, had raised them right.

Presley wasn't glaring at him any longer. She had decided to ignore him completely. From her perch on a plush red sofa, she grinned at his brother Gavin, who had just returned with a drink for each of them. Cash could deck his younger brother for inviting his ex-girlfriend to Beaumont Bay without telling him. Whose side was he on?

"You two are looking cozy," Cash said. "Though you've been in touch lately, so that makes sense."

"Ignore King High and Mighty, Pres," Gavin told her, unfazed by Cash's surly entry.

"No worries. I do." She flashed a tight smile Cash's way and he gave her the practiced half smile he reserved for fans.

"Beer, Mr. Sutherland?" A cocktail waitress approached. She was new if he wasn't mistaken.

In a town like Beaumont Bay, luxury and high-class living were the norm. It was unique for staff to stick around anywhere for long. Not that Cash frequented his brother's bar, but when he was here, he wasn't used to seeing the same friendly staff. Jobs around here were a means to an end, and once the fame-seeker found his or her opening, they left faster than you could say, "I'd love a beer." Which was what he told the waitress now.

"What kind?" She peeked flirtatiously through her lashes.

He grinned. "Surprise me."

She turned and wiggled away, making her classy black pantsuit look a hell of a lot more scandalous.

"Wow." Presley raised her auburn eyebrows. "You *can* be charming."

"Presley!" Hannah called from the bar. "Come over here. There's someone I want you to meet!"

Hallie, Hannah's identical twin sister, stood between Hannah and Will. Hallie was a carbon copy of her famous sister. Blonde and beautiful with bright hazel eyes and a wide mouth. They were easy to tell apart. Hallie wore a neutral beige dress, her hair tied back in a low ponytail, while Hannah practically glowed in a bright pink dress covered in twinkling rhinestones. Those two definitely had their differences.

"If you'll excuse me," Presley said sweetly. To Gavin.

When she was gone, Cash took her seat as the waitress delivered his beer. "Thanks, honey."

She didn't hover, which he appreciated. He took a long draw. Damn, that tasted good. He wasn't a big drinker, but it was tradition to enjoy a beer after a performance. By his calculations, he'd more than earned one.

"You want to tell me why Presley Cole is here yammering about interviewing me about my DUI?"

Gavin took a swallow from his gin and tonic and pretended to think about it. "No. I don't think I will."

"What are you not saying?"

"I know how you feel about the press, but when it comes to clearing your name with the public, she can help you."

Cash doubted her motivations were that noble.

"Your expression doesn't exactly scream that you're on board," Gav said with a grin. "Look, Pres wrote an article about Elite Records that was not only well written, it was fair. She didn't misquote Will, or play up a rivalry between Mags Dumond and the Sutherlands like *Rolling Stone* did."

Cash frowned. He recalled that magazine article. It'd had a ripple effect on social media that took a long while to peter out. If he disliked the press, he *hated* social media.

"She called a few weeks back asking if the studio had recovered from the storm, and we talked about your DUI. I told her it was trumped-up bullshit and she said she could've guessed and offered to help clear your name." Gavin shrugged. "She's on our side, Cash. And the timing is perfect since you're recording a new album. She can mention that alongside how Elite Records rose from the ashes after the storm nearly flattened it. Two birds. One stone."

"Your metaphors need work," Cash grumbled before returning to his point. "She's my ex-girlfriend and you should've told me."

"You dated her a hundred years ago."

"Did it occur to you she could be here to exact revenge on me for breaking up with her?" Cash asked under his breath after checking to make sure no one was listening. He could never be too careful.

Gavin leaned in. "Did it occur to *you* how it's a miracle this VIP lounge can hold both you *and* your enormous ego?"

Jerk.

"Revenge. Do you hear yourself?" His brother shook his head. "She's as sweet as apple pie."

Cash knew for a fact that she tasted equally sweet. He ground his molars together. Gavin wasn't stupid enough to flirt with her, but Cash delivered a threat anyway. "As wholesome as apple pie too. So, mind yourself."

Gavin couldn't comment since Presley returned at that moment. Cash moved down the couch to give her seat back, regretting it when she sat closer to Gavin than him.

"Hallie is so nice," Presley said. "Shy, though. I guess it's poor form to assume twins have the same personality. They are individuals."

"She's been around a lot more since Will and Hannah have been together, but she barely says two words to me." Gavin sounded slightly stung.

And Gavin thought *Cash* was the one with the ego? Gav hated when people didn't like him—women in particular.

"I wonder why? You're so easy to talk to." Presley

touched Gavin's leg. Clearly Cash's kiss hadn't been more than a blip on her radar if she was already flirting with his brother.

"I'm taking off," Cash announced abruptly. He'd seen enough. He set his unfinished beer on the table in front of the couch and stood.

"Pres is staying the week," Gavin said, his smile not at all innocent. "You should give her a full tour while she's here."

Cash's expression matched Presley's scowl, though he looked more comfortable wearing it than she felt.

"Where are you staying?" Gavin asked her.

"The Rose Something. In Greencamp?" When the name didn't spark recognition in either of them, she thumbed through her phone for the confirmation email. "Oh, here it is. The Dusty Rose."

"No," Gavin said at the same time Cash said, "Absolutely not."

"Well, the Beaumont—" she gestured around at the lush bar perched atop the hotel "— while quite lovely, is a *wee* smidge outside of my budget."

And Viral Pop's. While funds were *not* a problem for the Sutherland family, she was here partially on her own dime. The credit card she'd been given for "expenses" had a limit that was hilarious. But she was willing to dip into her savings to fund this trip, figuring that the pay raise after she won the contest would refill it and then some. Staying in Beaumont Bay proper wouldn't be dipping into her savings, it'd be scraping it dry.

Gavin and Cash exchanged dark glances and she shifted in her seat.

"Should I check into somewhere closer? There wasn't

much occupancy in neighboring towns given it's summer at the lake."

"You're right about that," Gavin said. "Occupancy is an issue right now, but the Dusty Rose isn't where you want to stay."

"It looked charming. And it's only a half an hour up the road."

"On those back-country roads, it'll take longer than that. And you can bet the Dusty Rose is about as charming as my brother." Gavin smirked, proud of the jab.

"I'm more charming than black mold and roaches," Cash commented.

Presley cringed. "It's that bad?"

"Yes," the brothers agreed.

"You can stay with me," Gavin said. "Free of charge."

"With you?" she and Cash asked in chorus. Except her tone was curious and his was…something else.

"Why would she stay with you if she's here to talk to me?" Cash snapped, suddenly defending the very interview he swore he wouldn't allow.

"Because *I* invited her here."

"Your apartment is the size of the elevator Pres and I rode up here in," Cash continued arguing. She didn't miss Gavin's sideways glance. Heat spread over her chest and climbed her neck as she relived what happened in the cramped space. "What are you going to do, share a bathroom?"

"Really, the hotel is fine," she tried interjecting.

"Cash's house is bigger than mine, but only because my *bigger*, *nicer* house is currently being built. I'm in temporary quarters right now," Gavin explained. "But, his place is on the lake. So while you'd be staying with the grouchiest Sutherland in Beaumont Bay, the view might be worth it."

"And I have a guest wing."

"Guest *rooms*. He's exaggerating." Gavin rolled his eyes. "But they are nice. I've stayed there a time or two."

"Uh…" What a choice. She could either add in extra travel time and risk roaches and black mold at the Dusty Rose, suffer a bit of awkwardness by staying—and sharing a bathroom—with Gavin, or stay in "the guest wing" of her sexy ex-boyfriend's lakefront house. Plus, if she wasn't mistaken, Cash had just agreed to the interview. "If you're sure it's not an inconvenience. I can pay you if—"

"Absolutely not," Cash repeated, then looked at his brother. "It's settled. She's staying with me."

Why, oh why, did his claiming her send a shiver of awareness down her spine?

"You'd better get going, then." Gavin clapped Cash's shoulder. "Make sure there are clean sheets on the guest bed."

Cash sent his brother one final dark look before pulling out his phone. It buzzed in his hand. "Looks like Rickie's already there anyway."

"His agent," Gavin explained to Presley.

"What's your phone number?" Cash asked her. "I'll text you the address. Then you'll have my number so you can call if you get lost."

She rattled off her cell phone number and Cash punched it into his phone before making his escape. She watched his confident swagger, unsure how she'd started off with hotel reservations and ended up agreeing to bunking with Cash.

Well, not *with him*. But in his house.

"You sure you're okay staying with him?" Gavin asked. "My apartment is tight quarters, but it's a hell of a lot better than the Dusty Rose."

"I'm sure we'll be fine."

Cash was a private person. The idea of staying with him—and it sounded like they'd be in separate parts of the house—wasn't as crazy as it'd seemed at first. She could observe the side of him he rarely showed in public. And that sort of closeness might lead to an intimate evening where he shared his secrets with her. Her neck grew hot again, prompting her to remind herself that intimacy in this case would not include more kissing. Or other…stuff.

She was here to do a job and that job didn't include a lengthy perusal of Cash's body—naked or otherwise. God, it really was hot in here. She fanned her face as her phone buzzed from inside her bag.

"Cash?" Gavin guessed as she checked her text messages.

"Yes," she said, her heart tapping out a hectic rhythm. She felt nineteen again. *A message from Cash Sutherland! Eee!*

But the text was merely an address. No *hi* or *drive safe* or even a smiley-face emoji. Disappointment took over where her excitement left off. It was just as well. There was nothing left between her and Cash but memories.

Six

Presley hung around in the VIP room and enjoyed appetizers with Hannah and Hallie while Will, Luke and Gavin stood in a manly huddle at the private VIP bar. So caught up in conversation with the Banks twins, she hadn't realized how late it was until she was hiding a yawn with one hand. Finally, at nearly midnight, she pulled up to Cash's house.

Well, she pulled up to *an iron gate in front of his* house.

"Seriously?" she asked no one. Except someone heard her.

"Door's unlocked, Pres," came Cash's deep, smooth voice through the box stationed outside the gate. She tried not to be aware of how sexy he sounded. Tried not to relive the searing kiss he'd placed on her lips earlier tonight. But here she was, thinking of both.

The iron bars swung aside and she drove in, a slightly cool breeze blowing her hair through her open window.

She was exhausted from a long day of travel and socializing. So exhausted that it took her a minute to absorb what was in front of her.

Cash's house.

Cash's *enormous* house.

House wasn't even the right word. It was more like a mansion. Beaumont Bay was littered with them. The Bay marketed itself as a bustling, high-octane town that never slept, but clearly the people living there had to, and they chose to do so in luxury.

Her coworker Ray had written an article on celebrity houses a few years ago, right before she'd come to Tennessee to interview the Sutherlands about Elite Records. Curious, she'd searched online for photos of Cash's home. This had not been the house in the photo. He must have upgraded.

The sound of trickling water drew her attention as she stepped from her Jeep onto the cobblestone drive. A fountain, lined with thick greenery and vibrant flowers, was splashing into an in-ground pond. She peeked into the lit water and spotted several orange-and-white and black-speckled koi fish.

She still couldn't square Cash with all this luxury. He favored cowboy boots and black T-shirts. Though she couldn't say he was as approachable as he'd been when she'd gone to school with him, he was a true family guy. Fame didn't suit him, but he'd seemed to settle into the fancy vibe of this town just fine. Probably because he was from here, a fact she'd overlooked when they were in college. She'd let herself believe he belonged in Florida with her.

She rolled up the windows of her Jeep in case of rain, grabbed her suitcase on wheels and, out of habit, locked the doors. Probably unnecessary considering the large iron gates at the front, but whatever. Hopefully her room wasn't far from the front door. She was damned near ready to collapse.

As instructed, she depressed the button on the big antique brass handle and let herself inside. The second she set foot in the house, a voice echoed across the expansive foyer. A female one.

"You know how I feel about it," the woman said, her tone clipped. She had an accent. English, maybe?

"Yeah, and you know how *I* feel about it," Cash returned sternly.

"Well after going round and round for the last two hours, we're not apt to agree."

Cash's voice dropped into a seductive husk. "Since when has that stopped us from making this work?" Presley could hear the smile in his voice. And it sounded like a real one. A genuine, kind one. The way he'd talk to a girlfriend. The way he used to talk to her.

"You're so full of it. I'm out of here, handsome," the woman replied.

"C'mon, Rickie, don't leave. I have plenty of space here."

At his cajoling, the English woman let out a laugh. Presley's stomach did a barrel roll. Rickie. His agent. Apparently, she was representing more than just his career.

How dare he kiss Presley in that elevator when he was attached to someone else? Her ire crept up, the rush of adrenaline waking her up. She could forgive his rudeness, his distance, but not cheating. That was unforgivable.

The soft scrape of clothing sounded like Cash and the woman were hugging. Presley braced herself for the smooching sure to follow, but the kissing sounds never came. What did come, as Presley stood in the foyer, her eyes squeezed closed, was a greeting from the woman that was much, much closer than before.

"You must be Presley."

Her eyes fluttered open to find the agent smiling at her. Rickie was older than Cash. Like, *thirty years* older. Her pale, ice-gray hair, cut into a long bob, was a beautiful fit with her bone structure.

"He told me you were staying here." Rickie shot out a hand and Presley shook it. She peered over the other woman's shoulder at Cash, who stood, arms folded, not the least bit concerned about being overheard. Not appearing the least bit guilty.

"I'm Cash's agent, Rickie Simmons. He's a complete bear, but I hope you'll go easy on him in the article." She cupped her mouth and stage-whispered, "Whatever you have to do to butter him up, love, feel free to do it."

"Rickie, for God's sake," Cash complained.

"You kids." She waved him off with a hand. "So sensitive. I'm teasing, of course. Good night, you two. Don't stay up too late!"

She shut the door behind her and the cavernous space echoed with her retreat.

"She's the worst," Cash said, his smile teasing. He stepped forward and reached out a hand and because Presley was dazed and really very tired, she reached her hand out, too. He gave her palm a gentle squeeze and murmured, "I was going for the bag."

"Oh! Right. Sorry. I'm—it's been a long day. First the drive and then the concert and then I was caught up at the VIP room…" She stopped talking, figuring it was silly to give him details about the concert he'd performed or the room where they'd mingled in following.

"Don't sweat it. Follow me."

They walked through what very well could have been

her dream kitchen if she'd ever bothered to dream up such an elaborate space. The gray granite countertops and rich brown wooden cabinets were high-end and gleaming. Textured stone flooring extended into a living room where a huge fireplace tracked up one wall to a high ceiling, and fat leather couches stood waiting for several guests to settle into their plush cushions. A staircase curved to a second floor, bisecting a hallway leading in both directions. The house was gorgeous and lush, manly yet stylish. A lot like its owner.

"Assuming you don't want a full tour right yet." He paused, one booted foot resting on the bottom step. His stance was casual and welcoming, definitely contrasting their interaction earlier.

She offered a head shake, too overwhelmed to say more. Today had been a lot to process already.

Upstairs they passed doors—a lot of them—and while her bedroom wasn't quite in its own "wing," it sat off by itself at the end of the hallway.

"How many guests do you usually entertain?" she asked as he wheeled her suitcase through the doorway.

"The band stays here sometimes, but this year they splurged for a houseboat on the water. They stay up late and party. I don't do that much anymore."

Much.

What'd it look like when he did, she wondered? Probably a lot like his mug shot, she answered herself. He was a crazy-famous bad-boy music star in a town of luxury and endless parties. Fifths of Jack Daniels, smoking pot and groupies must be commonplace for him. She frowned, hating picturing him dripping with faceless, nameless women.

"Rickie's a pill. Hope she didn't rankle you."

"I thought I walked in on a fight between you and your

girlfriend," Presley blurted out. His agent was pretty, and it wasn't *that* far-fetched to think she and Cash had... *you know.*

His laugh was hearty. "God, no. Her wife would strangle me, for one. For the other, I'd never compromise our working relationship. You know how hard it is to find good representation?"

"No."

His smile held for a beat. She didn't know if it was her unexpected response to his rhetorical question, or if his smile was left over from the idea of him and Rickie dating, but either way Presley liked seeing it.

"Bathroom is attached." He pointed at the en suite.

She took her first look at his guest quarters, which could comfortably hold a family of four. And their dog. "Don't you have anything bigger?"

"Too audacious for you?" His grin was a little knee-weakening. It was hard to be this close to him and not remember what they used to do together. Hell, what they'd done mere hours ago.

He lifted the suitcase and set it on a king-size four-poster bed, adorned with several plum-and-cream-colored pillows resting on a floral quilt. She touched the stitching, unable to help herself. It was beautiful work.

"Real Southern charm, courtesy of Dana Sutherland," he said.

"Your mom sewed this?"

"She decorated this entire room. You didn't take me for a purple-and-flowers type, did you?"

She shook her head. "No, not really."

A rolltop desk stood between a pair of tall windows. Layered drapes matching the quilt hung on either side of them. She peered out the windows and down at the driveway at her Jeep, admiring the tall, manicured line of hedges she'd overlooked when she'd driven in.

"This place is—"

"Audacious. I know," he murmured, directly over her left shoulder.

She whirled around and her mouth was closer to his than she'd planned. Her mind immediately went to the elevator. The kiss. Her hands on his body, his hands on her waist. The way he'd pulled her close. She'd been more than happy to press her hardening nipples against his solid form...

She took a deliberate step away from him.

"When, um, did you get the tattoo?"

He blinked, and it was a relief when his intense gaze left her face. He rolled up his short sleeve and revealed the rest of the colorful guitar and music notes looping his biceps. "The night I won a Grammy."

"Are the notes from any song in particular?"

"The one and only."

"'Lightning,'" she guessed.

"I peaked too soon." He rolled his sleeve down.

"You have a long career ahead of you." She plopped down onto a stuffed chair next to the bed and tugged off one high-heeled shoe. With a groan she rubbed one aching foot. "Thank you. For letting me stay here. I know you didn't plan on housing me. I sure didn't plan on intruding."

"Come on, Pres. It's not an intrusion."

"Well, after—"

He held up a hand. "An apology is not necessary."

"An apology?" What was he talking about?

"I mean it. Don't worry about it."

"Why would I apologize?" Shoe in hand, she considered throwing it at his head.

"For getting carried away in the elevator," he said, his tone set to *duh*.

Her grip tightened on her shoe. Seriously, she was going to brain him with it.

"*I* got carried away," she repeated, exasperated.

"I know. But it's okay. Happens all the time."

He pulled his hands over his chest and for once she didn't admire the snug fit of his T-shirt sleeves at the biceps or the way the soft cotton molded to his pectorals. At least, she didn't notice as much as she'd noticed earlier.

"Everything you need should be in here," he continued. "Except the coffeepot, but I'm up bright and early so there'll probably be some for you when you come down. Night, Pres."

He shut the bedroom door behind him. She sat alone in the massive room, her shoe in her hand, and blinked dumbly at the door. She thought about the easy way he'd smiled at her, the calm way he'd joked with her and, finally, the outrageous way he'd accused *her* of attacking *him* in that elevator.

"Does he have amnesia?" she asked the empty room. He was delusional if he thought this was the end of that subject. After she'd had a good night's sleep, she'd pour herself one of those cups of coffee he promised and set the record straight about what had happened in that elevator.

For good.

Seven

Presley slept like the dead.

She woke up later than her usual seven o'clock, but after a day filled with travel and socializing—and kissing Cash Sutherland—it wasn't that surprising she'd slept in a few extra hours.

She couldn't bring herself to regret it. Dana Sutherland's homemade quilt was cozy, and spread over a mattress that might well have been crafted out of clouds. Pres woke well-rested and with a smile on her face, but once she was in the shower working mango body scrub down her legs, memories of last night returned, and with them came a frown.

Cash had said she didn't need to apologize for kissing him. She chuckled anew at his audacity. He'd *very obviously* been the one who'd initiated the kiss in the elevator. Not that she'd resisted, but that was hardly the point. The point was it'd happened, and it wasn't happening again.

Leaving her hair damp, since it was already eighty-two degrees outside and the sun would quickly dry it the rest of the way, she jogged downstairs.

Last night the house had been gargantuan and gorgeous. It still was, but the sun streaming in through the wide windows, offering a droolworthy view of the sparkling lake, made the house feel more inviting. It was still a mansion with a kick-ass kitchen, but at the same time it gave off cozy bed-and-breakfast vibes.

She lifted the coffeepot to find only a small puddle of the precious brew left in the carafe. Luckily, she didn't have to do water-to-coffee math since there was also a one-cup-coffee-pod situation on the corner of the counter.

Thank goodness.

Coffee brewed, she mentally reviewed the speech she was going to give Cash. Before she had a chance to set off and find him, music lifted on the air.

Guitar strums to be precise. The sound grew louder then quieter, like the notes were being tossed on the wind. She crossed from the kitchen to the attached living room and squinted at the sun-dappled water beyond the French doors. Her eyes tracked down to the beach and then back to the house before she spotted him. He was sitting on the wide steps of the deck, his back to her, his guitar resting on his lap.

She opened one of the doors and quietly closed it behind her, not wanting to interrupt. His smooth voice drew her in like a siren's song, the familiarity wending in her brain and tangling up in a memory she'd been sure she'd repressed.

"Will you play for me?" She'd been dating Cash Sutherland for almost two weeks. She'd seen him perform. She'd gone to a party with him. She'd stared at him shamelessly on the football field before he'd even known her name. And last night, she'd kissed him until she was

breathless, simultaneously nervous, excited and finally disappointed when his hands failed to dip beneath the cups of her bra.

"What do you want me to play?" He strolled in from his kitchen, drying his hands on a dish towel. He didn't live in a dorm like she did. He had an honest-to-goodness apartment because, as she'd learned, his family had money. A lot of it. Good looks, musical talent and wealth seemed an unfair advantage over other guys, especially since Cash was also an amazing athlete.

Look at those guns. Yummy.

He lowered onto the couch next to her and she inhaled his spicy cologne. He lifted the guitar that was leaning against the wall and sent her a smile. At that second, she decided she was certifiably insane for holding on to her virginity.

It'd seemed like a good idea to be cautious when she'd started college—she'd heard horror story upon horror story from her girlfriends about how predatory college guys could be. And while she didn't think of Cash as "predatory" she did worry that once he slept with her he might realize he hadn't meant to court the chaste good girl. That he'd take her virginity and leave her behind, destroying her thoroughly.

Even so, she could think of almost nothing but shedding her clothes and being horizontal with him. Especially with his thick arms exposed, his deft fingers plucking the strings, and that low, sensual way he hummed in the back of his throat before he started singing... She was beginning to believe that the heartbreak would be worth the memories if the worst came to pass.

"Morning," Cash said now, head still bent over his guitar.

She snapped out of the memory, frustrated by her

naïve former self. She'd gone back and forth over the years about whether she should have or shouldn't have given him her virginity. In the end, she hadn't, and had ended up heartbroken anyway. On good days she told herself she was glad she hadn't fallen any deeper for him, and on the bad ones she wondered if he wouldn't have left her if she had slept with him.

"I didn't want to interrupt." She folded her arms over her chest. "I always enjoyed hearing you play."

He peeked over his shoulder at her, one eye narrowed against the bright morning sunshine. The hand that had been strumming came to rest on the body of the guitar as she sat on the step next to him.

"You found coffee."

"Well, someone drained the pot so I had to be resourceful." She sipped from her mug.

"Well, *someone* slept so late that the batch I made would have burned if I hadn't drained it."

She turned her head to smile and found him smiling back at her. Utterly attractive and utterly distracting.

"Nice view you have here," she said, reaching for an excuse to stop looking at his rough yet handsome face. The water appeared deep blue thanks to the sun, and a boat trolled by in the distance.

"I like it. It's peaceful." He went back to strumming, his eyes on the water. She wondered if he knew he was doing it, or if the instrument was a part of him. Her eyes tracked to the tattoo on his upper arm and she figured that it *was* part of him, quite literally.

"I didn't kiss you yesterday, by the way." If she didn't say it now, she never would.

"Beg your pardon?"

"Last night you said I didn't have to apologize for kissing you."

"You don't."

A growl sounded in her throat and then her voice went an octave higher when she argued, "I refuse to apologize."

"So you enjoyed it," he concluded.

"You're impossible." She had to laugh, because if she answered truthfully she'd say she'd enjoyed it very much. What she hadn't enjoyed was the way he refused to acknowledge his part in it. "For the record, you were the one who kissed me."

"'For the record' is a very journalist thing to say," he muttered, sounding displeased.

She was aware he was changing the subject, but she let him. She hadn't made much headway, and frankly it was probably best not to talk about kissing him. Especially since she was trying not to think about kissing him again.

"Gavin told me you weren't a fan of journalists."

"Ever since I became famous, the press has been challenging. Since the DUI, they've been as charming as a school of barracuda." His fingers moved over the guitar strings and he sang, "And I wasn't expecting the likes of you."

He grinned. She rolled her eyes.

"Gavin also told me you'd say no if you knew I was coming."

"I would have."

That hurt. She'd had just about enough of this conversation. Whenever she was around him, he found a way to hurt her feelings.

"This was a bad idea." She was delusional to think that spending this much time with him wouldn't leave her raw and vulnerable. When she moved to stand he placed a hand on her bare knee.

"I'm glad you're here."

"You're *glad*?" That sounded like an overstatement.

Gosh, it was hard to think when he was touching her. Thankfully, he pulled his hand away.

"Sure, why not?"

A million reasons why not. Like, she was his ex-girl-friend and he'd left her high and dry in Florida. Like she'd sneaked onto that elevator and he'd responded by kissing her senseless. And she must've been senseless; otherwise she wouldn't have slept in his house last night.

"You seemed upset with me yesterday," she said, unable to keep from steering the conversation back to them.

"Not at you. Clearly," he mumbled.

"So, you'll admit you kissed me?"

"You looked too damn cute not to kiss." His blue eyes burned straight through her as her heart pattered desperately against her rib cage. "But it won't happen again."

If it was possible to be thrilled and frustrated at the same time, she was experiencing that strange and yet-to-be-named emotion.

"That would be best." She took a sip of coffee and reminded herself that kissing Cash Sutherland...*again* would be the height of stupidity. She was staying in his house. He was speaking to her. She was halfway home. All she had to do was keep her wits about her a few days more. If he started talking about songwriting, maybe his guard would drop and he would casually admit the inspiration behind "Lightning". It was worth a shot. She cleared her throat and gave him a smile. "Do you practice every morning?"

"Lately, yeah. I'm writing." He pointed at a battered spiral notebook resting next to one of his thick thighs. "There are about five words on a page from this morning."

"Not going well?"

"It's going as well as it can go," he said. Cryptically.

"Can I help?"

His mouth slid into a half smile that was, like the rest of him, entirely too appealing. "You offering to be my muse?"

"I'm offering professional help."

"You mean like a therapist?"

"No, though you could benefit from one." She bumped her knee against his. He let out an easy laugh. He was so much less intense than he'd been yesterday.

"In case you haven't noticed, I'm a writer and words are kind of my thing."

"I noticed." The way his gaze locked on her implied he'd noticed more than just her profession.

A chill skated down her spine despite the warm summer sun. Him noticing her was only fair since she'd done nothing but notice him since she'd arrived.

"I like to write alone." He began strumming again, almost purposefully ignoring her. Just like that, he'd shut down. Smiling, friendly Cash was a memory.

"So do I. I'll be inside if you need me." She stood. He didn't try to stop her.

"The kitchen island has outlets if you want to work at the counter. Otherwise, there's an office upstairs. Doesn't get much use. I mostly work out here or in the studio downstairs."

"Thanks," she said, not meaning it.

At the door, she paused when he started singing "Lightning," the pull of his voice almost enough to make her linger and listen as he scratched out every heart-rending word. *Almost.*

Steeling her spine, she forced herself to walk inside.

Eight

The next morning Presley was downright chipper. The day was warm and sunny, the sky blue and clear. She practically skipped downstairs in her white gauzy cover-up, her bathing suit underneath.

After her run-in with Cash yesterday morning, she had retreated to the sanctuary of her laptop. The article about him was her priority, but the rest of her work hadn't magically stopped because she was here. She'd kept busy answering emails, writing blurbs and wrangling cute GIFs to post online celebrating a *Legally Blonde* remake. Thankfully, the assignments didn't require too much brainpower.

She and Cash had silently agreed on a truce and had reconvened by lunchtime. Will and Gavin stopped by to talk business around the same time Cash had opened the fridge in search of food.

Gavin had mentioned he was excited about a potential

sponsorship for Cash, but Will's focus had been solely on the progress of the album.

Watching their interaction as an only child had been a little overwhelming. While her parents doted on occasion, they were in no way as involved in her life as Cash's family was involved in his. Though he seemed to take their presence in stride.

Cash and Will had then filed downstairs to the studio, where Cash practiced a new song. Presley had been invited to watch but she'd made an excuse about needing to work. Which was true, but still an excuse. His singing on the deck had caused a full-on flashback, and she wasn't anxious to experience another one of those.

Cash also had a way of making her defenses climb sky-high. Being defensive tempted her to argue about the past, which would derail her goal while she was here. She hadn't come here to argue with him about the past. What was done was done.

Or at least it should have been.

As the practice sesh stretched into evening, pizzas arrived for dinner. She and Gavin had eaten upstairs. She'd asked a few softball questions about Elite Records and Gavin's star client list, typing notes into her laptop in between bites of her dinner. Cash hadn't emerged from the recording studio. She'd seen Will for a few seconds when he grabbed one of the pizza boxes, but he'd taken it downstairs.

Once Gavin left, Presley had retired to her room. She'd dozed off, waking around midnight when she heard Cash open and shut his office door, which was near the guest room on her side of the house. By then she'd decided to enjoy her stay here at *Chez Sutherland*, and stop worrying so damn much.

As work vacations went, she could do far worse than

a luxurious mansion perched on a lake, even if said mansion came outfitted with a surly musician.

That brought her to now, where she skipped to a stop in a kitchen. Cash stood at the countertop, his hair mussed, sleepily watching the coffeepot.

"Rough night?" she teased.

"Very funny," he replied, droll. "How'd you sleep?"

"Fine," she said, rather than tell him she'd heard him clattering around in the wee hours.

"Heading over to Elite in a bit if you want to come with." He sent a slow, thorough glance over her sunbathing attire. He still managed to make her skin sizzle with just a look. That was unfair. "You might want to change first."

She crossed one arm over her waist and bit down on her lip. The awareness permeating the air between them sure was inconvenient. "Are you sure you want me there?"

His head jerked on his neck, bringing his gaze to hers. "Why wouldn't I want you there?"

"Thought you liked to 'write alone,'" she repeated his words from yesterday.

"Write, yes, but I'll perform in front of you anytime, Pres."

The offer shouldn't sound nice, but it did. He was exhausting and she hadn't been here twenty-four hours. She was supposed to be wearing him down, not the other way around. "So you're recording today?"

"Yeah. Will and I eked out what we think is a workable song last night."

"You don't sound convinced."

He lifted his shoulders into a tight shrug. "Nothing feels right lately. There's usually a moment when everything clicks. When the words and the music come together. Sometimes that pours out at the beginning, other times not until the seventh or eighth time I lay down the track." His smile was almost sheepish. "That probably makes no sense."

"It does, actually. My articles don't come out great the first time, either. My boss, Delilah, says the magic is in the editing process."

"Do you agree?"

"Sometimes. Other times it's like you said, it pours out at the beginning."

He pulled two mugs from a cabinet and filled them with coffee. "Still take cream and sugar?"

"No sugar."

His eyebrows jumped like he hadn't expected that. He should have. People changed, and she'd changed a lot over the years.

He delivered her coffee with cream, leaving his black. His coffee hadn't changed. And maybe, she mused, neither had he. Maybe he was the same man capable of loving her and leaving her, the way he'd been on that long-ago rainy night.

Presley had changed from the gauzy white dress into a long, striped skirt, sandals and a white tank top. She looked good, but not as good as she had in a bright pink bikini that had been visible through the white sheer cover-up. If he closed his eyes, he could still picture it.

She'd pulled her hair into a high ponytail, her bright red locks glinting through the windows of his Bugatti on their drive over. She'd always been damn cute, but the cute he could handle. He didn't quite know what to make of her saucy, fiery attitude. She could turn it on when she needed to, that was for sure. She wasn't capitulating, didn't hesitate to tell him what she thought—or at least some of what she thought. He was sure there were plenty more thoughts bouncing around in her pretty head than what she'd shared with him so far.

They'd spent the better part of the morning at Elite Records. Cash had laid down a song he was calling "Fragile" and then he and his brother had gone over some of the other ideas for the album.

Will made a good sounding board. Not to mention he had a vested interest in Cash's album, specifically in the album going platinum. Success wasn't good only for Cash; it was good for his entire family. After college, success came at him like a tsunami, sweeping him up in the tide before he knew what happened. Some people had a slow and steady climb to the top. His was more like being shot out of a cannon.

He liked success for what it afforded him, so that he could do what he loved. The support of his fans gave him the freedom to write what he wanted, knowing they were along for the ride. After the DUI, it'd felt like that freedom had been taken from him. Like he was being corralled at every turn.

He'd rolled his eyes at his "bad boy" reputation at first, the moniker the result of desperate press grabbing for attention. Fans loved Cash, but they might have loved controversy even more. His reputation with women was far less scandalous than the gossip websites made it sound. Yes, he'd dated plenty, but he wasn't leaving a trail of broken hearts in his wake.

Though, he supposed Presley was the exception.

Since the mug shot, he'd been thrust into a different spotlight. "Bad influence" was a lot less charming than "bad boy." What pissed him off most was that he wasn't guilty of the crime he was currently paying penance for. Damned if he could prove it, though. The arresting officer hadn't changed a lick of his story since the night it'd happened, but Cash had been sober enough to notice the other man's shifty eyes.

Not that it mattered at this point. The damage had been done and had seriously messed with his head alongside his reputation. He'd been stuck on stupid for so many weeks, he wondered if he was capable of finishing this damn album.

Presley being in his immediate proximity wasn't helping him focus. Especially when she looked as cute and carelessly sexy as she did while doing nothing but walking across a room. More than once he regretted never making love to her while he'd had the chance. Maybe if he had, he wouldn't be so damn curious about her now.

He closed his eyes and blew out a breath.

"Don't sweat it," Will told Cash now, evidently noticing his frustration. Thankfully Will didn't know why his brother was frustrated, or Cash would never live it down. "You'll get there."

Cash was prepared to work well into the evening, but he'd left Presley in Gavin's empty office too long already. He headed down the hall, the telltale clacking of keyboard keys falling silent when he rapped his knuckles on the door.

He let himself in and she looked up, her blue eyes wide.

Damn. Cute.

"You want to grab some lunch?" He glanced at the half-eaten candy bar at her elbow. "Or was that it?"

"The commercials were wrong. It didn't satisfy me at all."

They left the studio for downtown, passing by the boardwalk and a league of barely dressed men and women on the shoreline. The sky was as blue as it'd ever been, the sun almost blinding considering he'd been stuck in a windowless studio all morning.

Every building they passed, Presley read the sign aloud. A tattoo shop, coffee spot and, finally, the restaurant she decided she'd like to try. "How can you not have lunch at a place called Cheatin' Eats? It's positively *naughty*."

It was more than that. Cheatin' Eats belonged to Mags Dumond. Typically he was dead set against lining the woman's pockets, but he'd promised to let Presley pick so here they were. At least he knew he wouldn't run into Mags here. Like most of this town, she owned the place, but didn't participate in running it.

He requested a table outside and they sat. Presley, sunglasses tilted up, sunshine glinting off the lenses, let out a breezy sigh. "This sure beats being stuck in my office in Florida."

"You there a lot?"

"Almost exclusively. Hopefully I'll be doing more traveling in the near future." She smiled at him. "This article is sort of make-or-break. No pressure."

She opened her mouth to say something else, but it didn't come. Her jaw dropped as she watched a couple stroll by. She leaned over the table and whispered, "Oh my God. Is that…?"

"Asher Knight? Looks like him."

Her lashes fluttered. "I loved his band Knight Time. I hear they're recording another album. Do you think that's true? Do you think it'll have country music vibes? Is that why he's here?"

Cash couldn't help chuckling. "He wouldn't be the first rock star to cross over. I thought you were cool under pressure with celebrities. Pull yourself together, woman."

Her cheeks pinked. "I am. Usually. Everyone gets starstruck sometimes."

"You're not starstruck with me," he fished shamelessly. Hell, he'd been the one struck dumb. He'd been the one who'd kissed her before thinking it through. He could blame decades-old claustrophobia and proximity all he wanted, but deep down he knew why he'd done it.

He glanced at her lips. He'd just…wanted to.

The waiter arrived and they both ordered cheeseburgers. Pres opted for sweet potato fries while he went for the beer-battered onion rings.

"Do you eat here often?" she asked.

"Never." He sipped his iced tea.

"Is the food bad or something?"

"Not at all. Mags Dumond owns it."

"The First Lady of Beaumont Bay?"

"One and the same."

Her lips quirked. Mags's bulldozing personality was infamous 'round these parts.

"You should have told me. We could have eaten anywhere."

"Yeah, but you wanted to eat here." And he'd liked giving her what she wanted. He'd liked seeing that sparkle of excitement in her eye.

"The name is like her record label," Presley said, figuring it out. "I should have put that together."

"I can't forget. She asks constantly if I'm going to jump ship at Elite and record with her instead."

"Even though your own brother owns the studio?"

"Even though."

"That's…ostentatious."

"That's Mags."

Presley's pursed pink lips wrapped around her straw and she sucked down some water. That wasn't so much cute as it was hot. Made him remember kissing her. Made him think of doing other things with her. *And to her.* He forced his eyes away.

"Weren't you at one of Mags's parties the night of the DUI?"

He stiffened, caught off guard by her inquisitive tone. He should have expected that question. Presley, a reporter, was doing her job. "Yeah. Black-tie fundraiser."

"Fancy."

"Around here, fancy's commonplace." He nodded in the direction Asher Knight and his wife, Gloria, had gone. "That wasn't the only celebrity in town who doesn't live here full-time. People clamor to be added to her guest list."

"Including you and your brothers?"

"Nah, we're permanently on that list. She keeps her enemies close," he said, only half joking. "And so do we."

"We'll fix it," she said, sounding confident.

"My reputation?" He let out a humorless laugh. "Unless you can erase the media's memory, not sure you can fix a bogus DUI."

"Bogus? So you're innocent?" She lifted her water glass.

"I'd never make that claim." He sent her a cheeky smile. "It was late. I was tired."

"Maybe you should've been charged with driving while up past your bedtime instead."

He chuckled. She'd always been clever.

"Did you have a date that night?"

His smile vanished. He'd do well to remember they weren't old friends playing catch-up. She was here to write about his family—him in particular. A prospect he'd never be fully comfortable with. "No date."

"I imagine it'd be hard to date when everyone around

you is speculating about your love life. Especially when you're writing an album. It's only natural to wonder about who influences the lyrics."

He sputtered into his iced tea and had to mop it from his shirt with a napkin. "Wrong pipe."

"Talking about exes does that."

So did his ex talking *to him* about his exes. For Cash, a private life was virtually nonexistent. But he hadn't expected Pres to bring up the one topic he'd refused to answer whenever it'd been broached by a member of the press. He wasn't sharing the inspiration behind "Lightning" with anyone. Especially her.

Their burgers were delivered. In between munching on a fry, she asked, "Is there someone special in your life right now?"

He lifted his sandwich. "You're nosy. Did anyone ever tell you that?"

"Everyone tells me that." She didn't take offense. Nor did she let up. "So, are you?"

"No. Are you?"

"I'm focusing on my career."

"Same," he said, then stuffed the burger in his mouth to keep from saying more.

The truth was he'd managed to live his life separate from the women he dated even while he'd dated them. They knew the score, honored the code, and he didn't have to worry about breaking another heart.

After breaking Pres's young heart, he'd consoled himself that at least they hadn't slept together. That would have made moving on harder, and he didn't only mean for her. He'd already been in neck-deep with her. Stripping her bare and taking her virginity would have made it damn near impossible to walk away from her, and by then he'd already made up his mind to leave.

Not sleeping with her was both the smartest thing he did back then—or didn't do, as it were—and also one of his biggest regrets. The other big one was selfishly dogging his own goals and leaving her in the wreckage. He'd been so focused on himself back then, on achieving success and stardom.

Presley, either too angry to speak to him or for her own self-preservation, hadn't reached out to him after he left. He hadn't reached out to her, either. When he'd heard she'd been in town two years ago talking to Gavin, he'd been pissed off. She'd sneaked back into town to talk to his family, never bothering to let Cash know about it. He'd blamed Gavin for the subterfuge, but it wasn't his brother's fault. No wonder Gav hadn't alerted Cash of her arrival this time. Cash hadn't exactly been gracious before.

What he'd never shared with anyone was why her avoiding him had bothered him so much. Seeing him would have hurt her, and he guessed that even years later, she hadn't been able to forgive him for destroying her heart while prioritizing his goals. Damned if he could blame her.

"Did you ever?" he asked. "Have someone special?"

She took a bite of her burger, proving she wasn't a big fan of answering questions about her personal life, either.

"Well?" he prompted. "Did you?"

"I've had a boyfriend or two since, you know, *us*." She shrugged and he wondered if it was to downplay her mentioning the "us" thing—the "them" thing. He didn't make it a habit to rehash old relationships either, which explained the awkwardness. "Nothing as impressive as a famous sitcom actor like Heather Bell or an award-winning singer like Carla Strouse."

He'd be damned if she didn't expertly steer the conversation back to him and his celebrity exes.

"I was the only famous person you dated, huh?" he asked, deflecting.

"You weren't famous when we dated. Only after you left."

He didn't think she meant it as a jab, but he felt the knife-slice all the same. Leaving her crying in her bed hadn't been easy. It'd nearly gutted him. Which was probably why he offered up a few details without her having to ask. "Famous people date each other because it's easy. We have the whole fishbowl lifestyle in common."

"So you dated Carla and Heather out of convenience? No sparks?"

Sex, yes. Sparks, not so much. He hadn't felt "sparks" in years. Unless he counted a certain elevator ride with his lunch date.

"The women you've dated are drop-dead gorgeous. You would have made beautiful babies together." Presley sounded nonchalant but her eyes swam with another emotion. That same hurt he'd just been thinking about.

"The women I dated were nice enough, but there wasn't more than attraction to glue it together. And... off the record?"

She nodded, leaning forward a little in her seat.

"You're prettier than any of 'em."

Her lips pursed. "I thought you were going to say something serious."

"I am serious," he defended. But she didn't believe him. Maybe it'd be easier if she thought the years between them had erased every emotion they'd shared. As if every memory of her in his arms had gone up in smoke the moment he'd crossed the Tennessee border.

Thing was, it hadn't worked out that way. Cash had told her he'd left to pursue the dream absolutely eating him alive. That was true, but what he hadn't admitted was that committing to her would have cost him both his time and attention—two things he couldn't afford to give up while throwing everything he had at being a musician.

It was an ugly truth he still hadn't forgiven himself for. And if he couldn't forgive himself, he had little hope that Presley ever would.

Nine

Not again.

For the last two mornings, Cash had been writing in his studio rather than outside. Sometimes the change of scenery helped him create. Lately, he'd been chugging along and, while writing was not seamless, at least he'd found momentum.

Also for the last two mornings, he had stopped cold on his way to the coffeepot for a refill after becoming completely distracted by the vision on the other side of the French doors.

Presley Cole had taken to sunning herself on his deck.

She wasn't naked but damn near. Dark sunglasses were perched on her nose, her red hair aglow under the noonday sun. She was on her back on one of his oversize bath towels, her pink bikini bright against crisp white terry cloth.

Today her arms were at her sides, one knee up, the other leg closest to him stretched long and straight. Perky breasts rounded the incredibly sexy string bikini top. A long time ago he'd had his hands on those breasts. He'd had his *mouth* on them. He'd made her come while touching them.

He blinked hard and forced his thoughts to the present, something he'd done a lot lately. Having her here was like opening a time capsule, one he'd prefer stayed sealed and buried. It wasn't easy to come face-to-face with what he'd missed out on in the years since they'd lost contact. Having her here, knowing she was as single as he was and sleeping in his guest bedroom and sunbathing on his deck, made focusing on anything hard. And that wasn't the only thing that was hard.

He glanced down at his empty coffee mug. He'd originally come up for a refill. After lapsing into a brief fantasy involving Presley minus her bikini top and with his mouth on her, perhaps a cold drink would be a better idea. He pulled a jug of homemade sun tea from the fridge, hesitating briefly before grabbing two glasses.

For three mornings, he'd attempted to push thoughts of her aside. He'd tried to keep up a wall, distancing himself from her like he would any other reporter. Problem was, she wasn't any other reporter. This was Presley Cole, and she'd crumbled his wall now the same as she had years ago.

In other words, his tactics weren't working.

She wasn't leaving for a few more days, so he was going to have to find a better coping mechanism than pretending he didn't want her. Today, rather than avoid her, he'd try something new and dive in headfirst.

He strolled outside with the iced tea glasses in hand. Walking the other direction—as in *away* from her— would be smarter than inviting her to dinner and seducing her, but he planned on doing both anyway.

Whether she forgave him for leaving her all those years ago or not, he saw no reason why they couldn't satisfy their desire for each other in some sort of in-between realm. A kind of sexual purgatory, that would be more like a reprieve. Then he could stop fixating on what he could have done with her back then and just freaking do it already. The what-if scenarios had lingered in his head for too long. At this point, he'd be better off knowing what he was missing. Now to get her to believe that too.

"Thirsty?" He was parched now that he stood over her glistening body. Her belly was flat and bare, sweat dotting her skin thanks to the hot, midday sun. She was as tempting as if she was lying on a platter. Answering beads of perspiration dampened his upper lip.

"How'd you know?" She pushed her sunglasses on top of her head and sat up. She blinked blue eyes the color of the lake before taking her glass and folding her legs beneath her.

He sat on the freshly stained deck boards, close enough to smell the coconut-scented oil on her skin. God, he wanted a taste of her. Just once. Just so he could settle the debate in his head about how good she'd tasted back then. He'd had his lips on hers the other day and that had proven his memory for shit. Her kiss had been far more potent and consuming than any he remembered from their past. Or maybe he'd forced himself to downplay her potency, knowing he couldn't satisfy both his desire to leave and his desire to have her before he did.

"I love the heat. It's the one tolerable element of Florida," she said.

"There's only one?"

She shrugged one freckled shoulder. He wanted to trace those freckles with his fingertips, slip the bikini top off and follow the path of his touch with his tongue.

He guzzled half of his drink and watched a boat zip by on the water instead. He wasn't stupid. Seducing Presley this time around required finesse.

"I love Florida but I'm tired of being there all the time. I've always wanted to travel. To see the world. Somehow the years passed and I haven't moved an inch. I thought I was on a journey up a mountain, but it ended up being more of a circular track. I looked up and realized I hadn't actually gone anywhere."

"You're here," he pointed out, a fact he hadn't been able to ignore.

"Yes. I am. I like this town. It's lush and beautiful. I can see why the rich and famous come here for leisure."

"It's home." It had been for his entire life. His parents had leaped on the real estate opportunities here, never expecting all four of their boys to go into the music industry instead.

"When I visited two years ago, I couldn't picture you here. I figured you must have changed, become a different sort of person who prefers luxury and the finer things in life."

"And now?" he couldn't help asking.

"Well, your house is luxurious, but you're…you. You love your family and songwriting and…" She bit her lip, seeming to think better of what she'd been about to say.

"And?" he prompted.

"It's corny."

"Honey, I write love songs for a living. Corny's my jam."

She blushed but held his gaze. The endearment, a by-product of Southern charm, called up the memory of Presley's honey-sweet skin.

"You make what could be a very snooty town seem laid-back." She sipped her tea before adding, "Comfortable."

So despite his attempts to be prickly, she saw right through him. He questioned the wisdom of seducing her after all, especially given how observant she was when it came to him.

Didn't change the fact that he wanted her. Badly. Lately, it'd been all he could think about, which was risky for him considering she was keen to ferret out his secrets. Letting her close could be disastrous for his career—and for another part of him he didn't want to examine too closely.

She straightened the center of her top and jostled those gorgeous breasts, and he told his second thoughts to go to hell. Some fires were worth the burn.

"Am I hogging your writing spot?" She sounded sincere. Like he'd come out here to reprimand her. She likely had no idea how she'd affected him this week, while she wore next to nothing or hell, even when she'd worn *something*. Her understated beauty had always been his weakness.

Frustrated, and not only sexually, he let her know exactly what he thought of her sunbathing in his "writing spot."

"Yes," he answered. "You're hogging my spot."

Her eyebrows flew up. He'd surprised her. He was about to surprise her more.

"I like it. I have liked it every day since you started coming out here. Wearing that tiny bathing suit, on your back, your hair spread around you like a fiery halo."

"Oh." Her mouth dropped open softly. He smiled. He'd been right. She had no idea how she tempted him.

"Do you want to go to dinner with me tonight?"

He wasn't sure if she'd say yes or hell no, but a jolt of satisfaction shot down his arms when he asked. He missed taking risks. He'd played it safe since becoming famous, recent bogus DUI aside.

He hadn't come this far to back off now. He was done resisting her.

"Sure," she answered, appearing way less affected than he was. Of course, she probably wasn't sitting here imagining licking him from head to toe the way he was imagining doing to her. "What's the occasion?"

"You have questions for your article I haven't answered. Figured we'd do it over dinner and get you out of this house. Into a nice dress. On the town."

All true, but not his main motivation for tonight.

Her pink lips pulled into a smirk he was dying to lean in and kiss. "How *nice* does this dress have to be?"

"Bord du Lac is jacket required. They have a coat check. A sommelier. I can't send you back to Tallahassee without experiencing the upper crust of Beaumont Bay."

"Well, who am I to turn down a fancy dinner with a famous musician?" Like before, she'd tried to sound nonchalant, but the sentiment didn't fly. He was too close to her to miss the excitement flickering in her eyes.

Eyes that dipped to his mouth and up again.

The glance was brief, but he'd noticed. Maybe she had been attempting to resist him after all. Trying to keep from fantasizing about *him*. There was a tantalizing thought.

She'd turned the elevator ride from hell into a slice of heaven the moment she'd kissed him back and pressed her body against his. If that happened now, he'd have a hard time not hiking her skirt up, pushing her back to the wall and begging her to take every inch of him.

It would be indecent. Inappropriate.

Fantastic.

"It's a date," he said, making sure there was no doubt

in her mind what tonight was about. If she gave him a second chance to kiss her, he'd take that kiss as far as she'd allow. He let his eyes trail down her body before shaking his head gently. "Damn, Presley."

Then he stood and went back inside before he changed his mind about tonight and attempted to seduce her right now.

Presley had successfully collected Hannah Banks's phone number from Gavin. She'd told him she needed a woman's advice on where to shop for a nice dress for the restaurant she'd be going to with Cash tonight.

Gavin had tried to placate her with, "It's Beaumont Bay, not the Oscars. Wear a dress. Any dress," To which Presley had replied, "Strapless or sleeves? Do I need a wrap? Is the air-conditioning usually cranked or is there outdoor seating? What about shoes? Are the floors shined to a fine polish, in which case I should skip the spiked heel in favor of a wedge, or—?"

That's when he'd cut her off and shared Hannah's number.

When she'd called Hannah's number, however, her twin sister, Hallie, had answered instead. It made sense given Hallie was Hannah's manager. Presley explained her predicament and was surprised when Hallie invited Presley to her apartment to "peruse" her closet. Presley hadn't wanted to be rude, so she accepted the offer, even though she doubted she'd find anything she liked from Hallie's neutral, conservative wardrobe. But she drove over there anyway, racking her brain for a way to politely decline when she didn't find what she was looking for.

Now, Presley stood in the closet of Hallie's first-floor apartment gawping at the clothes in front of her. On one side of the walk-in was what she'd expected: neutrals and black, demure hemlines and classic, timeless style.

On the other side hung the antithesis of "demure" and made her wonder if Hallie had a split personality. The clothes on the left were high-end, some with tags dangling from the sleeves. Some had sequins, others lace. Long formal dresses best suited for awards shows and shorter skirts perfect for a nightclub. They were in rainbow order, ranging from vivid reds and pinks to warm peaches and orange. Vibrant yellow to autumnal mustard to spring green, and sky blues fading into moody purples and plums. Beneath the gowns were rows of shoes in every color, size, shape and style.

"Wow," Presley muttered. What else was there to say?

"Hannah gives me the castoffs from her sponsorships. She receives tons of clothes from designers and companies who beg her to be photographed wearing them. She helps them sell a lot of clothes that way."

Presley stroked the skirt of an emerald green dress. The fabric was exquisite. "I can imagine." She frowned over her shoulder at Hallie, a copy of Hannah with her pert nose, warm hazel eyes and wide, sensual mouth. She wore a plain beige wrap dress and white sneakers, her blond hair in a braid down her back. Her style was understated, but she was every bit as beautiful as her sister. "You don't wear any of these?"

She shook her head and offered a small smile. When she did, a pair of dimples punctuated her cheeks.

"You have dimples." Presley hadn't noticed before. "Does Hannah?"

"Just me." Hallie blushed. "Dimples are a genetic defect. It makes sense that Hannah doesn't have them."

Presley wanted to hug Hallie and assure her there wasn't anything defective about her, but she didn't know the other woman well enough. She didn't want to make Hallie uncomfortable, but she couldn't keep from touching the other woman's arm in a show of support. "Most men would argue the defect thing. Dimples turn them into puddles. They melt at the sight of them."

"Really?" Hallie's smile lost some of the caution it held before. Presley wondered if there was a guy in particular who'd popped into the twin's head. She didn't have a chance to ask before Hallie went on to say, "Back to the task at hand. I may not look it, but I know how to dress for a nice dinner. I used to help Hannah before she hired a professional stylist."

Hallie slid a dress aside and then another, plucking down a red one and then a green one and taking turns holding them in front of Presley. This went on for another five minutes before Hallie decided they were done browsing.

"This one." Hallie's dimples reappeared as she pressed the hanger to Presley's front. "This is it. I'm sure of it."

Presley faced a tall mirror in the closet and tried to imagine herself in the gorgeous dress. Tried to imagine how Cash would react to seeing her wearing it. "It's not too much?"

"No way. Try it on. I can do minor alterations if needed. And please tell me you wear a size eight or eight-and-half shoe?"

"Eight," Presley answered.

"Perfect." Hallie bent to the shoe rack while Presley stepped into the adjoining bathroom and pulled on the very expensive, very finely made, very beautiful dress that Hallie had chosen.

As luck would have it, it fit like a glove.

So did the shoes.

Ten

Bord du Lac was jacket-required fancy, but there wasn't a tie requirement. Fine by Cash. He'd pulled on a dark pants and a jacket over an open-at-the-collar white button-down, threw on cowboy boots and called it a day. He didn't bother shaving since "scruff" was the look he preferred—and the look a poll favored according to a recent magazine article—and he did his usual hair routine, which was running his hands through it and letting it fall. A splash of cologne on his neck was the only fanciful part he bothered with, in case Presley leaned in for a whiff.

He stepped out of the master bedroom and jogged downstairs, expecting to wait for her for another ten or twenty or thirty minutes. He was surprised to find her standing at the kitchen counter, rummaging through a small sparkly handbag. She looked up when he reached the bottom step, where he was awestruck by the vision before him.

Her red hair was down, falling in big, bold waves around her deliciously bare shoulders. His eyes ate up her creamy skin on display, and there was a lot of it to enjoy. The dress was strapless, hugging her breasts and nipping in at the waist before flaring to allow for her luscious hips. He took in those long legs, capped by a pair of high-heeled shoes in the same slate-gray color of the dress.

She turned and the overhead lights caught the rhinestones—slate gray wasn't the only color on the dress. There were also icy-blue and almost-black bits, and the whole of it twinkled like the nighttime sky. When he finally managed to reroute his eyes to her face, her bubblegum pink mouth was parted innocently. Her thick, jet-black lashes weren't so innocent, closing down over blue eyes and causing parts of him to stir with interest.

Parts of him that wanted nothing more than to say *screw dinner*.

"I'm ready early." She sent one hand down the side of the dress. His gaze followed her hand hungrily. The dress stopped way before it should've—high on her thighs—and dipped low in the front, too, giving him a view of her cleavage.

Drawn in, he walked over until he was right next to her and could look down at her from his height. With great effort he unstuck his tongue from the roof of his mouth. "You look incredible."

She tipped her chin, sending her hair falling down her back. The woman was sex in stilettos.

"I have a wrap in case it's cold in there. I wasn't sure." She fiddled with a piece of material next to her purse, almost absently, but she never took her eyes off him. "Cash?"

He didn't know why she said his name, but he was already on the move. His lips touched hers for a soft, brief kiss. So soft, it shouldn't have turned him on. So brief, he wanted to howl when it was over.

Feeling like a dope for rushing in, and yet not the least bit sorry for it, he smiled and moved away. "It's a sin to hide those shoulders, but bring the wrap."

He collected his keys and followed her through the foyer, pulling open the front door for her. By the time she folded into his car, he wasn't sure how he was going to successfully drive to Bord du Lac with his eyeballs glued to her legs.

He succeeded, but only because he'd trained his gaze on the windshield like his life depended on it. Distracted driving wasn't limited to cell phones and fiddling with the radio. His ex-girlfriend riding shotgun and crossing one silky leg over the other while wearing tall, spiked, bad-girl heels was enough to send him flying off an overpass.

Inside the restaurant, they were led to a private back corner reserved for famous folks. Before Cash's fame peaked, he'd been mildly amused by the idea of famous people needing a "safe haven" for dining, but now he understood it. A visit to a nice restaurant could quickly become a nuisance. The few dates he'd been on in public were documented by every diner, whether they were a member of the press or not.

Even now, as he walked with Presley through Bord du Lac, he felt cell phone cameras pointing in their direction. He hoped he wasn't making her the topic of a tawdry headline. "Don't look now," he murmured in her ear, "but we're being watched."

She scanned the dining room before whispering up at him, "I can handle it."

Which reminded him that this was not the Presley from a decade ago. She hadn't curled into a ball and withered away. She'd followed her dreams just like he'd hoped, gaining newfound confidence thanks to her achievements.

Their table was hidden behind decorative privacy panels, the booth backs high and ensuring they wouldn't be bothered. Their nook was cozy, but big enough to accommodate multiple plates and glasses. The paneling extended on two sides with an opening wide enough for the waiter to stand and take their order or pour the wine, which he did before giving them privacy.

"This is very elegant." Presley lifted a balloon-shaped glass and sipped the red wine. He did the same. She'd already moved her silverware so that the ends lined up on the napkin, touched the edge of the candleholder to see if it was able to be repositioned and drummed her fingers along the leather-bound menu at her right elbow. All signs that she was nervous, and doing her damnedest to pretend she wasn't. "I'm glad Hallie loaned me this dress."

"*I'm* glad Hallie loaned you that dress." His words came out on a growl. "You couldn't look more beautiful if you tried, Pres."

She surprised him by smirking. "Is that why *you* kissed *me*? *Again?*"

He deserved that. "Yeah, but if you don't want me to kiss you again, say the word."

It was a test, but she didn't say no. Instead she relinquished her wineglass before leaning back in her seat to study him. "What's your favorite Cash Sutherland song?"

Back on the clock.

His guard climbed, a habit he'd honed after learning the press went for the jugular. He'd like to believe Presley wasn't after blood. Still, he gave her a canned answer.

"My songs are like my babies. I couldn't pick a favorite child and neither could I pick a favorite song. They're all a part of me."

"That's cute." She tipped her head in disbelief. She was the cute one. "Now the truth. Favorite song. And why."

When he didn't answer, she added, "I'm not publishing a recycled Cash Sutherland article a hundred other writers have penned. I want the real you. The public wants to know the man behind the guitar is a genuine person."

Genuine. He liked that word. He wanted to live up to it. Aspired to reach it. Fame, while it allowed him to share his most personal feelings on stage, could also be inauthentic. It forced him to smile when he didn't feel like smiling, or perform when he'd rather be sacked out in front of the television. His fans thought they knew him, but they only knew a version of him. *Genuine is the summit of the mountain I'm climbing.*

"One sec." He pulled his cell phone out of his pocket and pecked those words into the notes app on his cell phone. He wasn't sure if he'd stumbled across lyrics to a new song or if it was a flash of an idea that wouldn't pan out. Either way, he couldn't risk losing it.

"Did you suddenly have a burst of inspiration?"

He considered the sweet, beautiful redhead across from him and thought, *hell yeah I'm inspired.* "Hit me out of nowhere but I couldn't ignore it."

The same could be said of her.

"'Lightning,'" he answered belatedly, and this time, honestly. "'Lightning' is my favorite Cash Sutherland song. I wrote it and rewrote it for years. I agonized over every word and practiced it until my fingers bled. I can sing it in my sleep. I can perform it and call up the way it felt to put those words to music for the first time. It's part of me, that song—that's the truth. Indelible. Inseparable. Undeniable."

Her features softened. The facade of cunning and

eager journalist fell away, leaving just Presley. As if his honesty pierced the armor she hadn't known she'd worn.

"Pure," she said. "Your love for that song. That must be why it resonates. Why whenever you perform it, it's like you're singing a memory."

She didn't know it, but she had him dead to rights. He was singing a memory all right. A memory of a certain red-haired, blue-eyed and, yes, *pure* girl he'd been halfway head over heels for.

Presley Cole. The one who got away.

Or, more accurately, the one he'd left behind.

He couldn't let her go home to the Sunshine State without them finally sharing the one thing they hadn't. He couldn't live with another decade of regret. While he believed the lyrics of "Lightning," which said it never struck twice, he would accept a few distant flashes in its place.

A night or two with Presley in his arms would give him an idea of what he'd missed out on years ago, satisfying the hollow ache that had resided in the center of his chest since. And maybe, her walking away from him this time would heal the hurt from what he'd done to her. Win, win.

She was bold, smart. Driven. She could hold her own anywhere, and with anyone. He desperately wanted to find out if that would be true in his bedroom.

Throughout dinner she continued quizzing him. About his music and the new album. What it was like to work with his brothers closely. If there was any competition between them for Biggest Alpha Male—her words. That question made him laugh out loud. No, they hadn't competed. They were each in their own corner of this crazy industry and content to share the spotlight.

Halfway through dinner, his guard dropped, which

was less about the wine and more because of the company. Presley was still easy to talk to. The word *genuine* bounced around his head again, a few disjointed chords and notes bouncing with it. He wouldn't dare take his attention from her to write them down.

"How'd Will deal with the duet between you and Hannah Banks?" Presley swallowed the end of her wine and set the glass aside. "You and his wife-to-be essentially sang a love song to each other. Did it make him jealous?"

"No." Again, Cash laughed. "Hannah and Will are inseparable. He had nothing to worry about, and he knew it. As wonderful as she is, she's not my type."

"Famous and beautiful isn't your type?" She tapped her chin in faux consideration. "Your exes Heather and Carla might disagree."

"What about my ex-girlfriend from college?" he asked, his voice low. "Would she disagree?"

"I'm neither of those things."

"You are a *famous* journalist—"

"Hardly."

"—and the most beautiful woman I've ever laid eyes on."

Her delicate throat moved as she swallowed. She might not believe him, but he was telling the truth. As beautiful as the women he'd been photographed with were, none of them were Presley.

"Cash Sutherland," she scolded, her tone playful, "are you trying to seduce me?"

"Yeah," he answered. "I am." That wiped the smile off her face. "And if you want to end this night in my bed, your arms and legs wrapped around me, a light sheen of sweat coating our bodies after we've wrung each other out in the best way imaginable, I suggest you let me."

Eleven

Presley didn't make it two steps into Cash's house before her purse was taken from her hands, her back was pressed against the closed front door and her mouth was covered with his.

She reacted the way any red-blooded woman would, by wrapping her arms around his neck and accepting his tongue into her mouth. The kiss had the urgency of the one in the elevator, but none of the haste. As he proved a moment later when his hand tightened at her lower back and he slowed down.

Way down.

His lips moved over hers in a soft, rhythmic way before they moved to her neck and *oh yes*, that was so much better. She arched her back and closed her eyes, lost in the sensation of his hands on her waist and the scruff of his jaw scraping the sensitive skin of her throat.

"You smell good." His voice was a low rumble. She'd

always loved that deep baritone. It made her feel safe and it made her feel sexy, especially right before he nibbled on her earlobe.

When he backed away, her hair clung to his cheek. She liked seeing it there, the red strands mingling with his short, dark facial hair. His eyelids were low, his full mouth damp. He was so hot it was criminal.

"I see you decided to let me seduce you." A cocky grin slid across his mouth and she couldn't help smiling back at him. She hooked a finger into his belt loop and tugged him closer. His hips bumped hers, the sturdy ridge of his erection evident and tempting.

"What base are we stoppin' at tonight, Pres?" he murmured as his hands climbed her torso. He paused on her rib cage, just shy of cupping her breasts.

"Home run, cowboy," she breathed, trying to sound more confident than she felt. She felt a lot of other things. Jittery and excited. Impatient and willing.

After he'd left her in Florida, she'd cried her heart out. She'd also kicked her own rear end around campus for saving her precious virginity instead of sleeping with him while she could have. A year later she'd gifted her V-card to a guy in her Advanced Writing 202 class and had been as underwhelmed as she'd expected. He was nice enough, but she hadn't cared about him the way she'd cared about Cash.

The out-of-place memory made her sad and Cash, who was close enough to see straight through to her soul, noticed. His eyes flashed with concern and his mouth pulled into a loose frown.

No way would she let the past ruin this moment. "I'm not letting you escape this time," she said and then she kissed him hard enough that he'd forget what he saw.

It worked. The next words out of his mouth were, "Climb your sweet ass up the stairs and go to my room."

Liking his bossy side way too much, she turned and scurried for the stairs, her borrowed heels clicking along the way to the top. He caught her easily, linking their hands and leading her to his room.

She looked down at their arms, his deeply tanned skin and thick, calloused fingers looped with her smaller, paler fingers.

What are you doing?

Years ago, he'd broken her heart. It was big and it was unresolved. She'd sworn she wouldn't allow herself to be towed in by his magnetism when she began this assignment. So why wasn't she saying good-night instead of following him to his room?

Because.

She'd missed out on him once. She wouldn't miss out again.

What happened tonight would be a gift she gave her past self. And her present self. Her future self would have to learn to live without him, but she'd done it once. She could do it again.

At the entrance to his bedroom, he paused, leaned on the doorframe and gripped her hips with his palms. Those palms slid up her dress until they reached her breasts, but this time, he held them and drew his thumbs over her nipples. Without a bra, they leaped to attention. Then he moved those rough-feeling hands over her beaded dress and around, undoing the zipper at the back. When the front sagged, he tugged her top down and exposed her, his eyes going black as his widening pupils ate up the caramel brown of his irises.

She'd always loved when he touched her bare breasts. Her nipples were sensitive and currently shooting a zillion electrical charges straight to the apex of her thighs. Her breathing sped up and her fists clenched helplessly at his button-down shirt.

"Some things haven't changed. I know what you like."

Proving it, he dipped his head and took her nipple on his tongue. Slowly, he circled the tender bud as her eyes rolled back in ecstasy. Her hands relocated to his head, where she gave his thick hair a tug. He gently bit and then soothed her with his tongue.

After a few breathless moments of bliss, he backed her into the dark room, his mouth never leaving her breast. Then she was in the air, being tossed onto the bed. He climbed over top of her, his dark head lowering to her other breast, his finger plucking the nipple he'd rendered both damp and turgid. Her hips rose and fell, mimicking what she wanted most. Cash seemed content to make her wait.

Finally, he guided his hand up her skirt, fisted her lacy underwear and rolled them down her legs. There was a frustrating moment where they became tangled with her shoes, which he insisted she keep on. Since he insisted while sliding his fingers up her inner thigh, she decided not to argue.

He stroked into her and, wet and ready, she easily accepted his finger. His tongue went back to work on her breast, sucking and pulling while his thumb joined the action, stroking her clit. She jolted and felt his smile against her skin. He knew what she liked, all right.

They hadn't had sex years ago, but he'd made it his personal mission to find a way around her rules. He'd found all the loopholes—and had managed to gift her the best orgasms of her life. She'd given herself several since, sometimes imagining his fingers between her legs, his mouth on her breast, but those imaginings paled in comparison with the real Cash Sutherland.

"Come for my fingers and I'll give you my mouth," he murmured against her nipple as she shook in his arms.

He continued his sensual assault and not long after she orgasmed as he'd commanded. The release was long and easy and freaking *fantastic*.

"Good girl," she heard him say and then vaguely became aware of him unzipping her dress the rest of the way, his hand at her back. "Arms around my neck, sweetheart. I have more kissing to do, only lower this time."

"Cash, you don't h-have to," she stammered, overwhelmed by what he was suggesting. He'd never gone down on her. And now, with a fresh Cash-induced orgasm lighting her bloodstream, she wasn't sure she could handle more.

"*Have to* has nothing to do with it." On his knees in front of her, he unbuttoned his shirt and pulled it off his shoulders. He'd stayed in shape over the years, filling out with muscle. The width suited him, the dark hair over his pectorals unashamedly masculine.

He'd been good-looking then. He was hotter than hell now.

Not only was his chest deliciously defined, so were his abs. She wouldn't mind exploring every hill and valley on his torso. A perfect innie belly button sat just above a trail of dark hair that disappeared into his pants. Behind his fly, his cock gave a peppy jerk and she squeezed her knees together. Then she nearly hyperventilated when he undid his belt and drew down his zipper.

"You're not making this easy on me."

"Looks pretty hard, actually," she said with a grin.

He gave her an admonishing glare as he stood and

pulled off his clothes. He returned to the bed, still wearing black boxer briefs.

She shoved his chest with her high heel. "Those, too. Take them off."

He grabbed her ankle, pulled her leg to one side, took a long-enough-to-make-her-squirm gander at her naked body and then said, "And if I don't?"

"Don't make me come up there," she warned.

He laughed and any residual nerves faded away with it. To her delight, he stood again and shoved his fingers into the sides of those briefs, pushing them down his legs. His erection was on display, hard and glistening at the tip. She bit down on her lip. She was done being patient.

"Let's have sex. Don't worry about that other part." She nodded to encourage his agreement but he didn't agree. Not at all.

Grabbing both her ankles, he gently spread her legs and wedged his shoulders between her thighs. He looked good there. Really good. Her heart pattered out a desperate rhythm.

"Haven't you ever had anyone do this for you?" he asked, his eyes on her most private part, his thumb stroking her folds.

"Cash," she gasped. She licked her lips, her nerves returning. "It's okay, really."

She lost his touch and when she looked down at him this time, he was frowning. "Seriously?"

"I—it's not a big deal. I just, it's not something I enjoy?" She didn't mean to ask, but she'd asked. Over the years she'd convinced herself she wasn't missing out, but with Cash poised over her, preparing to deliver a tongue lashing that would be her first—and probably the best—she was positive she'd enjoy it.

His smile widened, a feral glint in his eye. "Damn, I'm excited. Here I've been thinking you experienced everything without me and I'm the first one who will—"

"Don't say it." The words were rushed out, and he obeyed her request in the best way imaginable. His tongue slicked over her center and a long moan escaped her throat. That was… That felt very nice. Incredible. *Indescribable.*

He cupped her ass and yanked her closer to his face, and then reached behind his head to pull off her shoes and toss them on the floor. "Second thought, you might impale me given you've yet to experience this."

"Safety first," she murmured. This time when he laughed it reverberated down her legs since he'd already set his mouth to her.

He toyed with her at first, delivering light, even strokes before picking up the pace and then slowing down again. Meanwhile she fisted the bedsheets helplessly, her hips lifting and rising to meet each stroke. When he homed in on one particular spot, her next exhalation was no more than a feathery rasp.

"Hang on tight. Here we go," he advised, and before she had a chance to tighten her grip on the sheets, he picked up the pace. Her hips rose to meet his thrusts, her heels scraping down his back, and in no time at all, she came on a cry. Her entire body hummed, the electric current from earlier still flowing through her veins.

He eased up, allowing her to enjoy the release. Without his shoulders for support, her legs collapsed uselessly to one side. In fact, her entire body felt boneless. Sparks danced along the surface of her skin and entire cosmos burst behind her eyelids.

He left her briefly, but by the time he returned to bed his smug smile was locked in place.

"That," he said, lazily stroking his fingers up her arm, "was worth the fucking wait."

She laughed, but it was wheezy. She blamed the orgasm. It'd been a wringing one. She'd thought his hand was nice? His tongue should be bronzed.

"Guess I enjoy that after all." She faced him.

"Guess so." He flicked on the nightstand lamp and pulled open a drawer.

Her eyes on the foil packet, her breaths tightened.

"You're sure—" he started but she snatched the condom from his hand. No way she was going to say no to him.

"Get your ass in here," she demanded.

"Look who got bossy."

"You ain't seen nothing yet." She tore the condom open with her teeth, her hands shaking—her entire body shaking. When he climbed over top of her, she reached for him.

He helped her roll on the condom, which shouldn't have been sexy but somehow, with him, it was. Once it was in place, he moved her hand with his over his sheathed cock and down to the crisp hair encircling it. Up once more. Down once more. Her eyes turned up to his and what she saw there nearly stopped her cold.

Cash Sutherland. In the flesh. Several inches of him about to be joined with her for the first time. She'd convinced herself tonight was just sex but already she questioned if he could ever be "just" anything to her.

She shut her eyes against the thought. His lips kissed her nose before he said, "Presley. Look at me."

She fluttered her lashes, taking in his handsome face, his thick arms bracketing her. He appeared golden in the lamplight, a beautiful fallen angel.

"You good?" he asked.

"So good," she answered.

Then she reached up and cuffed his neck and pulled his mouth to hers. At the same time, he tilted his hips, entering her that first amazing, agonizingly perfect inch.

Twelve

He eased into Presley's sweet, giving body slowly, which was an exquisite form of torture.

There was no need to ease—she was wet and ready for him—but he didn't want to rush. He finally had her, had her approval, and had been the first man to give her an orgasm with his tongue on her clit. That alone was enough to make him blow.

So, by the time he'd eased in to the hilt, he'd had to breathe low and slow and remind himself he was a grown man who could hold out longer than a few pathetic minutes.

Presley wasn't helping in that endeavor.

She stroked his hair with her fingers, rocking her hips against his in a rhythm that was both gentle and deep. He wedged his teeth together when she touched his chest. Now she was murmuring words like "you're so hot, you feel good, I like your mouth the most," and he had to pause to issue a warning.

"Pres," he grunted as the pressure in his balls built to a dangerous level, "honey, you have to stop talking dirty or I'm going to lose it."

Her eyebrows rose. "I'm talking dirty?"

"Yes. And I like it. Way too much."

Upon hearing that, his vixen crossed her ankles at his thighs and arched her back. Her nipples were alert and begging for a kiss. He delivered one to each of them before she started again.

"I had no idea how big you were," she purred into his ear. "You used to be able to make me orgasm with your mouth on my breasts, but now that I know how good you are between my legs, I'm going to demand that from now on."

"Presley."

"Seriously. So *big*."

"Dammit," he begged.

"Don't stop."

Like he could? His hips pistoned between hers, desperate to find the release he'd sought since he entered her.

"Huge, actually," she breathed.

"Honey, shut up." He stamped a kiss onto her mouth.

"Not on your life." A flicker of challenge lit her eyes. "Tell me, what else can you do with your—*oh!*"

Her startled "oh!" was because he'd decided to teach her a lesson, lifting her leg and hooking her knee over his elbow. He tilted his hips and drove deep, loving watching her blue eyes darken to navy.

He might be at her mercy, but he wanted her to know she was also at his.

"Yeah, 'oh,'" he teased. Her eyebrows scrunched, the whimper she released a melody he'd not soon forget. "You first, then it's my turn."

"I...already...had a turn," she breathed, with effort, given he hadn't stopped moving.

"You had two turns. This makes three." He seated himself again and her face contorted in a pleasure-pain expression. She was close. And, thank God, she went over after he doled out one more stroke.

He let go of her leg and propped himself on his elbows. Her arms lazily looped his neck and then she continued murmuring about how sexy he was and how hot he was and how big he was. This time he didn't stop her.

He found his own release shortly after hers, finishing on a growl, his face in her neck, his nose buried in her hair. His breath was shallow. His mind blessedly blank.

He surfaced after who knew how long, the sweat from their bodies cooling on their skin. That was when she turned her head and kissed his cheek, giving him so much sweet he could hardly stand it. Too much sweet after what they'd done. But that was Presley. She was sweet. Even when she was naked and talking dirty.

Before he could let that thought take root, she murmured, "Wow" into his ear and for some reason that hit him and he laughed.

Hard.

She joined him, her shoulders bouncing beneath him, which was when he became aware he was crushing her into the mattress. He pushed up, slipped free of her tight hold and rolled to his back. Hand on his chest, he pulled in a deep breath.

"You wore me out, wildcat."

"I'm not a wildcat."

He rolled off the bed and went to the bathroom, calling over his shoulder, "Dirty talker, then."

Her chiming laughter followed.

When he returned to his bed, he found her sitting

up, her breasts hidden behind his gray sheets, her sparkly dress in hand. He plucked the garment from her and tossed it onto the chair by the window.

"Got somewhere to be?"

Her hair was untamed after she'd rolled around on it for the last hour. And here he didn't think she could look any hotter than she had sunbathing on the dock. He was wrong. She looked hottest after she'd been sexed up, down and sideways and was wrapped in his bedsheets.

Mine.

He tried to shove out the thought when it came but he didn't succeed. Instead, it curled up in his chest and made itself cozy. Presley had been his once. It'd been a long time ago, and she'd been waiting to gift him exclusively what she'd given him just now.

That Wayne Gretzky quote about missing 100 percent of the shots you didn't take felt really damn true. He hadn't taken a shot with her and now knew what he'd missed.

But that didn't mean he would allow fantastic sex to distract him from finishing his album. Nor would he allow her to be distracted from what she'd come here to do. Long ago, they couldn't have slept together without becoming deeply entangled. Now that was not the case. They could—and they would—walk away intact. Even if the sex was so good it should be illegal.

"I was going to take my borrowed shoes and dress and go back to my room," she answered. "Did you expect me to sleep in here with you?"

And there it was. The line he hadn't thought to draw but, obviously, he needed to draw it. He eased back on the bed, shoved a pillow behind his back and curled her into his side. Arranging the blankets over both of them, he leaned over and kissed her wild hair, smiling against it when he thought about the tangles she'd have to comb out later. He hoped she thought of why they were there when she did.

"We should talk about that, yeah?" He felt her stiffen in his arms. "I want you here, Pres. In my bed. Naked in my arms. I want you on my dock, driving me crazy in your tiny pink bikini. But we should be clear about what this is...and what it's not."

She shifted and looked up at him, her blue eyes wide and innocent, her lips pursed gently. "What it's not."

"Yeah, honey," he continued, gentler than before. "What it's not."

"You mean..." She licked those pink lips and rested a hand tenderly on his chest. "You mean you aren't going to make an honest woman out of me now that we had sex?"

Cash's face broadcast myriad emotions. They ranged from regret to nervousness to confusion and finally to what she could only describe as "oh, shit."

Much as she was enjoying this, she let him off the hook with a laugh. Holding the sheet over her chest, she sat up. "I'm kidding! Cash, honestly."

His confused expression held a moment longer than it should have. "I knew that."

"I'm not the girl you left at Florida State. I grew up too, you know. I learned how the world worked."

She still cared about him, but she didn't expect a marriage proposal just because they'd slept together. She had a life separate from his. And she knew better than to fall for him this time around. He was a famed heartbreaker, and she didn't care to relive that experience.

"That was fun," she continued. "I had a great time. You had a great time. I'm looking forward to doing it again if you're up for it."

"If *I'm* up for it?" He let out a disbelieving chuff. That was better. She couldn't have him looking at her like she was precious, or who knows what mixed messages her heart would receive.

"You were the one begging me to stop talking dirty to you."

"I was not begging."

"Please, Presley, please stop talking dirty before I lose my mind!" she totally misquoted. Then she was dissolving in laughter, Cash having dug his fingers into her sides with the single-minded intent of tickling her to death. She squealed and then gasped for breath before managing a strangled apology.

When he finally let up, the sheet had fallen to her waist and her breasts were exposed. His leg rested heavy on one of hers and his erection was nudging her hip.

"You're different," she said, and didn't miss when he bristled. "Less bitter than when you left school. Happier, but somehow sadder at the same time."

His eyebrows closed over his nose in warning. She ignored that, too.

"Your family's success is important to you." She ruffled his hair away from his forehead, smoothing his furrowed brow with the tips of her fingers. "Have they always been? Did you accept that football scholarship to Florida State to make your parents happy?"

His jaw tightened. A muscle jumped in his cheek. She pressed on, curious.

"Are you writing this album for you, or are you doing it to bolster the success of Elite Records? I imagine it'd be a lot harder to be inspired if you are only trying to help the record company. Unlike your first album that birthed 'Lightning,' which came straight from the heart."

A thundercloud swept over his face. He no longer

looked confused or nervous, but angry. "You in my bed gives you access to my body, not my personal life."

She flinched, but he kept going.

"You want to interview me, Ms. Cole, make an appointment."

"Cash—"

"Best you sleep in your own room after all."

She watched through narrowed eyelids as the stone wall formed around him. He stared at her calmly, not taking back a single sharp word he'd said.

"Fine." She hustled out of bed and collected her clothes and shoes. "We both got what we needed tonight anyway. We can talk more tomorrow if *your schedule* allows. How's ten in the morning work for you?"

A dab of regret washed over his features. "Wait—"

"Good night."

She wasn't waiting for whatever explanation he was going to offer. She was irritated with herself for letting him affect her this much. She should have shrugged off his grouchiness and left with her dignity intact.

Well, screw that. She could still leave with her dignity intact.

The couture dress wadded against her chest and strappy shoes dangling from her fingertips, she marched naked down the long hallway, her hair billowing behind her. She hoped he was watching her strut away from him. She hoped he was missing her body pressed against his. She hoped he was regretting that they weren't halfway into round two.

She shut her bedroom door, threw her clothes on the chair and climbed into the shower.

She was wrong. He hadn't changed. He was the same guy who, given half a chance, would shut down and send her away.

And even though she knew she'd crawl back into his bed again to experience more of what she'd had tonight, she was properly armored up this time.

Hopefully her heart knew better than to allow fanciful ideas about how he'd changed to take over like weeds in a garden bed.

Thirteen

Cash rapped on the guest bedroom door the next morning aware of two things. One, Presley was nowhere near waking up since it was before seven o'clock, and two, he'd been a dick last night and that required an apology.

He'd realized that last bit the moment she'd strolled away from him down the hallway, her bare, heart-shaped ass wiggling.

He'd had no idea how to make up for his temper or overreaction at the time, so he'd sat on it. By the time she'd closed her bedroom door—she didn't slam it, which was somehow worse—he'd muttered to himself about being an idiot and proceeded to lay staring at the ceiling trying to think of a way to make it up to her.

The answer had hit him about an hour ago. He'd been biding his time waiting to go to her room, but he couldn't wait any longer.

"Pres," he called, along with another knock.

Her sleepy, slightly grouchy voice sounded through the door a second later. "Go away."

He shouldn't, but he smiled. "C'mon. I have coffee."

Silence. Then, "The coffee I'll take."

"Well, you have to answer the door, honey, because my hands are full." He waited for what felt like a full minute before the door opened a crack. She appeared in the gap all bright blue eyes, a mess of red hair and an FSU T-shirt that'd seen better days. It wasn't his, but he'd had one like it when he'd gone to school with her.

She couldn't look any sexier if she tried, but he sure as hell couldn't open with that.

"Mornin'." He held up his hands—one of them holding the handles of two coffee mugs and the other wrapped around the neck of his guitar. "The rest of my gift is forthcoming. Can I come in or do I have to serenade you from the hallway?"

He'd been kidding, but she looked as if she might make him stand there while she glared at him through the crack. Luckily, she pulled the door wider, shameless about wearing nothing but a blue pair of panties beneath her T-shirt. Sexy. *Damn.* She did it for him. Even in a threadbare T-shirt and cotton underpants.

He settled the mugs on the high dresser and then handed her one. "Creamed, like you like it."

She mumbled incoherently and traipsed back to bed, jamming her legs under the covers, her back propped against the headboard. Her eyes closed as she took the first sip of coffee, a small moan communicating her gratitude. Another thing he'd learned about her years ago: if you show up early, show up with coffee.

He left his own mug and walked to the bed. She braced, but he kept coming until he'd lowered on to the side of the bed, his hip nudging her leg.

"This is called the apology song." He cleared his throat. Hummed for effect. Then he strummed a few chords and sang.

Dear Presley.
This is my apology.
I didn't mean to be so mean.
I didn't mean to be so much me.
Dear Presley.
I brought coffee.
And I'll do it gleefully.
Until you forgive me.
Will you forgive me?
I hope you forgive me.
I'm so sorry, Presley.

He hummed at the end, set his fingers to the strings and waited. He didn't have to wait long. Her lips curved up at one corner and she didn't waste any time taking him to task.

"Gleefully?" she repeated.

"Yeah. You should feel special since I don't do *glee*."

Her small laugh faded fast. For good reason. He couldn't expect to be out of the doghouse with a hasty, questionably funny song.

"Last night was—"

"Don't." She shook her head.

"I'm gonna," he informed her. She sucked in a breath that she let out in a huff and he continued. "Last night was good, Pres. Better than good. I wasn't prepared for... how good."

Meaning: the blast from the past that was Presley Cole had carried with it a truckload of memories.

"And because I wasn't prepared, I wasn't ready to deal with the crap that came up. Including you talking about those days again. And how I deal with my family. My defenses climbed sky-high and I blew it big-time. Laid in my bed and swore and stared at the ceiling long after watching you walk away."

"You did blow it," she murmured after a beat.

"I know." He rested his arm on his guitar. "Hope you don't regret it, though."

"I don't." She lifted her chin.

He could have guessed. She was strong. Strong enough to deal with the fit he'd pitched.

"I pried, though, and I shouldn't have. Insatiable curiosity is one of my traits. Not a great one."

She had that backward. He was the insatiable one when it came to her. "You didn't do anything wrong. I was just…being me," he finished lamely. He thought he'd be able to ignore their past, but when she'd mentioned "Lightning," he realized that was an impossibility.

He strummed the strings on his guitar and clumsily sang, "Come with me to a Fourth of July party. On Friday, Friday. Yeah, on Friday."

She raised her eyebrows. "For real?"

"For real." He continued strumming nothing in particular. "There's a party at Mags's mansion before the fireworks. After, we'll take the boat out, watch them light up the lake."

Will had called to ask if he'd like to join, along with Hannah, Hallie and Gavin on his boat, but Cash had declined. Then Luke had asked if Cash wanted to join him on his boat, and Cash had declined that invite, too. Reason being, he wanted to show Presley the lake and the fireworks and, if he could get her to forgive him, he preferred to be alone with her on his own boat.

He hadn't told his brothers that part.

He kept strumming. "The party will be a pain but after, you can change out of your formalwear. We'll have the boat to ourselves. Fireworks overhead."

"Formalwear?"

"Formalwear. Mags," he explained, which was the entire explanation.

"I love fireworks."

"I know." He stopped playing. Her eyes went to his hands on the guitar.

"I liked the part where you admitted you were mean."

"Figured you might."

"The coffee was a nice touch."

"Figured you'd think so."

"I don't want to fight with you while I'm here." She sighed. "But I'd like to keep doing what we were doing. If you're willing."

His mouth dried out. He'd hoped she'd accept his apology. Hoped he could convince her to attend the party with him. And yeah, he'd hoped he could have sex with her again. Eventually. He hadn't expected to be propositioned, which she did next.

"Are you? Willing?" She set her coffee mug on the nightstand.

"Now?" This was too good to be true.

"Now."

He wasted no time setting his guitar on the chair by the window and then yanked the blankets off her lap.

"With you, Pres, I'm always willing." He kissed her and she tasted like coffee. "This shirt." He feathered his fingertips beneath the hem and touched her bare stomach. "It's hot."

"You're crazy." She laughed.

He was. And his not being able to stay away from her

was proof. He didn't care what she thought about him, just so long as she accepted him in her bed.

She did, and he spent the next hour and a half doling out part two of his apology.

Friday arrived. Presley tore the tags off the little black dress she'd purchased. It was short and classy, but also comfortable. She paired it with black high heels, also new, and packed a small bag like Cash had suggested. The bag contained her swimsuit, beach towel, a pair of shorts and a T-shirt. He assured her the water would be warm enough to dip into if she wanted to do so, and if she didn't want to do so while naked, to bring a suit. She didn't plan on climbing into the water, but she would rather be prepared. When it came to Cash, she'd surprised herself a few times already. She simply hadn't expected to enjoy him quite as much as she had. Lately, every time she was around him, *naked* was exactly how she'd ended up.

After he'd serenaded her in her room two days ago, they'd had another round and a half of fantastic sex. They didn't argue when they were done either, which was a nice change of pace. What followed had been a "normal" day, and he'd encouraged her to ask the questions she'd asked the night before. She did, tentatively, but he'd answered without much fuss.

Yesterday they'd sat on the dock and wrote. Cash, guitar in his lap, humming and strumming and occasionally jotting down words into a spiral-bound notebook that had seen better days. There were paper shreds stuck in a badly bent coil and she'd teased him, asking if that was the same notebook from when he went to FSU. That'd earned her a low laugh and a kiss, which she returned without argument.

Tonight was the formal affair at Mags Dumond's house, and would include her first boat ride since she'd arrived. She was ready for a night off, but acutely aware that tonight wasn't a night "off" at all. Her article was coming along, but she still needed some key information so she could end it with a bang.

As luck would have it, Hannah Banks and Cash Sutherland wouldn't be country music's only superstars in attendance. A source had confided that Carla Strouse would be there—as in Cash's ex. That source was Hallie, who hadn't a clue what Presley was up to and if Pres had her way, never would. Alas, when she published her article, everyone would know that she'd been seeking the truth to the inspiration behind Cash's hit song. She hoped Hallie and her sister, Hannah, Cash and the rest of the Sutherlands could forgive her for it someday.

"Slip out of those shoes," Cash said as she came downstairs.

She looked down at her black high heels. "Why?"

"We're taking the boat to the party. It'll be easier for you to navigate the docks without three-inch heels." By the time he finished talking, he was standing in front of her and smiling. "Four inches," he corrected, moving her hair away from her face to tuck it behind her ear. "Like you this tall."

"Thanks."

He kissed her. She lingered. When he released her lips, brushing her jaw with his thumb, she somewhat dazedly slipped out of her shoes and into the flip-flops she'd stowed in her bag.

On his deluxe pontoon boat—which was the fanciest pontoon she'd ever set foot on—she sat on one of the cream-colored vinyl seats and admired the shine glinting off every surface. How did he keep it this pristine?

He drove slowly since there were several boats dotting the water and they were in a "no wake" zone. The wind was at a minimum, so she wouldn't have to fix her hair when they arrived at Mags Dumond's mansion.

They passed other giant houses on the water, some towering with multiple balconies, others low and sprawling, partially hidden by thick, green-leaved trees.

"Come drive," Cash invited, holding out a hand.

"Really?"

"I'm insured."

"You're hilarious." She gave him a playful slap on the arm as he pulled her onto his lap. She took the wheel, and he moved her other hand to the throttle, murmuring instructions into her ear. Those instructions turned into praise for how good she smelled and then advanced to kisses on the side of her neck. By the time she closed her eyes, he teasingly reminded her she was going to wreck them into the rocks.

A short while later they arrived at Mags's lakefront mansion and docked in one of the few available spots left. She carried her shoes in one hand, leaving her boat gear on the pontoon, and walked barefoot up the dock. By the time they reached the walkway cutting through a grass-covered hill, her jaw was on the ground. She toed on her shoes, holding on to Cash for purchase, while watching many, *many* well-dressed people file into the massive house.

"Let's get this over with." His tone was hilariously bored. As if the fanciest, most well-attended party in town was nothing more than a nuisance.

Her stomach jumped as she thought about speaking to Cash's ex-girlfriend. Tonight might be the night Presley found out if Carla was the woman fueling the sentiment behind his hit song.

Presley told herself she was simply satisfying her own curiosity, but that was a lie. She would have to write about what she learned tonight. Uncovering secrets was part of her job—Delilah had made that clear. And uncovering one this big would not only win her the contest at work, but also catapult her career *and* make her travel dreams come true.

She'd share what was in the article with Cash before she published it, though. She wasn't a monster. But she *would* publish it. And if he couldn't understand the reasons behind why she needed to, then he'd never understood her at all.

Fourteen

Presley was underdressed.

Who threw a Fourth of July party that was a suit-and-tie affair? Mags, apparently. Cash didn't care about dress code. He was dressed country cool in black jeans, cowboy boots and a black button-down shirt with bold, stitched embellishments on the chest. The women at the party were dressed grander in gowns or pantsuits bedazzled with glittering rhinestones or sequins or a combination of both.

Only when she saw Hallie did Presley let out a breath of relief. The other woman looked chic and professional in a sophisticated black pantsuit with a sash tied at the middle. Her high-heeled shoes were not as tall as Presley's, but enough to lift her so that the wide legs of her suit didn't brush the marble floors.

"I'm underdressed," Presley confessed instead of saying hello.

"No, you're not." Hallie smiled. "You look amazing. Hey, Cash."

"Hey, Hal. Seen my brothers?"

"I came with Will and Hannah, so yes. Luke popped in, but I don't know where he ran off to."

Presley searched the well-dressed crowd, spotting an incredibly famous country singer who had aged really, *really* well. "And Gavin?"

"Gavin?" Hallie squeaked, a blush stealing her cheeks. "I—uh, why would I know where Gavin is?" She sucked down an inch of her wine.

Well. That was an interesting reaction. Presley folded her arms over her chest and studied Hallie carefully, having the distinct impression that the blonde was hyper-aware of Gavin's whereabouts while pretending not to be. "Why would you know where Gavin is, indeed?"

Cash picked up on none of this, his eyes traveling the room.

"If you need to mingle, I'm good here," Presley told him.

"Yeah?"

"Yeah."

He gave her a soft smile, followed by a softer kiss, and then let her go. He walked across the room, but not before promising, "Be back."

"Are you two," Hallie started, moving closer to Presley to whisper the rest of her question, "back together?"

"No. Yes. Sort of." Presley winced. "I'm not sure I can have this conversation without a glass of wine."

"That can be arranged."

Hallie was not only beautiful and kind, she was also good company. Each with their own glass of champagne, they mingled among the famous, Hallie introducing

Presley and making a smooth getaway so they weren't trapped in any conversation for too long.

Knowing Presley wanted to meet and speak with Carla Strouse, Hallie was sure to include the famous singer in their rounds. After an introduction, the twin excused herself and left Presley and Carla alone. Presley felt a ping of guilt that she hadn't been forthcoming about why she wanted to meet Carla, but she couldn't very well blurt out that she was going to grill Cash's ex about "Lightning," now, could she?

Hallie had found Carla Strouse on one of Mags Dumond's many balconies. This one was on the second floor and less populated than the patio below, where guests had spilled out into the yard and were littering the beach, as well.

"Anyway, enough of my gushing. I'm sure you're tired of me standing here reciting all the reasons I adore you," Presley said with a chuckle. That was the truth. She had always loved Carla's music. Gushing came naturally. "I assume at these parties it's gauche to morph into a fangirl."

"Please." Carla, both pretty and friendly, rolled her eyes. "I nearly *died* when I spotted Louise Hatton here. *Louise Hatton*, the woman who inspired me to sing when I was six years old! We're all fangirls deep down."

Carla, with her short, layered hair, full mouth and twinkling green-blue eyes, was more beautiful in person than she was on stage, which was quite the feat. She was also really freaking nice. Presley didn't know the reason for Carla and Cash's breakup, and she couldn't imagine one, either. They were both famous, attractive. They'd looked good together, too. There was no shortage of flattering photos of them online.

"You're here with Cash, right?" Carla brushed her hand along the shiny silver dress fitted to her lithe body.

"I am." Presley drank the rest of her champagne in a rush. She wondered if Carla was sizing her up and comparing. There was no comparison, really. Carla was a glowing beacon of perfection whereas Presley was, well, *not.* "We went to college together."

"In Florida." Carla's light eyebrows lifted.

Presley wondered how much Cash had shared with the other woman about those days. A petty part of her wanted to trumpet that she'd been with Cash first, but she hadn't technically been with him first, had she? She'd been with him only a few nights ago. Knowing that Carla had also been with him made Presley feel more than a little self-conscious.

"He's wonderful, isn't he? I mean, he's complicated. He is a man," Carla added with a delicate snort. "But he's great."

"He's, uh, he's all of those things." Before she lost her nerve, or her dinner, Presley decided to get to the point. "I've always thought you were the one, you know?"

She let the bait dangle.

Carla cocked her head, smiled quizzically and then bit. "'The one'?"

"Yeah. The woman he wrote 'Lightning' about. You two made a cozy couple. And you were together, what, eighteen months?"

"On and off." Carla's smile faded.

"Oh." Presley hadn't uncovered that nugget during her online research. "I just assumed… I didn't ask him about you, or anything. He doesn't talk about his past."

"Believe me, I know. He never told me details about anyone he dated before me."

"Really?" Presley was both surprised and unsurprised.

Cash wasn't exactly an open book, but she'd expected him to be tight-lipped with her, *the reporter*. He hadn't shared his past with the woman he'd dated for a year and a half? Carla and Cash must not have been as close as the press had everyone believing. The words *on and off* suggested distance.

"Oh, to be the woman who inspired 'Lightning'..." Carla's smile didn't seem forced, but amused. "I wish he'd felt a fraction for me of what he sings about in that song. Whoever she is, she's a lucky girl."

"Indeed." Presley nodded tightly. One starlet down, one to go. Too bad Heather wasn't also in attendance at the party tonight. The actress lived on the West Coast. She and Cash had met while Heather was filming a movie in Nashville. Presley wondered if Heather and Cash were also "on and off" in the six or so months while they dated.

Presley and Carla moved on to tamer topics, talking fashion and hors d'oeuvres and music. Carla introduced her boyfriend, also her producer, who seemed like a decent guy. Cash meandered over and met Carla's boyfriend too, shaking the other man's hand and politely kissing Carla on the cheek. No longing glances were exchanged, no stiff, nervous smiles, either. Presley was beginning to believe what Carla had said about the nature of her relationship with Cash.

It was oddly relieving to know that during the brief time Presley shared Cash's bed, he wasn't having any lingering feelings for the likes of the beautiful, famous, likable Carla Strouse.

They returned to the bar and Cash handed Presley another glass of champagne. He ordered a Coke with lime, hold the Jack Daniels, for himself.

"Staying sober for the press?" she teased.

"I have to drive the boat." He bent and whispered into her ear, "And talk you into doing a host of bad-girl things on that boat." Now he was grinning and she understood why. He wasn't going to have to try hard to talk her into anything. "I have to be at the top of my game if I hope to…"

His words trailed off, his attention elsewhere. His arm at her back stiffened. "Get ready."

"For what?"

But then Mags Dumond slithered over to stand in front of them and Presley knew exactly *what*. The First Lady of Beaumont Bay had finally made her way to them.

Mags had to be around seventy, but her smooth skin betrayed her age. Her plastic surgeon was good. The woman looked every year of fifty, but not much older than that.

"Well," Mags drawled, the tassels on her ice-blue gown shimmering under chandelier light. The dress was weighed down with beads and rhinestones and should have made Mags look gaudy. Instead it only made her look *wealthy*. She was a woman who knew herself, knew her power in this town and reigned like the queen she believed herself to be. "Look who decided to grace us with his presence."

"Mags," Cash said through clenched teeth.

The woman turned to Presley. Her smile didn't budge, her pearlescent teeth practically aglow. "Mags Dumond. Most people around here know me as—"

"The First Lady of Beaumont Bay," Presley finished, offering a hand.

Mags's eyes narrowed. "Why, yes." She moved her martini from one hand to the other. When Presley took the other woman's hand, cool metal pressed her fingers from Mags's many chunky diamond rings, not one of them understated.

"Did you know—" Mags released Presley's hand "—Cash refuses to record at my studio? Even after a storm knocked Elite Records to the ground. I'm all for loyalty but that's just silly."

"Elite Records wasn't on the ground," Cash muttered, the flash in his dark eyes a warning Mags ignored.

"Close enough." Mags guffawed. "You're Presley Cole, aren't you? You're interviewing our boy for your hometown paper or whatever."

"Viral Pop is far from a hometown paper," Presley defended. "They have eighteen locations all over the globe, and a reach of over 100 million." Presley realized belatedly she'd stepped into the same snare as Cash. This woman was good.

"Huh. Who knew?" Mags shrugged with her mouth. "Well, I'll leave you two to…whatever it is you're doing. Anyway, Cash, even in the wake of your DUI and subsequent PR nightmare, my offer stands. Cheating Hearts Studio is not petty. Are you sure your brothers have your back no matter what?" She made a show of peering down at Cash's drink. "I hope there's no alcohol in that glass."

Cash's nostrils flared. If he hadn't been sucking in a breath through those nostrils, Presley would have sworn rigor mortis had set in. His arm at her lower back was positively rigid.

"I'm staying with Elite." He emitted a low exhalation that was a borderline growl, followed by, "Mags. Always a pleasure," before excusing himself and leading Presley in the opposite direction.

"The pleasure was mine!" Mags called after them, loud enough to be heard over the entire party. Forget the storm that smashed into Beaumont Bay a few months ago, Mags was a force of nature with twice the wallop.

Cash steered them to the bar, set his Coke down and instructed, "Jack Daniels, rocks." Then to Presley he promised, "I can still drive the boat."

Once he'd taken a hearty sip of his drink and they'd moved to a less populated room in Mags's mansion, they walked out onto a small landing. Presley rested her forearms on the railing and looked down at the guests milling around below. She could feel that Cash had something to say, so she gazed up at the stars and waited for him to come around to it.

"She doesn't give up," he finally said. "She's been pressuring me for years. Went as far as offering me a movie role with one of her director friends in Hollywood. She doesn't care about my success. She wants the clout. Wants to be tied to every big name in the business. She went after Hannah the same way a few months ago. Nearly broke up Will and Hannah in the process. There's nothing magnanimous about what Mags does. Not ever."

Presley had zero doubts that Mags was the complete opposite of magnanimous after their brief meeting.

"That woman could drive the soberest man to drink," he muttered.

"Why do you guys come to these things?"

"You met a lot of people tonight. Famous people."

She had.

"Relationships are forged at these parties. Friendships made. Mags is the price of admission, and everyone is willing to pay. When Cheating Hearts was the only recording studio in the Bay, Mags was... Well, she was never *nice*, but she wasn't as villainous. When she had competition, she got worse."

"So on the one hand Elite Records makes connections

at these events, but on the other they are forced to play by Mags's rules."

"Lest we suffer her wrath." He sipped his drink.

Presley blinked, a lightbulb of an epiphany flipping on in her head. "Literally, in your case."

Cash frowned, not following her train of thought.

"At that last party. You said she approached you to record with her?"

"Yeah."

"And you said no."

"I said 'hell no,' but close enough."

Presley touched his forearm. "And it was Mags who goaded you into one more drink when you were about to leave."

"She's persistent."

"That checkpoint, the questionable reading on the Breathalyzer. Could that have been part of her 'wrath'?"

His frown deepened, his eyes unfocused like he was thinking back to the night in question. "Earl."

"Earl?"

"The officer who pulled me over. They've been seen in town together lately." Cash's lip curled. *"Romantically."*

"Maybe he did her a favor. He set you up for her. That way she could approach you, claim to overlook your bad reputation and represent you anyway. Knowing you wouldn't want to harm Elite Records." It wasn't so far-fetched to believe. Mags would do anything to stay on top. "I can blow this wide open. My article can be your saving grace. I can demand a public apology for you. I can—"

He pressed his finger to her lips before shaking his head. "Let it lie, Pres. It's done."

"It's not done. It's an outrage."

"Past is past. No sense in dredging it up." He tipped

her chin and she tried not to look into his eyes, tried not to see clear through to the sentiment behind it, and how it reflected her own need to dredge up the past. To find out who had inspired him to write the most heart-rending lyrics she'd ever heard in her life. To slay that mystical beast Closure, no matter what it cost her in the short-term.

"I have an album to focus on," he continued. "Elite Records is primed for a comeback. Write about that. No good can come of stirring the pot."

"But your mug shot," she tried.

"What's done's done." His tone communicated he was also done having this conversation. "You ready to leave? It's almost time for the fireworks."

Heat shimmered in his eyes. She guessed he didn't mean only the fireworks in the sky. He meant the ones that would happen once he set his lips to hers.

Fifteen

Cash anchored the boat away from a fleet of other boats volleying for the best spot to watch the show. The fireworks hadn't started yet, so most of the noises bouncing off the water were the hoots and hollers and whistles of partiers on the lake.

The sky was dark. The crickets were singing and winged bugs large and small bounced off the lights on the front of the boat. That left Presley and Cash in the semidark, but she could still see nearly every inch of the boat's interior, which meant so could anyone else.

"Guess I won't be changing clothes since I have an audience," she told her captain.

"You sure about that?" He moved her to the side and pulled open a small compartment on the side of the dashboard. Up popped a privacy panel that stood taller than him and was twice as wide. The lightweight fabric was pale in the moonlight and billowed gently in the breeze.

He opened a gap in the fabric and gestured. "Your changing room, miss."

She eyed the ample private space created by the fabric, "Okay, that was impressive."

"I aim to please." His hands on her hips, he followed her in and promised she was about to be more impressed. His lips hit hers and he unzipped her dress.

"How," she asked between kisses, "are we supposed to maneuver *this*?"

A whistling sound streaked up high, and because the fabric panels were open at the top, she watched as a colorful explosion burst overhead.

"We'll maneuver just fine," he assured her.

She returned his grin and began thumbing open the buttons of his shirt. He kicked off his jeans and she let her dress drop.

"I don't know what to hold on to." She scanned the tight, hot and getting hotter space.

"Hold on to me."

There was a pause as she considered her inability to hold on to him at one point in time. She pushed the thought aside as he shoved his boxers off his legs. She was going to give in to the magic of this moment. And, like a magician, he made her bra and thong disappear.

He wrapped her arms around his neck and then palmed her ass and lifted her. The tip of his erection nudged her center and she gasped. She was wet and ready for him after only a few kisses.

"You're like a drug, Cash Sutherland," she whispered against his mouth. "You should come with a warning label."

"Speaking of, I should probably grab a condom." He kissed her swiftly. "But I don't want one."

"I don't want one, either." She stuck out her bottom lip. "I'm—I can't get pregnant since I'm on the pill. So…"

She was nose to nose with him so she didn't miss the moment his gaze darkened with lust. *"Presley."*

"If it's safe. Are you? Safe?"

"Yeah, baby, in the way you mean. Totally safe."

She didn't think too hard about what other ways he wasn't safe. He was the bad boy of country music, after all. "Safe" didn't describe him.

He didn't give her a chance to overthink before he slipped past her folds and erased her mind.

"That's nice," she breathed, hugging his neck.

"Fucking fantastic," he agreed, lifting her off him before dropping her down. His arms shook with effort as he made love to her standing. She held on as he'd requested, her fingers in his hair and her truncated breaths in his ear. Sweat slicked her chest and she glided against his torso each and every time he slid into her body.

"Do you…want to…put me down?" She didn't want that. He was in deep, felt too good. She was ready to explode from pleasure.

"Never. Touch yourself, Presley. Help me out."

She untangled one of her arms and wedged her fingers between their bodies. After a few tender strokes from her own fingers and a few more thrusts from Cash, she found her release.

Her moan vanished under the sound of another firework explosion, the faint smell of smoke tickling her nostrils. She fought for her breath as he found his own release. He groaned into her ear, a deep, appreciative guttural sound lost under yet another firework going off overhead.

"I'm heavy. I can feel you shaking." The tremble in his arms and legs was apparent.

"That's not why I'm shaking," he muttered before capturing her lips in a consuming kiss. "You make me weak, Pres."

Boy, could she relate. She had the will of a wet paper bag around him. Tenderly, she unhooked her legs from his waist. He slipped free, making sure she was steady on her feet before letting her go. But he didn't leave right away. He bent his head and rested his lips against her neck, his arms holding her tight.

Being naked on his boat under the fireworks should have led to naughty, kinky sex. The kind of sex they'd just had was far more intimate. In the small, overheated space with his breath on her neck and his hands on her body, she came to an unpleasant realization. Somehow, even though she'd tried to stop it, Cash had burrowed past her defenses. He'd buried himself in her body, but he hadn't stopped there. He kept going until he'd wedged himself into her heart.

Yeah, baby, in the way you mean. Totally safe.

She trusted he wouldn't impregnate her or put her in any physical danger, but if she allowed herself to fall for him... Well, there wasn't anything safe about that, was there?

"Grand finale." He kissed her neck again as cracks, pops and whistles dominated the night sky.

"Thought we did that already," she joked, not feeling like joking at all. Not with the complicated emotions clogging her chest.

"You're amazing. Completely amazing." His top half vanished out of the privacy panel. He returned with a pair of board shorts and stuffed his legs into them. Then he stepped out, leaving her to pull herself together.

In more ways than one.

She cleaned up with a beach towel, tied on her bikini

top and tugged on a pair of shorts followed by a T-shirt. Her arms shook, a warning that the mistake she'd made was bigger than forgoing prophylactics. Her chest felt too full. She missed him already and he was standing right outside the privacy panel.

She heard motors rev to life as boats left in search of another party opportunity. She emerged and Cash folded the fabric dressing room back into the dashboard before cramming his party clothes into a bag.

"Now where do we go?" She felt jittery, anxious to return to his house. Maybe then she could relax. Or at least retreat to her room.

"Nowhere." He lay on his back on the wide sunbathing bench on the back of the boat. "Come here."

She couldn't say no to him, which was most of her problem. She crawled onto the platform and tucked herself against his side.

"Best fireworks ever, don't you agree?" he murmured.

She inhaled the fragrant chemical smell of spent fireworks. "Incredible."

"Agree." His lips were close to her ear.

When she turned her head, she caught him watching her. She was propelled back to her dorm room, his bulky body taking up most of her twin-size bed, his eyes on hers while she apologized for making him wait to have sex with her. He'd always said the same thing.

You're worth the wait.

"You were worth the wait, too, Cash."

He knew exactly what she meant. His hand cupped her neck and then he was kissing her again. A boat blazed by and some guy shouted, "Get a room!"

He grinned against her lips, not letting the interruption ruin the moment.

They watched the sky in silence for a minute until

she said, "I had a great time at the party. Despite Mags being horrible."

His low laugh was relaxed and easy. Quite a departure from his demeanor at the party earlier. She was feeling the equally relaxed. She could slip into a deep sleep while bobbing on the water with naught but his arm supporting her head.

"Carla is nice."

"She's a good person." He gave her a quick squeeze. "But she's no *you*."

Presley wanted to argue with the compliment, especially since she was planning on finding out his secret and exposing it to the world.

"I wish you'd let me help you with Mags," she tried again, unable to stop herself. "She deserves to be called out. You deserve to be happy."

He *was* happy.

Right now, with Presley in his arms, he was happier than he'd been in a long time. And because that light, easy feeling was a rarity for him, he didn't want to talk about his DUI or Carla, and he especially didn't want to talk about Mags Dumond.

"I don't want to talk about the past," he said. "You're here. I'm here. Let's talk about that."

She drew in an unsteady breath. "Okay."

After months of trying to control the media—impossible—and monitoring his every facial reaction and posting carefully online—annoying—he was more than ready to let the past go. Easier to do when it came to Mags or Carla. Letting go of Presley was proving harder.

"You should stay a while longer." He blurted out what he'd been thinking for most of the evening.

"S-stay?"

"Yeah. Another week, at least."

He'd told himself he was blowing off steam with her, that they'd have their fill and move on. But they'd had sex multiple times, and he was as steam-filled as a hot kettle. He was beginning to wonder if it was possible to have his fill of her.

He wasn't through with her yet, and he hoped like hell she wasn't through with him. Once she went home to Florida, he knew that would be it. She'd go back to her life and he would go back to his. She had her sights set on traveling. He was destined for more awards. But he wasn't ready to release her from his hold. Not just yet.

He wished he could read her mind. He sure as hell couldn't read her expression.

"You're not done writing the article," he said, figuring that was true. "Isn't there more you need from me?"

Her smile was slight, but it gave him hope.

"I'll keep bringing you coffee in the morning," he said into her hair. She reinvigorated him, made him feel new. Fresh ideas had been bouncing around in his head since she'd climbed into bed with him. "You're inspiring."

She sat up on an elbow and this time he read her doubtful expression clearly.

"I'm not feeding you a line," he argued with the accusation in her eyes. "Come back here."

She muttered something about him being "impossible" but snuggled into him again, this time lying on her side and draping her arm over his chest.

"I haven't felt this alive in a long time," He rested his chin on the top of her head. The smoke above had cleared, revealing a sea of twinkling stars. "You make me better, Pres. At everything."

But no matter how much she meant to him, he had to have limits with her. How could he possibly ask her to trust him after he'd demolished her trust so thoroughly? After he had proven his success came first, regardless of what she'd meant to him.

"I'm sure Delilah would give me a week's extension to close some of the gaps in my article," she said.

"And you can write about the new song I'm recording next week."

"A new song?" He heard the excitement in her voice. He loved how much she loved his music. It was the highest honor. "Which one?"

"One you haven't heard." He kissed the top of her head. "But you will. I mean, if you stay."

He felt her smile on his bare chest. "You're such a tease."

"Not teasing." If anyone was teasing, she was teasing *him*. She was giving him everything he wanted that he couldn't keep. Everything he shouldn't have left behind and couldn't get back.

Those were sad words, cut him right to the core. But they were also honest. He mentally noted to add them to his new song. No one knew better than him that heartbreak was a big seller.

"If you're sure?" She was back to tracing circles on his chest again—his favorite sensation. Her fingers, his bare chest, her soft exhalations tickling his skin.

Another boat motored by as a shooting star streaked across the sky.

"Yeah, Pres. I'm sure."

Sixteen

"This is your job," Presley said to herself, her eyes on her laptop. "Do your job."

The cursor on the screen waited for her decision. She bit her lip, reread the email for the umpteenth time and doubted herself anew.

"This is what you came here to find out," she whispered. "So, *find out*."

Granted, she hadn't planned on emailing Heather Bell. It just so happened the new intern at Viral Pop came across Heather's private email. Ray was very much Team Presley when it came to the content contest. She appreciated his having her back, and saw no harm in attempting contact with the actress. She was running out of time.

In the email to Heather, Presley played up how she was helping repair Cash's reputation with his fans. She also might have told a teensy-*weensy* lie about how she and Cash were a couple. She'd even hinted at the idea of "ring shopping" this week, which, admittedly, was a little over the top. But if Heather believed Presley and Cash were serious, that might help sell the assumption that Pres had his best interests at heart. Which she did, ultimately. In her defense, it wasn't an out-and-out lie. She was technically "coupling" with him.

Presley also mentioned assisting with media attention for Heather's upcoming TV series by promising Heather a timely interview. Whether or not the actress trusted or believed Presley, Heather had to be familiar with Viral Pop. The amount of exposure wouldn't be small and could definitely boost any career.

Finger hovering over the send button, Presley tapped Send and sat back, feeling moderately satisfied with her many justifications.

The back door swung open and in walked a dripping-wet Cash, rubbing his hair with a towel. His lashes were spiked, rivulets of water running down his naked chest and over the bumps of his ab muscles. He looked ridiculously hot. He rarely didn't. Lake water rained off his board shorts and soaked the rug by the door.

"Hey," he said.

She slammed her laptop lid down guiltily. "Hey! How was your swim?"

"Wet. You busy?"

"Nope!" She stood and stuffed her hands into her shorts pockets, worried he might read the guilt on her face. "I was about to take a break."

"Good. Water's warm. Come swim with me."

Why was it whenever he commanded she "come" do anything, she did it? Staying in his house, or in his bed the way she had last night, put her directly in the path of an emotional tornado. Not that she could, or would, take cover.

Whenever his dark eyes were trained on hers, she remembered why she came to him. She'd forgotten what it was like to have his undivided attention. It was heady.

When she was within arm's reach, his arm snapped out and tugged her against his wet, warm body. Water soaked through her gauzy white cover-up and then that was gone when he lifted it over her head and tossed it on the floor. Then he was carrying her outside to his sandy, man-made beach at the edge of the water.

"Watch for sharp sticks," he advised, settling her into the waist-deep water.

"I can't think of anything to say that's not dirty." The sun kissed her skin, the water as warm as promised.

"Well, by all means." He scooped her up again and carried her deeper into the water. "Don't hold back on my account."

"Throw me," she instructed, reaching up to hold her nose.

"Yeah?"

She nodded and he adjusted his hold, first giving her a pinch on the butt, before tossing her a few feet into the air. She squeezed her eyes closed, hit the water with a splash and resurfaced with a smile.

He was laughing and coming toward her again. He caught her easily. This time when he lifted her, he kissed her mouth hard.

"Wildcat," he accused.

Yep, she was falling in love with him again.

He didn't toss her but held her against his warm, solid body. She wrapped her legs around his waist and pressed herself flush to his torso.

"Hmm," she said, nuzzling his nose with hers, "I think I found one of those sharp sticks you were talking about."

"Tree trunk, baby. Tree trunk."

She threw her head back and laughed. He was too much. Too hot, too funny, too sexy, too good at absolutely everything. He was her specific brand of catnip. He drove her crazy in the best way possible, and she didn't think he was even trying.

"Mom and Dad are having a family barbecue on Saturday. You're invited."

"I am?"

"Course you are. They want to meet you."

Gulp.

"That's thoughtful." And terrifying. How should she introduce herself? *Hi, I'm Cash's ex-girlfriend who refused to sleep with him only now we're doing it nonstop and it's great. By the way, I'm also sniffing around to find and expose a secret he's never told anyone.*

She couldn't shake the guilt about the damn email. Maybe there wasn't anything to worry about. Her request might go unanswered or be lost in Heather's spam folder for eternity. Once she received a response, she'd know how to approach Cash. Although she might want to write her own version of his apology song, in case he wasn't feeling magnanimous.

"Did you see how Hallie reacted when you brought up Gavin?" she asked, mainly to stop her incessant worrying.

Predictably, Cash's eyebrows lowered in confusion. "How do you mean?"

"She likes him. *Likes* him, likes him."

"You could tell that by talking to her for a few minutes last night?"

"A woman knows."

"Is that so?" He watched her for a long beat that felt almost accusatory thanks to her guilty conscience. "I don't know, Pres. She's the consummate good girl and Gavin…"

"Gavin what?"

"Gavin's not interested in settling down."

"Seems to run in the family. I mean, except for Will. But his 'one' was Hannah Banks, so what choice did he have?"

"She's a force. And, as you've noticed, Hallie isn't like her."

Presley's neck jerked. "Are you saying Hallie can't handle the likes of *Gavin*? He's charming and friendly and—"

"With you, maybe." Cash frowned, seeming irked at her list of compliments about his youngest brother.

"With me, definitely. He offered to let me stay with him first. He's nice."

Cash's visage darkened, even in the bright sunshine. He adjusted his hold on her, his hands wrapped tight at her thighs. "He was being *nice* so you'd stay in his house with him."

"What? No, he wasn't."

"Gavin is charming and friendly, but he also likes his relationships short and sweet. If Hallie's smart she'll stay away from him."

Well, Presley knew firsthand that "smart" had nothing to do with it.

"No way was Gavin trying to convince me to stay with him. He gave in with hardly a fight when you demanded I stay with you."

"I demanded?"

She ignored that. "And anyway I'm not interested in Gavin the way I'm interested in…"

Cash grinned, satisfied that she'd walked into his trap.

"I'm not interested in Gavin."

"Good." Cash stamped his mouth on hers.

"How could you be jealous of Gavin—" she twirled her fingers in Cash's hair, where a few unruly curls looped at the base of his neck "—when I'm here with you?"

"Presley," he groaned, and she felt her belly drop in delicious anticipation.

"Yes?"

"Honey, get ready."

"Ready for what?"

He untangled her arms from his neck, kissed one of her palms and murmured, *"This."*

Then the bastard tossed her into the air. Before she had a chance to hold her nose, she splashed into the lake water. When she surfaced this time, she was sputtering and he was laughing.

She swam after him, catching him before he could dive beneath the water. She climbed on his back and dunked him, satisfied with her payback. But when he exploded out of the water and pressed her against his front, she wondered if she'd ever truly be satisfied when it came to Cash.

Eventually she'd leave Beaumont Bay and resume a new life of pay raises and wanderlust. She'd probably forget all about him once she was stationed in Italy or France.

But then he kissed her, opening his mouth to allow his warm tongue to tangle with hers, and she knew she'd been lying to herself all morning.

Forgetting him would take more than a trip overseas. She wasn't sure a trip to Mars could erase Cash from her memory bank, but she was still going to try her damnedest to forget about him.

Seventeen

The rest of the week zoomed by.

Presley and Cash had developed a routine of sorts. Coffee on the deck, although sometimes he brought her coffee to bed. His bed, since she hadn't slept in the guest room since the Fourth of July.

Once she was out of bed, they'd either sit side by side and write on the dock, or if it was raining, at the kitchen counter instead. She'd had trouble focusing since Cash was plain distracting. Whether perched on a stool and singing bits and pieces of the song he was composing, or chewing on his pencil while reading his notes, his bare feet resting on the bottom rung of the stool. Just completely distracting.

Yesterday afternoon his low, rocky voice had stolen her attention from her writing. She'd leaned on one elbow and stared at his beautiful profile while he stumbled, started and stumbled again. He'd shot her a grin, but it faded when he noticed her staring.

"What?" he'd asked.

"You're so talented. It would have been a waste for you to have become a football player. Or if you'd pursued the business side of music like your brothers. You'd have robbed everyone of your incredible voice. I've never heard anyone who sounded like you."

"Pres—"

"I mean it." She turned on her stool to face him. "You sing and I forget the world around me. I'm completely lost in your music. Not everyone has that ability. Just you."

He blew out a breath from his nose, his fingers curling around the neck of his guitar. The rain picked up, beating the windowpanes and painting the outside a moody gray-blue.

"Get over here," he'd told her. She'd hopped off her stool at the same time he left his. He set the guitar on a stand in the living room and then pulled her onto the couch with him.

First, she'd been on top, his rough jaw scraping her soft skin while he made out with her long and slow. Then he'd reversed their positions and pressed her into the leather cushions. They'd kissed for a long, long while as distant thunder rumbled. They'd advanced to heavy petting by the time the storm blew in.

She'd climaxed with his mouth on her nipple, his fingers in her underwear. Then she'd pushed him onto his back, and tried something she hadn't experienced with him yet. She kissed a trail from his chest to his flat stomach and took him into her mouth.

She loved the heft of him, the taste of him on her tongue. She loved more the way she'd driven him to the brink. He nearly lost control but had stopped to haul her up by the elbows and kiss her deep and hard. They'd made love on the couch, but that hadn't been hard or fast. Their lazy pace had matched the ebbing rain outside.

It was a memory of their rainy-day lovemaking that consumed her on Saturday morning. Not the sexy shower or the way they'd slept curled into each other afterward. They'd savored one another.

Like they both knew the end was coming.

When she'd first arrived in Beaumont Bay, she hadn't expected to miss Cash when she left, but now she didn't see how to keep from it. He was…consuming. And the last thing she wanted was to be consumed by anyone.

She climbed out of his comfy bed and carried her empty coffee cup downstairs, humming Cash's new song, "Back for Good."

He'd been piecing it together all week, and had finally laid down a track he and Will were happy with. It was by far her favorite song from the new album. It was soulful and, when sang in his rough, low, damn sexy voice, practically *orgasmic*. Since he'd sung it on repeat this week, and then several times in the studio while she'd watched and listened, the tune was on a loop in her head.

In the kitchen she hummed the chorus, passing by Cash, who stood, his back to her while he looked outside. Capable, attentive, sexy Cash. It really was too bad she was leaving for home tomorrow. Delilah had been generous about giving Pres extra time, but she needed to be back in the office for the release of the article. An article that didn't have much of a chance of winning the coveted pay raise and internship. Not without the scandalous reveal she'd been plotting—she hadn't heard a peep from Heather.

Not that Pres would have revealed the truth anyway.

Last night, while she listened to him sing his heart out, she'd decided to stop trying to figure out the inspiration behind "Lightning." She'd written a robust article about Elite Records, with an exclusive behind-the-scenes peek at Cash recording his new album. She had weaved in details about the way he was at home—leaving out that she'd shared his bed, of course. And she'd outlined how generous he was with fans whenever they bumped into him downtown.

The fresh focus of her article had nothing to do with scandal or secrets, but she was proud of it anyway. It would give readers an honest look at an honest man, and whet their appetites for his next big hit. There was no way "Back for Good" wouldn't go to number one.

If the new angle of her article cost her the contest, she would simply have to find another way to convince Delilah to grant the raise and transfer Presley deserved. Pres had known deep down she wasn't doing the right thing, and the guilt had been eating her alive. She wasn't going to sneak around behind Cash's back anymore, not after how intimate they'd been. Not after that sexy afternoon on the sofa when their very souls had been involved in the exchange.

She cared about him too much to hurt him. The decision had set her heart at ease.

As she refilled her coffee mug she became aware of a searing gaze on the side of her head. She turned to find Cash watching her, his phone pressed to his ear and his expression fierce. He didn't give her a panty-melting smile nor did he deliver a cheeky wink. And he didn't crook a finger and invite her to come to him.

His shadowed brow matched the low-hanging clouds outside. His frown, edged by a day's worth of growth on his jaw and cheeks, was just as dark. He was *pissed* and that sent a shimmer of fear down her spine.

"Guess who just walked into the room?" he said into

the phone. His eyes narrowed to slits fringed by thick, black eyelashes as he watched her round the counter. "You guessed it. My *fiancée,* Presley Cole. You want to say hi?"

He offered the phone but she leaped away from it like he'd offered her a live rattlesnake. Evidently, Heather had read the email and had taken that "ring shopping" hint to heart. Explanations and excuses piled up in Presley's mind.

"Never mind." He returned the phone to his ear. "She can't talk right now."

True. Her mouth might as well be stuffed with cotton balls for how speechless she felt.

He said goodbye, lowered the phone and prowled over to her. She backed up a step for every one he advanced. Until she bumped into the countertop and she uttered a weak, "Ow."

She expected him to yell at her, which she deserved, but maybe she could explain herself before he started. Explain how she was no longer planning on writing about "Lightning" at all. How she had already written the piece and had instead focused on his new album. How she was telling the story of how amazing he was with his fans and his brothers—

"Heather Bell and I had a physical relationship and nothing more," he boomed, speaking first and robbing her of the chance. "Unlike Carla, who gave me the physical but could also hold a conversation."

Presley's stomach did a barrel roll.

"Heather was so far in my rearview I didn't expect to hear from her again. *Ever.* We burned hot, but fast. And then it was over." His eyebrows were two angry slashes as he went on. "Imagine my surprise when she calls to tell me a reporter is asking if Heather inspired my song 'Lightning.' Excuse me, not a reporter. My *fiancée!*" He roared the word and Presley winced.

"Cash, listen to me. I didn't think she'd focus on what you and I were to each other. I just hoped she'd trust me enough to—"

"You could have asked *me*," he growled.

She flinched. Not because he was scaring her, but because he was right. She could have. She *should* have.

"You and me in my bed, on my boat, on my couch while it rained, Presley."

His words, and the hurt lingering in the depth of his eyes were as good as an accusation. He'd trusted her, and now it appeared as if she'd slept with him solely to gain his trust. Why hadn't she just been honest in that damn email?

Because you never dreamed Heather would call him and rat you out. A huge oversight, to be sure.

Her heart sank as tears warmed the backs of her eyes. Heather's timing couldn't have been worse. Pres had wanted to find the truth, but sleeping with him had never been about playing him. Now how was she supposed to convince him otherwise?

"So this—" he tossed his cell phone onto the counter "—is what you're doing when you're not having sex with me?"

"Cash, I swear," she started but he cut her off again.

"You reached out to my ex-girlfriend and asked her instead of coming to me." His voice, quiet but lethal, was ten times scarier than when he'd been shouting.

He loomed over her, fists balled at his sides. Guilt made her defenses climb sky-high. Rather than sing her version of his apology song, she yelled back at him.

"Would you have told me if I'd asked you?"

He straightened his spine and said nothing.

"That's what I thought." She folded her arms. "What do you care if the world knows if you sang 'Lightning' about Heather, or Carla, or both of them? It's just gossip anyway. No matter what some reporter writes or doesn't write, you could deny it."

"Don't you mean whatever *my fiancée* writes?"

"I was trying to sound credible. That was wrong," she admitted, her voice small.

"You think? The meaning behind that song is personal, Presley, and none of the world's goddamn business. I'm not protecting myself. I'm protecting the woman I wrote the song about. I've performed it a thousand times and I'm the only one who knows. I *like* that I'm the only one who knows."

He wasn't yelling anymore, but watching her with sad eyes. And instantly she knew she'd made a big mistake.

"You're protecting her?"

He didn't respond. He didn't have to. His disappointed expression said it all.

"From people like me," she concluded. "Ugh."

She sank on one of the stools at the counter, her head hanging. Even though she'd changed her mind about pursuing the truth, at one point she'd intended to write that story. Somehow, she'd become the kind of person she least respected. A reporter who would compromise everything to get the story. Including her own integrity. The truth, in Cash's case, wasn't hers to share.

Double ugh.

"For what it's worth, I gave up trying to find out."

He was silent, but still looming. She peeked up at him.

"You put people ahead of yourself a lot," she pointed out. His hands rested on the countertop and she admired his knuckles. His blunt nails. The hair on his forearms. How was it that every inch of him was undeniably attractive? She thought of his hands and his arms on another woman. Knowing he'd written "Lightning" about someone he'd cared about deeply made her want to wail. But this wasn't about her.

"Honestly, Pres. What were you thinking?"

"I wasn't." She let out a defeated breath. "I'm sorry. I was just…carried away. Blind ambition and all that," she said, which sounded like an excuse even to her own ears. "That probably sounds lame."

He let out a deep sigh. "Believe it or not, I understand how chasing success can make you do something stupid."

Was he talking about the way he'd left her in Florida to chase his own success? That seemed like too much of a leap, so she instead rerouted to ask, "Do you want me to stay home today rather than go with you to the barbecue?"

She'd been looking forward to spending the day with the Sutherland family, and not only because she'd planned on snapping a few candid photos for her article while she was there. She wanted to meet Cash's parents, hang out with Hannah, who was arriving with Will. And she'd wanted to say goodbye to Luke and Gavin, and Hallie if she showed up. But, given her egregious behavior, she wouldn't blame Cash if he disinvited her.

His hand cupped the nape of her neck and he looked down on her, sadness still swimming in his eyes. Then he bent and kissed the crown of her head.

"We leave at noon." He let her go and walked to the staircase.

"Cash?"

He paused at the foot of the stairs, head down, fists clenched.

"Are you all right?"

He didn't look at her. He simply repeated, "Noon."

Eighteen

In his parents' backyard, Cash sat, a glass of iced tea sweating in his hand. His brothers surrounded him in a semicircle. Dad manned the grill, chatting with their mom, Dana, who micromanaged Dad in her own irritating, sweet way. Travis Sutherland informed his wife of this moments before he dipped her over one arm and kissed her. Dana giggled and swatted him when he set her on her feet again.

Cash didn't feel like smiling, but he smiled. His parents had such a laidback, loving relationship. How did they do it?

Though he'd been trying to shake it, frustration coated him like a sheen of oil. As pissed off as he was that Presley had circumvented him and lied, he knew there was nothing evil behind her intentions. Oversights happened. He knew how badly she wanted to win. At one point he'd been as blindly ambitious as she was, and it'd cost him the ultimate price: *her*. How could he fault her for doing the same now without being a total hypocrite?

He wanted to believe she'd have come to him before running the article. He was angrier that she'd been poking around about "Lightning" at all. The truth—that Presley had inspired the song he'd written while high on heartbreak after their brief relationship—was one he'd intended to take to his grave.

He'd been in love with her back then. In love and in complete denial. Until they'd made love on his couch, the rain hitting the windows behind him, did he realize what he'd lost to her. That hollow, empty feeling in his chest was because his missing heart had gone to Presley Cole.

He'd been so focused on his dreams back when they'd been in college, on escaping the football-and-business degree trajectory he'd been on, that he'd been single-minded about leaving. He'd convinced himself then that what he and Pres had shared was too short-lived to be real and lasting love. Only in hindsight had he realized he'd blown it with her, and only recently had he realized that falling in love with her was easy when he'd never fallen out.

"Things are going good," Luke, his hand wrapped around a beer bottle resting on his knee, remarked.

Cash jerked out of his thoughts and focused on his brother. "At the bar?"

"No, man. With your girl. Things are going good with Presley."

Cash followed his brother's gaze across the yard to where Presley stood with Hannah and Hallie. Pres was wearing a green dress with tiny pink flowers on it, and a pair of bright white sneakers. Her hair was back in a ponytail, showing off her cute ears and sun-kissed cheekbones. She was girl-next-door irresistible, but capable of being his bad girl whenever he slipped her out of her clothes. And when she made mistakes, she apologized for them. She tried to make everything right even when it didn't serve her best interests.

She was perfect.

"She's going home tomorrow," Cash told Luke. No matter how perfect she was, or how he felt about her, she wasn't staying.

"And you're letting her?" Luke chuffed.

"This proves it," Gavin butted in. "I'm the smart one. You let her go again, you're an idiot."

Cash sipped his iced tea and decided silence was his best ally. At this rate his *only* ally. Then he opened his mouth to defend himself anyway. "She was never staying. You knew that."

"I didn't know you'd talk her into staying longer and show up in town with her hand in yours." Gavin's eyebrows lifted, daring Cash to argue.

"Florida's not that far away," Luke commented. "It's a day's drive. A shorter flight."

"And when would I have time to drive or fly to Florida?" Irritated, Cash shifted in his lawn chair. "Between albums? Or during the tour?"

"Damn, sorry I brought it up." Luke took a swig from his beer.

So was Cash. His darkest worry was that a precious part of Presley would forever hate him for leaving her that dark night in her dorm room. That she'd never truly trust him since she knew firsthand he was capable of walking away and never looking back.

"Meat's done, thank God. I'm starving," Will announced, rejoining his brothers. "Damn. What did I miss? Cash looks grumpier than usual. What are you worried about? We have the album on lock. You guys hear 'Back for Good' yet?" he asked Gav and Luke.

"Yeah," Luke confirmed at the same time Gavin said, "Not yet."

"Well, you should. I think Presley's right," Will said. "She thinks it should be Cash's first single."

"It's a ballad," Luke said, wrinkling his nose. "Guess it depends on the month it drops."

"Country music is nothing but ballads and bar songs," Gavin put in.

"It's a hit. Trust me," Will said.

Sick of everyone talking about him like he wasn't sitting there, Cash barked, "I'm trashing that song."

"What?" Will asked, predictably incensed.

"You heard me. I'm rewriting it. That track we laid down is no good."

"No good? Are you insane?"

"Yes," Gavin and Luke answered in tandem.

"I can't let you do that, man," Will stated.

"It's happening," Cash informed him. "I'm rewriting 'Back for Good.' It's a shit song and I can do better."

A lie. "Back for Good" was one of his best. But it was too honest. And it depressed the hell out of him considering it would never come to pass.

"Are you insane?" came a sharp, feminine voice from behind.

This time Will, Gavin and Luke all said "Yes" at the same time.

Cash turned to find Presley coming from the direction of the house, a dish of potato salad in her hands. Behind her, Hannah and Hallie completed their journey to the picnic table.

"I can't let you rewrite that song," Presley said.

"That's what I said," Will agreed.

Presley only had eyes for Cash. "That's the best song

on the album so far. Hell, it might be your best song *ever*. Even better than 'Lightning.'"

"That's a big statement," Gavin said.

"You must not have heard it yet," she challenged before her gaze jerked back to Cash.

"Ladies and gentlemen, start moving to the picnic table. Time to eat!" Travis hollered.

"Give us a sec." Cash slid a meaningful glare to his brothers.

Luke stood, Gavin with him. Will snagged the bowl from Presley's hands and followed his brothers, granting Cash and Presley a dab of privacy while the family arranged themselves on the long wooden benches.

"It was a mistake to contact Heather," Presley said. "I didn't expect her to call you. I really am sorry."

"It's done, Pres."

"'Back for Good' is the best song I've ever heard and I'm not just saying that. Your fans deserve to hear it."

He wedged his teeth together.

"Back for Good" was a fantasy. And he'd been a fool to believe he'd release that song and proceed to sing it for years to come without thinking of and missing the redhead gazing up at him now. "Back for Good," like "Lightning," was inspired by Presley. Except "Back for Good" was the happy ending to the sad story "Lightning" had started.

How the hell was he supposed to tell her *that*? Especially when their story ended with her leaving him this time around.

"We're about to say grace, Cash," Travis called.

"Coming," Cash stood. "Pres, let it go."

She didn't.

"I forbid you from changing a single note of that song. A single *word*." She touched the center of his chest.

He leaned in close, his nose almost touching hers. "That's not up to you."

"I'm your muse so it kind of is." She poked him as she spoke as if punctuating each word.

"Seriously guys, I'm starving," Luke offered. "You know Dad won't let us eat until we pray."

Cash ignored him.

Presley's features softened. "I'm going home tomorrow and I'm going to publish an article about Cash Sutherland, the man. A man who is dedicated to his craft, his family and his friends. I'm going to share your writing process and what it was like to be there when inspiration struck you in the middle of dinner. Or while you're making coffee in the morning." She blushed when she added, "And other times, but I won't share those. Not with anyone.

"I'm going to show your fans you're more than a sex symbol or an award-winning performer." Her hand flattened on his chest. "I'm going to show them you. The real you. And when they see that, they're going to forget about the mug shot and the bogus DUI. And if they don't forget, they won't care. Not once they see the guy beneath the glitz."

His heart sank. The longer she talked, the more sincere she sounded, and the worse she made everything. She had no idea how hard she was making it for him to let her go when all he wanted to do was beg her to stay. How could he ask her to trust him again after how badly he'd abused that trust? Simple. He couldn't.

"Don't forget the part about how I walk on water," he muttered.

Her gentle touch, her profession that she loved his song and forbade he change a word of it, was too much to take.

Especially when a profession dwelled deep inside him—an "I love you" he wouldn't dare speak.

No matter how sweet her words were, or how true the sentiment behind them, he knew she wouldn't take a chance on him again. The hell of it was, he couldn't blame her. A few weeks of bliss wasn't enough to erase years of hurt. She'd built her own life, separate from his, and she deserved to live it. Even if he could coax her into coming back for good like he sang in his new song, he wouldn't make her choose between him and her dreams. Hadn't he been selfish enough for a lifetime?

"Do you hear me?" She had to know he'd heard every word she'd said since he hadn't taken his eyes off her yet. "I'm not writing about 'Lightning' and if you like, I'll call Heather Bell and personally apologize. I'm not going to *out* whoever you wrote that song about, Cash. I...care about you. I have always cared about you."

And he cared about her—still. He'd laid himself bare in "Back for Good." He'd written snippets of it when Presley was in his bed, in his arms. When she'd been sunbathing on his deck. He'd been consumed and inspired and, what was the word? Oh, right. *Stupid.* He'd been stupid to pretend for a second he could allow this fairy tale to go on.

"Cash, honey," this from his mother. "I'm sorry to interrupt."

His mom wasn't the least bit sorry, but evidently he wasn't going to have the chance to finish this damn conversation without interruption.

"We're coming," Presley called cheerily, snatching his hand and dragging him to the table.

"Finally!" Gavin said, reaching for the potato salad.

"Not yet," Travis scolded. "Grace."

While his father said grace, Cash bowed his head, but

he wasn't paying attention to the prayer. He'd been arriving at a decision. Tonight, once he returned to his house with Presley, he'd tell her the truth.

It was time for the fantasy to end. She wanted to know the inspiration behind "Lightning"? He'd tell her. She could share it with the world and claim the prize at work. It was the least he owed her for leaving her in the dust years ago. And, if he were being honest with himself, it wasn't only his secret. It was hers to do with what she wanted.

He'd leave out the part where he still regretted leaving her. He wouldn't admit he knew he'd ruined his one shot. And he sure as shit wasn't going to tell her that "Back for Good" was inspired by what could have been. It was a great song, but he'd see to it that it never saw the light of day.

He'd do that for her. Because of what he'd seen shimmering in her eyes as she'd begged him not to change a word of that song.

Love.

He saw it now, and he'd seen it on the couch yesterday. While they'd spent long, intimate moments together as it rained cats and dogs. He'd felt it, too, eating into him. It was heavy and undeniable, but he had to deny it.

He'd had his shot. His flash. Like his own song said, lightning never struck the same place twice. He didn't deserve her forgiveness for the mistake he made years ago. Arguably he hadn't deserved her company while she was here.

Whatever chance they might've had was over. He refused to hurt her twice.

Nineteen

On the drive home from his family's house, Presley chatted about his brothers and how good his parents' cooking tasted. Cash seemed a million miles away, giving one-word answers rather than committing to conversation.

She didn't want to leave town on a low note, but she was leaving in less than twelve hours, so that was a definite possibility. She was fairly certain he was still upset with her for contacting Heather, and honestly, Presley understood why. What she'd done hadn't been nefarious or calculated, but it'd been a breach of trust.

Hopefully by the time she left he would be able to forgive her for it.

At his house, he parked in the garage and rounded the sleek sports car to open her door for her. She followed him into the kitchen, intending to revisit the conversation they'd started at his family's house. She couldn't let him even *consider* rewriting "Back for Good." She *forbade* it. It was his best work and she should know. She was a Cash Sutherland superfan from way back. From before he was *The* Cash Sutherland.

Rather than put off this discussion another second, she faced him and asked, "Do you believe me?"

He tossed the car keys on the counter and then ran a hand through his hair. "About what?"

"About me not writing about who inspired 'Lightning.' I mean, I still don't know who inspired it, but if I did, the secret would be safe with me. I promise not to mention Carla or Heather."

He watched her for so long, she wasn't sure if he'd fallen asleep with his eyes open, or zoned out while thinking of something else. Either of those possibilities would have been more expected than what came next.

He closed the gap between them, leveled his eyes with hers by bending slightly and hugged her neck with one palm. "I wrote 'Lightning' after I left FSU. I wrote it about the shot I could have had if I hadn't left behind the woman I loved. I wrote it, Presley Cole, about *you*."

Lost in his dark, penetrating gaze, especially since he hadn't moved so much as an inch away from her, she had to blink to break the spell. His expression bordered on agonized and she felt similar. She had no witty response in her toolkit to deal with his admission.

"M-me?"

"We had something then, but I was too young and stupid to see it. I had big dreams and goals and I couldn't handle being in love and pursuing those dreams. I was too tangled up in my own circumstances. In one fell swoop I erased the possibility of a football career, dropped out of college and left Florida for Tennessee. Left you. In short, Pres, I fucked up. And that's what 'Lightning' is about. We had a shot. I blew it."

With a sigh, he stopped touching her and walked away. She watched him unlock one of the French doors and step outside. Numbly, she struggled to wrap her feeble mind around what he'd told her. He...loved her back then?

She'd listened to "Lightning" on the radio every time she'd come across it, and that song got a ton of airplay. She knew every word. She'd cranked it and sang along loudly, often with the top off her Jeep. She'd bobbed her head to the music while she sat at her desk with her headphones on. She'd *ached* over those lyrics, remembering how she'd felt about him back then and lamenting that she hadn't touched him as deeply. More than once she'd wished "Lightning" was about her. Wished that Cash had felt an iota of what he felt for the mystery woman in the song.

And now he was saying *she* was the mystery woman who'd inspired it?

He'd written a love song about lightning striking once, yet here she stood. In his house, hours away from leaving for Florida, and completely, irrevocably in love with him yet again.

And apparently, he was content to let her leave.

She yanked the door open and marched out to the dock, where Cash stood, silently staring out at the lake. Clouds hung low in the sky, and without the help of stars and the moon, the water appeared murky black.

"Weather's clearing up tomorrow," he said without turning around. "You should have decent roads for traveling out of the mountains. Are you going straight through or will you stop for an overnight on the way down?"

Instead of responding to his irritatingly detached words, she stated, "You weren't in love with me in college."

He faced her, his arms crossed, his expression neutral. So, she went on.

"When you broke up with me, you told me you were leaving everything behind in Florida, including me. You told me I'd be okay because we'd never been serious. You told me you had fun with me and that you hoped I didn't regret the time I spent with you."

Time they'd spent being intimate but never going past the point of no return. Time they'd spent together *not* having sex, which she sometimes believed was the reason he'd been able to walk away without looking back.

"You had no regrets, Cash." Her voice shook. She almost needed that to be true. The alternative was unbelievable. "I spent the entire next year wishing I would have slept with you, wondering if you would have stayed with me then. And now you're telling me your most popular love song is about me?"

"I had regrets, Presley. You didn't corner the market on those." His stubborn jaw was set. "I wrote about them in that song."

She replayed the lyrics in her head. The part about his walking away when he knew lightning struck only once. About not being able to catch lightning in a bottle so he'd had to let it go. The part about how he'd never have again what he'd found all those years ago.

"I was in love with you back then," she said, not willing to admit she was now, too.

"I know." She could read the regret in his features. It glowed like the neon in a sign.

"And you're saying…you loved me, too? But you didn't stick around. You didn't tell me. You let me believe I was this…this…silly, naïve girl who fell in love with a guy who didn't give a damn about me!"

"I thought a clean break would be easier for both of us," he countered, his voice raised. "I had a lot to deal with back then, Pres."

"Oh, did you? You had a lot to deal with coming home to your beautiful family and living in the lap of luxury while you found yourself? Meanwhile, I was heartbroken and trying to pick up the pieces of a life I didn't recognize anymore, while trying not to fail every exam that next quarter. And then I slept with someone hoping I'd finally get over you and you're telling me the whole time that you were in love with me and *you left anyway*?"

Sick. She was going to be sick. She'd wasted not only the time they'd dated, but years after thinking of him. For a while she'd pined for him, for a longer while she'd mourned. And then when she was finally over him, she'd traveled to Beaumont Bay and allowed herself to be talked into his bed.

You're smarter than this, Presley.

"What was your plan this time around, Cash? Were you testing a theory? Or did you need inspiration for another hit song? Don't tell me you were actually hoping I'd be 'Back for Good'?"

His head snapped up and his mouth pulled into a frown.

"My God." She wasn't as far off the mark as she'd hoped. "Is that what your new song is about? Me staying?"

"Presley."

"But I'm leaving. An-and you're encouraging me to go. Is this a game to you? Do you enjoy stringing me along and then pushing me away?"

"Pres, listen to me."

Which begged another question. "Why did you tell me about 'Lightning'?"

He licked his lips. Sucked in a deep breath. "You gave up New York."

She blinked. "What?"

"The internship. You stayed in Florida because I was in Florida. Your grades were slipping. Because of me."

She shook her head, but the sentiment was weak. She wanted to accuse him of being cocky and self-centered, but she *had* turned down New York for him. She had put her life on hold once she was in his orbit. That's what you did when you loved someone. Or at least, that's what *she* did.

"I can't give you anything else, but I can give you the truth. Now you know the answer to the question behind who inspired 'Lightning.' Do with it what you will. If it helps your career and allows you to travel the world like you dreamed, then maybe I can live with myself for letting you leave. If it's a secret you want to keep to yourself, so be it. I'm not telling anyone."

"You can't give me anything else," she repeated, her voice trembling with anger. "What the hell does that mean?" But she knew. He'd clearly said he was letting her leave—that he could live with himself now that he'd told her the truth. But what about her? What about what the truth was going to do to *her*? He'd practically guaranteed she would spend years pining and yearning and mourning him all over again.

"I know it was a mistake to let you go, Pres. I do. I know you care about me. I also know that you never truly forgave me for walking away from you. And I don't blame you. Not one damn bit. I was so focused on my own success, I left and didn't look back. You'd be crazy to trust me again."

She was stunned silent, her heart aching at the truth behind those words. The truth was she had struggled to forgive him. And even though she told herself she had, it was hard to trust him now.

"You've heard 'Lightning,' you know how I feel about you."

"Felt," she corrected. "That song was about our past, not the present. And I'm not sure what to think of 'Back for Good.' Was it some warped fantasy or did those feelings from years ago come up again recently?"

Her heart hammered as she waited for him to answer. Those feelings had definitely resurfaced for her. And now, hours before she was heading home, he decided to drop a bomb on her, and for what? His own egotistical reasoning? So he could pay his penance for leaving her back then by telling her the most inconvenient truth ever?

"Songs are one of two things for me," he said. "Fantasy or remembering. 'Lightning' is me remembering who we were, what we had before our lives happened to us. 'Back for Good' is the fairy-tale ending to 'Lightning.'"

"What's so unbelievable about me coming back for good?" She had to ask, at least once.

"This isn't real." He shook his head. "That's why I'm rewriting the song." He delivered her the felling blow on a butterfly's wing. "I was caught up in the fairy tale of you in my bed and back in my life."

"You were caught up," she repeated, her limbs going numb. A protective instinct. She didn't want to feel this pain—couldn't handle it. "And telling me the truth behind 'Lightning' is what, my parting gift?"

"Now you know calling my ex-girlfriends won't clear it up for you."

"No, Cash, *you* cleared everything up for me." Tears burned her eyes but she refused to let them fall. "You took the inspiration you needed and now you're through with me. I was just the idiot falling in love with you again."

She stomped inside and jogged to her room, locking the door when she heard his boots on the stairs. He knocked. She ignored him.

He'd already said enough. Too much.

She could have gone home not knowing he'd loved her once and wasted years of their lives—and her virginity in the process. She could have gone a lifetime without knowing that.

But now she knew the truth. Lucky her! She could share his secret and boost her career. Which she was angry enough to do, but she loved him too much to do that to him. He thought he owed her?

He owed her, all right. He owed her his heart.

But nowhere in his speech had he mentioned his feelings for her in the present. It'd been about his healing as he walked away one more time. Cash was cutting her loose so she could move on with her life. Like she didn't know her own heart and mind. Like she needed him to tell her how to proceed.

God, she really was an idiot.

He stopped knocking, giving up after a few minutes. She pulled her suitcase from the closet and threw it on the bed. Once he fell asleep, she'd leave. She'd drive as far as she could without falling asleep at the wheel and then rent a room in whatever hotel was closest.

She wasn't spending another minute in this house with Cash—the man who'd loved her, but not enough to stick around. The man who claimed he wanted her "back for good," but only as fodder for a hit single. As if their sleeping together for the last two weeks had meant nothing.

She should have known better.

She *did* know better.

Apparently, that was a lesson she'd needed to be taught more than once.

Twenty

Cash's beat-up spiral notebook sat next to his right thigh, its pages blowing in the breeze. He watched them flutter, the many lines and scribbles from where he'd been attempting to rewrite "Back for Good" mocking him. A lot of it hadn't worked.

Any of it, in fact.

Presley had left eleven days ago and he'd been a miserable asshole since. Worse, she hadn't said goodbye when she'd left. She'd packed her bags and sneaked out in the early hours of the morning before he'd woken up, or maybe shortly after he'd fallen asleep. He'd called when he noticed her Jeep missing to make sure she was all right, but she hadn't answered.

He'd called over and over again for the last week-plus, but she hadn't answered his calls then, either. On day three of her being away, he'd asked Gavin to check on her for safety's sake. She'd answered Gavin's text to let him know she was home. She'd also made it clear she didn't want to talk to Cash.

He didn't know if she meant she didn't want to talk to him now, or if she meant she didn't want to talk to him ever, but it felt like the latter.

He plucked a few strings and tried out the revised lyrics to "Back for Good." Unsurprisingly, they didn't flow. He set aside his guitar, snatched up his notebook and flung it into the air. It sailed on the breeze before hitting the water, pages open, where it bobbed on the undulating surface.

"I give your form a six, but the distance a solid nine-point-zero." Gavin walked down the dock, hands in his shorts pockets. "Thought I'd find you out here. Writing not going well?"

"You could say that." The notebook sank below the surface, now nothing but bleeding ink and soggy paper held together by a piss-poor spiral coil. Words had meant something to him before Presley left. Now they were meaningless.

His fault. He'd been the one who hadn't given her a reason to stay. Cash walked back to the deck. Gavin followed, Cash's guitar in hand.

"Soft drink sponsorship is a go, by the way." Gavin sat, guitar in his lap, and played a few clumsy chords. "How do you do it, man?"

"Do what?"

"Lay out your feelings so cleanly. Express them so genuinely in your music. Perform them so openly in front of thousands of strangers." Gavin attempted another few chords before giving up and setting the guitar aside. "You have a gift."

"Keep practicing and you'll get better."

"I'm not only talking about your musical talent,

brother. I'm talking about you knowing what's going on in here." Gavin tapped his temple and then his chest. "And in here."

Cash grunted. He didn't know about that.

"What is going on in there when it comes to Presley?" Gavin didn't wait for an answer. "Far as I can see, ever since she left you've been one miserable bastard. And if that's any indication—" he nodded to the spot where Cash had winged the notebook "—you're not having much luck rewriting her song."

"It's not *her* song," Cash lied.

"Yeah, okay. You didn't write 'Back for Good' for the girl you wished was back for good. I heard it. It's your best work."

"I told Will to destroy that track."

"You signed a contract with Elite Records," his music attorney brother reminded him. "Will didn't destroy that track. And you shouldn't force our hand. We'll sue you."

Cash rolled his eyes.

"Nah, we won't," Gav smiled. "But if you change it, I'll be tempted. I can't play or write, but I know a winner when I hear it."

"I don't need to make bank on another Presley Cole–inspired song," he muttered.

"He admits it."

He wasn't admitting anything. Okay, maybe one thing. "I've done a lot I regret. I'm not adding Presley staying when I don't know how it's gonna end to that very long list."

"That crap about artists writing their best stuff when they're depressed is just that. *Crap.* You wrote 'Back for Good' when Presley was here and falling in love with you. And you're pretending like you didn't love her? That's just stupid."

"What it is, is pointless. She's gone, Gav. Look around. She told you she didn't want to speak to me."

His brother said nothing, which in a way was worse. Then he stood, seeming to come up with an idea.

"In that case, you have to start dealing with the heartbreak. And I know one very good way to do that. It might be the only way."

Cash cocked his head. "And that is…"

"Day drinking." Gavin grinned. "I'll drive, so no danger of a DUI."

"You're a funny guy."

"Thanks." Gavin grinned, ignoring Cash's sarcasm.

"Anyway, I'm busy."

"Doing what? Going to throw the guitar in next?" His brother hefted the instrument. "I'd pay to see that."

Cash snatched his guitar. He'd sooner die than sacrifice her to the lake's bottom.

"Luke's at the Cheshire. Asked me to call you and invite your sorry ass. We'll have the rooftop to ourselves. You could use a break. Bring the guitar. And your notebook. Eh, a new notebook. Maybe inspiration will hit after a few whiskeys."

Cash studied the blue lake and bluer sky, the trees on the horizon. Laughter of vacationers on a boat in the distance carried on the wind. If he wasn't inspired here, he didn't hold out hope for being inspired elsewhere, whiskey or no.

"What's Luke *really* want?" Cash asked, suspicious.

"I'm not supposed to say."

"Gavin."

"He wants you to play the original 'Back for Good' at the Cheshire. I'm supposed to fetch you, bring you there, get you drunk and make sure you agree."

Cash was already shaking his head.

"Don't change the song, Cash. But not because of Will, or Luke, or me. Keep it for the album. For the fans. They deserve the truth. They appreciate that sort of thing, which is why they appreciate you. You're talented, but your superpower is your honesty."

"What about Presley? What does she deserve?"

"She deserves the truth, too."

The truth.

He hadn't been able to admit the truth about her to anyone—not even himself. Maybe that would be the start of healing. Maybe not. Only one way to know for sure. He took a breath before committing, and then said, "Me loving Pres isn't going to change anything. We can't be together for a lot of reasons, the least of them me not telling her how I feel."

"Maybe you're right," Gavin agreed, and Cash realized he'd been hoping his younger brother would argue. He'd hoped for a few reasons to pursue Presley. To try calling her again. To fly down to Florida and beg her to give him a second chance. No. A *third* chance.

Gavin's smile was tight and Cash understood why his brother hadn't encouraged him. Presley must have said more than Gav was letting on.

It was official. Cash had lost her. For good this time.

"Let's go to the Cheshire."

What did he have to lose? His song ideas were at the bottom of Mountain View Lake. Presley wasn't speaking to him. The song he desperately needed to rewrite wasn't coming to him.

If there was ever a time to bury his sorrows in the bottle, it was now.

Delilah rarely smiled the way she'd smiled when Presley's article had been published. Since the timing had coincided with Cash Sutherland and Hannah Banks's duet going gold, the interest in both artists had an organic spike. Presley's article was currently Viral Pop's most popular piece of content.

It'd been picked up and shared countless times on social media. The contest was in the bag, her raise forthcoming and she'd been given the green light to book a flight to wherever in the world she'd like to transfer with the company.

She'd done it.

And it felt nothing like she'd imagined it would. There was no parade, though her fellow writers had surprised her with cupcakes. She'd thanked them, of course, and pasted on a smile, but it was hard to feel celebratory when she'd spent most of her days split between being miserable and angry.

She felt similar to when Cash left the first time, except then she hadn't known what it was like to have sex with him, or be held in his arms all night. Now she did, which made the memories harder to deal with. Especially since she had lost him forever this time.

At least that's what she'd told herself at first.

A few days before the article went live, she'd been re-reading it for the umpteenth time, hurting so much she was tempted to take Cash out of the article altogether and focus only on Elite Records and the other Sutherland brothers.

But that would do a disservice to his fans, who deserved to know the man behind the music. So, Presley put her own hurt feelings in the rearview, and poured her heart into the article.

She knew he believed what he'd said about not deserving her forgiveness, but the truth was she was tired of holding onto that grudge—of bearing the oppressive weight of it.

He'd made a mistake. So had she, for similar reasons and far more recently. He'd forgiven her without a second thought. And she hadn't been able to blame her recent bout of selfishness on being a clueless college kid.

But she wasn't the same hearts-in-her-eyes girl she used to be. She'd taken a chance, and had chased her dreams and her heart. Why should she have to choose between them? He'd told her the truth recently, and damn the consequences. She would do the same.

So she wrote the truth about Cash Sutherland. She revealed him for the loving, giving man he was. People didn't need to know who had inspired "Lightning" to understand the sacrifices he'd made for those he loved.

He'd been punishing himself, but also protecting Presley by sending her home to Florida. So focused on doing the right thing for her, he hadn't noticed she didn't need his protection. What she needed, what she deserved, was his heart.

Her article would give him a chance to change his mind.

If he didn't realize what he'd lost this time, then she would book a flight to Viral Pop's London office and she wouldn't look back. She'd traverse the globe. Visit Tokyo. Live in San Francisco for a while. The moon, if the company managed to wrangle an office at Elon Musk's space station. She'd go unhappily, but she'd go knowing she'd left nothing on the table. She'd go knowing she'd said everything. Even if Cash had been the one to sing it first.

Inside the Beaumont Hotel, she pulled off her sunglasses and stepped into the fancy bathroom.

"Déjà vu all over again," she told her reflection in the

sitting room. Then she pulled out the bag she'd brought with her so she could freshen up after her long drive from Tallahassee to Tennessee.

Her phone buzzed in her hand and she looked down to see a text from Gavin. There was one word on the screen: Here.

She said a little prayer and then shut herself into a stall to change. She was going to ride the elevator straight up to the Cheshire bar and give Cash one final chance not to blow it.

Then, for better or worse, she'd have her answer.

"What'll it be?" Luke asked as Cash sat on a barstool.

"What are you doing back there?" Cash asked as Gavin sat next to him.

"I like to play bartender on occasion. Revisit my roots. Whiskey?"

"Make his a double," Gavin said.

Luke smiled and poured three doubles, one for each of them.

Hand wrapped around his glass, Cash stared down at his drink for a long moment before Luke pointed out, "You look like something the cat ate, barfed up, ate again and then barfed up again."

Gavin chuckled.

"How go the rewrites?" Luke asked Cash.

"You have any snorkeling gear?" Gavin asked Luke.

Cash grumbled a string of creative swear words as Gavin explained why snorkeling gear was needed. Luke laughed.

Everyone seemed damned amused by Cash being a sorry sack. He swallowed a mouthful of whiskey. Day drinking was definitely a better idea than writing.

"Will's not going to let you rewrite that song," Luke said. "He'd sooner die."

"That can be arranged." Cash downed the rest of his drink like a shot. Luke did the same and refilled their glasses.

Gavin chugged his and shoved his glass across the bar.

"I know why I'm here," Cash informed Luke.

"Are you serious?" Luke glared at Gavin.

"He knew something was up," Gavin defended.

Luke's eyes narrowed, and next he focused that glare on Cash. "So, he doesn't know everything?"

"Of course not." Gavin sipped from his refilled glass.

Cash looked from Gav to Luke. "What are you—"

"You didn't read it, did you?" Luke pulled his cell phone out of his back pocket and fired off a text. "That'd have been the first thing I'd have done, but I don't have your sense of self-preservation."

Cash's phone dinged and he checked his messages. Luke had sent a link to Viral Pop's website.

"Click it," Gavin advised.

"I know what it says."

"You don't," Luke assured him.

The whiskey must have done its job since Cash felt curious instead of defiant. He clicked the link. The article opened with a photo of him on his own deck, guitar on his lap. The sun was shining, his now-trashed notebook sitting intact at his side.

Presley had taken that photo. He remembered her asking if she could use it in her article. He'd agreed to let her.

The headline read "Cashing In."

Beneath that read "Everything you wanted to know about singer-songwriter Cash Sutherland. Except for one secret that will forever stay buried."

His heart thudded as he skimmed the article. She didn't write about "Lightning"?

Dammit, he'd gift-wrapped that for her. Then again, if she hated him, she probably didn't want to be hounded by the press about being his inspiration, he thought miserably.

The article began with details about Elite Records and the harrowing rebuild after last season's storms. Then it mentioned Hannah and Cash's duet and how it was sure to bolster the label. She wrote about his struggle following a "bogus" DUI. She cited a source in the Beaumont Bay police department who corroborated that they were investigating the charges, as they'd suspected a faulty Breathalyzer.

By the time he read the words "Back for Good," he saw that Presley had thrown him under the bus as well, stating the song was "the first single from his highly anticipated second album." She then mentioned she'd been granted an early listen, which made him remember her in his bed as he lazily strummed his guitar.

He didn't know how much more he could take, but his brothers clearly weren't going to let up.

"This part." Gavin stabbed the phone's screen.

Cash kept reading.

I uncovered the inspiration behind Cash's most famous song. I had my own theories about whom he'd written it about, but his answer surprised me. I have no doubt that if I disclosed the mystery woman, you would be equally surprised. I never saw it coming. And while I could disclose what I've learned, I wouldn't feel right about doing that here. But I do know one thing for sure. Cash's muse loves

*him to this day, and she'd light her whole world on
fire to be his forever. No regrets.*

There was more to the article but Cash had stopped
reading. He was still staring at the "loves him" part and
trying to decide if that was hyperbole or if she was telling
the truth. Surely, she couldn't be in love with him after...

The service elevator rattled to a stop and Will stepped
out. Then a vision walked in behind him, and Cash's heart
became lodged in his throat.

Presley was wearing a black dress and high-heeled
shoes. The very same, if memory served, as she'd worn
when she'd shut herself into the elevator with him that
past fated night.

"Look who I ran into in the lobby," Will said. "Small
world. How far behind am I?"

"At least one," Luke said, pouring a whiskey for Will.

Cash stood from his seat, his brothers forgotten. She'd
come back. To him.

She'd put her whole heart out there for him to see.
He'd never had the guts to do that for her. He'd been too
busy protecting himself. She said she'd set her world on
fire for him. She said she'd have no regrets. Had she forgiven him after all?

"Hiya, cowboy," she said with a smile.

He reached her in a few long-legged steps and scooped
her against him. Before he said a single word, he kissed
her lips and hoped for the best.

He got it.

She wrapped her arms around his shoulders and wound
her fingers in his hair and kissed him back. And damn,
did that feel good. No, better than good. It felt *right*.

"Guessing you read my article?" she asked, her big
blue eyes turned up to him.

"I love you, too."

Wetness clouded her eyes. "Cash."

"So much."

She grinned, and it lit up her entire face.

"Guessing you didn't win the contest," he said.

"Oh, I won."

"Yeah?"

"Yeah. I'm holding off booking my flight to London in case I'm needed in Tennessee."

"You're needed and not just in Tennessee." His turn to grin. "Just so happens my upcoming tour includes international stops."

"How convenient."

"I'm so sorry, Presley. For putting you through this not once, but twice. For not telling you how I feel about you. For not recognizing it at first, and then when I did, denying it. I had no idea the heavy feeling in my chest was you, crushing my heart into a million pieces."

She palmed his cheek. "You don't have to say anything else."

"I do. I should have told you the second I knew I was falling in love with you." He dropped his forehead to hers and murmured, "Which happened at the same moment you were falling in love with me. That rainy day on my couch."

He earned another longer, hotter, wetter kiss. It must have gone on a while. From the bar, he heard his brothers clear their throats and mutter under their breath.

When Presley's lips left Cash's, the only thing on his mind was taking her home. Taking off her dress. Taking his time once he had her underneath him.

"By the way, 'Lightning' is the song that needs to be rewritten."

"Beg your pardon?" He frowned.

"Well, see, you were wrong." She tightened her arms around his neck. "In our case, lightning struck twice."

"Does this mean I'm forgiven?"

"Yes."

His chest expanded.

"I'm not wasting another minute on regret or what-ifs."

"Aw, honey." He kissed her smile off her face, earning more mild protesting from his brothers. "You're my one in a million. Thanks for giving me another shot."

"Not so fast. You have some lost time to make up for," she whispered against his lips. "Let's get out of here."

"Good idea." He intertwined his fingers with hers and led her to the elevator, no need to steel himself for the ride down. After fearing the worst, that he'd lost her permanently, everything else that scared him was a joke. She loved him and he loved her and that was all he needed to feel ten feet tall and bulletproof.

"Hey!" Will called as Cash and Presley stepped onto the elevator. "What about the rewrite for 'Back for Good'?"

Cash glanced down at Presley, who squeezed his fingers and offered a gentle shake of her head. Then he looked up at his brothers and answered, "Think I'll leave it the way it is."

Epilogue

At the Cheshire, to a packed VIP crowd, Cash performed "Back for Good" for the first time in public.

In the front row stood Will and Hannah, Hallie, who had been peeking through her lashes at Gavin for most of the evening, and the love of Cash's life: Presley Cole.

Cash finished singing and Pres put her fingers between her lips and blew a loud whistle, the sound riling up the crowd.

"Hope you liked that one," he murmured into the microphone, letting his voice dip low. Pres loved it when he did that. She'd told him recently it sent shivers over her entire body. He'd personally checked every inch to be sure. "I have a bonus track to perform tonight. No one's ever heard it before. If that's okay with you all."

Predictably, the crowd cheered its approval.

He strummed his guitar and nodded to the band to go forth as they'd planned. Laughing, he returned to the mic and corrected. "I take it back. Presley Cole has heard a version of this song. I called it the 'Apology Song' but I've since changed a few lyrics. Pres, honey, you'll have to tell me if you like this one better."

She cocked her head, obviously curious. More whistles and cheers rose on the air, as Cash steeled himself and played the first few chords.

He cleared his throat and, eyes unwavering on his girl, he sang:

Dear Presley.
Will you marry me?
Make an honest man of me.
You mean everything.
Dear Presley.
I'll bring you coffee.
Every morning, gleefully.
Until you agree.
To marry me.
I hope you marry me.
You mean everything, Presley.

The crowd's cheers and whistles rose to ear-bleeding decibels, but he allowed them to fade into the background. There was only Presley, her gaze on him, her eyes welling with tears. She'd risked everything for him. He owed her the same.

"Irv," he said into the microphone. The beefy security guy cuffed Presley under the armpits and set her on the stage.

Demurely, she pushed her hair behind her ear and bit her lip. Cash, his grin unstoppable, turned his guitar facedown and gave it a good shake. He caught the diamond ring in his hand before it hit the stage.

She covered her mouth with her palms before shakily offering her left hand. The crowd roared their approval.

He heard his brothers over all of them, shouting their encouragement the loudest. Cash slid the ring onto Presley's finger and then she hugged him so tight he had to fight for his next breath.

Viral Pop would beg her for weeks to disclose what she'd whispered into his ear at that moment, but she refused to confess.

She and Cash would argue for years about whether readers would be disappointed if they knew what she'd said, or if not knowing made the story better. In the end they decided it didn't matter.

Cash and Presley had each other, and there was nowhere he'd rather be than in her arms. Whether on the dock writing songs, on the couch making love while it rained, or on his boat, floating under the starry, nighttime sky.

He'd found his forever.

Twice, as it'd turned out.

* * * * *

COMING SOON!

LET'S TALK
Romance

For exclusive extracts, competitions
and special offers, find us online:

 facebook.com/millsandboon

@MillsandBoon

@MillsandBoonUK

Get in touch on 01413 063232

For all the latest titles coming soon, visit
millsandboon.co.uk/nextmonth

MILLS & BOON

THE HEART OF ROMANCE

A ROMANCE FOR EVERY READER

MODERN — Prepare to be swept off your feet by sophisticated, sexy and seductive heroes, in some of the world's most glamourous and romantic locations, where power and passion collide.

HISTORICAL — Escape with historical heroes from time gone by. Whether your passion is for wicked Regency Rakes, muscled Vikings or rugged Highlanders, awaken the romance of the past.

MEDICAL — Set your pulse racing with dedicated, delectable doctors in the high-pressure world of medicine, where emotions run high and passion, comfort and love are the best medicine.

True Love — Celebrate true love with tender stories of heartfelt romance, from the rush of falling in love to the joy a new baby can bring, and a focus on the emotional heart of a relationship.

Desire — Indulge in secrets and scandal, intense drama and plenty of sizzling hot action with powerful and passionate heroes who have it all: wealth, status, good looks…everything but the right woman.

HEROES — Experience all the excitement of a gripping thriller, with an intense romance at its heart. Resourceful, true-to-life women and strong, fearless men face danger and desire - a killer combination!

To see which titles are coming soon, please visit

millsandboon.co.uk/nextmonth

MILLS & BOON
True Love
Romance from the Heart

Celebrate true love with tender stories of heartfelt romance, from the rush of falling in love to the joy a new baby can bring, and a focus on the emotional heart of a relationship.

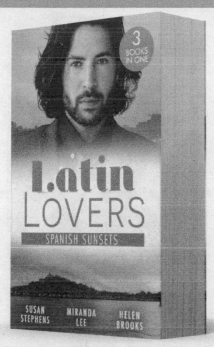